LUCKY'S BLUES

LUCKY'S BLUES

Thomas Bontly

Bruin Books

LUCKY'S BLUES by Thomas Bontly

A portion of LUCKY'S BLUES (Chapters 10 and 11) was first published in the *Sewanee Review,* vol. 104, no. 3, summer 1996. Reprinted with permission of the editor. Additionally, a portion of Chapter 5 previously appeared in *Northeast* (Juniper Press, La Crosse, WI, John Judson, editor).

Other than the following exceptions, all lyrics appearing in the novel were written by the author. The lyric appearing on page 91 is from the jazz standard "Up A Lazy River" written by Hoagy Carmichael and Sidney Arodin in 1930. The lyrical fragment appearing on page 248 is from "Rock Around the Clock" written by Max C. Freedman and James E. Myers in 1952, recorded by Bill Haley & His Comets for Decca in 1954. The lyric appearing on page 283 is from "My Handy Man" written by Andy Razaf & Eubie Blake prior to 1928 (date uncertain). The first known recording of the song was by Ethel Waters in 1928.

Author's Photo courtesy of the Milwaukee Journal.

The Bruin Books edition of LUCKY'S BLUES is published under the full authority of the Thomas Bontly Literary Estate.

Illustrations by Culpeo S. Fox

Publisher: Jonathan Eeds

Cover Design: Michelle Policicchio

This book was crafted in the USA but is printed globally.
Printed in the USA
ISBN 978-1-7349759-9-4
Published March, 2021
Bruin Books, LLC
Eugene, Oregon, USA

LUCKY'S BLUES

Thomas Bontly

Dedication

To my agent, Emilie Jacobson, who has stuck by me almost as long as my wife.

Disclaimer

Lucky's Blues is a work of fiction. Its characters are imaginary and have no living counterparts.

Acknowledgments

Portions of this novel have appeared, in somewhat different form, in the following journals: Chapter 5 in *Northeast* (John Judson, editor); Chapters 10 and 11 in *The Sewanee Review* (George Core, editor). The author thanks them both for giving Lucky a breath of life.

Acknowledgments from Bruin Books

The team at Bruin Books would like to thank Marilyn Bontly and Thomas D. Bontly for their continued support in bringing *Lucky Blues* posthumously to print. We first worked with the Bontly family to republish Thomas Bontly's single foray in the supernatural realm, *Celestial Chess*. (And what a fine foray that was!) At that time, we became aware that the author left behind an unpublished manuscript. In Marilyn's own words: "This book went through multiple revisions as many books do in its search for a publisher. The last revision by the author was in 2007. It is very gratifying to think that 14 years later the book is about to meet its public."

"The term 'blues' is often used to refer to any sad or mournful song. As such it is one of the most frequently misused terms in music."

Ted Gioia, *The History of Jazz*

"Heard melodies are sweet, but those unheard
        Are sweeter; therefore, ye soft pipes, play on;
Not to the sensual ear, but, more endear'd,
        Pipe to the spirit . . ."

John Keats, *Ode on A Grecian Urn*

Author's Note:

Though not an historical novel, *Lucky's Blues* does presuppose some familiarity with the American popular music scene of the late 1950's, in many ways a pivotal time in the history of jazz. The "Dixieland Revival" of the late forties was still attracting its devoted fans, especially in the Midwest, though both musicians and audiences were growing older. Except for a few established names (Duke Ellington, Count Basie), the big bands of the thirties and forties had disappeared, while "modern" or "progressive" jazz (sometimes called "bee-bop") had reached a degree of complexity and virtuosity few musicians could master, and fewer listeners could enjoy. Meanwhile, a scruffy, grassroots, generally disreputable kind of rhythm and blues had begun to dominate the AM airwaves, attracting a younger, and perhaps less discriminating, audience. It was called Rock and Roll, and its king was Elvis Presley.

During these years many lesser-known musicians—some of them quite talented and dedicated to their art—continued to find part-time work in their home venues, playing for weddings and for college and country club dances, in bars and nightclubs, and at occasional jazz festivals. These musicians resisted, for the most part, the new wave favored by the young. They continued to play their own kind of music, for as long as they could, and wherever they could, under conditions that were often less than ideal. This is the story of one such man, a product of the Roaring Twenties and the Swing Era, who late in his career made a desperate gamble with fate for "one last fling" as a jazz musician.

Madison, Wisconsin

Late Summer, 1956 . . .

1.

First Chance/Last Chance

"END of the line, mister," the bus driver said over his shoulder. "You'll have to get off here."

Laurence turned from the window. These east-side streets were lined with memories, an old tune on every corner, and he hadn't noticed he was the last person on board the bus. He slid out of his seat and made his way to the front, guitar case in hand. Though not a tall man, he was so slender and moved with such careful grace that he seemed tall in the close confines of the bus, and he hovered over the driver with an invalid's habitual stoop. "Sorry, friend, I thought this bus went out to Lake Edge."

"Not on weekends," the driver said. "On weekends I turn here for the barns. It says so right on the window." He pointed to a placard which Laurence had failed to notice when he boarded the bus a scant dozen blocks up Atwood Avenue.

"Does that mean I have to walk all the way out to my brother's place?" His soft baritone registered a mixture of annoyance and resignation, as if the world had been playing these little tricks on him for years.

"There's another bus in forty minutes," the driver said. "You'll need a transfer."

He tore off one of the pale green slips and gave it to Laurence, who held it in his long, slender fingers and looked at it with a puzzled frown. "And *that* bus will go out to Lake Edge? You're sure about that?"

"You betcha—regular route. You can catch it right here." The driver shifted his weight behind the wheel, put his hand on the lever that would shut the doors.

Laurence pulled his peeling leather suitcase out from behind the driver's seat, placed it at the exit, then climbed down two steep steps to the street. He put the guitar case on the curb and reached back for the bag, knowing it would require both hands. A good yank and he got it down the first step, but the pain made him gasp. He braced himself for the next assault, but by this time the driver had left his seat and together they wrestled the bulky suitcase down to the curb.

Laurence brushed back several strands of fine gray hair, already damp with sweat. "Thank you kindly, friend. I guess I'm a little out of shape."

The bus driver cast a glance over the quiet, Sunday afternoon street corner.

"You'll be okay, won'cha? The next bus'll be along in forty minutes, like I said."

"I'll be fine, thanks. No problem." He gave the driver a wink and felt his face wrinkle in some new places, like a mask. These days he wore his skin like a rented suit.

The driver got back on board, resumed his seat and pulled the lever to close the wheezing doors. Laurence tried to hold his breath as the bus pulled away from the curb, but the cloud of bitter blue-gray fumes lingered in the heavy air. He coughed harshly into his handkerchief, then sat down on his suitcase and waited for the pain in his chest to subside. In a moment he recovered and looked around the empty intersection with a tentative smile, ready to greet anyone he might've missed when he stepped off the bus.

There was no one. The mid-afternoon sun blazed down out of a sky so bright it seemed bled of color. Its warmth was tainted by the sour smell of algae roasting on the nearby lake. Laurence had forgotten what a steamy swamp Madison could be in the summertime. Tough breathing for a man with one functional lung, and that half-calcified by its resident colony of *tubercle bacillus*. A tune bobbed to the surface of his thoughts:

> *I got the dog-day blues, just sittin' in the sun.*
> *Can't go swimmin', can't have no kind of fun . . .*

The bus had deposited him right outside a tavern. Laurence knew the place. He knew most of the taverns in Madison—the older ones, anyway—and this one had been standing on this corner for at least twenty years. It had the same Pabst Blue Ribbon sign above the door it had worn back in the forties, when it was one of his favorite hangouts. Beneath the neon tubing there hung a small black on white panel that could be read from either direction. If you were coming down Atwood Avenue and headed out of town, it said "The Last Chance." But if you were coming the other way and just entering the city from the suburbs, it said "The First Chance."

Cute, Laurence thought. He'd seen signs like it in other towns around the state. In fact, there were probably "Last Chance/First Chance" taverns all over America. Which made you wonder, was a man's first chance also his last? How many chances did a guy get in this life, and how did you know when you were on your last one? You could ponder those questions over a tall, cool one, if you weren't already on the wagon.

"On the wagon"—now there was another funny expression! As if staying sober was as easy as hitching a ride—all you had to do was climb aboard and your troubles were over. So far, Laurence hadn't found it quite that simple. Back in Madison barely two hours and already stranded outside a tavern in the hot August sun with a mouth as parched as a buffalo's bunghole. Was this the way his luck was going to run?

There was a drug store kitty-corner across the intersection, and that drug store surely had a pay phone. Probably had a soda fountain, too. He could buy himself a nice cool Coca-Cola, then call his brother and ask for a ride. *That would be the smart thing to do*, Laurence thought. On the other hand, the plan had several disadvantages. First, he'd have to lug this goddamn heavy suitcase clear across that broad intersection, and second, he might get over there only to find the store was closed. In the several minutes he'd been sitting here, not a single customer had gone in or out. And even if the place was open, he wasn't sure he wanted to call Leo. That would give Leo time to talk to Maggie, and Laurence knew his sister-in-law. She'd be all right, once he got himself in the door. It was getting himself in the door that presented the problem.

So maybe the drugstore wasn't such a good idea after all. There was something to be said for the tavern, however. It would be cool as a farmhouse cellar and nearly as quiet on a Sunday afternoon, and of course taverns sold soft drinks as well as hard. A fellow didn't *have* to order anything alcoholic in order to sit at the bar for a little while. In fact, he could see how it might be really good practice for the life that lay ahead of him to wait for the next bus *inside* the tavern.

"You take one drink," Doc Steinmetz had told him before he was discharged from the san and sent off to Lake Tomahawk for the summer, "and you'll take six. You take six and you'll go off on a six-weeks' bender. One more bender and they won't be bringing you back here, chum—they'll just wheel your worthless carcass off to the morgue."

Now that was putting it plainly enough, Laurence thought as he tucked his dark blue shirt into his light gray trousers. But nobody was going to make it easy for him now that he was back in the real world. There would be taverns to the right of him, taverns to the left of him, all over this town. He might as well find out right now if he had the guts to make it on his own terms, or if he should have them reserve that slab in the morgue.

He set his guitar case beside the door and went back for the suitcase. He yanked the bulky object free of the pavement, but the muscles in his back and shoulders, sealed with scar tissue where they had been severed years ago, screamed a protest. He winced off the pain, got his balance, and lunged forward. There were two steps up to the entrance, but already he was in the building's shadow and he could feel the cool darkness of the interior reaching out to welcome him. He pushed the latch and nudged the door with his hip; it opened easily, letting him into the cavernous damp and gloom.

After the glare of the street, the murky interior

seemed banked with large, fuzzy, blue and yellow flow-
ers. A garden. Lucky stood just inside the door, waiting
for his eyes to adjust, and the air sacs in his single lung
expanded gratefully, sucking in the smoky, booze-
scented air. Gradually, he made out the long bar with its
row of stools, only two of them occupied at this hour of
the afternoon. The blue-white ghost of a TV screen
offered a ball game. A long row of bottles were lined up
like toy soldiers on the shelf behind the bar, their red
and blue helmets reflected in the mirror. From the dark
recesses of the tavern, back by the washrooms, shone
the winking lights of a pinball machine, the glowing red
and green tubing of a juke box.

Lucky left his suitcase and guitar beside the door—
nobody was likely to run off with them in this place—
and made his way to the bar. The bartender had a pair of
flat, unfriendly eyes and a poker player's stony face.
Lucky slid unto the stool and leaned over the bar, his
long thin fingers bridged just beneath his chin, as if he
might be about to ask a blessing.

"Friend, I'm thirsty as hell, but I'm not supposed to
drink alcoholic beverages. What would you suggest on a
hot day like this?"

The bartender looked at him suspiciously. He
turned and opened the cooler in which the soft drinks
were stored. "Well, we got root beer, cream soda, Dr.
Pepper, Royal Crown Cola, grape soda, Orange Crush—"

"Ah, that sounds good," Lucky said. "Give me an
Orange Crush. In a glass with lots of ice, please—I want
to make it last."

The bartender took out the bottle, uncapped it, put
it down before Lucky, then supplied a glass half-filled
with ice cubes. Lucky put a dollar bill on the bar. "And

change for the juke box, please."

The bartender took the dollar. "Can't let you play the box now," he said, jerking his thumb at the TV set. "Ball game's on."

"Ah, the ball game," Lucky said. He glanced down the bar at the other two customers. "Those fellows follow the Braves, do they?"

The bartender raised his bushy eyebrows. "Mister, in this town *everybody* follows the Braves! You just get here or something?"

"S'matter a fact, yes. Last time I was in this city, the Braves were still back in Boston. Some folks followed the White Sox and some liked the Cubs. Me, I always preferred a good juke box."

"Too bad," the bartender said, and carried off his dollar.

Lucky sipped his Orange Crush. A bit too sweet, but it would have been all right with a little gin in it. Most things were all right with a little gin in them. He put his eyes on the flickering TV screen and watched dutifully as some Brave struck out. The bartender came back with his change and slapped it down on the bar.

"So where you been?"

"Hospital," Lucky said.

The bartender nodded. "Drying out?"

"That, and other things. Curley Swenson still own this place?"

"Naw, Curley sold out nearly two years ago. I own it. Name's Jim Murphy."

"Pleased to meet you, Jim. My name's Larry Lantz. People used to call me Lucky."

The bartender peered at him closely. "I thought you looked familiar. Didn't you used to play banjo with Marty

Hogan's band, back around '45, '46?"

"That was me," Lucky said. "I played with a lot of bands around town here. Were you bartending at one of the clubs?"

"Nah, I was in the service then, stationed out at Truax Field." Murphy picked up a rag and began to mop a space of bar just to Lucky's left. "We used to go to the Idle Hour and those other clubs along U.S. 51—you know, chasing skirt. I remember your band because I met my old lady the night you guys were playing at the Midnight Sun. My old lady thought you were a hell of a banjo-picker."

"I was," Lucky said simply.

"We kept asking you for her favorites—'Tiger Rag' and 'The World Is Waiting for the Sunrise.' She was some jitterbug, let me tell you. The more you strummed that box, the hotter she got. And I got all the benefit of it later, when I took her home. A few weeks later we were married."

"Glad I could be of service," Lucky said. "How's the lady doing these days?"

"I don't know—we split up about four years ago. She turned out to be a tramp." Murphy's expression remained unchanged as he mopped the bar around Lucky's place.

"Sorry," Lucky said. He reflected that it was the tramps who always seemed to like his music the best. Or maybe it was the music that brought out the tramp in a woman, maybe that was it. Every woman had a little tramp in her, and you could find it if you tried hard enough.

"Wasn't your fault," Murphy said gruffly. "So how'd you get sick, anyway?"

"It's an old family ailment. I've had it off and on for years. I'm cured now, though."

"Oh yeah?" Murphy took a step back. "You ain't a lunger, are you?"

Lucky inclined his head. "Non-infectious, at present. I've passed all my sputum tests for the last six months. They sent me to a rehabilitation camp in the north woods, so I could learn a trade and make an honest living."

"Oh yeah? You mean, no more banjo-picking?"

"Nope. Nor piano-playing, neither. The late hours are bad for me, friend. Also the company I keep when I'm on the road. Also the stuff that would make this orange pop taste like something the dog didn't puke up. You know what I mean?"

Murphy nodded and put his elbows on the bar. "I got an ulcer myself. The doc tells me to get the hell out of the tavern business, get away from booze altogether, but I said, 'Hell, what else do I know?'"

Lucky leaned forward earnestly. "That was always my problem, friend. I dropped out of school in the sixth grade. Now my brother, he's a smart boy—went to college and everything—but me, I never knew anything but music. Between gigs I'd take whatever jobs came along— no heavy work, not since I first got sick back in '29—but a man does what he has to in order to survive, you know what I mean?"

Murphy nodded, solemnly. A bartender always understands.

"But now, you see, I got something else I can do. I've learned a respectable trade."

Murphy looked as if he thought Lucky might be pulling his leg. "Yeah, so what's that?"

"Shoe repair," Lucky said proudly.

"Shoe repair? They teach you that in the hospital?"

"At that rehabilitation camp, up on Lake Toma-hawk. I'm certified by the state of Wisconsin, got my papers and everything. One year as an apprentice and I could open my own shop."

"Is that right?" Murphy seemed to be wondering if they had something similar for ulcer patients. "You like it, fixing shoes?"

Lucky sipped his Orange Crush. "Well, friend, let me put it to you this way: it beats lying on your back in a sanatorium, choking on your own blood and listening to the guy in the next bed coughing his lungs out. It beats that, any time."

"Yeah, I suppose it would," Murphy said, and gave the bar another wipe.

Lucky slid off his stool. "You don't mind if I just take a look at the tunes on your juke box, do you? I won't play any of 'em—I just want to see what's current."

"Sure, go ahead "

Lucky took his drink across the room, pulled up another stool, and sat down before the red and green tubing. Behind the glass panel there were several metal racks on a spindle. Each rack held the cards for twelve different numbers. You turned a knob and the next rack came down with twelve more. The records were stacked up above, in the little glass bubble like a robot's head. When you pushed the buttons a record slid out of the stack and set itself down on the turntable. *Just like a brain,* Lucky thought, *selecting memories and playing them back.*

He turned the knob and the first rack fell into place. Lucky read the titles with disappointment. Tex Ritter and Tennessee Ernie Ford—hillbilly music. That kind of junk always was popular with the rednecks on the east side of town. He turned the knob and the next rack came down, this one featuring recent selections from the Hit Parade: Pat Boone's "Ain't That A Shame," Perry Como's "Don't Let the Stars Get in Your Eyes," "Sincerely" by the McGuire Sisters. *Spare me,* Lucky thought. He turned the knob and the next rack descended. Ah, the jazz selections. Not bad—a little Benny Goodman, Count Basie, some Artie Shaw and Stan Kenton. Lucky had filled in with Kenton's big band once when they came through Madison on tour and their second guitar took ill from too much local loco-weed. Kenton had been impressed. Said he might give Lucky a call if something came up later. He never did, though. Or maybe when he called Lucky hadn't been at home.

There was nothing on the juke box by Gary Ames. Too bad, because Lucky might have played it anyway, screw the ball game, just to hear if it was one of the cuts he made with Ames' Sharpshooters at that Chicago studio back in 1951. He'd know if it was. A musician could always tell his own style, just as he recognized his own face in the mirror—there was nothing else that was really you.

He turned the knob again and the last rack descended. Ah, the torch songs. For the guys who were crying in their beer, black at heart because some dame took 'em for a ride, and there, sure enough, Lucky found a Jo Stafford rendition of "Stormy Weather". Remembering the gal who used to sing that song (not as well as Jo would sing it—Ruby's real talents lay elsewhere), Lucky nearly failed to notice the door opening behind him, the glare on the juke-box glass, then darkness again.

"Hey, Lucky," Murphy called from the bar, "there's somebody here says he knows you."

Lucky turned on his stool and saw the newcomer grinning at him. A large man, yet soft-looking—not really fat, just soft and pudgy all over, like a well-fed woman. His low, slanted brow was framed by thick, dark hair, heavily oiled and combed back over his large ears, and his small dark eyes glittered with a hustler's slick assurance. He wore a lizard green suit with a fluorescent sheen, a purple shirt, a lavender tie patterned with pairs of dice. A gaudy, gold and ruby ring flashed as he held a match to his huge cigar, then waved away a cloud of harsh smoke.

Of all the people I had to run into on my first day back in town, Lucky thought sadly, as he slid off his stool and crossed to the bar. "So how you doin', Eddie?" he said, without offering his hand.

Eddie King looked suspiciously down at his glass. "What's that slop you're drinking, Lantz? They haven't turned you into a teetotaler, have they?"

"'They' didn't," Lucky said. "I did it myself, so as to keep alive." He put the glass on the bar. "Hit me again, Murph."

"Shit, give him a man's drink," Eddie King said and put another bill on the bar.

"Thanks but no thanks," Lucky said. "Do I look like a man to you?"

"Well, you've shrunk a bit," Eddie said. "You're mighty scrawny, I'll admit that. But otherwise you look okay. How old are you, Lantz?"

"I was fifty-five last month, if it's any business of yours. But there's parts of me that are a lot older than that. The doc says my one good lung has started to calcify—you know what that means? It means one more go-round with the TB bug and I'm a worm-farm, that's what it means."

"So what are you doing in this dump?"

"Waiting for the bus. I was on my way out to my brother's place in Lake Edge, hoping he'll put me up for a few days, till I know for sure if I got a job."

"A dance job?"

"Naw, a cobbler's job," Murphy said, putting Lucky's bottle of Orange Crush on the bar. "They taught him an honest trade, Eddie. That's what you and I need, you know that?"

"I got an honest trade," Eddie said indignantly. "Fact, I got four or five of 'em. But what do you mean, a cobbler? You mean, like a fucking shoe repair shop?"

"Yeah, like that," Lucky said.

"Bull shit," Eddie said. "Bull shit, man!"

"Hey, tone it down," one of the guys at the other end of the bar called out. "We're trying to watch the ball game."

"Fuck the ball game," Eddie roared at them over Lucky's head. "Hey, you hear me, assholes? Fuck the ball game!"

"Take it easy, Eddie," Murphy said. "They don't mean anything."

The guys at the other end of the bar turned away. From this Lucky concluded that Eddie still carried his switchblade. He was famous all over town for his eagerness to use that blade on anyone who tried to call his bluff, which explained why he was free to shoot his mouth off in bars—until he met somebody with a blade bigger than his.

"So what the fuck you wanna repair some asshole's

shoes for?" Eddie asked. "You happen to be one of the best banjos in the business, my man."

"Used to be," Lucky said.

"You played a pretty mean piano, too."

"I used to all right," Lucky acknowledged.

"And now you're giving it up for a goddamn cobbler's bench?"

Lucky reflected that Eddie King really wasn't worth the breath an explanation would cost him, but he was one of several people in Madison who owed him money —something like a hundred and fifty dollars, though he'd have to check his little black book to make sure. There wasn't much hope of getting that dough out of Eddie on such short notice, but he might just give Lucky a ride out to Lake Edge. Eddie always had a set of wheels.

"So, you got a band these days, Eddie?" Lucky asked.

Eddie drew himself up and put on his big-time bandleader's face, which looked a lot like his small-time hoodlum's face, only funnier. "I'm putting together a new one, see. The last outfit I had became too successful —the big-name bands started raiding my personnel, so I said 'fuck it' and got involved with other things. Right now I'm getting ready to open a new club—out of town a ways on U.S. 12. Figure I'll book in a few groups, see what goes over with the hayseeds."

"You've got the money to invest in a night club?" Lucky asked, thinking maybe he could get his hundred and fifty smackers after all.

Eddie shrugged, as if money were the least of his problems. "A guy I know, a new player in town, he's willing to bankroll me. We picked a place out in the sticks, see, where the local yokels don't take their licensing laws too seriously. That way we can have a little action in the back room, you know what I mean?"

Lucky knew. He'd been playing in joints like that, and leaving his earnings behind, more often than not, for most of his life. "And what kind of a group are you looking for, another big band?"

"Naw, big bands are out of style. Besides, the payroll kills you. It's gotta be something small and jazzy—Dixieland, maybe, or rock and roll."

"Rock and roll, what's that?"

"Shit, you *have* been gone awhile! That's what's making the charts these days, my man. That's what all the kids want to hear."

"Jigaboo jazz," Murphy said contemptuously.

Eddie drew himself up. "Naw, there's white bands play it, too. Ain't you lunkheads ever heard of Wild Bill Haley and the Comets? *Rock Around the Fucking Clock?*"

"That garbage," Lucky said. "That's twelve-bar blues, that's all that is. Anybody can play that crap."

"So why aren't you playing it? You'd rather fix shoes for a living, right?"

"Right," Lucky said.

"Well, fuck," Eddie said, with great disgust.

"Look," Lucky said, "tell you what—why don't you give me a lift out to my brother's place, and you can tell me all about this new club of yours on the way. I may want to put a little money into the place myself."

"You? Where would you get any money in bug-bin, for Chrissake?"

Lucky shrugged. "Guys have a lot of time on their hands in the san. Sometimes they get money from home —enough for a little game . . ."

Eddie chuckled. "So you fleeced a few suckers in the

san—*that* sounds more like the old Lucky! But I don't need your money, pal—keep it for your old age. Mr. Holiday's bankroll is plenty thick enough."

Murphy pursed his lips. "Is that your backer—Frank Holiday?"

Eddie acknowledged the power of the name with a wink. "Keep it under your hat, Murph. Mr. Holiday wants to be a silent partner, see?"

Lucky knew he wouldn't be silent for long—not with a big-mouth like Eddie fronting for him. "Who the hell is Frank Holiday?" he asked.

"A good guy to stay away from, according to what I hear," Murphy said. "Mob connections, Milwaukee and Chicago—pretty heavy stuff."

"Aw, that's all just talk," Eddie said. "Frank's okay, once you get to know him. He's just a smart business-man who likes to play a little poker now and then. So how far out of town does this brother of yours live, Lantz?"

"Not far. I couldn't walk it, though—not with that big suitcase you see over there by the door. It's got my tools in it—the tools of my new trade."

Eddie looked at the suitcase, then back at Lucky. "Okay, what the hell? Let's have one for the road first. Why don't you have a real drink this time?"

"I'm fine with this," Lucky said, "but I'll buy you one. Fix him up, Murph."

"Sure," Murphy said, and took Eddie's glass. A shot of whiskey at the Last Chance cost thirty-five cents these days, and Lucky had already paid for his bus-ride, but Eddie would probably carry his suitcase for him, and provide delivery right to Leo's door. Besides, it was just possible that he might find some way of getting his money out of the big lug. It would be like taking a bulldog's bone away from him, but if you were quick enough, and clever enough, it could be done.

Lucky didn't know how quick and clever he was any more, and he wasn't in any hurry to find out. But you never knew what opportunities fate might throw your way. First chance or last chance, it was all the same—you had to see the cards before you knew how to bet your hand. He took a sip of Orange Crush and waited patiently for the big man to down his shot. Over his shoulder, he could see the red and green tubing of the juke box throbbing with silent melodies, music aching to make itself heard.

2.

Ain't Misbehavin'

IT WAS GOING on five, the sun frying like an egg in the sky's greasy skillet, when Lucky finally coaxed Eddie King out of the Last Chance. Eddie's Cadillac convertible was sprawled over most of two parking spaces, looking like a beached whale with its big tail fins and shiny chrome teeth. Eddie had left the top down and Laurence lowered himself gingerly onto the molten seat-cover, then helped himself to a Pall Mall from the pack on the dash, next to the little hula dancer with a shimmery cellophane skirt. "Just go out Monona Drive and I'll tell you where to turn," he said as Eddie settled himself behind the wheel.

The Caddy rumbled away from the curb. Eddie charged the yellow light at the corner and plowed through the intersection on red. He accelerated up a short, steep hill, then coasted down the long slope to Olbrich Park. Laurence saw the lake winking sunlight through the weeping willows that lined the shore. The grass in the park was brown; cyclones of dust rose from its empty baseball diamonds. They crossed a bridge over a narrow channel clogged with algae and floating litter, and Laurence puffed on his cigarette to cover the smell.

The radio was playing the Top Twenties—nothing he hadn't heard before—and Eddie was jabbering about this new partner of his, this Frank Holiday character, and some tramp he'd picked up who called herself a vocalist, but Laurence wasn't paying much attention. Downtown Madison had come into view, a blue silhouette between the sparkling water and hazy-bright sky, and he was glad to see the city's skyline hadn't changed much in the years he'd been away. The state capitol still rose above the other buildings like a solo clarinet springing up from the ensemble work of a good swing band.

Of course there would be changes, Laurence understood that. He felt like that guy who took a nap in the mountains and came back a hundred years later . . . Rip Van Winkle, that was the cat's name:

I got the Rip Van Winkle blues, been sleepin' in the hills.
Forgot all my troubles and cured all my ills . . .

"So I told Frankie, I said, that gal needs a piano-player who can keep her on key and cover her bloopers—a real pro, you know what I mean?"

Lucky spotted the turn-off to Leo's place up ahead. "Next left," he said, in plenty of time for Eddie to slow down, but the big jerk still hauled the Caddy off Monona Drive with squealing tires, a semi blasting its horn in their wake. The little hula dancer on the dashboard went through some impressive gyrations and Laurence ran a comb through his wind-snarled hair. "Next right," he said.

Hegg Avenue was shaded by overarching elms and

Lucky spotted his brother's house while they were still well down the block. Like most of the homes in Lake Edge, it was a modest, pre-war bungalow set on a large lot, but somehow it looked spiffier than its neighbors. Leo always took a lot of pride in his home, Laurence recalled; he would rather putter around the place than do most anything. He wondered if Leo still played the sax on occasion, and if they still had that old upright piano in their dining room.

"Stop here," he told Eddie, and the Caddy skidded to a stop in the loose gravel at the end of Leo's long driveway.

"This it, huh?" Eddie raised his sunglasses to survey the premises. "Don't look like much of a house. Where they gonna put *you,* in the garage?"

"That's a thought," Lucky said. "Would you mind getting my suitcase out of the trunk, Eddie? I'm a little weak in the shoulders since my operation."

Eddie obliged, and they shook hands at the side of the road. "Thanks for the lift," Lucky told him. "Nice car."

"You got money, you spend it," Eddie said, as if that summed up his whole philosophy of life. "So like I said, you get sick of mending them smelly old shoes, you gimme a call and I'll set up an audition with Savannah."

"Savannah?"

"Frankie's torch singer—the one I just been telling you about."

"Oh yeah, right." Laurence had noticed somebody on the front porch and he wanted to get rid of Eddie before he had to introduce him to the family. Leo and Maggie always said he hung out with the wrong sort of people and Eddie King wasn't likely to change their minds. "I'll give you a call," he promised, "just as soon as I'm settled."

"Don't put it off," Eddie said. "The club opens the end of the week." He got back in the car, gunned the engine, and roared off in a blue cloud.

Laurence covered his nose with his handkerchief. Tucking it back in his breast pocket, he heard a screen door slam and saw a boy coming toward him across the front lawn. A good-looking kid, about sixteen and fully grown, with lots of wavy brown hair and a soft, uncertain smile. Laurence decided to have a little fun.

"Excuse me," he said politely, "does the Lantz family still live here?"

"They do," the boy said, and hooked his thumbs in his belt, eying Laurence suspiciously.

"Ah, good. And you must be, what, the young fellow they've hired to mow their lawn?"

"No," the boy said, "I live here. I'm Jack."

Laurence took a step back and stared in astonishment. "What? *You're* little Jack? Why, it can't be! You're a grown man!"

Jack grinned broadly, and Laurence could tell he'd won the boy over. He extended his hand. "I'll bet you don't know who *I* am."

"Sure I do," Jack said, stepping forward to take his uncle's hand. "You're my Uncle Lucky—how the heck *are* you, anyway?"

Jack had his mother's full, open face, but there was something about his eyes and mouth—something both innocent and inward, yet quick as a young fox—that reminded Laurence of Leo as a boy. He felt a sudden need to testify on his own behalf:

"I'm fine, Jack, just fine. Cured, you know . . . cured

of a lot of things. Are your folks at home?"

"Sure—Dad's out back, in the garden, I guess, and Ma's just starting supper. I'm sure she's got enough for one more." Jack reached down to pick up the suitcase. Its weight surprised him, but he hefted it resolutely and started down the driveway. Laurence followed at his side with the guitar case. A small dog, chained to the open garage, began to bark at their approach, and in another moment Leo came around the garage from the back-yard.

If Laurence hadn't known better, he would have thought his brother was the one who had fallen on hard times. But he knew Leo's frugal habits and guessed that frayed and tattered outfit was his brother's gardening clothes—Leo believed in "wearing things out." Still, he was surprised at how old Leo looked, how slender and frail. A few strands of pale hair lay loosely across his naked scalp, and his blue eyes nested in a thicket of fine wrinkles. Everyone had always thought Leo's cure was permanent, but you never knew about TB—it could come back on you like a bad debt, when you least expected it.

"Hey, Dad," Jack sang out, "look who's here!"

Leo's expression didn't change. He might have been advancing along his driveway to confront a bill collector or salesman, or one of those Jehovah's Witnesses with a pamphlet in hand. Laurence hadn't expected a red-carpet welcome, but Leo's hostile squint was certainly disappointing. Didn't he remember what pals they used to be?

They came to a halt outside an open window and Laurence caught the aroma of frying bacon and onions. He hoped Maggie was fixing some liver to go with that bacon and onions, because that was just about his favorite dish in the whole world. Determined to get a free meal out of his brother, if nothing else, he stuck out his hand and put a hearty note in his voice: "Leo, by golly, it's good to see you! I hope you don't mind me dropping in like this—I just got back in town."

"Hello, Larry," Leo said, his right hand still in his pocket. He came a step closer, his blue eyes leery, his nostrils narrowed like a fox's, sniffing the air. Then Laurence understood: Leo was trying to get a whiff of his breath. Detecting no hint of alcohol, he let his face relax. His hand came reluctantly from his pocket and Laurence seized it in both of his, shaking it vigorously.

"So how are you, Larry?" Leo asked politely. "Just back in town, you say?"

"This afternoon," Laurence said. "I was discharged from the san last spring and spent the summer at the state camp up on Lake Tomahawk. You remember Tomahawk, Leo—best place in the world for a lunger, lots of fresh air and outdoor exercise. I'm in better shape now than I've been in since my twenties, and what's more—" he paused to make sure he had Leo's eyes locked onto his— "I haven't had a drink in over two years."

Leo took that in, and for the first time he showed his buck teeth in a smile. Those teeth had gotten him the nickname "Chippy" as a kid, but they weren't really a chipmunk's choppers, Laurence thought. They were more like beaver's teeth, and Leo had a disposition to match—sober and industrious, and quick to sound an alarm.

"That's very good, Larry," he said cautiously. "That's certainly good news—"

His voice trailed off and Laurence knew what his brother was thinking: two years was not *that* long—not if you were cooped up in a san and couldn't get a drink if you wanted one. "You can believe it this time," he told him. "This time I've really made up my mind to change my life. I've even learned a new trade, so I can get out of the music business and stay out of trouble. I'm a new man, Leo—a brand new man!"

Leo seemed to find the idea puzzling, as if he hadn't known you could trade in a worn-out life for a new one. "You've learned a trade?" he asked dubiously.

"That's right," Laurence said. "I took one of those special courses they offer up at Tomahawk and got my certificate. I'm a shoe repairman, Leo. That suitcase your boy is carrying, the reason it's so goshdam heavy is it's got all my tools in it. The state bought 'em for me, and they've lined up a job for me, too. I've got an interview with the guy first thing tomorrow."

"A job—here in Madison?"

"A place called Abe's Shoe Repair, near the Milwaukee Road station. Not a very classy part of town, I grant you, but beggars can't be choosers. I have to serve a year's apprenticeship, see, before I'm *fully* certified. Then I can go anywhere I want—even open my own shop, be my own boss—"

"Your own shop," Leo said, as if he was finding all this a bit hard to follow.

"Well, if I save up for it. The pay's pretty poor, but if this guy Abe takes me on as his apprentice, the state will supplement my salary—sixty bucks a month. I reckon I can live on that. Until then, I'll be a little on the short side, so I was wondering if, possibly—"

Laurence paused, realizing that he'd pushed a little

too far. At the first mention of money, Leo's eyes had slipped away to the vacant lot next door. A bumper crop of dandelions had recently gone to seed and their pale fluff was drifting on the warm wind, settling onto Leo's well-kept lawn.

"Jack," Leo asked sharply, "can't you quiet that damn dog?"

"Sure, Dad," Jack said, and left Laurence's suitcase sitting there on the cindered driveway, as if it had dawned on him that his long-lost uncle might not be spending the night in the family castle, after all.

"I can't give you any money, Laurence," Leo said quickly. "You should know that by now. We're just barely making ends meet as it is, and I promised Maggie I'd never give you another loan."

Laurence nodded, wondering why he had thought Leo's response could be any different. Maggie ruled this particular roost, and Maggie was probably watching them even now from the kitchen window. He resisted the temptation to look over his shoulder and give her a wave.

"Sure, Leo, I understand. I can get by for awhile— there's plenty of people in this town who owe me money. But the thing is, I don't have a place to stay just yet, and I was wondering if maybe you still had that old army cot out in your garage . . . that would be plenty good enough for me, this time of year."

Leo turned to look at his large double garage. Even from here, Laurence could see it contained just one car. The other half still seemed to be used for storage, as it had been the last time he'd stayed with his brother's family. A lot of that stuff, he now recalled, had been their mother's—family heirlooms she'd carted from town to town after the old man's business failed and he took them on the road like a band of gypsies.

Leo turned back, his face gone stiff once again. "I guess you heard about Mother," he said, and Laurence realized he should have known this was coming, too. In fact, he should have said something sooner . . . there was just so much ground to cover!

"I got your letter," he said. "I wanted to get back for the funeral, but I was flat on my back in the san—they never would have let me out." He could see that wasn't Leo's main beef, so he added, "I guess you and Maggie had a pretty hard time with the old girl, at the end?"

"We had to put her in a nursing home," Leo said. "She had hardening of the arteries and lost her memory. Got some really strange notions, too—'senile dementia,' the doctor called it. She couldn't take care of herself, and I couldn't ask Maggie—"

"No, of course not," Laurence said quickly. "I'm sorry I wasn't here to help."

Leo poked at the driveway cinders with a shabby, scuffed-up shoe. "Well, her pension took care of most of it, but we had to make up the rest. We could have used that money you got for her furniture, Larry—"

Ah, that, too! Laurence shut his eyes for a long moment. When he opened them, he saw that Leo was willing enough to forgive him if only he would accept his guilt. That was easy—guilt had been his only capital for a long time now.

"I'm really sorry about that, Leo. Taking a loan on that furniture was just about the dumbest thing I ever did, but I was sure I could pay it off before Ma needed the money . . . what can I say? I know you've had to carry the burdens in this family for a long time, but I hope to change all that now. I'm a new man, Leo, and I'd like to prove it to you, if I could."

"You don't have to prove anything to me, Larry," Leo said. "As long as you can prove it to yourself, that's all that matters."

Jack had returned with the dog in his arms—some kind of a terrier mutt, who was quiet now and eager to make friends, once he got a sniff of Laurence's fingers. *Don't worry,* Laurence told the dog, scratching behind his ears, *I won't steal the goddamn furniture—not this time!*

A screen door slammed and both Jack and Leo turned expectantly. The game wouldn't really start, Laurence knew, until they'd dealt Maggie in. She came around the corner of the house, a full-figured woman in a flowered housedress and apron. Her dark, curly hair was cut short, showing just a little gray at the temples, and her cheeks were flushed from a hot kitchen. Her green eyes were as lively as ever, her teeth white and even behind a dimpled and mischievous grin. Laurence could see why his brother had always been nuts about her.

"Maggie, my wild Irish rose!" he crooned, and extended his arms.

"Well, hi there, stranger," Maggie said, and accepted his light embrace, the brotherly kiss he put on her warm cheek. There was no hostility in her eyes, but Laurence knew her jolly good nature was joined to a quick temper and an iron will. His fate, for the moment, was in her hands.

"Of course you can stay in our garage," she said with a quick glance at her husband, and Laurence understood that Leo had been waiting for her permission. "It's dusty and dirty, and the roof leaks, but I guess you'll be all right if it doesn't rain *too* hard. And of course you'll have dinner with us. It's nothing special—just liver and bacon, but I know that's one of your favorites. What can we get you to drink? Leo never drinks anything before dinner, but I like a glass of sherry."

"Oh, nothing alcoholic for me, Maggie," Laurence said, sure she was testing him. "I'm on the wagon and I mean to stay there. Have you got a soft drink?"

"I reckon we do. Jack, put your uncle's suitcase in the garage, and then bring him one of those Squirts you like so much. Would you like to come in the house, or would you rather sit out in the backyard until supper's ready?"

"The backyard sounds great," Laurence said, deciding not to press his luck. He saw now how to play this hand. Take what was offered—whatever Leo and Maggie felt comfortable giving him—and don't ask for anything more. At least not until they were satisfied that he really had changed his life. He was going to have to show a lot of people that, so he might as well start with his own family.

Leo led the way into his large, shady backyard. Of course he had to give Laurence the complete tour: his vegetable garden, his raspberry patch, his fruit trees, his flower beds, even his compost pile. *A lot of farmer in that boy,* Laurence thought. They came from a long line of Swiss dairy farmers and had both worked on farms as boys, but Leo had loved that life and Laurence hadn't, it was as simple as that.

After he admired Leo's home-made picnic table, and the stone fireplace he had built in a corner of the yard, Laurence was allowed to settle down in a webbed lounge chair and put his feet up. Jack brought him his Squirt, then went off to help his mother set the table. It was a bit cooler now, the sun behind the trees, the breeze blowing through the feathery foliage of a Chinese elm.

"You've done wonders with this place, Leo," Laurence said. "It's like a Garden of Eden back here, a little piece of Paradise."

"Thanks," Leo said. "We like it pretty well. At least, we *did*. Lately, Maggie's got it in her head we should sell the place and move back to town. She thinks it's too much work for me."

Laurence saw that haggard look on his brother's face once again, that haunted expression in his eyes. "Well, you always did work too hard," he said, "even when we were kids. Can't you get that big, strapping boy of yours to do some of that work for you?"

"Oh, Jack helps me a lot," Leo said. "But he's got a full-time job this summer, doing yard-work around the neighborhood. Anyway, I enjoy working in my garden. It's my hobby—my escape from my other job. They promoted me, you know—taught me how to wire the IBM machines. Now I run the payroll for the whole damn plant."

"Congratulations," Laurence said, thinking a good raise must have come with that promotion. Maybe Leo wasn't as poor as he liked to let on.

"It's a lot of responsibility," Leo said, "a lot of pressure." He leaned forward and spoke confidentially. "The truth is, Larry, I've been having some pains lately in my chest and anus. It's probably nothing—just heartburn, or gas. But they've been getting a little worse lately, and I've got an appointment to see the doctor this coming Saturday. Don't say anything to Maggie—she's got enough worries already, and I don't want to get her started on me."

"What has Maggie got to worry about?" Laurence asked. It had always seemed to him that, if any woman ever had it good, with a loving husband ready to please her every whim, it was Maggie Lantz.

"Oh, plenty of things," Leo said, leaping to his wife's defense. "She's not as healthy as she looks, Larry. She was never completely cured of her TB—they've had her in the san for observation two or three times since her last breakdown, and she's terrified they'll make her go in again. Then there's her change of life—that's pretty hard on some women, you know. Depresses the heck out of them—you have to find ways to cheer 'em up. And lately, of course, she's been worried about Jack."

"Jack? What's wrong with *him?*" Laurence had seldom seen a healthier, happier looking boy than Leo's only son.

"Nothing," Leo said, "except that he turned sixteen this summer and got his driver's license. Now he's got this job and a bit of money, so of course he wants to go out with his friends . . . we know he's a good boy, but Maggie worries when he's out late with the car." He paused, squinted off across the garden. "And then, of course, there's this latest thing—this idea he's got in his head that he wants to be a jazz musician."

"Ah," Laurence said with a smile, "that *is* bad."

"He's been taking piano lessons for years," Leo said, "and he's got a little talent, how much is hard to say. He wants to work his way through college playing dance jobs, like I did—or like I tried to, before I got sick."

"Does he know what happened to you?"

"Of course, but like most kids his age he thinks he's

indestructible. And he idolizes *you*, Larry—you've always been one of his heroes."

"Me? For God's sake, what does he know about me?"

Leo peered at his brother. "Not everything, that's for sure. I don't guess any of us knows that! But I've told him a few stories about the old days, when we had our band. I'm sure he'll want to talk music with you, maybe even jam a bit this evening, and that's all right, we play together a lot, only—"

The screen door slammed and Laurence saw Jack motioning for them to come in to supper. Leo finished quickly: "Only don't encourage him, okay?"

Laurence smiled and got to his feet. "Leo, the only advice I've got for anybody is not to wind up like me. I think that about covers it, don't you?"

They walked across the lawn to the back door. As they went in, Laurence turned to see the sun smoldering like a big red coal in the bed of ash-colored clouds that had risen in the west. A slightly cooler breeze moved through the treetops and a promise of rain was in the sultry air.

3.

Family Jam

LAURENCE speared his last, bite-size piece of liver, slid it through the congealing swirls of gravy on his plate and onto his last strip of bacon. Raising the tasty morsel to his mouth, he realized he was the last person at the table still eating. It was growing dark in the dining room, but Maggie had yet to turn on the lights. A gentle breeze billowed the lace curtains and, along the shadowy inner wall, the old upright piano gleamed in the darkness like a family ghost.

Laurence swallowed, lay down his silverware and put his napkin to his lips. "Maggie, if that's not the best dinner I've had in years, I must have amnesia, because I sure as heck can't think of one to beat it. And Leo, those green beans were delicious. Right out of the garden— what a treat!"

Maggie beamed. "Well, we may not be able to afford the luxuries of life, but we eat good, healthful food in this family. You're welcome to join us, Larry, any time you feel like a square meal."

"Ah, be careful, Maggie," Laurence laughed. "I might

just take you up on that—I might move right in!"

There was an awkward silence and Laurence knew they were all remembering that *other* time he had moved in on them, that summer after the war, when he came back to Madison to find his mother living in Leo and Maggie's large, unfinished attic. The old girl had lost her flat and couldn't find another she could afford on her widow's pension. Accustomed to staying with his mother when he was in town, Laurence moved in, too—though whether Leo had actually *invited* him was an open question. In any case, it hadn't worked out so well, and Leo finally asked him to leave—none too gracefully, as Laurence recalled. There were hard feelings all around after that incident.

"Don't worry, I was only joking," he said hastily. "I'll want a place downtown, close to my shop—a furnished room will do. But maybe you folks will invite me out to dinner now and then."

"Of course we will," Maggie said. "We'll do whatever we can to help you get settled, Larry. Dishes, linens, whatever you need—we really hope this new career works out for you, don't we, Leo?"

"We sure do," Leo said. "We're all for it, Larry—one hundred percent."

"Thank you," Laurence said, "that means a lot to me." But he had seen the look that passed between husband and wife and understood that their offer of support didn't extend to financial assistance. Leo might be making a little more money these days, but that wouldn't alter *his* credit rating.

"I warn you," Maggie added, "out here you'll have to work for your supper. Ever since you arrived, I've been looking forward to a little concert."

"A concert?" Laurence rolled his eyes until they landed on the old piano, its heavily varnished wood shining dark as molasses in the dim light. "Good gracious, Maggie, I haven't touched a keyboard in nearly three years! I don't think I could find middle C."

Maggie just smiled, as if she knew well enough that he could.

"Say, wasn't that a guitar case you had with you this afternoon?" Jack asked. "I hear you used to play a couple of different instruments, Lucky."

"Oh, that's just an old thing I picked up cheap in Tomahawk," Laurence said. "I like to pick out a tune now and then. But I hear *you've* turned into quite a piano player, Jack. Your dad says you're pretty good."

"He's been taking lessons with Lennie Marx," Maggie said proudly. "Maybe you've heard of him—he's got his own band and a TV show on channel 27."

Before Laurence could say he hadn't had the pleasure, Jack added, "I've learned a few Dixieland tunes from Dad, too. In fact, we usually have a little jam session after supper—if I'm not going out, that is."

Laurence turned to his brother. "Do you mean to tell me you've still got the breath for that old licorice stick, Leo?"

"Oh, I can manage a few squeaks," Leo said, "when Jack gets me going. Maggie usually keeps time for us on the old snare drum I salvaged when I sold off my set."

"Say, sounds like we've got the makings of a real band here," Laurence said happily. "The Lantz family quartet."

"Dining room performances only," Leo said with a laugh, and reached for his ashtray and pack of Raleighs. "Jack, why don't you pick up the dishes? Maybe your mother will bring us some coffee."

"Coming up," Maggie said, and turned on the over-head light as Jack began clearing the table. Blinking away the sudden glare, Laurence noticed a crucifix on the wall and recalled that Maggie was a devout Catholic. Fortunately, it had never kept her from enjoying a good time, like some folks he'd known.

Leo passed around his cigarettes and soon tendrils of smoke were wreathing themselves around the chandelier. Jack was running water for the dishes in the kitchen and Laurence, wanting to compliment something besides Maggie's cooking, said, "Good boy you've got there. Seems to have a good head on his shoulders."

"We think so," Leo said. "Of course he wants to grow up too fast, like most boys his age. Nothing we can do about that, I suppose." He looked at his wife, whose green eyes seemed to turn a little frantic at the thought of losing her only child.

"I don't think you've got anything to worry about," Laurence said. "Jack will be just fine, as long as he keeps his health."

"I pray to God for that," Maggie said. "There's been entirely too much illness in this family. Sometimes I wonder what we ever did to deserve that curse."

They sat silently for a moment, listening to the clink of dishes and silverware in the kitchen, and then Leo said, "Well, I guess every generation has its problems, but ours certainly seems to have had more than its share. For some it was the depression, for some the war; for us it was tuberculosis. It ruined our lives."

Maggie forced a little laugh. "Well, I wouldn't say 'ruined,' exactly—unless you're sorry you ever met *me*."

"I didn't mean it *that* way," Leo said quickly, and

reached across the table to pat his wife's hand. "You know I'm glad we found each other, Mag! I'm just sorry it had to be in a sanitarium, that's all."

"Where else *could* we have met? I didn't go to college, like you, and my family couldn't afford to vacation at those ritzy resorts you and Lucky used to play at every summer . . ."

Laurence saw they'd stumbled across an old sore spot and tried to show them an easy way around it. "Hey, we had some good times though, didn't we? Even in the san. Remember how we used to sneak out after bed-check, the three of us and Lou? We'd hitch a ride to that speak-easy up the road and dance the night away."

"We *did* have fun," Maggie agreed.

"At least I thought so, and Lou was crazy about you, Larry. You broke that poor girl's heart, you know."

Laurence didn't remember it quite that way, but he didn't argue. You couldn't have found two prettier gals, back in 1930, than Maggie and Lou Malloy. Full of the devil, too, cooped up in a sanitarium while all the other girls their age were out having fun. Lucky and Leo were just the guys to show them a good time, and it wasn't quite clear at first who was dating who. For some time Laurence had thought that Leo was sweet on Lou, and that Maggie was his girl.

"So how is Lou?" he asked, helping himself to another of Leo's cigarettes.

"Oh, she married that fly-boy she took up with when she got tired of waiting for you," Maggie said. "He's a crop-duster now, down in Illinois. I don't get to see her very often, but I think they're having their troubles— turns out he's another womanizer."

"Sorry to hear that." Laurence let Maggie glare at

him for a moment before he added, "Well, we were all young then." What else could you say after you'd said that?

Leo, however, was not done brooding on the past. "Sometimes a man gets to thinking, you know . . . he starts wondering what he might have done with his life if certain things had been different. If I'd finished college, for example—"

"You would have been a high-school history teacher," Maggie said promptly, "and a darn good one, but you wouldn't be making any more money than you make right now, thanks to the union. We wouldn't be any better off."

"No, I guess we wouldn't," Leo said. "But maybe I wouldn't have to dread going into work every goddamn day . . ." He scowled, then ground out his cigarette. "Say, are we going to have that jam session, or aren't we?"

"I'll go get my guitar," Laurence said, and left the table.

It was good to get outside—the atmosphere in the dining room had been getting a little too close for comfort. *That's what comes of looking over your shoulder,* Lucky thought, taking a few deep breaths. A man could drive himself crazy, worrying about things that were over and done with. He was surprised at his brother, because Leo usually tried to look on the bright side— even when there wasn't one. Maybe it was those chest pains he'd mentioned before dinner—a thing like that could weigh on a man's mind.

He entered the garage by the side door and groped along the wall until he found the light switch. Two overhead bulbs revealed the bleak interior, its bare walls hung with gardening tools, its windows curtained by cobwebs. His guitar case was sitting on the bare concrete next to the rickety canvas cot that would have to serve as his bed for the next night or two. He put it on the cot, snapped the clasps, and opened the lid.

There was a rip in the satin lining and Laurence slipped in two fingers, found the old leather coin-purse in which he kept his savings, and brought it out. He took out his roll of bills and counted them quickly. It was all there. One hundred and forty-seven dollars—all the money he had in the world, except for the change in his pocket and whatever he might be able to raise by pawning his wristwatch, the guitar itself, and a few keepsakes. Not much to show for fifty-five years of living, but he'd known guys with less. *A stake is a stake,* Lucky thought. *You can't afford one game, you find yourself another.*

He put the money back in the purse and returned it to its hiding place, then snapped shut the case and carried it from the garage. Fireflies winked in the deeper darkness of the yard and lightning flickered faintly in the west. He came in through the kitchen where Maggie was drying the dishes.

"Don't keep them up too late," she said as he passed. "Leo has to get up early tomorrow."

"Don't worry, I go to bed with the chickens myself," Laurence said. "I'm an old man now, Maggie, and totally harmless."

"*You'll* never be harmless," she said with a laugh, and he understood it was meant as a compliment.

He went into the dining room, where Jack and Leo had pushed the table aside to make more room around the piano. Leo had his saxophone case open on the floor and Laurence recognized the sharp, metallic scent of tarnished brass. Leo took out the stained and ragged scarf that held the pieces of his clarinet, unwrapped it carefully and fit the sections together. He wet a reed and slid it into the mouthpiece. Meanwhile Jack was spreading out his cheat-sheets. Someone had written out a lot of tunes for him—just the melody and chord progression: C, G, F7, B ♭. That was all a piano-player needed, if he knew how to improvise.

Laurence took out his guitar and tried to adjust the shoulder strap. As he expected, it was too loose and couldn't be tightened any further. That hollow place in his back, where they'd collapsed two of his ribs on his right lung, left too much slack. He found a sofa pillow in the living room and slipped that under the strap. The pillow filled in the hollow and made the guitar fit snugly over his shoulder. He asked Jack for an A, plucked a string, listened briefly, tightened one of the thumb-screws. "Now an E Flat." The piano was woefully out of tune, but who was he to complain?

"So what'll it be, Lucky?" Leo asked, fingering his keys.

Laurence noted the use of his old nickname. Leo had never liked it much, saying it only encouraged his brother's bad habits, but on the bandstand was different. He was always Lucky on the bandstand—everyone called him that.

"Well, you fellas better take it easy on me until I get warmed up," he said. "Have you heard that tune that's so popular these days? Louis Armstrong's got a recording—I think it's called 'Mack the Knife'."

"Hey, that's one of our favorites," Jack said. "We've got a neat arrangement for that one—I do an eight-bar intro"

"Let her rip," Lucky said, and winked at Leo.

Jack hunched over the keyboard, tapped his foot on the pedal, and punched out a standard blues intro. His style was a bit heavy-handed but certainly exuberant, and Leo picked up the melody on the first chorus. As promised, the old clarinet produced several squeaks and more than a few sour notes, but Lucky could see his brother was just warming up. You couldn't get pure sweet water till you'd primed the pump and run out the sludge.

Lucky began strumming along with Jack's boom-chick accompaniment. The chords were easy enough, and he saw, or rather heard, how you might vary them a little, work in a little more harmonic interest, maybe even a counter-melody or two, but it wasn't his place to take over the kid's instruction. They played four uninspired choruses, just getting acquainted, and by then Maggie had finished in the kitchen taken her place at the snare drum.

"'Whispering,'" she demanded, always been one of her favorites. Jack hopped obediently into the old chestnut and Maggie took up the beat. She played a simple rat-a-tat-tat, but she *could* keep time, which was good, because Jack had a tendency to goose the tempo. Leo had warmed up his clarinet by now and heard what Lucky was doing with the chords. He began to swing a little. Lucky nodded his head, keeping time with his foot, his ears alert to the possibilities in Leo's solo. No one could swing a tune like Leo, even if he was a bit off his mark on a few notes. If only Jack would lay off those ham-fisted chords . . .

Lucky could see that Leo and Maggie didn't have too much to worry about: their son lacked the talent to play piano professionally and would figure that out for himself soon enough. In the meantime, let the kid get it out of his system—maybe he could chase off a few of those devils that tormented young fellows his age. Lucky knew all about devils, and he knew it wasn't music that brought them on. It was music that kept them from taking over the world.

They played a few more oldies—"Margie," "Indiana," "Bye-Bye Blackbird"—and then Jack wanted to play something "more modern." Lucky feared the worst, but the arrangements he and Leo had worked out for "Foggy Day in London Town" and "How High the Moon" weren't half-bad. Somebody had taught the kid a few good licks —maybe that guy with the TV show—but what Jack needed to learn most of all was a little restraint. Leo played a lighter style. You had to know how to set him up, when to layoff and let him fly, and when to fill in the gaps, the places where even a skilled clarinetist needed to take a breath. There wasn't much Lucky could do for Leo on his cheap guitar, so he just strummed along and enjoyed the music.

They'd been playing for maybe half an hour when Jack finally asked Lucky if he'd like to take a turn on the piano. "I can take over the drums and Ma can get us all something to drink," he suggested.

"Thanks a lot," Maggie laughed, but then she added, "I should check the windows anyway—I think I heard thunder. Let's hear you play something, Lucky—I'm sure you haven't forgotten *that* much."

"Well, I'll give it a try," Lucky said, and took his place on the bench.

He tried a couple of chords, then a run. The action was a bit stiff, but workable, and if you laid off the pedal the old piano didn't ring quite so much, didn't sound so out of tune. There was thunder rumbling somewhere far off, and a smell of rain came in the windows, but Lucky knew how to chase those clouds away. He turned to Leo. "Blue Skies, one flat."

"Gotcha," Leo said, and tapped his toe to set the pace: *one, two; a-one-two-three-four-*

Jack picked up the beat and Lucky began laying down a solid foundation of chords, a launching pad for Leo's solo. He knew what his brother liked, what it took to get him rolling, and it wasn't long before Leo took off with the melody. At first just a few short flights, but each one made him stronger, gave him more confidence. By the third chorus Leo was soaring up into that sunny blue sky, way up there with the puffy white clouds and cruising eagles. *Now that's the way a clarinet ought to sound,* Lucky thought. The kid still had the gift—all he needed was a good piano to set him up.

That was all most guys needed. Lucky had never considered himself much of a soloist, but he did know how to bring out the best in the people he played with— that had been his stock-in-trade for years. "Get Lucky Lantz for your piano," they used to say around Madison, "and your whole band will sound better." He took pride in his reputation, even if they sometimes said other things that weren't so nice: "Provided you can keep him off the sauce, that is, and away from the chicks . . . and God help you if he finds a hot poker game anywhere in town!"

Yes, that was the book on Lucky Lantz, and the reason so many bandleaders had given him the sack, even though they always said he was one of the best. And now here was Leo, who hadn't played professionally since 1929, and he was swinging that old Irving Berlin tune as if he'd never been away. A nice pure tone, too, now that he was warmed up—one of the sweetest Lucky had ever heard. A man who could coax music like that out of a clarinet had no right to keep it wrapped up for years inside a ragged scarf.

Leo brought his solo to a close and nodded to Lucky: *Your turn, brother—show 'em what you can do!*

Lucky began carefully, like a man on a tightrope, feeling that wide-open sky all around him, wondering if he might lose his balance and tumble to his death. He stretched the rope a little tighter, tried a little more, and then, just when the void seemed about to swallow him up, he scrambled back to safety. He found a graceful way to get himself down from the high-wire and then Leo and Lucky took one more chorus in close harmony before they went out with that jazzy little flourish they had worked out nearly thirty years ago.

Maggie and Jack clapped enthusiastically. "Gee, you guys really are good together," Jack said, as if he never would have believed it without a demonstration.

"We weren't too bad in our day," Leo said happily.

"Best band in the North Land," Lucky said, reciting the slogan they'd painted on the old touring car that once carried them to the resorts of northern Wisconsin. A slight exaggeration, maybe, but not a great one.

"I don't suppose you remember the way we used to do 'After You've Gone'?" Leo asked, tightening his reed.

"Are you kidding? I've taught that arrangement to three or four guys who weren't half as good as my brother. We take the first two choruses slow and easy, Jack—then at my signal you give the rim a hard rap and we double the tempo."

"Oh, like on that Benny Goodman record Dad likes so much," Jack said.

"Yeah, like that," Lucky said, and gave Leo a wink. They played Benny's version—not as well as they once did, but with some of the old zip. The fire was still there, Lucky could see that. It just needed a little stoking, a decent draft, and it would grow. They played several more Goodman tunes, sounding better on each one, and then Leo said he'd better switch to the saxophone, which was easier to blow than the clarinet.

"You set a mean pace, Lucky—I haven't worked this hard in years." He looked plumb tuckered out, but proud and happy, as if he'd proved something to himself he'd been wanting to prove for a long time.

"We can quit any time you want," Lucky said. His own wrists were aching, his fingers tingling, as if he'd been pounding shoe leather at his last all day.

"Hey, we're just getting a good start!" Jack protested. "I want to sit on the bench with you, Lucky, so I can see what you're doing."

So Leo warmed up his sax and Lucky altered his style to fit that moodier instrument. They played some blues and ballads, nothing too strenuous, and the storm, which had been rumbling nearby without ever quite arriving, produced a few big boomers that rattled the windows, but nobody suggested it was time to quit. Lucky was reminded of an evening back in '27 or '28, when he and Leo were playing the Veterans' Ballroom in Eagle River, a big Fourth of July dance, and the lights were knocked out by a sudden storm. The thunder roared and the wind howled, but the band was so hot that night they just kept right on playing, and the people kept on dancing, and in the flashes of lightning you

could see couples fox-trotting around the dance floor—
an eerie sight, as if they'd conjured up a ballroom full of
spooks. They were just dumb farm kids from southern
Wisconsin, but they'd heard all the hot bands of the day,
on radio and records and sometimes even in person, and
for one night, at least, they were good enough to keep a
crowd dancing through the teeth of a storm.

Once again this storm seemed to pass off and Leo
and Lucky kept playing old favorites, another tune
coming to mind as soon as they'd finished the last. Then
Maggie asked for 'Stardust', always one of their best
numbers, and as Lucky built a flight of stairs he knew
Leo's sax would climb, all the way up to the Milky Way,
he found himself remembering another time they'd
played this tune . . .

The year was 1930. The band had long since broken
up, the country was sunk in a terrible depression, but
Leo and Lucky were safe and secure, sharing a sunny
room on the second floor of Lake View Sanatorium.
When the san's social director found out they were both
musicians, she suggested a Sunday afternoon concert for
the other patients, a supplement to the weekly bingo
party. So that was how the brothers first met Maggie and
Lou Malloy—two gals with stardust in their eyes and
mischief in their smiles, who hung around after the
concert to flirt with the musicians. Lucky was an old
hand at romancing the ladies from his piano bench, but
he was a little surprised at Leo, who was usually too
bashful and too much the gentleman to chase skirt the
way he did. Once the kid confessed that he had fallen
hard for Maggie, Lucky did his best to help him out by
wooing her sister. He didn't think he'd broken Lou's
heart, though. She found out soon enough what kind of

a guy he was, and she didn't seem to mind one bit.

It was 1930, after all, and nobody expected the good times to come back, least of all the patients of Lakeview Sanitarium. You had to make your own good times, and nights after lights-out Lou would sneak downstairs for a nightcap and a petting session with her beau in the broom closet by the stairwell. They'd neck standing up, wedged in between the vacuum cleaner and the dust mops, the scent of cleaning fluid and furniture polish making them dizzy after the bootleg hootch, and every night Lou would stay a little longer, let him go a little further, give him a little more of her body before she spooked and ran upstairs to her room. And one night, just for the hell of it, she sent Maggie down in her place, and Lucky couldn't tell the difference in the dark. He had her half-undressed before he realized he was sucking the tongue and squeezing the tits of Chippy's girl . . .

The dining room was lit by a brilliant flash. An explosive crack shook the house and Laurence and Maggie exchanged a startled look, as if they'd been sharing the same memory. The lights went out, and in the darkness they could hear the rain pounding the rooftop and hissing on the driveway cinders outside the open window.

"Well, I guess that's the end of *that* concert," Maggie said, and went to get candles and flashlights from the kitchen. Once they had some light, they went out on the front porch to watch it rain, and Lawrence inhaled the rich, musky odor of steaming asphalt and dampened soil, the earth soaking up moisture after a long hot spell.

"Well, we sure needed the rain," Leo said, and put

his arm around his wife. They stood side by side, watching the lightning flicker and dance across the night sky. Laurence hung back by the inner door. He wasn't superstitious but, after the life he'd led, he saw no point in tempting fate.

"No yard work for me tomorrow," Jack said happily. "Think I'll go uptown and pick out some new records. Want to come along, Lucky?"

"Gosh, I'll be starting my new job tomorrow, Jack. I reckon I'll be gone before you're even awake, if your dad will give me a ride into town."

"Glad to," Leo said, and gave his brother an approving look.

By the time they'd had their dessert and coffee, the rain had stopped and the lights were back on, so Maggie dug out some sheets and a blanket and Leo took Laurence out to the garage, where they made up the cot. The roof *had* leaked some, but not right on the cot, and not on Laurence's suitcase.

"I'm sorry to park you out here for the night," Leo said, the muscles in his jaw twitching. "If there was anywhere else you could sleep—"

"Don't worry about it," Lawrence said. "Warm weather like this, I'll be just fine. When do you leave for work?"

"Around seven. You want some breakfast first?"

"I'll get it uptown. Just wake me when you're ready to go. Goodnight, Leo, and thanks for everything. And thank Maggie again for that swell dinner."

"Our pleasure," Leo said. "Sleep well!" He gave Laurence a last guilty look and then slipped out the side door.

There was too much to say, and neither brother had

ever been good at expressing their feelings. *Not in words anyway*, Laurence thought, sitting down on the cot to take off his shoes. They never needed words when they had their music.

And, it appeared, they still didn't.

4.
Nice Work if You Can Get It

THE SHRIEK of rusty hinges woke Laurence with a start. Sunlight poured in through the open garage door and in the slanting rays stood a hazy figure with bright wings— an angel come to carry him off? Laurence rubbed his eyes and looked again, relieved to see it was only Leo, his wings a trick of sunlight in the dust-riled air.

"Sorry to disturb you, Larry, but I have to leave for work in a few minutes. Still want a ride into town?"

Laurence sat up and stretched. The cool damp air of the summer dawn had seeped into the garage, stiffening his joints and muscles under the light blanket. His body seemed made of woven twigs—once false move and he'd snap. "Can I shave first? Don't want to show up for my new job looking like a bum."

Leo checked his watch. "I guess I can spare a few minutes. There's some coffee on the stove and a box of doughnuts on the counter. Maggie and Jack are still asleep."

"Be right out," Laurence said, and pulled his trousers on over the underwear he'd slept in. He took his shirt and shaving kit into the house. The only bathroom was in the hall between the two bedrooms and Laurence did his business as quietly as possible, then ran a little hot water at the tap. He washed, shaved, and ran a comb through his graying hair—combing it straight back to accentuate his high forehead and long, straight nose. That forehead kept getting higher and that nose longer with each passing year, and tiny red veins had begun to show across his cheekbones. Still, it was a face women seemed to like. When he was young, they used to say he looked like Rudolph Valentino. These days, Laurence figured it would be more like Bella Lugosi.

Leo was waiting in the driveway with the engine running. Laurence grabbed his sport coat from the garage and settled down beside his brother in the '52 Plymouth. "Nice car," he said, as Leo backed down the driveway.

"Thanks—I bought it last year when the old Lafayette finally gave up the ghost. Had to take a big loan from the Credit Union to pay for it."

Well, at least you've got credit, Laurence thought of saying, but didn't. They drove over to Monona Drive, where a steady stream of cars was flowing into the city. Leo edged forward, watching for an opening. When a tiny gap appeared, he gunned the Plymouth into the stream and drove intently, both hands on the wheel, his eyes fixed on the road ahead where red lights flashed periodically.

So this is what it's like to go to work everyday, Laurence thought. Already he could feel the magnetic power of the city with its thousands of jobs drawing them along bumper-to-bumper, a long line of box cars pulled by a single engine. But was this train on the right track? That was the question nobody cared to ask.

"That was a nice little jam session we had last night," Leo said. "It was fun playing with you again, Larry—I'd forgotten what a good set-up you are."

"Oh, not as good as I used to be," Laurence said, "but I enjoyed it, too. Don't you ever miss it, Leo? Playing with a real band?"

"Not a bit. Jack and I play together a lot, and sometimes I get together with some guys from work—other ex-musicians. We did a stint at the union's Christmas party last year—won first prize. That's enough for me."

Laurence wondered if that would ever be enough for him. A settled life had never appealed to him in the past, but he could see its merits for a man his age. Last year a young social worker had come to see him in the san. "I've taken an interest in your case," she said, "and I wonder if I might be of help. Have you given any thought, Mr. Lantz, to what your problem *really* is?"

"Yes, I've got TB," Laurence said.

She shook her head. "TB is a curable disease these days. Many former patients live productive and healthy lives. Your problem is that you've lived an irregular life— a life, if you'll permit me to say so, rife with temptation."

Laurence smiled. The temptations had always been the best part of it, in his opinion, but he didn't expect this little missionary to understand that. She explained that, in order to rehabilitate such "hardened cases" as himself, the state had set up a series of vocational courses, which he could take free of charge. They would even supplement his salary if he were serving a bona fide apprenticeship in an approved trade. This was all news to Laurence and, always on the look-out for a free ride, he agreed to look through the social worker's loose-leaf notebook, which described the various courses.

Carpentry sounded interesting; he had always enjoyed working with his hands, but the social worker thought that, given his age and physical condition, carpentry was a poor choice. Electronics repair also appealed to Laurence—he'd built his own crystal set when he was a kid—but the social worker doubted that he would have the mathematical skills he needed for such a course. That left watch repair and shoe repair, and of the two Laurence definitely leaned toward watches, but the social worker said the course in watch repair took longer and required an elaborate set of tools—investments she didn't think the state would be willing to make for a man his age.

So shoe repair it was. Laurence supposed that, if you couldn't be a musician, one job was probably as good as any other, and he was used to letting the state make his decisions. At least he'd had a pleasant summer up at Tomahawk and won a little money playing cards with the guys in the bunkhouse. Strictly recreational, of course.

They were driving past the park now and Laurence noticed how bright and clear the air was after last night's storm. Across the dark blue waters of Lake Monona, the dome of the state capitol gleamed like a beacon in the morning sun, yet here on Monona Drive the traffic crept along in double rows. Drivers gained a car-length now and then by changing lanes, then lost it when the cars in the other lane surged ahead. Laurence sensed his brother was getting ready to say something.

"You know, I'm really sorry I can't help you out with a loan," Leo finally said as they neared the city limits. "If a few bucks would do you any good—"

"Don't worry about it," Laurence said. "I'll see if I can't collect on a few old debts."

"Gambling debts aren't collectible in a court of law," Leo observed.

"They weren't *all* gambling debts," Laurence said. "I earned an honest buck now and then—when I had to."

"Of course you did. But I hope you won't go back to any of those jobs, Larry—especially tending bar. That wouldn't be a good idea if you're serious about staying away from the booze."

"I understand that," Laurence said. "Tending bar is out. So is hustling pool, shooting craps, dealing cards, playing the ponies—"

"You never made any money that way," Leo said. "You just thought you did."

"Well, then I thought I spent it, too. I thought I had a pretty good time with it. But don't worry, Leo, I'm putting all that behind me. I'm determined to live a few more years, if I can." He paused a moment, then asked, "So when did you say *you're* seeing the doctor?"

Leo kept his eyes on the road. "This Saturday. It's my annual check-up."

"I was thinking . . . maybe you shouldn't wait that long. I mean, if those pains are still bothering you, it could be something serious."

"I doubt that," Leo said. "Anyway, I can't take time off work this week—we're running the payroll and there's a ton of vacation-pay to figure in. It's going to take two nights of over-time as it is. My boss would scream if I asked for time off."

Laurence didn't argue; he knew how stubborn his brother could be. Back in '29, Lucky was in the san a month before Leo finally saw a doctor about his own cough. By then he was hemorrhaging in both lungs and, when he arrived at the san, they put him on the corridor known as "death row" because they didn't expect him to live out the year.

"Say, do you mind if I just drop you at Schenk's Corners?" Leo asked as they drove up Atwood Avenue. "You can get a bus uptown from there, and I'm running a little late—"

"No problem," Laurence said. "I'll see you for dinner tonight—if I'm still welcome, that is."

"Of course you are. We'll want to hear all about your new job. Good luck today, Larry. I hope you and your new boss hit it off."

"You know me," Laurence said as the Plymouth pulled up to the curb. "I can get along with anybody. Thanks for the ride, Leo—and thanks for giving me another chance."

"That's what you're giving yourself, Larry. You know, I probably shouldn't say this, but I always believed you could quit drinking any time you really wanted to."

Laurence gazed up the street. From where the Plymouth was parked, he could see three taverns, each one extending its neon beer sign over the sidewalk like a white flag of surrender. "Take it easy, Leo," he said, and got out of the car.

~§~

Thirty minutes later the crowded bus labored up King Street and swung onto the Capitol Square. Laurence was surprised to see how busy Madison was at eight o'clock in the morning—not an hour he saw often in his former life. He climbed down from the bus and began to stroll along with the crowd, feeling as fragile as a sheet of glass. One good bump and they'd scatter his pieces all over the sidewalk.

He was ready for some breakfast, but the lunch counters on the square all looked pretty crowded. Fortunately, he remembered a nice little place by the railway station where they used to go for flapjacks and eggs after an all-night jam. He was headed in that direction anyway, so he crossed over to West Washington and started down its broad, tree-lined sidewalk. In the first block he passed the Cambridge Hotel—a massive, red-brick fortress where he skipped bells in his younger days, whenever he was between gigs. A lot of traveling salesmen stayed at the Cambridge, also lobbyists and politicians, a few on-the-road musicians and assorted entertainers. There was always plenty of sporting action at the Cambridge, and Lucky supplemented his tips with the odd night of poker in one of the top-floor suites.

He paused at the corner, looking up Fairchild Street to the canopied entrance with its red carpet and potted shrubs. A liveried doorman—Ernie Hansford, it looked like—stood guard before the revolving doors. Lucky was tempted to mosey up and have a word with him. If memory served, the Cambridge was still holding his last paycheck. He seemed to recall some unpleasantness over a craps game in the laundry room, and he had left town in a hurry, without supplying a forwarding address. That sort of thing had happened to Lucky Lantz fairly often in the old days.

Let it go for now, Laurence thought. He'd come back later, when he could present himself as an honest craftsman, gainfully employed. He proceeded downhill from the square and the buildings became smaller and shabbier the further he got from that hub of commerce. After four blocks the street leveled out, the trees were gone, and Laurence could see the Milwaukee Road switch yards up ahead. In the block before the depot stood a small, shabby diner that catered to train crews and assorted night-owls. It was named after the Milwaukee Road's streamliner, the Hiawatha.

Laurence was pleased to see the Hiawatha was still open for business, and doing quite a bit of it, to judge by the aroma that came from its exhaust fans. He entered and found himself a stool midway along the crowded counter, then took a menu from the rack. A hard-pressed waitress gave him an over-the-shoulder glance as she poured several coffees. "What'll it be, mister?"

She was broad-bottomed and buxom, with sharp dark eyes and the embittered air of a woman who had trusted one man too many. Lucky was not daunted—he'd been charming dames like that for most of his life.

"Good morning, dear. Do you suppose I could get a couple of eggs fried easy over, three strips of crisp bacon, a side of toast, jam, a glass of freshly squeezed orange juice, and a nice cup of hot black coffee?"

The waitress seemed mildly amused by this recital. "Sure, I don't see why not. It's called the Breakfast Special."

"Ah, but you see"—Lucky leaned forward and spoke softly, as if he didn't want the other people at the counter to hear—"if your cook can't do a decent easy-over, I'd really rather have my eggs sunny-side up. I like the outside firm and the inside nice and soft, you know what I mean? It all depends on how deft your man is with a spatula, and how hot he keeps the griddle."

The waitress gave him a level look. "So which way do you want 'em?" The nametag on her full, well-supported breast said "Ginger." Her hair was short and curly, a faded red-gold color that matched the light down on her thick freckled arms.

"Well, Ginger, which would you recommend? I suppose you've served a lot of eggs in your time?"

"Oh Lord," she said, and rolled her eyes, "I've served a few, but I try not to look at the damn yokes."

"A wise policy," Lucky said. "Tell you what—I'll try them easy over. Better a hard yoke than a runny white, I always say. What about the jam? Do I get a choice?"

"It's all strawberry today," Ginger said.

"Ah, good thing strawberry is my favorite. Do you suppose you could sneak me an extra packet or two? I've got a real sweet tooth."

Ginger gave him a crooked half-smile. "I'll bet you do," she said, and went to place his order. A moment later she was back with his juice and coffee, her dark eyes making brief contact with his before she moved on.

Lucky watched her proceed along the counter, refilling coffee cups. Not a bad looking broad for a gal in her fifties. He liked the way that uniform clung to her rounded hips and plump buns. He drank his juice and sipped his coffee, keeping his eyes on Ginger as she took care of her customers at the other end of her section. Though she didn't look his way, he knew she was aware of his gaze. When she brought his bacon, eggs, and toast, there were four packets of jam on the plate instead of the usual two.

"Thanks, sweetheart—I can see you've got a good heart."

"I hope the yokes are the way you like them," she said with a quick bold look, then hurried off. He watched her suddenly mobile ass swing down the aisle.

The bacon was crisp and the eggs satisfactory. Lucky ate with pleasure, sopped up the yoke with his last slice of toast, then slid the plate aside and lit one of the cigarettes he'd filched from Leo's pack last night. With a good breakfast under his belt, he was ready to think about business, so he got out his little black book and removed the rubber band that held several loose pages in place. Each page contained a column of figures, neatly entered in pencil, the earliest ones so faded he could barely read them. They represented his earnings as a musician over the past thirty years, plus any wages from tending bar or skipping bells. Later entries also included the loans to which he'd been a party—the money he owed and the money other people owed him. Whenever a debt was paid, it had been carefully crossed out, but there weren't many crossed-out lines in the book, and none after 1950. Lucky had never tried to add it all up, and he had no idea how it would come out if he did— whether the world owed him money or he owed the world. Something told him it was better not to know. That way a man never got to feeling too sorry for him- self, or too guilty about his debts—he could go on thinking that it probably all came out about even.

There was one debt, however, that far outweighed the others, and Laurence knew it tipped the scale the wrong way. If he was ever going to get back in good with Leo and Maggie—that is, *really* good—he would have to find some way to make it up to them. The entry was dated October 12, 1947, and it said simply, "Capitol Savings and Loan, $800." And in parenthesis, "Ma's furniture, collateral." This line had been crossed out and written beneath it, wedged in between the lines, were the words: "I.O. Ma $800." A damn shame, really, because if his luck had held he could have paid off that loan with plenty left over—he could have put the old gal on easy street.

Laurence shook off the memory, turned back a few pages, and found an entry for the Cambridge Hotel. Ah, just as he thought: $72.35—two weeks' wages—owed since April of 1944. He didn't suppose they had saved that check for him, but if any of the old gang still worked there—anyone besides Ernie the doorman—he had a chance of collecting. Not much further along was an entry for Eddie King, who owed him $150 for one weeks' work at King's House of Cards, one of several joints Eddie had opened after the war, all with great fanfare, all going dark when Eddie couldn't meet his payroll. There it was: two hundred and twenty dollars—his stake, if he could only collect it. Lucky raised his eyes and there was Ginger, refilling his coffee cup.

"Everything okay?" she asked him.

"Just fine. Good service, too. I may become a regular customer. I take it you're here every day?"

"Monday through Friday, seven to three, and every other Sunday." She rested one hip against the counter, signaling her willingness to stop and talk a moment. The lunch counter had cleared out a good deal since his arrival. "You work around here, do you?"

"Not yet, but I'm hoping to."

"New in town, huh?"

"So to speak. I used to live in these parts, but I've been out of circulation for a while."

She looked at him sharply. "In the slammer?"

Laurence smiled. "No, dear. Various hospitals, mostly. Then I was at a school this past summer, learning a new trade. Say, do you know a shoe repair shop near here, a place called Abe's?"

"Sure, it's just around the corner from my apartment. What about it?"

"Well, I'm hoping to become Abe's apprentice. What can you tell me about him?"

She stepped back and folded her arms, sizing him up. "You're a little old to be starting out as an apprentice, aren't you, pal?"

"I'm a little old for a lot of things," Lucky said pleasantly, "but sooner or later a man has to settle down and pay his way through life, don't you think?"

She shrugged. "As far as I can tell, most men put that off as long as they can."

"I knew you'd say that. But we're not all like that. My brother, now there's a hard-working man, if you ever saw one. Good family man, too. Takes good care of his wife and son."

She stared at him. "I take it you ain't your brother."

"No, I'm not. But I aim to be a good deal more like him, if I can. Anyway, Abe Slovinsky agreed to take me on as his apprentice, sight unseen. I'm just about to drop around and introduce myself. What do you think? Have I got a chance?"

Her eyes showed that she understood his question might have a broader meaning. "I wouldn't know about that," she said carefully, "but from what I can see, Abe doesn't get a lot of business. I don't know what he'd need with an apprentice, except that he's getting older— like the rest of us. Walks with a limp, and he's got one of those blue tattoos on his forearm—I think he must've been in a concentration camp."

"Yeah? Jewish fella, huh?"

She shrugged. "I never asked about his religion. You got anything against Jews?"

"Nothing at all. In my former line of work I knew a lot of Jewish gentlemen. They were all nice fellows— tough bosses, sometimes, but fair."

"And what line of work was that?"

"I was a musician," Lucky said.

"Oh," she said, and looked away, as if he'd told her he robbed banks. "You got anything against musicians?"

"Nothing, except my ex was one. I swore I'd never get mixed up with another." She paused a moment to let that sink in. "So do you know how to find Abe's place?"

"I believe it's south of here a few blocks. Kind of a tough neighborhood, as I recall. We used to call it 'the Bush' back in the thirties, when somebody got knifed there every other Saturday night. It was an Italian neigh- borhood, in those days."

"It ain't changed much," Ginger said, "except for its color—but then, I suppose you ain't got nothing against colored folks, neither."

"Honey," Lucky said earnestly, "the only color I ever cared about was the blues. And any race that includes Louis and the Duke is all right by me." He paused and smiled. "Besides, if *you're* living in the neighborhood, I guess it can't be all bad."

"What would you know about *that*?" she asked, with an edge of sarcasm that suggested a long trail of defeat. His kind of woman, all right—he knew that trail well enough himself.

She looked down the counter toward the kitchen, where a burly cook was watching them. "Hey, I got to get

back to work. I hope you get the job. What'd you say
your name was?"

"Lantz—Larry Lantz, but folks used to call me
Lucky."

She turned back. "And are you?"

"Only in love, Sugar, only in love."

"I guess I should a seen that one coming," she said,
and walked away.

~§~

It was a small, one-story building, wedged in
between a corner grocery and an out-of-business dry-
cleaner's. Behind it stood the switch yards, an expanse
of tracks and box cars bordered by coal piles, storage
tanks, and warehouses. The morning sun glared off the
shop's peeling clapboards and tattered yellow awning,
which bore the faded letters "Abe's Shoe Repair" along
its fringe. The single window was covered by a layer of
grime that nearly hid the decals for Esquire polish, Cat's
Paw soles, and various other products. To Laurence the
place looked just about perfect. No pressure in a joint
like this, he thought. If the guy needed an assistant, he
must be about ready for the undertaker.

Feeling confident, he entered beneath a tinkling
bell. At first all he could see was a dark figure hunched
over a bright square of window at the back of the shop.
The figure rose at the sound of the bell and lumbered
forward, dragging a foot which, Laurence saw as he
came closer, had been permanently twisted to the left.
He was an old man, large-framed but stooping, with a
few wisps of dirty yellowish hair still clinging to a waxy
scalp. His mild brown eyes peered cautiously out from

behind thick, dusty lenses. His fingers and teeth were stained yellow-brown from the pipe which smoldered in an ash tray near his stitching machine.

"Can I help you, maybe?" he asked, as if Laurence might have had some other purpose in entering his shop.

Sensing the presence of an old and abiding fear, Laurence made his voice as gentle as possible. "The question, friend, is can *I* help you? The folks up at Tomahawk said you might be in need of an apprentice, and I just finished the course they offer up there. My name's Laurence Lantz—that ring a bell with you?"

The old man took in his words and wondered at them, as if Laurence had told him he'd just won first prize in a lottery. "Me? Need an apprentice? For all the work I got in this place? Is that what they told you?"

Laurence cast an eye over the empty shelves that should have been lined with shoes waiting for repair. "Well, I can see you're not too busy right at the moment, but I might bring you luck. The fact is, I know a lot of people in this town. If the word got out I was working here, things might pick up. Anyway, what have you got to lose?"

The question brought a grimace to the old man's face. He sat down on his stool and blinked at Laurence. "Yeah, I remember when they write to me, and I say 'Sure, I could use some help,' but I figured maybe a young fella, just needs some training. Him, I could help, but this is no place for a man your age—a man who wants to make money."

Laurence put his elbows on the counter and leaned forward. "I'll level with you, friend. I'm a bit old to be starting out in a new trade, but I've made a lot of mistakes in my life and this is my last chance. I'd like to start out kind of slow, you know what I mean? I'm not as strong as I used to be, and some of these shops would run a guy like me into the ground."

The old man nodded. "A man's body is his worst enemy. His spirit is indestructible, but his body gives up too quickly. And when the body is gone, what happens to the spirit, huh? Tell me that."

"Nobody knows the answer to that," Laurence said, feeling himself in the presence of another philosopher. "That's the sixty-four dollar question, Pops."

The old man looked at him shrewdly.

"You're a drinker, maybe?"

"Used to be," Laurence said. "That's behind me now—I haven't had a drink in two years."

"Two years is not so long. Wait another ten years, maybe you can say you're cured. So what happens if I make you my apprentice? How you going to live on what I pay you? This shop can't support one man, let alone two. We going to eat shoe leather, maybe?"

"The state will supplement my salary," Laurence said. "I just have to get somebody to sign these papers." He took them out of his jacket pocket and spread them open on the counter. The old man leaned forward to look at them through his dusty glasses. He ran his finger along each line, proceeding slowly, as if he were translating the words into another language. While he was still reading, the bell over the door jangled and, wonder of wonders, a customer entered the shop.

He was a black kid carrying a pair of black and white wing tips, a sporting man's shoe. Laurence saw at once that the soles and heels were badly worn. The uppers had begun to pull away from the welts where the young man's bunions had applied too much pressure to the light-weight stitching. Cheap leather—it cracked easily, but buffing would bring back its shine.

"Can you do anything with these muthas?" the young man asked the proprietor.

Abe took the shoes and looked them over carefully, turning them in his hands like a doctor examining a sickly child. "Yes, yes, I can fix. Cost you one fifty for half-soles, a dollar for rubber heels, another dollar to sew this welt.'

"Good. I need 'em by tonight, okay?"

"Yes, okay." Abe tore the tab off a ticket and gave it to the man, then tied the ticket to the shoes.

"You undercharged that guy by three or four bucks," Laurence said, after he'd left the shop. "A kid like that has money in his pocket—you might as well get some of it.'

Abe shrugged. "My prices are the same for everybody." He held up the shoes. "You want to give me a sample of your work?"

"Gladly," Laurence said. He went behind the counter, took off his jacket and hung it on a hook. The old man cleared a space for him at the bench and showed him where his tools and supplies were kept. Laurence rolled up his sleeves and went to work.

Twenty minutes later he had replaced the soles and heels, sewn the welts, and applied coats of black and white polish, which he buffed to a glossy shine. He presented his handiwork to Abe, who looked it over carefully.

"Not bad," Abe said. "You do good work."

"I had a good teacher," Laurence said. "Besides, I'm the kind of guy who likes things neat. There's no satisfaction in a messy job. So, am I hired?"

The old man sat down at a battered desk and relit his pipe. "Mister, I'd like to help you, and I'd be glad to have a helper—someone I could talk to when there's no work in the shop—but I'm an honest man and I got to tell you the truth: next week I may be out of here. The city, they say I owe them taxes. The bank, they say I owe interest on the mortgage. I pay one, I can't pay the other. Every month it's the same, every month it gets worse. What am I gonna do? They see I got another man working here, they'll think I'm making money. They'll say, 'Abe, you got to pay up in full.' Then we're both out of work."

"So how much do you owe?"

"Two hundred the city, another hundred and fifty the bank. You know what I make here in a week? Twenty bucks, I'm lucky. I save what I can, but it's never enough."

"And if you pay them off, how much time does that buy you?"

Abe shrugged. "A year, maybe less, I don't understand these things. They send the bills, they come and talk to me, I always pay what I owe when I got it. When I haven't got it, they give me a little more time. Not this time, though. This time they say, 'Abe, you got to pay up by the end of the month or you lose the shop.' I lose the shop, how am I going to make a living at my age?"

He sat staring out his small window, as if he could see the numbers he'd recited on the box cars that filled an adjacent siding. Laurence got out his little black book and the pencil stub he kept in his coat pocket. A hundred and forty-seven in the coin purse, plus that seventy-two bucks they owed him at the Cambridge, plus the hundred and fifty Eddie King owed him—that came to three hundred and sixty-nine dollars. Even if he only got. seventy-five out of King, he might be able to come up with the rest.

"Tell you what, Abe—let me make you a business proposition. Suppose I took care of the taxes and the bank for you—what could you give me in return?"

Abe spread his arms wide. "You want this shop, it's yours. Let me be *your* apprentice, you got such money to spend. I work for you, okay?"

Laurence smiled. "No, I think I'd rather let you run the show. But say I bring in some extra business—say we start doing better than twenty a week. Anything over that is mine, okay? If we top forty, we'll split it down the middle, half for me and half for you—how does that sound?"

"Forty dollars a week in this shop? You got big dreams, Mister."

No, just little ones, Laurence thought. A two-bit gambler's dreams, that's all they were. His problem was that he hated to drive a hard bargain with someone worse off than himself. He'd let guys go light on the pot when by rights he should have driven them out of the game. You couldn't get rich that way. But what the hell, he saw possibilities in this location. There was always the chance of a profitable sideline, given the clientele. And Abe wouldn't complain if he wanted to take a day off now and then. No pressure, that was what he liked about it—no pressure at all.

"Listen, I'll need a few days to raise the money. You've got till the end of the month, right? That's still five days off—in fact, with the Labor Day weekend, you've probably got until next Tuesday before they come after you."

Abe shook his head. "There's something I haven't told you yet. A real estate developer, he's been buying up lots around the neighborhood. He wants this whole block, so he can tear down what's here and build something else. He made me a good offer for the land, said he'll be in this Saturday for my answer. I can't wait past then, Mister. Next week I got nothing."

"All right," Lucky said, "I'll have three and a half big ones for you by Saturday morning at the latest. Then you can tell this developer to go piss up a rope, sign my papers, and we'll be in business. By the way, my friends call me Lucky—Lucky Lantz."

The old man raised his eyebrows. "Lucky? That's your nickname? You're going to lose your luck working here, my friend."

"It wouldn't be the first time," Laurence said with a smile. "Put her there, partner."

He extended his hand and the old man, after a moment's hesitation, took it in his large, calloused paw. Then he looked at Laurence earnestly. "This shop is all I got in the world, Lucky—my wife, my children, my past, present, and future. You won't take it away from me, will you?"

"No way," Laurence promised him. And for once in his life, he almost believed he was on the level.

~§~

The day was heating up and Laurence was feeling a mite tuckered out, so he decided to walk over to Park Street and wait for a bus uptown. There was a chance he could catch Eddie King at his favorite hangout, the

Pastime Billiards Emporium. Or he could drop by the Cambridge and see if anyone there remembered him. The sooner he got his stake together, the sooner he could settle into his new life.

All along Regent Street and off to the south, the old three-story flats were being replaced by low-cost public housing—plain boxy buildings that were already starting to look a little rundown. Between the housing projects there were vacant lots filled with piles of rubble and discarded appliances, a few playgrounds where black children jumped rope and shot baskets. Laurence found a shady place to wait for the bus, and eventually one came along Park Street from the south.

He rode across the University of Wisconsin campus, still quiet during the last week of its summer vacation, and got off at State and Johnson, just a few blocks from the square. He was about to head up Johnson toward the pool hall, when his eye was caught by a flickering neon sign on the next block of State Street. Say, was the old Buccaneer back in business?

Laurence strolled up the shady side of the street, feeling like a kid sneaking up on a carnival peepshow, and, sure enough, there was a red neon "open" sign in the window. Next to it stood a brightly colored poster:

LIVE JAZZ every Mon.Weds.Fri.
JOEY MARCH and his Dixieland Paraders.

Lucky was glad to see the reborn Buccaneer still featured Dixieland jazz. Three nights a week, too—not bad for this town. Joey March was a good kid and a damn fine trumpet, but even more important was the fact that Joey owed Lucky money. He got out his little book and thumbed through it once again. Yes, here it was: "April 12, 1949. Joey March, $100."

He remembered the incident well. The kid had a chance to audition with Bob Scobey's Frisco band and no way to get out to the coast. The guys all chipped in and Lucky, flush after some good nights at the poker table, chipped in the most. Joey got the job and stayed on in Frisco, and Lucky never expected to see that C-note again, but here it was just waiting for him to come by and claim it.

Laurence decided to put off the Cambridge and Eddie King for another day. He felt his luck coming around and it wasn't running in that direction. Better to drop by the Hiawatha and let Ginger know he'd gotten the job. Then he'd see what she was doing this evening. Lucky Lantz always did like to show up at one of his old haunts with a new lady on his arm.

5.

Up A Lazy River

THE DAY was coming to a close in shadows and soft breezes as Laurence escorted his date along State Street. A parade of gaudy neons had upstaged a bashful sunset, but the sun's warmth still rose from the sidewalk and in the window of a florist's shop Lucky saw their reflections strolling arm in arm through a grotto of ferns and bright, exotic blossoms. Ginger had dolled herself up for the occasion and didn't look half-bad for an old hash-slinger from the Hiawatha Diner, but what he lacked in heft and girth she more than made up for.

"So what is it we're going to do again?" she asked him. "Hang out all night in some jazz joint, jiving with your old cronies, or collect on a bad debt?"

"I wouldn't call it a 'bad debt,' just yet," Laurence said, "and it won't take all night, I promise."

"And then what?"

"Well, that's up to you," he said, though actually he had something in mind. Under his other arm he carried a paper bag containing two 78 r.p.m. records he'd picked up at Leo's before catching the bus uptown. If Ginger was in the mood for more music, maybe they could find a place to play them.

They were still a block away from the Buccaneer when he caught the first faint bleat of Joey March's trumpet. *It's always the trumpet you hear first,* Lucky thought—especially a brash, hard-driving trumpet like Joey's. Personally, he preferred a somewhat mellower tone, but if Joey got to blow his horn three nights a week in a downtown club, he had to be doing something right.

Lucky held the screen door open for his date. Entering behind her, he surveyed the long, narrow room, a bar along one wall and a row of wooden booths along the other. It was the bandstand at the far end of the room that made the Buccaneer unique among the clubs Lucky had played in his long career. Built to resemble the deck of an old-time pirate ship, it featured wood and brass railings, a mast and poop deck, rope ladders, and even a cannon that could fire blanks. The shimmering blue backdrop was lit by hidden spots, and when the joint was jumping you could almost feel the deck heaving beneath your feet, hear the sails snap taut overhead, smell the sea breezes or the perfume of tropic isles. Every band played better at the good old Buccaneer!

Even though Monday nights were supposed to be murder in the club business, the booths were full and most of the bar stools taken. Ceiling fans swirled lazily overhead, but they couldn't disperse the layer of smoke above the bar or the sweet-sour scent of booze and sweat. Lucky found a stool for Ginger and leaned his elbow on the bar as he sized up Joey's group. It was a standard dixie ensemble: trumpet, trombone, clarinet, piano, bass (taking the place of a tuba), and drums. The piano player and the drummer were both kids, neither very good, but the bass player was an old pro—a black gent by the name of Bill Williams. Bill was working hard, trying to hold the rhythm section together, and the sweat glistened on his hair and face. The trombone and the clarinet were also manned by old-timers, and Lucky remembered their names—Pete Staley and Tommy Morris. Good musicians in their time, but they weren't putting much effort into these old Dixieland tunes.

It was Joey March who was the real star of the group. Lucky listened to him blast out the solo on "St. James Infirmary" and had to admit it was done with real authority. He was glad he'd loaned the kid that hundred bucks to get his audition back in '49, because working with Bob Scobey's Frisco Band had really cleaned up his style, given it a bite and force it never had before. *That's what working in the big-time will do for you,* Lucky thought. He'd been there once himself, but too late in his career, and not for long.

He signaled a passing bartender. "Howdy, friend. The lady would like a mixed drink, I believe, and do you have a bottle of Squirt for me?"

Ginger requested a bourbon and seltzer. "So you're an alcoholic, too," she observed, when there was a break in the music.

"Well, that's a matter of opinion," Lucky said. "Let's just say I used to take a drink now and then, but I gave it up because it was bad for my health. I never considered myself a true alcoholic."

"True alcoholics never do. My ex was one, so I ought to know."

He laughed. "I seem to be striking out on all counts. Anything else you want to hold against me?"

She peered closely at him. "I'll probably think of

something. You've got good manners, but there's something odd about you—something a little spooky. I can
tell you've been through some bad times."

"Sister, haven't we all?"

The bartender brought their drinks and Lucky
nursed his Squirt through the next set, enjoying the ensemble work of the veterans but getting pretty impatient
with the out-of-synch piano. The kid wasn't paying
enough attention to the other musicians, wasn't pulling
it all together the way a good piano should. That was the
trouble with these younger players—good technique, but
lousy instincts. They needed to think less and listen
more.

The band took its break and Joey March came down
to the bar for his usual shot of brandy with a beer
chaser. Evidently Joey still thought he could punish his
body night after night and get away with it. He was a
heavy-set man with an unhealthy flush and a cloudy
look in his green eyes.

Lucky leaned over the bar and waved. "Sounding
pretty good tonight, Captain."

Joey's red face creased around a broad smile. "Well,
I'll be damned—look who the cat dragged in!" He
brought his beer down the bar and shook Lucky's hand
vigorously. "Good to see you again, old-timer! I heard
you were back in the san. Hope it wasn't as bad as they
said it was."

"It's never that bad," Lucky said. "Fact is, the san's
not a bad place to be when you need a little time off—I'd
highly recommend it."

"No thanks, I'm too busy making a buck in this
dump." Joey wiped his brow with a damp handkerchief
His gray-black hair glistened with sweat and his chunky

body radiated heat, the energy left over from his hot-to-trot solos.

"You're sure packin' 'em in, kid," Lucky said. "How long have you been here?"

"Couple a years now. We get a good crowd from the campus, even on weeknights, and a lot of old-timers. It's great having a steady gig, Lucky—beats life on the road, any time."

"I reckon it does, if they pay you enough to live on."

"Oh, I got a day-job. I'm the band teacher out at Evergreen grade school. Can you imagine that? Me, teaching Sousa marches to a troop of snot-nosed little twerps? But I'm a married man now, Lucky—raising a family. Gotta put bread on the table."

His gaze turned questioningly to Ginger, so Lucky provided introductions. Ginger and Joey shook hands.

"Pleased to meet you, ma'am. Any friend of Lucky's is a friend of mine. You two known each other long?"

"This is our first date," Lucky said. "I'm trying to make a good impression."

"Jeez, and you brought her to a dump like this? Let me buy you both a drink. What's your poison these days?"

"No poison," Lucky said. "I'm drinking Squirt."

Joey laughed. "How long is *that* going to last?"

"Forever, I hope. Doc gave me orders, Joey. I'm out of the music business, too. Decided it was time to take care of my health."

"Yeah, so what is it now? Selling refrigerators to Eskimos? Heaters to Zulus?"

"You know that little shoe repair shop over on Regent Street—Abe's? Starting tomorrow. I'll be Abe's apprentice. Gotta get myself home to beddy-bye soon, but we saw the sign in the window and wanted to catch your group. You make a good sound—real nice."

"Yeah, except for the piano and drums," Joey said. "Best I could get this time of year, with a lot of bands on the road. The piano's pretty hopeless, don't you think?"

"Oh, I could teach him a few things," Lucky allowed.

"Damn, I wish you would! Why don't you sit in for a few numbers and we'll see if he pays attention?"

Lucky turned to Ginger. "Would you mind? Just one set, for old times' sake?"

She smiled at Joey. "I think he wants me to hear him play."

"Smart move," Joey said. "You'll see the old man here is a real pro—the best in the business."

"Oh, I never doubted that for an instant," Ginger said.

There was still time before the end of the break to ask Joey about that hundred dollars, but Lucky knew already it was hopeless. A young fellow with a wife and kids, a job at a grade school—he wouldn't be able to fork over a hundred smackers on a moment's notice. *Maybe,* Lucky thought, *I never really lent him that hundred dollars. Maybe I only meant to lend it to him, and then spent it on something else.*

Lucky entrusted Ginger with his paper bag—"Something for later," he explained—and left some money on the bar so she could order herself another drink. Then he followed Joey up the steps to the bandstand, where Joey introduced him to the other musicians. Pete and Tommy remembered him. So did Bill Williams. "Welcome back, Lucky—where you been hidin', man?"

"Oh, I've been retired," Lucky said. "This here's my big come-back."

The kid on the piano was not exactly pleased to be pushed aside. "What is this," he asked Joey, "old-timer's night? If you don't need me, I'll take my pay and go home."

"The hell you will," Joey said. "I want you to sit right there and listen to this guy. If you can learn something from him, you might be able to keep your job."

"Just humor me for a set," Lucky told the kid. "And stay close, in case I get in trouble—you might have to take over." He turned to the other musicians. "How about 'Up A Lazy River'? Key of F."

"Take an eight-bar intro," Joey said.

Lucky flexed his fingers over the keys. The first chord and he knew he was going to get along with the piano just fine. It was the kind of instrument he liked—a little resistance in the keys, but a quick response from the hammers and a nice, solid tone. He was glad he'd had that jam session at Leo's last night, because now he knew how far he could trust his aging fingers to give him what he asked for. He set the tempo at an easy pace, punched out a standard intro, then turned to the chords as the rest of the band joined in. The first chorus was nothing spectacular. They were like six guys thinking about putting a boat in the river but afraid to get their feet wet. Lucky could feel the drummer getting restless, trying to goose the tempo, but he and the bass were holding him back. *No, Junior, no—we're stronger than you. Just relax, for once, and get with the music!*

Joey took a solo on the second chorus and they finally got their leaky old vessel afloat. Lucky entrusted the rhythm to the bass while he worked out a counter-melody to Joey's solo. He found a little theme, tested it, repeated it, gave it to the trombonist, who picked it up readily enough and built his own solo on it. Lucky could see his eyes twinkling an acknowledgment: *Thanks, pal, I needed a fresh idea for this old chestnut!*

The clarinet took the fourth chorus, building on the trombone's solo, as Lucky had known he would. By now their little boat was gliding along smoothly, but their rendition was becoming a shade too predictable for Lucky's taste. A lot of guys had played the piece this way; it was time to try something different.

The fifth chorus was his. He tried putting a little more blues into his version of the melody. Nothing fancy, just a few blue notes where you hadn't heard them before. Now the river wasn't quite so lazy—there was another current flowing and the water was deeper in this channel he'd found. Lucky began to wonder if anyone had ever drowned in this river. Maybe a beautiful young woman who had thrown herself off the bank when her lover deserted her. Lucky began looking for the woman in the darker pools and channels, along the willow-shaded shoreline. As he neared the end of his first chorus, he began to glimpse her death-pale face beneath the surface.

Hey, lady, I see you down there. You can't hide from old Lucky. I see you, babe, and I'd keep you company if I could, but I'm not quite ready for the river—you'll have to wait awhile.

Joey heard what Lucky was doing, liked it, and signaled him to take a second chorus. Then he put a mute on his trumpet and began playing softly underneath, a somber counterpoint, which the trombone joined after a few bars, so that now they made up a little funeral procession for the drowned lady. Lucky built his

solo phrase by phrase, chord by chord, talking to the
face beneath the water, telling her that she was
beautiful, that he'd be with her by and by. And then
something extraordinary happened—the kind of thing a
musician lives for. The clarinet answered with the lady's
voice. Lucky got goose bumps, as if he'd called her spirit
from its watery grave. She was calling to him now and he
was hanging back, afraid to let her take him in her
watery embrace. They worked it back and forth through
another chorus, calling to one another, an eerie duet,
and then Lucky knew it was time to break the lady's
spell. He nodded to the drummer, raised a hand to
signal the other musicians, then hit a hard chord to
announce a break.

Let off the leash, the kid went after his snares and
cymbals, revved up his tom-toms, pounded out his
sixteen-bar Solo, then led the group enthusiastically into
the last chorus. The trumpet, clarinet and trombone
played ensemble and Lucky just gave it the old blues
boogie, leading them all toward home.

> Blue skies up above—
> Everyone's in love!
> Oh, up a lazy river, how happy you will be—
> Up a lazy river with me!

When the last cymbal had crashed and the last
boom of the bass drum had rolled away, there came a
modest patter of applause from the drinkers in the long
narrow room. Lucky hadn't expected an ovation. He
knew that the best things a musician did often went
unnoticed by the audience. Not that this had been one of
his best things, but it wasn't bad. He'd had a pretty good

time with it. Joey was beaming at him over his trumpet.

"Nice, old-timer. What's next?"

Lucky suggested "Mack the Knife," because there were some ideas he'd had last night that he hadn't gotten to try out. They played several choruses, Joey giving a fair imitation of Louis Armstrong and Lucky doing a little Fats Waller on his own chorus. For the third number he suggested "Mood Indigo," one of his all-time favorites. He coaxed a nice solo out of the trombone, got the clarinet warmed up, then he and the bass took a chorus all to themselves, probing the moody depths of Ellington's melancholy tune. They finished in a minor key and the audience didn't quite get it—it was little too close to the bone for the college crowd, maybe a little too much like real life.

Joey said they ought to finish the set with something upbeat, so Lucky suggested "Rampart Street Parade." Joey tapped his heel five times and they set off at a brisk pace, banners flying, batons twirling, a hundred leggy showgirls strutting their stuff through the streets of New Orleans. It was a city Lucky knew only from its music, but one he loved with all his heart, and he leaned over the keyboard of the rattletrap piano and tried to grasp all its color and magic with his ten fingers as they brought their parade to a slam-bang, fried chicken, speeches and fireworks finish.

The audience clapped enthusiastically. They always like the fast ones best, Lucky reflected. Even if you muff half the notes and slur the rest, the crowd always loves speed, mistaking it for virtuosity. Lucky's fingers were tingling, his wrists nearly numb. He felt short of breath and there was a peculiar pain behind his breastbone, as if he'd swallowed a pin, but the smile Ginger was sending him seemed to suggest that it had all been worth the effort.

Joey shook his hand. "By God, Lucky, you've still got the gift. This group never sounded better." He turned to the kid piano player. "I hope you learned something, boy."

The kid looked a little insulted. "I thought the style was a little old-fashioned, to tell you the truth, but if that's what you want—"

"Of course it's what I want," Joey said. "We're a Dixieland band, for Chrissake—or hadn't you noticed?"

Lucky was inclined to stick up for the kid. "Everybody's got to work out their own style, Joey. You've got a solid group here. Thanks for the seat, kid."

He stepped down from the bandstand and started along the bar, feeling a little weak in the knees and hoping there would be a the barstool next to Ginger's, when suddenly a massive figure loomed up in his path. Lucky tried to go around but the figure side-stepped to cut him off, put a pair of a heavy hands on his shoulders. Eddie King's oily mug emerged from the haze of cigar smoke encircling his puffy pompadour.

"Lantz, you lyin' bastard—I thought you said you were all done playin' in dives like this!"

You might know he'd be here, Laurence thought sadly. He could see that anywhere he went in this town to have a night out and listen to some music, Eddie King would be there—or guys just like him, determined to drag Lucky back into that chummy little world of hotshots and hustlers.

"I *am* done, Eddie. You just heard my last set, played for old times' sake. Now let me go sit down."

"Bull shit," Eddie said. "Hey, there's somebody here

who wants to meet you. Come say hello, for Chrissakes."

There were two people in the booth behind Eddie: a man with a cigar and a woman in a low-cut summer dress—the pleated, cross-my-heart style Marilyn Monroe had worn in *The Seven Year Itch*, a movie Laurence had seen three times when it played the Rialto in Tomahawk back in June. This gal had Monroe's knockers, but her hair was midnight black, a glistening cascade of waves and ringlets. Her skin was a dusky tan and she fixed Laurence with a pair of warm brown eyes, a smile that told him to take his best shot, because one chance was likely all he was going to get.

Laurence figured one was more than he had any use for, at his age. Besides, he could see the lady was mostly window-dressing for the sharp-shooter at her side. He wanted to rejoin his own date, but Eddie wouldn't let him pass, so finally, with an apologetic wave to Ginger, he slid into the booth. Eddie slid in beside him and now he was trapped in the dark booth with the two people across the table. The panels of gleaming wood reminded Lucky of an ebony coffin.

Eddie said, "Frankie, this is the guy I was tellin' you about, Lucky Lantz. Lantz, meet my new partner, Frank Holiday."

Holiday put a small pink hand across the table. A well-manicured, gambler's hand. "Pleased to meet you, Lantz. I enjoyed your set—that's the best this group has sounded since I've been coming here."

"Thanks," Lucky said, "glad you enjoyed it." Holiday had a deep, manly voice for a shrimp—sort of like Alan Ladd or one of those tough-guy actors. He also had wavy blond hair and a trim blond moustache. His teeth were white and even, his eyes a glittering, metallic blue. *A gambler's eyes*, Lucky thought, and that was a two-hundred dollar suit, if he ever saw one. The tie was genuine silk, with a diamond stick-pin. Lucky hadn't seen duds like that since he'd run a little game in Chicago and the high-rollers used to come up from the south side to try their luck against him.

"I thought Eddie said you were retired," Holiday said, courteously blowing his cigar smoke over Lucky's head.

"I am, as of now. That was my swan song."

The brunette seemed to find this remark funny. She laughed harshly, expelling cigarette smoke from her crimson lips.

"I'm sorry to hear that," Holiday said. "Aren't you sorry, Savannah?"

"I thought he sounded . . . promising," the girl said, and looked off across the bar, as if the whole conversation had suddenly begun to bore the hell out of her.

"This is Miss Savannah Jones," Frank Holiday said. "She's a blues singer with a great deal of talent—a potential star. We're looking for an experienced piano-player to back her up when she makes her debut later this week."

Lucky reflected that he had seen gals with Savannah's talents before, and they seldom had much to do with music. He smiled politely and said, "I'm sure you can find lots of good musicians in this town, Mr. Holiday. Eddie here knows most of them."

Holiday drew on his cigar and let the smoke escape from between his teeth. "Eddie says *you're* the best back-up piano in town, and after what I just heard I'm inclined to agree with him. He also says you play a mean game of poker."

"Naw, just a friendly game now and then," Lucky said. "I was never in your league, Frank."

Holiday's eyes glinted light from the bar, like a reflection on ice. "What do you know about my league? I'm just a fellow who likes to lose his money—strictly an amateur."

"Sure," Lucky said. "Only you've got the bank roll to ride out my hot streak and find one of your own, and nobody can win against odds like that."

Holiday smiled. "You're no dummy, Lantz. You change your mind, there'll be a place for you at my table."

"Hey, you guys forget about *me*?" Savannah asked, putting an elbow none too gently into Frank Holiday's rib cage. Holiday's quick glare made Lucky wonder if she knew how close she was to getting her pretty nose broken. Yet the gambler's voice remained gentle.

"We haven't forgotten about you, doll. How could we? I was just about to tell Lantz that we're opening a new club this Friday night. 'The Blue Swan'—how's that for a classy name? We're going to showcase this little lady in appropriately elegant surroundings." He put his five agile fingers around Savannah's swan-like neck and squeezed just hard enough to make her wince. Lucky's impulse was to slap the hand away, but he knew better than to try a dumb stunt like that.

Eddie gave a guffaw, while up on the bandstand the boys had jumped into their next number—"Sweet Georgia Brown"—and Lucky wished he was up there with them, in charge of the keyboard and at peace with the world.

"So if you'd like an audition with our gal here," Holiday said, finally relaxing his grip on Savannah's neck, "just let Eddie know. And if you'd care to give us a demonstration of your skill in other areas—"

Holiday left the words hanging as he relit his cigar, and that gave Lucky a chance to say, "Gee, Frank, I appreciate the offer, but the truth is I just can't do it any more. It's my health, you see. Eddie knows the problem. I'm living on borrowed time, as they say. Well, I guess I'd better be going—I left a friend at the bar . . ."

He pushed against Eddie, hoping the big jerk would let him out of the booth, but Eddie didn't move. For a moment, nobody said anything, and Lucky felt a twinge of panic, as if the coffin he was trapped in was about to go into the ground. Then Frank Holiday said, "Let him out, Eddie. The man wants to go home."

Eddie reluctantly slid out of the booth and let Lucky escape, but he followed him back to the bar. "You dumb fuck—don't you know you just blew the chance of a lifetime?"

"First chance or last?" Laurence asked him. "I ain't got that many left."

"You're an asshole," Eddie said, and went back to the booth.

Laurence smiled at Ginger. "Sorry about that. My fan-club."

"No problem," Ginger said. "A musician's date gets real friendly with the bartender. So who's the thug— another old friend?"

"I wouldn't call him a friend. In the music business, you sometimes have to deal with people like that. That's why I'm glad I'm out of it."

"You didn't sound much like you were out of it. You had the joint jumping, pal—you brought that bunch of loafers to life."

"I'm a little out of practice. Wait till you hear my records."

"Records? Is that what you've got in the bag? And where do you expect to play them, I'd like to know?"

"Your place, if you've got a record player, and you'll invite me up for coffee later this evening. Haven't I convinced you I'm harmless?"

She arched an eyebrow. "That was *not* the music of a harmless man, Mr. Lantz. Why does everyone call you Lucky, by the way? You a gambler, too?"

"It's just an old nick-name," Laurence said. "You know how those tags stick to a guy."

Joey completed the next set and came down to talk with them again. "You can sit in with us any time you like, Lucky. In fact, how'd you like to take over the piano on a regular basis?"

"Couldn't do it, Joey—I'm just not up to this kind of life anymore. Besides, the kid is all right. Stick with him and you'll have a good piano player by and by."

Joey walked with them to the front door and sucked in a few gulps of the slightly cooler air of the street. "It's great having you back in town, Lucky! We've all missed you. Say, did you ever get that money I sent you?"

"Money?" Laurence asked.

"Yeah, from out in Frisco. I sent you a check for a hundred smackers, but I don't know if it ever reached you. That was right about the time you left town."

"No, I never got it—or if I did, I must have cashed it and spent it when I was drunk. I don't suppose you've got that kind of money these days, Joey?"

"God, no, not with my mortgage! But I feel damn bad about this, Lucky. You really helped me out with that loan."

Laurence could feel Ginger's knuckles digging into his rib cage, but he didn't look her way. "Well, maybe you can do the same for me sometime, Joey. I'm trying to get together a stake, but don't worry—there's no big hurry. Bring your kids' shoes in when they need repair—Abe needs the business."

"We get paid on Friday night," Joey said. "Drop by around closing time—I'll have fifty bucks for you, and then I'll take you out for some of the best pizza in Madison."

"Wow, some Mr. Tough Guy," Ginger said as they set off down the street. "How do you expect to raise the money Abe needs if you keep letting guys off like that?"

"Oh, Abe will get his dough," Laurence said. "It's only three fifty. I ain't seen the day when I couldn't raise three fifty in this town, sugar."

"It's not just Abe I'm worried about," she said, taking his arm and letting him feel the fullness of her breast against it.

They stopped at the Brat Haus for a sandwich and coffee.

"So," she said, when they were settled down in a back booth, "I heard you tell Joey you were in the sanatorium. Not your first time either, I'll bet."

"I've had TB off and on since I was twenty-eight," Laurence admitted. "You're never entirely cured, but sometimes the disease goes dormant. Then you get to lead a normal life until it kicks up its heels again."

"We had TB in our family," she said. "I used to visit one of my cousins who was in a san, down in Tennessee. You've got that same spooky look my cousin had before she died, like there's something nibbling away at you from the inside. I suppose you've got a wife somewhere, just waiting for you to come home."

Laurence shook his head. "I was married once, years ago, but it didn't work out. I heard she got married again, so there's nothing left but a few bitter memories. You're the first woman I've seen, aside from my sister-in-law, since I got out of the san."

"Maybe that's why I look good to you," Ginger said. "A few days back in circulation and you might see somebody you like a whole lot better." Laurence started to protest, but she waved his compliments aside. "I know what I look like. You don't have to sweet-talk me, Lucky, and don't feed me a line, okay?"

"No lines," he promised her, but he wondered if a man ever really knew when he was feeding a woman a line, or just doing his best to be a nice guy. There were shades, niceties, he'd somehow never understood. But he had a notion Ginger would let him know if he ever laid it on too thick.

They left the restaurant and walked to Ginger's apartment, which was over on Mills Street, just a block or so from Abe's shop. Laurence had checked the schedule and knew the last bus left for Lake Edge at eleven thirty. Of course he could always take a cab, but he was hoping that wouldn't be necessary.

"So, I suppose you want to come up and play your records," Ginger said at the side door of a decaying building.

"That's up to you," Laurence said. "We can do it another night, if you're tired."

"Tired isn't the problem," she said—and then, after a moment's thought—"Oh well, once a sap, always a sap, I guess. C'mon up."

They climbed a stairway that smelled of sauerkraut

and cat piss to a door on the second floor. The apartment was plainly furnished; Laurence noticed the absence of personal items—plants, photographs, souvenirs. Ginger hadn't been living there long, and she hadn't brought much of her former life with her.

"I'd offer you a drink but you don't," she said. "Want me to brew some coffee?"

"I'm fine," Laurence said. "Where's your record-player?"

"In the bedroom—I don't play it often. Should I bring it out?"

"Not unless somebody's in there sleeping." He followed her into the bedroom and found the portable phonograph sitting on a flimsy stand near the window. There were a few records—hit parade stuff, mostly—stacked up beside it. Laurence took out one of his 78 rpm's and showed Ginger the label.

"'Gary Ames and His Sharpshooters,'" she read aloud. "You played with *them*?"

"For about six months," Laurence said, "back in the winter of 1951. We made six singles altogether, but these two are all I could find at my brother's place. You see, right there on the label, it says 'Piano solo, Lucky Lantz.' This was just before I got sick the last time. I was on the verge of my big break, and I blew it."

"Tough," she said. And then, "So let's hear it."

Laurence placed the disk carefully on the turntable. He started the motor, then lifted the needle-arm off its cradle and lowered it gently onto the outermost groove. He adjusted the volume, then sat down on the bed.

Ginger sat beside him and they listened in silence to the first side—"Satin Doll." Lucky hadn't listened to the record years. The quality of the recording was poor, but

the musicianship was as good as he remembered, even
better in places. That was old Johnny Coleman on the
sax—a damn nice solo. His own part was coming up:
thirty-six bars of piano, just a little brushstroke from the
drum and a steady bass underneath. Here it comes now,
here it comes . . .

Hearing his own music, the notes he'd struck in
November of 1951 at the little recording studio off Rush
Street, Lucky was carried back to that moment at the
keyboard when the whole world was soft wet clay beneath his fingers, and he shaped it, molded it, gave it his
own special stamp. *Ah, now that's the way a jazz piano
should be played,* he thought. There were other ways,
sure, but his way had always been the best.

When the record ended he removed the needle,
then lifted the disk with his fingertips along its edges
and flipped it over. "This side's for you," he told Ginger.
"An expression of my current sentiments."

The arrangement for "I've Got A Crush on You" gave
Lucky a full chorus intro. His touch and timing were as
good as he remembered. The effect was moody, pensive:
a man who should know better, falling in love against his
will, enchanted by a lovely woman. By the time the tenor
sax picked up the melody and the bass and drums took
over the rhythm, Lucky had made his statement. He
turned to Ginger and saw tears shining in her eyes.

"You wouldn't try to con an old lady, would you?"
she asked, letting her hand rest on his knee.

For answer he slipped his arm around her waist and
brought his face down to her waiting lips. Eventually the
record came to its end and the needle began to scratch
across the inner grooves. "Do you want to put on the
other record?" she asked, her breath warm in his ear.

Lucky reached over to remove the needle, then put his mouth back on the soft skin of her neck. "Later," he said. For this next part, they really didn't need any music.

6.

The Sunny Side of the Street

LUCKY walked into the saloon. The old gang was there; it felt good to be back. "Set 'em up, Mike," he said to the bartender, "drinks all down the line. Make mine Four Roses, neat."

"Comin' up, Lucky," the bartender said.

"Don't do this, Larry," Leo said at his elbow. "Don't spoil it now, when I'm almost starting to believe in you."

"Blow it out your ear, kid. Since when do I give a damn whether *you* believe in me or not?"

"Then don't do it for my sake," another voice said at his elbow. "You know *I've* always believed in you, dear, even when no one else did. You were always my good boy."

Lucky recognized the voice but didn't turn his head. "Relax, Mom. I'm just taking this one drink. Just for old times' sake. You know I can always stop with one."

"You take one, you'll take six," old Doc Steinmetz told him. "You take six, you'll go off on a week-long bender—"

"Yeah, yeah, stuff it, Doc," was all Lucky said,

watching eagerly as the bartender poured a tumbler full of the amber liquid and set it before him. What a lovely color, what a seductive aroma! Lucky closed his fingers around the glass, looked down into the shimmering red-gold depths as if into crystal ball. It was all there, his past, his present and his future. What else did a man need?

"Down the hatch, Lucky," the bartender said.

Gratefully, he raised the glass to his lips, but before he could drink he saw the whiskey evaporating into a thin pinkish cloud that rose above his head and blew away. Only a few tantalizing drops tingled the tip of his tongue, and those drops only intensified his thirst. He turned angrily to the bartender:

"What kind of a dirty goddamn trick—?"

But already the bartender had vanished; the saloon's walls were dissolving, leaving him all alone in a pool of bright sunlight. Lucky dove for cover, seeking the shadowy depths of his deeper dreams, but it was too late—the sunlight had him now and dragged him slowly back to consciousness. He woke up with the brightness of another morning in his eyes.

Ginger's bed was a lot softer than his old bunk up at Tomahawk and a lot roomier than the cot in Leo's garage. The lap of luxury, Laurence would have called it, but Ginger's ample lap was no longer there beside him, only her scent and the deep imprint of her body on the rumpled sheet. He reached to the bed table and found his watch. A quarter to eight, and she had said something about being at work by seven. Which meant she hadn't gotten much sleep, though he supposed she wouldn't mind too much—not after the night they'd had. Laurence shut his eyes and, hoping to block out the after-thirst of his dream, pictured Ginger's large, soft breasts in the palms of his hands, her plump, nicely rounded buns, their fullness like the curve of two half-moons. He always had liked a big woman, the bounty of her, the ample luxury of her flesh. And ah, that old jellyroll—a man could live till ninety and never get tired of that!

He'd been worried at first that his scar might put her off, the hollow place in his back where his ribs should have been. But Ginger scarcely noticed his deformity; she'd been much too busy with those parts around in front. *Not a bashful lady,* Lucky thought with a smile, *not a bashful lady at all!* Just thinking about it now in the morning light had given Laurence another erection. He would ignore this one, however. When a man latched onto a gal like Ginger, he did well to conserve his resources.

He got out of bed and crossed the sticky linoleum floor to the small bathroom, where he emptied his bladder, then inspected his face in the speckled mirror. *Not bad, old-timer!* Apparently the old Valentino still had a few miles left in him. He got dressed and made for the kitchen, where he found an electric percolator still plugged in. Propped against it was a note, and taped to the note was a key:

> *"Morning, lover! Hope you slept well after your labors. Help yourself to breakfast and lock the down-stairs door when you leave. See you for supper? –G."*

Well, at least she's still friendly, Laurence thought. That key was an invitation to move right in, but he wasn't sure he wanted to start playing house at his ripe old age. Whenever he moved in with a woman trouble soon followed. On the other hand, he didn't want to spend any more nights in Leo's garage if he could help it. Maybe a week or two with Ginger would be all right, just till he got on his feet.

The coffee was bitter from having sat on the stove for too long; its gritty burnt taste reminded him of his dream. Not the first time he'd dreamed about booze, and every time he woke up with a terrible thirst and also a kind of remorse, as if he'd actually managed to knock back a few in his sleep. He found some orange juice in the refrigerator and tried to quench his thirst with a big glass. He noticed there was no wine or beer in the fridge, and none in the cupboard, either. *Trying to make it easy for me*, he thought, a shade resentfully, until he remembered that her first husband had been an alcoholic. Probably she didn't like to have the stuff around.

He fried an egg and toasted a slice of bread to put under it. The apartment smelled of something spoiled, as if the garbage didn't get taken out often enough, but after all the joints he'd lived in it was practically a luxury suite. He could make do with it. Maybe later today he'd find some way to get out to Leo's for his suitcase—he could sure use some clean underwear. But first he needed to raise that three fifty.

Too bad about Joey—even if the kid came across with fifty bucks on Friday night, it would still leave him a hundred and fifty short. He'd have to drop by the Cambridge later today and see about that old paycheck. Laurence wiped the plate with his crust, popped it in his mouth, and chewed thoughtfully. It had already crossed his mind that Ginger might have a little money she could lend him, but he didn't like to borrow from the woman he was sleeping with—that would really make her think she owned him.

All these people to deal with, to try to get along with, and all of them expecting something from him! It was a lot easier on the bandstand, where you had a tune you could follow, a rhythm and a key that held it all together. If the guys in the band knew their business, they could play with anybody. Nobody criticized anybody else's style—they just found a way to harmonize and blend in.

He rinsed the dishes and left them in the sink, then returned to the bathroom, where he found a safety razor and can of foam in the medicine cabinet, compliments of one of Ginger's former boyfriends. Shaving, it occurred to him that there was, of course, another way he could raise the money Abe needed: there was Frank Holiday and his torch-singing sweetie. No doubt Holiday would pay top dollar for the right piano-player; a few nights at the Blue Swan and he'd have his three fifty.

No, you're not ready for that, Laurence told himself, rinsing off his lather. *Just forget about it!* But he knew that wouldn't be easy; neither Holiday's money nor his woman was likely to be far from his thoughts for the next several days.

He took the key Ginger had taped to the note, went down the back stairs and out the door into yet another hot, steamy day. A pair of old women, chatting over their back fence, looked at him with interest as he went up the alley. Laurence gave them a smile and nod. Best way to get along in a new place, he knew, was to act like you belonged there. People got used to you soon enough.

He walked down Regent Street, no breeze blowing

and no shade to soften the glare of the sun, a blind white eyeball hovering over the shabby storefronts and vacant lots. Laurence was glad to make the shelter of Abe's little shop. Even though it was as hot as an oven, it was at least a dark oven.

Abe looked up at the tinkling of his bell and reacted to the arrival of his new apprentice with pleased surprise, as if he'd never expected to see the man again. Maybe he thought Lucky's offer was just one of his better dreams. Laurence figured he had to have a few good ones to space out his nightmares, just like everybody else.

"So, what can I do for you today, old-timer?" he asked. "I've got a couple of hours before I need to see some people about that money I promised you. Anything come in this morning?"

The old man pointed at the empty shelves. "What we got we can split down the middle," he said sadly. "Nothing for you and nothing for me."

"What you need," Laurence said, "is something to bring in some business. How about we run a special?"

Abe looked skeptical. "A special? In this place?"

"Sure. You got all this shoe polish just sitting here, taking up space and drying out in the can. You won't sell it if you don't get some customers. How about we offer a free can of polish with every pair of half-soles? You can sneak the price of the half-soles up a quarter to cover it."

The old man shook his head. "If I say 'free,' it's free. But how are we going to let people know?"

"Easy—I'll make a sign to put in the window. How about another special: 'two for the price of one'? We're a two-man shop now, so we might as well each do a job as sit around and watch the other guy work. I'll make a sign

that says: 'Repair one pair, get the second pair fixed free'
—how does that grab you?"

"You got wild ideas, Lucky, but sure, go ahead—
what's to lose? I'll probably be out of here by next week,
anyway."

"Not if I can help it," Laurence said, and found
some old cardboard boxes beneath the counter he could
tear apart for his signs. Abe had no paint or marking
pencils, so Laurence used his finger and some ox-blood
polish to letter the signs. When they were taped to the
window, they sat back and waited for the business to
come in.

"So how long have been in this country, Pops?"
Laurence asked him.

"Since '47," Abe said, and fell into a moody silence.

"1947," Laurence said, as if that was a remarkable
fact. "And before that? You were born in—?"

"Czechoslovakia, but during the war the Nazis sent
me to a camp in Poland. I don't like to talk about that so
much, Lucky."

"I suppose not. Must've been rough. So where'd you
learn shoe repair?"

"In another camp, for refugees, in West Germany.
In Czechoslovakia I was a jeweler."

"A jeweler! Say, that's interesting. Did you repair
watches, too?"

"I could, yes. But I lost all my tools during the war
and now my fingers are no good for that kind of work."
He held up a hand to show Laurence his crooked, knotty
fingers. "The Nazis did this to me. The bones didn't heal
so good and now the arthritis makes it worse. Some days
I can barely sew."

"Well, that's all right," Laurence said. "I can do the

sewing. My fingers are still good, anyway. The one part of me that never got damaged, Pops. We might make a good team, you know that?"

Abe shrugged, as if afraid to admit he was hoping the same thing.

"So tell me, how'd you get over to this country?"

"My wife's brother—he escaped to America before Hitler took over Czechoslovakia. He wrote to me for news about Rachel and the children. I had to tell him the truth—they all died in that prison camp. He came to see their graves, then offered me a job, a ticket to New York. I worked for him three years but we didn't get along so good. I saved up my money, became a citizen, then set out on my own. As soon as I saw this city with its beautiful lakes, I knew this was where I wanted to spend the last years of my life. Also here you have a university, culture, educated people—"

"Yeah, if you can live in the right neighborhood," Laurence said. "Too bad you picked this one for your shop."

Abe shrugged. "It was all I could afford. I got nothing against black folk—they got to have shoes, too."

Just then the bell tinkled and a large black woman entered the shop, her massive arms full of children's shoes. "I seen your sign," she said. "How much you charge to fix all these?"

She dumped the collection of worn sandals, sneakers and oxfords on the counter.

"Let me handle this," Laurence said to Abe, and edged him gently away from the pile.

"Well now, let's see—" Lucky fell easily into the voice he used with jazz musicians, black and white—a voice that copied the rhythms and some of the locutions of the black dialect— "Looks like you got yourself one big family to provide for."

She chuckled ruefully. "Oh Lordy, six young'ns at the last count, and they keep on out-growin' their shoes! I can't afford to buy new ones, so we pass 'em down from one chile to the next. But I hates to see 'em wearing shoes as beat-up and sad as these."

Laurence completed his survey of the little pile of shoes: eight pair altogether. Three would need new soles; four needed their straps re-sewn; there wasn't much he could do about the sneakers, except to glue down some loose welts and replace the tongues. The assembled shoes released the sorrowful aroma of childhood and poverty; Laurence could imagine the young black faces that belonged to these shoes, the skinny bodies that ran, walked, skipped and scuffled in them.

"All right, young lady, tell you what I'm gonna do. You look like a good steady customer to me, and that's the kind we want coming to this here shop. So I'm gonna make you a special offer. Most shops, they'd nick you for twenty, twenty-five dollars to fix all these. I'll do the whole lot, have 'em bright and shiny new by tomorrow morning, for ten bucks. I'll even throw in three cans of polish and some laces for the sneakers—how does that sound?"

"That sound pretty good," the woman said. "I'm glad to see there's *one* shop 'round here that 'preciates my business!"

Abe sighed as the woman left the shop. "You're some businessman, Lucky! How we going to make any money fixing all these shoes for just ten bucks? The material alone costs more than that."

"I know, Pops, but sometimes you have to lose a little to win a lot. That gal will sing our praises all over this neighborhood. Business will pick up in a day or so—you wait and see if I'm not right. Goodwill—it's the most valuable commodity a merchant has. My old man was a shopkeeper and I know what I'm saying."

Abe still looked dubious. "Three, four days is not much time to build up a business. If you haven't got that three fifty by Saturday, I'm going to have to sell out, Lucky. I can't wait no longer."

"Don't worry, you'll have it," Laurence said, and set to work on the first pair of sandals.

At a quarter to twelve, Laurence surrendered the stitching machine to the old man. He was hot and tired and had other things on his mind. "I'll grab some lunch, old-timer. And then I'll have to spend an hour or two chasing down your money. You can finish this batch. I'll be in later this afternoon."

Several more jobs had come in since morning, and Abe looked happily at the little row of shoes waiting on the shelf "I guess I can keep busy," he said. "Thanks, Lucky. Maybe you'll bring me some good luck after all."

"We'll see," Laurence said, shrugged into his sport coat and left the shop.

The Hiawatha was crowded and he could see Ginger was plenty busy, so he went on by, figuring he could stop for lunch someplace else. It wasn't a long walk to the Cambridge, but most of it was uphill and Laurence took his time, trying not to exhaust himself in the mid-day heat. He knew he'd have to do some fast talking when he reached the hotel, if he could find anybody there who even remembered him. Aside from old Ernie Hansford, that is, who was still stationed beneath the blue canopy as Laurence came up Fairchild Street. Ernie had put on a few pounds and his close-cut hair was grizzled at the temples, but he still commanded his post with a doorman's serene dignity. One look at Lucky and he deftly side-stepped to block the entry.

"Sorry, lobby for hotel guests only."

"Hey, Ernie, it's me—Lucky Lantz. Don't you remember me?" Lucky extended his hand. Ernie debated a moment, glanced over his shoulder at the hotel lobby, then gave the hand a quick slap.

"How you doin', man? I heard you was in the hospital, pretty near dead."

"That's true, Ernie—I was laid up over two years, but I'm all recovered. Alive and kicking. Say, who's the manager here now?"

"New guy, you don't know him. Name's *Mister* Brockington. He don't take no lip from the hired help, but he's a straight shooter, more or less."

"Anybody left from the old days?"

"Oh, a few. Tom Cotter's still the house dick. And Glenda still keeps the books."

Lucky knew he was on Cotter's shit-list—that fat Irishman never did like him—but with Glenda he had a chance.

"You take care of yourself, Ernie," he said, and made to step around him. Ernie, however, continued to block his way.

"Sorry, Lucky, but I gotta ask—what you come here for, anyway?"

"Maybe I want a room for the night."

"At our prices? I don't think so. I know you can't be looking for no bell-hopping job, not at your age. Mr. Brockington don't allow no hustles in his hotel. We clean as new-fallen snow, now."

"Relax, Ernie. I just want to talk to Glenda for a minute, that's all. Just lookin' up an old friend." Ernie stepped reluctantly aside. "If there's trouble, I'd hate to be the one to throw you out of here, Lucky. I'm afraid I'd break whatever you got ain't broken yet."

"No trouble," Lucky said with a wink, stepped around him, and pushed through the revolving door. The large, ornate lobby hadn't changed much since the last time he saw it—maybe a little more wear on the oriental carpets, a few less fronds on the ferns. Those mirrors were looking a little scummy, and the gold cherubs could have used buffing. The Cambridge wasn't exactly on the skids, but it wasn't quite what it used to be. Laurence walked up to the front desk, where he was greeted by a balding young man in rimless specs.

"Yes sir. May I help you?"

"Thanks, friend—it could be you can. Is Glenda in today?"

"Glenda?" The young man seemed suspicious, though Laurence knew he looked presentable. Maybe he didn't smell so good, after a morning's work in Abe's sweaty shop, but there wasn't much he could do about that until he got his suitcase.

"Tell her it's Larry Lantz. She'll remember me—I used to work here."

The clerk went into the back room. Lucky looked over the keyboard behind the desk. Less than half the rooms were booked. Of course, it was the beginning of the week, and salesmen didn't usually check in till evening. Maybe the rooms would fill up later—or maybe those new motels out on the beltline were cutting into business. Lucky would have been happier if the place had seemed a little more prosperous—prosperous enough to want to buy him off.

A stocky, middle-aged woman with bright red hair came out of the back room. She took off her horn-rimmed glasses the better to focus a pair of glittering green eyes. "Lucky! It *is* you!" She leaned across the counter to embrace him and he put a light kiss on her powdered cheek. As usual, Glenda had doused herself with perfume. Laurence had to pull away to get some air.

"Glenda, you haven't changed a bit—still as lovely as ever."

"Oh, go on with you! I've put on a few pounds, I know it. And my hair—"

"It's a lovely shade," Lucky said. "Very becoming. I think it suits you."

"You always were a flatterer," Glenda said happily. "Come on back to my office where we can talk."

Glenda's cubby hole behind the front desk was thick with cigarette smoke. She quickly lit a Pall Mall and offered the pack to Lucky, who declined, knowing he'd have trouble enough breathing in such close quarters as it was.

"So where have you been, Lucky? I heard you went to Chicago to cut some records—"

"I did, baby. That was supposed to be my big break. Didn't work out that way, but I hung around, played some clubs, worked a few hotel jobs . . . I stayed there nearly three years. Then I got sick."

"Same old problem?"

Lucky nodded. "First they had to dry me out. Then they gave me eighteen months of bedrest, then rehabilitation. They taught me a trade, Glenda. I'm going to be a shoe repairman from now on."

Glenda giggled. "Oh sure, tell me another!"

"It's the God's truth. I'm on my lunchbreak right now, but I couldn't walk past the good old Cambridge without dropping in to see if any of my friends were still around. So how's life been treating you?"

"Oh, pretty well." She lowered her lashes, then added proudly, "I'm married again."

Lucky was delighted to hear it, though he put on his long face. "Well, I knew you couldn't wait forever, babe. Who's the lucky guy?"

"You don't know him. His name's Harold Royce—he's a retired policeman."

"Glenda—you married a cop?"

"He's a very nice cop, and besides, like I told you, he's retired. He gets a good pension and we live very well. Steak every night, if we want it."

"I'm real happy for you," Lucky said. "I'd like to meet Mr. Royce sometime. Of course I don't suppose he'd approve of an old con man like me."

She looked dubious. "Well, Harry can be a bit of a stickler. And he *does* get jealous, sometimes—not that I'd ever play around—"

"Of course not, but I'd get jealous, too, if you were my wife. You find a good thing, you hang on to it, right? Still, he wouldn't object to your helping an old friend, would he?"

A veil seemed to descend over Glenda's dark eyes. She regarded the smoke curling away from her cigarette. "I guess it would depend on what my friend wanted. Some things I couldn't do. Like if he wanted to set up a game at the hotel here—"

"Nah, it's nothing like that," Lucky assured her. "I'm trying to collect on a few old debts, and I've got a pretty good idea the hotel owes me money. I wonder if you could check your pay sheets for 1944. You keep them back that far, don't you?"

"Oh, we keep them back to the dawn of time," Glenda said, "but they're all boxed up in the store room—it would take me a while to dig them out."

"Well, I was hoping maybe you could check the sheets for April of that year. You may remember the incident: I was running a little craps game down in the laundry room, and some poor loser complained to Cotter, said the dice were funny. I took off in a hurry and never came back for my last paycheck. I figure it comes to about seventy bucks."

"I do remember the incident, Lucky. Cotter wanted to send the cops after you but Ernie and I talked him out of it—said it wouldn't look good for the hotel if you got hauled into court."

"Good girl—I always knew you were a pal. Besides, the guy was a stiff. I never rigged a game in my life."

"I always thought you were an honest man, Lucky— deep down inside."

"So, you'll see I get that money?"

She frowned. "Gee, I don't know about that, Lucky. It was a long time ago; you should have come back sooner . . ."

Lucky heard what she was saying: *you should have made love to me, you schnook! You should have saved me from the old geezer I wound up with.*

He gave her one of his rueful smiles. "You know me, babe—easy come, easy go. I didn't want to get into any big hassles. But now I really need that money. This guy I work for, he's a refugee, a nice old codger, and I promised I'd help him out. It's a good situation for me,

Glenda, the best chance I've had in years to get my life back on the straight and narrow. In fact, it might be my last chance. I either make it this time or they can pick out a verse for my tombstone."

She gazed at him for a long moment, then leaned forward to cover the back of his hand with her pudgy, ink and tobacco-stained fingers. "I really think you mean it, Lucky. If I'd known you were going to come out of the san a new man, I might have waited for you, after all."

Lucky smiled. "I'm heartbroken you didn't, babe. But maybe it's just as well. You've got a good life and I'm just starting over. That's not so easy, as my age."

"A good woman could help," Glenda said, as if she was thinking of dumping old Harold Cop-face, after all.

"Yes, that's true, she could . . . but I never had much luck with good women—only the other sort. By the way, you haven't seen Ruby lately, have you?"

Glenda rolled her eyes. "You still carrying the torch for *that* piece of trash?"

"No way," Laurence said earnestly. "Ruby's the one dame I could never figure out—which is why I married her, I guess, and why we drove each other nuts. When we split up I left a few things in her possession—a beautiful pearl-handled banjo, best one I ever owned, and some phonograph records. I'd sure like to get them back. Any idea how I could find her?"

Glenda shrugged. "She's in town; try the phone book. Should be listed under the name of that guy she married—Claymore, that's the name. Chester Claymore."

"Sounds like an undertaker," Laurence said. "Maybe I'll look her up. In the meantime, will you see what you can do for me here at the hotel?"

"I don't know, Lucky. Mr. Brockington is one tough

hombre. He's not going to like shelling out for an un-
claimed paycheck—even if I can find it on the ledger."

"Well, maybe you could talk to him about it. Tell
him I've got a lawyer and I'll go to court, if I have to. A
few unsavory details about the history of this place could
come to light, if we had to hash it all out before a judge."

Glenda smiled. "You're as crafty as ever, Lucky.
Okay—I'd like to see that stuffed shirt squirm. You come
back tomorrow around noon—I'll have him all primed
for you."

"Thanks a million, babe—I knew I could count on
you!" Lucky leaned over to put a kiss on her cheek and
found her painted lips waiting for him instead, so he
gave her a quick smooch, what the hell, and moments
later was wiping the lipstick off his chops as he sought
the fresh air beyond the revolving doors.

Ernie saw him tucking his handkerchief away and
smiled knowingly. "Same old Lucky!" he cackled as
Laurence went down the street.

Yeah, the same old Lucky, Laurence thought. *And
the same old bullshit.* Sometimes he got a little disgusted with himself, but then, he'd always believed it was
better to be nice to people, if you could, than to hurt
their feelings, and if a little kindness worked to your
advantage now and then, what was wrong with that? He
figured that seventy-two bucks was practically in his
pocket.

The Greyhound bus station was just down Fairchild
Street from the hotel, so he stopped in for a hot dog and
a Coke. There was something about bus stations, train
stations, any place where people were on the move, that
Laurence found soothing and peaceful. A musician spent
a lot of time on the road and after a while you really got

to love that kind of life. Lonely, yeah, but there was always a sense of freedom on the road and hope for maybe a better gig at the end of the line.

So old Ruby was still in Madison! He was tempted to check her out, just for the hell of it, but he knew that was another street he'd better not walk down. There were just too many of them by now—all these streets marked "do not enter," as if some flood or tornado had torn up his life and left it a shambles.

After lunch he lounged on the square for awhile, watching the traffic whirl around the stately capitol with its park-like grounds, then stopped in a record store. Everything was L.P. these days. Too expensive for his wallet and he didn't know if Ginger's record-player could play them, but he liked to look at the covers anyway, and study the personnel listed on the back. He took a Count Basie album into one of the booths and listened with great pleasure until the clerk started giving him the evil eye. Then he returned the record to the counter. "I'll stop back for this on pay-day," he told the clerk, and left.

It was going on two when he got back to the shop and right away he could tell from the look on Abe's face that something was wrong. The old man looked as if he'd just seen Adolph Hitler strolling down the sun-baked street.

"What's up, Pops?"

"Bad news, Lucky. I hate to break it to you, but your nephew was in here earlier, looking for you."

"Jack was in the shop?" He was a little sorry the kid had seen what a dump he was working in, but maybe that was just as well—let him see where this kind of life led. Then he realized that Abe was holding something back. "So what did he want?"

"I guess he wanted to take you to the hospital," Abe said, that baleful look in his runny old eyes.

"The hospital?"

"Saint Mary's. That's where they took your brother Leo. He collapsed at work, Lucky. I been trying to tell you, he had a heart attack."

"A heart attack! Is he still alive?"

"He was, an hour ago. Your nephew said he couldn't wait any longer, but it's not far to the hospital. You can walk it easy. I'd go right over there, if I was you—the family, they may need you."

That would be a new one, Laurence thought. But of course he wanted to be there. Leo was his buddy, his pal—and it suddenly struck him that Leo, Maggie and Jack were the only family he had left in the whole world. Somehow he was never there when people needed him, but maybe this time it would be different.

"Okay, old-timer, I guess I'll have to take some more time off. I'll stop back later, if I can."

"Don't worry about that," Abe said, waving him toward the door. "Just go, go!"

So Laurence went.

7.
Heart O' My Heart

LAURENCE arrived at St. Mary's foot-sore and exhausted. He limped into the lobby and sat down for a moment to catch his breath. Fans were positioned around the large waiting room, stirring up breezes that chilled the sweat on his face and neck. He could see the registration desk, a gift shop, coffee shop, and, further down the hall, a nurses' station where women in bright white uniforms bustled about, doing important things.

Laurence had seen a lot of hospitals and sanitariums in his time and thought of them as places where people took care of you, muttered over your X-rays, and carried on as if they really could save you from that little colony of bugs nestled in your lungs. Of course they couldn't. Nobody ever saved anybody in this life, and by now his sensitive nostrils had picked up a familiar odor, that disinfectant or whatever it was they used to cover up those *other* smells—the ones you weren't supposed to notice. He pushed up from the couch and approached the registration desk.

"Excuse me," he said to an elderly woman who

seemed to be in charge, "I wonder if you could tell me about my brother, Leo Lantz. He was brought here this morning after a heart attack."

The woman checked her records and said that Leo had been admitted to the cardiac wing from the emergency room. He was in room 345. "You can go right up," she said. "The family isn't required to observe visiting hours on the first day."

"Then he's all right? He's out of danger?"

She gave him a kindly smile. "I'm sorry, we don't have that kind of information, but he's not in intensive care. That must mean his heart-rate has stabilized."

Laurence thanked her and went to the elevators. A statue of the Virgin in an alcove by the elevators caught his notice. He must have been in this hospital before, because that statue seemed awfully familiar. Maybe when the old man died. Stomach cancer, 1941. Will Lantz was fifty-two years old and everyone said he drank himself to death, but Laurence knew there was more to it than that. His father never got over the loss of the family business. It was a two-bit store in a one-horse town, but it meant a lot to the old man. You could just as well have said he died of a broken heart.

Laurence pushed the up-button and waited, his gaze returning to the statue. The Virgin was wearing a white robe with a blue cape and cowl; she had a sweetly innocent face and a smile so serene it made you want to smile back, to say something nice and friendly. What really got him, though, was the casual way the Virgin had pinned the head of a sizable snake beneath one of her small bare feet. Now that took some nerve! Some women were like that, he thought. His mother, for instance. All through the old man's disgrace, she never complained, never spoke a harsh word against him. She just made a home for the family wherever they happened to be. Laurence thought there really ought to be a heaven for people like his mother. For most everybody else, a hole in the ground would be good enough.

The elevator doors slid open, revealing an old man in a wheelchair, a husky young orderly, and some sort of machine on wheels. The machine was attached to the old man's body by several tubes that snaked under his hospital gown. The gown gaped open in front to reveal the old man's bony knees and thin thighs. Laurence stepped in and the old man's baleful, discolored eyes looked at him with a silent plea: *Get me out of here, friend. Unplug me and let me die.*

Now there was a tune, Lucky thought—not a happy one, but the blues weren't about happiness. They were about love and death, the two saddest subjects in the whole world. Only fools thought music was always supposed to make you feel good. The best tunes made you want to cry.

He got off on the third floor and went down the corridor, following the numbers toward 345. As he approached, he saw a red sign on the door: *No Smoking —Oxygen in Use.* A young nurse's aid was just coming out with a lunch tray.

"Excuse me," Laurence said as she passed, "that's my brother in there. Leo Lantz—how's he doing?"

"Oh, just fine," the aid said brightly. "Ate all his lunch, see?" She lifted the lid to display an empty plate. "The oxygen tent is just a precaution—he only needs to have it on when he's sleeping. You can open it up to talk to him—just close the valve beside his bed. And don't stay too long—he's supposed to get lots of rest."

"So what's the prognosis?" Laurence asked, using the term his doctors had often used when discussing the course of his own disease.

"We don't know that yet," the aid said. "Doctor Fisher will be around later this afternoon, after he's read the EKG's. But so far all the signs are good."

"Thanks," Laurence said. He approached the door, tapped lightly and went in. Leo was in the second bed—the one near the window. Stretched out beneath the shimmering canopy of his oxygen tent, he looked like a creature wrapped in its cocoon. Laurence had seen a science fiction movie once where aliens from outer space put themselves into just such a contraption in order to assume human form. Leo's face was vaguely visible beneath the plastic.

"Hey Leo," he said softly, "it's me—Larry."

Leo unzipped the plastic sheath from inside and peered out, his face crinkling to a smile. Despite the smile, Laurence saw evidence of recent, intense pain in Leo's eyes. That pain seemed to have baked his already sharp features to a hard, ceramic glaze, leaving them brittle and breakable, a face made of glass.

"Larry, thanks for coming. I told Jack not to bother you at work—you see, I'm not dead yet."

"Good thing," Laurence said. He turned off the valve on the tank and folded back the plastic sheet, then sat down at Leo's bedside. "Was it bad?"

"Worst pain I ever felt in my life," Leo said. "Like a freight train ran over my chest—ran right over me and dragged me about a hundred yards. I'm all right now, though. Just a little woozy from all the drugs they've given me."

"I could tell you didn't look good Sunday evening,"

Laurence said. "I should have told Maggie about those chest pains you were having and made sure she hauled you to the doctor that very evening. Some brother I am."

"You did your best—you told me not to wait," Leo said. "Anyway, if things hadn't been so hectic at work today, I might have made it through the week. Crank me up a little, will you, Larry, so I don't have to raise my head?"

Laurence cranked him up. "So how are Maggie and Jack taking this?"

"Oh, Maggie's upset, of course, but Jack is looking after her. They went down to the cafeteria a little while ago for some lunch."

"I'll stay until they come back," Laurence said. "I understand you're supposed to get plenty of rest."

"Oh, I'll get enough of that," Leo said. "Six weeks, they say, before you can go back to work after a heart attack—at a minimum."

"Enjoy it," Laurence said. "You deserve a vacation."

"Well, if was a *paid* vacation . . . but this one may not be." Leo's eyes turned to the window, as if he might try to fly away home, or back to his IBM machines.

"You've got some kind of insurance, don't you?" Laurence had always heard that one advantage of steady employment was the insurance—something he'd never had himself, and hadn't needed, since TB care was provided by the state.

"Right now I do," Leo said. "The problem is, I opted to remain in the union after my promotion, and our contract expires September first. The company's not budging on it's latest offer and there's a strike vote scheduled for tomorrow night."

"So?" Laurence didn't see the problem.

"So if the union goes out on strike, I'll lose my health insurance, and then how do we pay for all this? And what do Maggie and Jack live on till I can get back on my feet and find some kind of work?"

"You mean you won't even get sick leave?"

"Not if we're out on strike. The company won't owe me a dime."

"What about unemployment compensation?"

"Doesn't apply to striking employees. There's a law —if you're out on strike, you're not eligible for benefits."

"Jeez, what a screw," Laurence said. What good did it do to hold down a job for twenty years if something like this could happen to a guy? "There must be *some* kind of government program that would bail you out—"

"If there is, you'd probably know about it," Leo said sharply, but then reached out to touch his brother's arm. "I'm sorry, Larry, that was a cheap crack. It's just that, after all the years our family spent on welfare, I don't want to end up like that. I've worked too hard to get where I am."

"You've worked too hard, period," Laurence said. He knew Leo had never forgiven their father for putting the family through a long period of poverty and disgrace. For Laurence it was easier, since he saw most of the old man's faults in himself.

"So how's *your* new job going?" Leo asked.

"Just fine—I put in a good morning's work. Abe's a decent old codger—I think we'll get along just fine." He decided not to mention the money he needed to raise to keep the shoe repair shop in business.

"Good, I'm glad to hear it," Leo said. "You didn't come home last night," he added, as if that cot in the garage gave him the right to set a curfew. Laurence saw he would have to be careful: Leo had certain scruples where women were concerned.

"Oh, I ran into an old friend and he offered to put me up for a few days, until I can afford a place of my own. It's close to the shop, so I took him up on it. Sorry I didn't call, but it was getting pretty late when I made the decision—I didn't want to wake you."

Leo frowned. "This old friend, is he a former drinking buddy?"

"Yes, but he's on the wagon now. He'll be a good influence on me." Laurence figured that was only half a lie, because he did expect Ginger to keep him on the straight and narrow.

"Sounds good," Leo said, and just then Maggie and Jack entered the room.

"Hey, Lucky's here," Jack said, coming around the screen and catching sight of Lucky first.

Maggie's green eyes, red and moist from a morning of tears, flared at the sight of her brother-in-law. "So you got the message. We had no idea how to reach you—just that shoe repair shop you'd mentioned, and it doesn't have a phone."

Laurence rose from his chair and went to her with his arms extended. "I was on my lunch break, but I came straight over when I heard about it. If there's anything I can do—"

"Like what?" She slipped past his embrace and approached Leo's bedside. "You've got a thousand dollars, maybe, to pay for this room?"

"Ma," Jack said, "for cripes' sake!"

Leo tried to change the mood. "Larry says the job looks good, Maggie. Says he's bunking with a friend for a few days, till he gets his own place."

"Well, this is no time for you to have a house guest," Laurence said. "No need to worry about me—I'll be fine where I am."

"I wasn't worried about you in the least," Maggie said, sitting down in the chair he'd given up. "It's my husband I'm worried about."

"Of course," Laurence said, taking a place at the foot of the bed. "He's looking better, though, isn't he? Doesn't he look better?"

"He looks terrible," Maggie said with her usual bluntness, and stared at her husband as if he were already in his coffin.

"Ma," Jack said, "don't you have any sense? Tell him he looks fine. You look fine, Dad. You're going to be all right."

"Your mother always tells me the truth," Leo said. "You be good to her."

"He bawled me out all through lunch," Maggie said. "He says I nag you too much—that it's all my fault you had this heart attack."

Leo glared at his son. "That's nonsense, Jack. You shape up now! I don't want to have to lie here and worry about you two quarreling all the time I'm in the hospital."

"Sorry, Dad," Jack said. "It's just that she never thinks about anybody but herself."

"That's not true," Maggie said, her voice rising. "A lot you know about anything, you miserable pup!"

Jack was about to respond, but Laurence took him by the arm and turned him aside. "Say, let's you and me step out in the hall for a minute, Jack—there's something I need to ask you about."

Jack allowed himself to be ushered from the room

and Laurence caught Leo's grateful glance. *One at a time, brother—that's enough for me right now!*

Once outside, Laurence guided Jack toward a small visitor's lounge at the end of the corridor. "This must be tough on you," he said, still holding onto his nephew's arm. "I know how much you like your dad."

"He's a good man," Jack said, his voice tight with emotion. "Too good for what's happening to him."

"Well, I guess that's true for a lot of people," Lucky said. "It's hard to understand, sometimes, the way life deals out the cards. One guy gets a great hand and doesn't know how to play it. Another guy gets a lousy hand but he knows how to bluff. You have to play the cards you're dealt, you know what I mean?"

"Yeah, I suppose that's right," Jack said, and Laurence could see that his nephew was too polite to say what he really thought: *Life as a card game—yeah, sure. Spare me the corn.*

"Your dad knows how to play this hand," Lucky went on. "He knows how to handle your mother. Those two have been taking care of each other since before you were born. Why, I never saw two people as much in love as your dad and ma. It was beautiful to see, the way they felt about each other."

"Yeah?" Jack seemed impressed, but then his scowl returned. "But that was back in the old days, when they were both young. These days, Ma's so wrapped up in her own problems she doesn't give a damn about what he's going through."

"I'm sure that's not true," Laurence said. "Your mother's an emotional woman, and right now she's frightened. She needs your strength. . ." They had come by now to the lounge area and he noticed ash trays, a sure sign that smoking was permitted. He'd also noticed the smell of tobacco on Jack's breath. "Say, you haven't got a cigarette, have you? I could sure use a smoke."

Jack fished a flattened pack of Lucky Strikes out of his jeans. "Don't let Dad know I got these. I just started smoking this summer, hanging out with the guys. I'll probably give it up when school starts."

"Good idea," Laurence said, extracting a somewhat battered cigarette from Jack's pack. "Your dad and I started smoking as teenagers, when we worked summers on the farm, and now look at us. Got a match?"

Jack lit Lucky's and his own and they sat in the chrome and vinyl chairs to smoke. "You think smoking's really bad for you?" Jack asked, as if he respected Lucky's opinion on a whole raft of subjects—everything from music to foreign affairs.

Lucky took a long drag, felt the harsh smoke tingle what remained of his left lung.

"Well, son, let me put it this way. If you can do without it, you're surely better off. But you could say that about a lot of things. The one thing I've learned about life is that it's too damn short. And the more hell you raise along the way, the shorter it gets. There ain't no other rule, that I can see."

"Yeah, but look at Dad. He hardly ever takes a drink. Goes to bed early every night, gets up early, never has any fun—"

"Well now, you see," Lucky said, "that's the thing you don't understand about your father. He does have fun, in his way. And he loves your mother, too. Might be hard for you to see, being her son and all, but Maggie Lantz is a hell of a fine woman. A lot of men would've been glad to marry her, but your dad won the prize. And now he's counting on you to take good care of her while he's in the hospital."

Jack was silent a moment. Then he said, "I'll do my best."

"Fine. Now there's something else I need to ask you about. That suitcase of mine, and the guitar—are they still sitting out in your garage?"

"They were this morning," Jack said, "but we don't usually lock our garage door. I didn't think about it when they called about Dad—"

"Understandable," Laurence said, "but I think I'd better make some arrangements for picking them up. You suppose I could hitch a ride out to your place with you and your ma when you leave here this afternoon?"

"Sure," Jack said, "and then we can drive you back to town when we come out to see Dad tonight."

"That's sort of what I was hoping," Laurence said.

They put out their cigarettes and went back to Leo's room. Maggie was just coming out. "Say goodbye to your father, Jack, and then we should let him rest for awhile."

While Jack was in the room, Laurence explained to Maggie his plan for collecting his suitcase. "You won't have to feed me any supper," he added.

"You can have whatever we have," Maggie said, "but it's going to be simple. I have to start looking for ways to stretch our grocery budget. I guess Leo told you about the strike vote tomorrow?"

Lucky nodded. "Tell you what, let's stop at the store on the way out to your place and I'll buy some steaks. Jack and I can grill them at that outdoor fireplace and you won't have to do a thing."

"Oh, I can make a salad, at least" Maggie said, and seemed to cheer up a little. It was always good for Maggie to have company, and Lucky figured he could serve as a buffer between her and Jack. A man had to find some way to make himself useful, at a time like this.

~§~

It was a tense ride back to Lake Edge. Jack hadn't had his license for long and Maggie kept telling him to slow down and to watch where he was going. As a result, Jack drove too fast, both to defy his mother and to show Laurence he knew how to handle a car, though Laurence would have been glad to take that on faith. They stopped at a supermarket on Monona Drive and he spent the last five bucks in his wallet on three nice T-bones. It was about time he started paying Maggie back for all the good meals she'd given him over the years.

He was relieved to see his suitcase and guitar were still in the garage. As soon as Maggie and Jack went in the house, he opened the guitar case and fished the old coin purse out of the lining, took out the roll of bills, and sat down on the cot to make sure it was all still there. Good thing Leo lived in an safe neighborhood.

It occurred to him that he could give some of this money to Maggie—a down payment on the eight hundred he owed them—but then he'd have to raise that much more to cover Abe's bills. No job, no income—and he'd never raise any money that way. The eight hundred would just have to wait.

He replaced the purse and got a clean pair of briefs and tee shirt from his suitcase. Then he went in the house. "Mind if I take a bath?" he asked Maggie, who was peeling potatoes at the kitchen sink. "I'm starting to smell like a polecat."

"Go right ahead," Maggie said. "Those are lovely steaks you bought. I thought maybe I'd fly up some potatoes to go with them."

"Fine," Laurence said. He paused at the door to Jack's bedroom. Jack was stretched out on his bed reading a paperback novel with a lurid cover, his little 45 rpm phonograph playing Dixieland jazz.

"Think you could build me a nice hot fire out in that fireplace about five o'clock? I'd like it to settle down to coals before I put the steaks on."

"Sure, Lucky. You like this record? It's Turk Murphy."

"Good old Turk, I knew him well," Lucky said, and went into the bathroom.

He ran a tub full of hot water, peeled off his clothes, and lowered himself carefully into the steaming liquid. Once he was in, he stretched out and let the hot water soothe his aching body. All this traipsing around town was damn hard on a guy his age—be nice when he could afford a car. Of course, first he had to raise Abe's three fifty. And then he had to start repaying that eight hundred he owed Leo . . . Jesus, everywhere he turned, there was something he needed or somebody he owed. It was like that song he'd composed once:

> *Broke and busted, can't pay my dues,*
> *I guess I got them old greenback blues!*

In the old days, he would have known just how to make a quick score. First he would've taken Eddie King to the cleaners at pool, and then he would've sat down at the poker table with Mr. Hotshot Frank Holiday. It wouldn't have taken him long to find out if Holiday was any kind of gambler. Even if he was, nobody could stand up to one of Lucky's hot streaks. Four, five hundred a night was not out of the question for Lucky in his prime.

Of course you had to expect bad nights—nights when you really got burned. And if you couldn't pay up, there would be various unpleasant consequences. He was getting too old for consequences like that. Besides, he knew he'd never get through an evening of poker without taking a few drinks, and that, as Doc Steimetz assured him, was his ticket to the morgue. There was no way he was going to play poker again, no matter how much he needed the dough.

Music was different. He could play piano sober, he'd found that out, and he might risk a few nights at Frank's club, just to get Abe's stake. He wondered if Savannah Jones could really sing well enough to get by as a solo. And then he remembered her lush dark hair, her dusky skin and full breasts, and he realized nobody, including himself, would care much whether she could sing or not, and the next thing he knew the purple head of his battered old dick was poking up out of the water and he thought, *Lordy, child, you are achin' for a breakin', if you go after that little piece of change!*

~§~

It was going on five when he came out of the bathroom all fresh and clean, and it occurred to him that he ought to give Ginger a call. The phone was in the dining room; Maggie was in the kitchen and Jack had gone out to build the fire. Laurence dialed the number he'd copied down this morning, just in case.

Ginger's husky voice came on the line. "Hello?"

"Hi, it's me," Laurence said.

"Hi, you. Didn't know whether I was going to hear from you again or not."

"Sorry about that. My brother Leo had a heart attack—"

"So I heard. I stopped at Abe's on the way home from work. Is he okay?"

"Seems to be, but the family's kind of upset. I thought I ought to stay for supper, make myself useful, but I can be over to your place around eight or nine this evening—that is, if you're still willing to put up with me for a few days."

"Why just a few days?" Ginger asked. "You don't like the accommodations?"

"They suit me just fine," Laurence said, "but I didn't think I ought to presume. I figured we'd try it for a while and see."

"See what? I don't like that 'try it for a while' stuff, Lucky. Guys been pulling that crap on me for years. "

Laurence shut his eyes for a moment and tried to chart a path through the minefield. "Well, then, let's say we give it a week. If you don't want to boot me out by the end of the week, we'll talk about something more permanent, how's that sound?"

"It ain't exactly a commitment," Ginger said, and then she added, "I see you took the key."

"Be there around eight," Laurence said, and hung up. He wasn't sure how much of that conversation Maggie had heard, but she gave him a sharp look as he entered the kitchen. "That didn't sound like any 'old friend' to me, Lucky Lantz. You had that 'sweet-talkin' a new woman' tone in your voice."

Laurence smiled. "Never could slip anything past

you, Maggie. Matter of fact, I did meet a gal yesterday. She offered to put me up for a few days, but I didn't think I ought to mention it in front of Jack."

"Jack knows the facts of life," she said. She was slicing vegetables for the salad and a glass of sherry was on the counter. Her face had that rosy flush once again and she seemed a good deal more relaxed. "Leo's the one who might be upset. He thinks you're always looking for some woman to take care of you."

"Well, that's what men do, isn't it? You take care of Leo."

"I do my best," Maggie said. "Though to hear Jack tell it, I'm driving the poor man to an early grave."

"Jack's just a kid. He doesn't understand these things. You should be glad he likes his dad so much. Most kids his age hate their fathers."

"Yes, he just hates his mother," Maggie said. "I don't know what I ever did to that boy to turn him against me—"

"He doesn't hate you," Laurence said. "He's a teenager, Maggie. He has to talk tough to hide his true feelings. He's afraid to show how much he really loves you."

She sniffled, then wiped her eyes on her apron. "That's what Leo says, but I have a hard time believing it." She turned and gave him one of her old smiles. "Thanks anyway, Larry—you know how to cheer me up. I hope it works out for you and this gal—you could use a good woman to look after you."

Laurence sat down at the kitchen table. "Well, Maggie, somehow I never seem to get that kind, but I think Ginger's all right. I'd like to do right by her—something tells me she's had a pretty hard life."

"It won't get any easier with *you* around," Maggie said, but he could tell she was feeling better. You had to know how to handle old Maggie.

"Say, that salad looks plenty big enough for three people. Why don't you set it aside for now? I'll bet there's a cribbage board somewhere in this kitchen."

"You'd be right about that," Maggie said, sliding open a drawer. "But do we have time for a game? I'd like to get back out to the hospital by seven."

"Fire won't be ready for half an hour yet," Laurence said. "I reckon I can beat you two out of three in half an hour."

Maggie rose to the challenge. "Oh yeah?"

She brought her sherry glass, the cribbage board, and a deck of cards to the table. They cut for the deal and Maggie won. Watching her plump fingers shuffle the cards, Laurence remembered how they used to play cribbage by the hour that winter she was pregnant with Jack. Leo was working a lot of over-time at the plant and Lucky, as usual, had only a few weekend gigs, so he'd drop by their flat to see if there was anything he could do for his sister-in-law. Sometimes he'd take her shopping or to the movies, or they'd take a walk around the neighborhood. His own marriage was on the rocks, and it was nice to pretend that the pregnant lady with the rosy cheeks and bright green eyes belonged to him. Sometimes it almost seemed that she did.

8.
Bum's Rush

ABE was just unlocking the door of his shop Wednesday morning when Laurence came up the street. Another hot day in the works, by the feel of that sun poking between the old two-story houses, though the sidewalks and shabby little yards still gave off the cool, musty scent of last night's shower. Laurence was carrying his heavy toolbox and could feel the sweat already dampening his brow.

Abe waited for him at the door. "Lucky, I'm glad to see you. How is your brother?"

"He's doing fine, Pops. Doc said his heart is still okay—it's his arteries that are causing the trouble. They're giving him something to thin his blood, and something else he can use if the pain comes back—that stuff they use to blow up bridges."

"Nitroglycerine—yes, yes, I heard about that. Modern medicine is wonderful, Lucky. We live in an age of miracles."

"Yeah, well, there's a few things they can't cure yet," Laurence said. "So how's business?"

Abe ushered him in and turned on the light. "Look!" He pointed to the shelves behind the counter, which had been empty yesterday morning. Today they were lined with shoes, little red or white tags dangling from each pair.

"Those signs you put up, and the bargain you gave that woman, really did the trick. More work came in yesterday afternoon than I could keep up with. We got enough to keep us both busy all morning."

"That's great," Laurence said. "I brought my own tools this morning." He put his toolbox on the counter and snapped it open. "Just about everything I need, except a stitching machine. Clear me a spot on the bench and we'll get a regular production line going here."

"You bet, Lucky. Looks like you're going to change my luck, after all."

Well, if I do, Laurence thought, *it'll be the first time.* He hadn't gotten his nickname for bringing other people luck—that wasn't how it worked. He had no objection to helping a guy out when he was in the chips, but if you tried to pass your luck on to somebody else you ran the risk of killing a hot streak. And it was way too early in this particular game to start counting his winnings. When he had served his apprenticeship and opened a shop of his own, *then* he could feel like a winner.

They worked side by side all morning, mending pair after pair of abused and battered shoes. *The weight of humanity,* Laurence thought, *resting on scraps of leather and canvas and thin slices of rubber—no wonder the world limped along on sore feet. Maybe shoe repair wasn't as interesting as watch repair, but you could still feel good about a job well done.*

Still more business came in, drawn by the signs he

had put in the window, and by word of mouth. Heavy black women with paper bags full of their children's shoes, elderly Jews and Italians from the other side of Park Street, even some college kids back in town early and looking for a cheap fix for last year's loafers and saddle shoes. By a quarter to twelve he was plumb tuckered out and ready for a break—good thing he had an excuse to knock off for a while.

"Say, Old Timer, I've got an appointment uptown in a little bit. It's got to do with that stake I'm trying to rustle up for you. I'll grab some lunch while I'm out."

"Fine, take as long as you want," Abe said. "I can handle what's left here—you've been a big help to me, Lucky."

"Well, it's going to take me awhile to get used to working an eight-hour day," Lucky confessed. "Up at Tomahawk we generally just worked mornings. But I'll get adjusted, don't you worry about that."

"I'm not worried. I haven't seen the shop this busy since I opened up eight years ago, and it's all thanks to you."

"Well, a little goodwill never hurts," Laurence said, remembering one of his father's maxims. "We don't sell just hardware and dry goods," the old man used to say. "We sell good will, first and foremost." And there wasn't a more popular merchant in all of Good Hope than Will Lantz, as long as times were good. But when times were bad . . . Laurence put on his sports coat and went to the door.

"Just keep smiling, Old Timer, and the folks will keep coming."

"For once I got something to smile about," Abe said, and began unpacking his lunch of salami and cheese.

Laurence wasn't really hungry so he bypassed the Hiawatha and headed up West Washington toward the Cambridge Hotel, stopping every so often beneath the elms to catch his breath and mop the sweat from his brow. He kept thinking about the old man, and how, when bad times hit Good Hope, a few years before they hit the rest of the country, that good will quickly evaporated. The store went on the auction block and the family left town in disgrace. Laurence was eighteen at the time and had been working for his father since he dropped out of school. People naturally expected him to take over the business, and he might have done all right with it, but he was already playing the banjo at local dances and he had an entirely different career in mind.

He approached the canopied entrance of the Cambridge Hotel at ten past twelve. Ernie was hailing a cab for a pair of businessmen, but he broke away to intercept him at the revolving door. "Watch your step, Lucky," he said in a hoarse whisper. "Old Cotter's on the watch for you."

"Thanks, pal," Laurence said and entered the artificial chill of the lobby. The same smarty-pants in specks was at the desk. He took one look at Laurence and nodded to someone across the lobby. Lucky saw Thomas T. Cotter, the burly house detective, pushing himself up from one of the deep armchairs. Cotter had put on a few pounds since Lucky last saw him, but he looked as if he was still trying to stuff himself into the same rumpled brown suit he'd worn back in the forties.

Laurence turned back to the clerk. "Would you tell Glenda I'm here, please?"

"Sorry, Glenda's gone home for the day. Mr. Cotter will take care of you."

"That's what I was afraid of," Lucky said, as Cotter put a heavy hand on his arm.

"Well, well—Lucky Lantz, as I live and breathe!" The dick's voice rumbled in his throat like a load of coal going down a chute. "How you doing, son? They told me you were back in circulation."

Lucky tried to smile. "I'm fine, Tom. How's yourself?"

"Can't complain, son, can't complain. Say, I believe the bar is open. Why don't we go on in and have a little drink for old times' sake?" There was a broad smile on Cotter's meaty chops, but his dark eyes were as hard and sooty as briquettes. Lucky had never found it easier to turn down a drink.

"Sorry, Tom, I'm on the wagon. I just stopped by to see Glenda."

"Glenda don't want to see you again, son," Cotter said, still holding onto Lucky's ann. "She asked me to tell you that. Now, if you'll just step over here out of the way—"

Laurence saw an elderly couple with suitcases waiting to check in. He let Cotter guide him across the lobby to a service area near the elevators, where they were out of sight of the lobby.

"Now what was it you wanted to see Glenda about, son? You weren't trying to start up an old romance, were you?" Cotter winked, as if encouraging Lucky to confide in an old mend.

"Of course not, Tom. This is a business matter— Glenda was going to check some back pay sheets for me."

Cotter raised his bushy gray brows. "Pay sheets? You think the hotel owes you some money, is that it?"

He made it sound like a pretty silly idea, and by this time Laurence was beginning to think it was.

"That's right—seventy-two dollars. Two weeks' work back in April of '44. Things came up and I never got around to collecting it, but I earned that money, Tom, fair and square. I understand you've got a new manager and I'm sure he'll want to make good on an honest debt."

Cotter smiled. "Think again, son. Mr. Brockington has already reviewed your claim, and he asked me to tell you there's no record of your past employment here—nothing to show the hotel owes you a nickel. I guess you'd just better figure the money you took off those suckers at that craps game of yours made up for it, because nobody's going to take your side around here—not Glenda, not Ernie, not me, not nobody—you understand what I'm telling you?"

"Maybe, if I could talk to Mr. Brockington personally—"

"Mr. Brockington ain't got the time to talk to no-account bums like you. He told me to say that he doesn't want to see you around the hotel again. In fact, he gave me orders to give you the bum's rush if you ever stick your nose in the door."

"He may regret that," Lucky said. "I can get legal assistance, Tom. I can take the Cambridge to court."

Cotter laughed. "That'd be the day! If you can find a lawyer in this town who's got the time to chase after a measly seventy-two bucks, you're welcome to try."

"The thing is," Lucky pointed out, "a lot of dirt could come to light if we started talking about all this in front of a judge. Things Mr. Brockington might not want to get out—things *you* might not want aired either, Tom.

You had your fingers in a few pies, as I recall."

Cotter scowled, then shook his head sadly. "I sure wish you hadn't a-said that, son. What good's it gonna do to drag up all that ancient history, huh? Why, a man could get himself in a peck of trouble, shootin' his mouth off thataway."

"Or maybe he could get what he's got coming to him," Lucky said.

"Oh, I reckon he'll get *that* all right," Cotter said with a slow smile, "I just reckon he will! Now why don't you follow me, and I'll show you out the back entrance—"

"I'd prefer to go out the front, if you don't mind," Lucky said, but Cotter still had a grip on his arm and was already walking him down the corridor behind the kitchen and the cocktail lounge—a route that led, as Lucky recalled, to the alley.

Suddenly frightened, Lucky tried to wedge words between himself and the approaching exit. "Hey, you don't have to get tough with me, Tom. I'm your old pal, remember? We had a lot of laughs in the old days—I won't cause you any trouble—"

"That's right, son, you won't," Cotter said. He fished out a ring of keys and unlocked the heavy fire door. As the door swung open, Lucky spotted the squad car parked in the alley and thought for a moment that he was saved, since Cotter surely wouldn't rough him up in front of the cops. Then he realized his mistake.

"Tom, is this any way to treat an old friend? Let me go back out through the lobby and you won't see me around here again, I promise you. Just let me walk away in one piece, all right?"

"Sorry, Lucky, the boys in blue want to have a talk with you. Glenda's hubby is their pal, see—spent thirty years on the force. They just want to make sure you don't get too friendly with his wife. Don't give 'em any lip, and you should be all right."

"Cotter, for Christ's sake—"

"Sorry, pal. Maybe this will help pay for the band-aids." Cotter tucked a five-dollar bill into Lucky's breast pocket, then pushed him out the door and into the alley. The service door shut with a solid thunk, it's lock snapping into place.

Lucky surveyed the situation. The alley led to a loading dock, but its steel door was down and padlocked. The squad car blocked the only exit to the street: a narrow channel flanked by two brick walls. There were windows and fire escapes, but too high above the pavement to provide a means of escape. Nothing to do but bluff, so Lucky put his hands in his pockets, began whistling an old tune, and strolled nonchalantly toward the square of daylight waiting for him beyond the squad car.

I got plenty of nothin', and nothin' is plenty for me . . .

As he drew closer, he could see there were two officers in the front seat. At first they didn't stir and he thought maybe they would let him pass. Then the passenger door swung open and one of the cops got out. He was a husky young fellow with blond hair, a blunt nose and a square jaw. His dark blue uniform was clean and looked freshly pressed, as if he hadn't gone on duty for the day. Nonetheless, he had his big police revolver riding in its holster, his badge, and his night-stick. He peeled off his dark sunglasses to reveal a pair of bright young cop-eyes.

"Yo, there—mind telling us what you're doing in this alley, Mac?"

"Why, I just came out that door," Lucky said, pointing behind him.

"That's a fire exit," the cop said. "Is the hotel on fire?"

"No, I don't believe so."

"Because if there's a fire, we ought to call it in, get a fire truck over here on the double—"

"There's no fire," Lucky said. "I was asked to leave by the back way."

"Oh, and why was that?"

He paused. "I guess the management didn't like my looks."

The cop moved closer. "Well, I don't like your looks, either. Lean against the hood of the vehicle and spread your legs."

Lucky did as he was told and the cop patted him down, firms hands running quickly up and down his thin body. *Public Enemy Number One*, Lucky thought. Over the years he'd been run in a time or two, never formally charged, but he knew that when a cop had you in his power he usually wanted one of two things. If there was money to be had, he wanted the money. And if there was no money, then he wanted an excuse to punch your face in. The trick was to avoid giving him that excuse.

"Get in the car," the cop said, and opened the back door.

Lucky climbed reluctantly into the back seat and the young cop slid in beside him. The other cop backed the car out of the alley, bulling his way into the heavy traffic along West Washington Avenue with his red light and a short blast on his siren.

"Looks like we're in a hurry," Lucky observed.

"Yeah, we got better things to do than fart around with guys like you," the cop said. "You got some identification?"

Lucky got out his wallet and extracted his driver's license. The cop peered at it closely as the squad car turned onto the square. Traffic moved aside; people on the sidewalks stopped to stare at the flashing red light. Mad-dog Lantz, in custody at last. No doubt they could all breathe easier now that Lucky was off the streets.

"This license expired two years ago, Mac," the cop said.

"Was I driving a car? I've been in the hospital for two years, so naturally I haven't needed a renewal."

The cop seemed to think it might be a serious offense to let your license expire in any case. "This your current address?" he asked.

"No, I just got back in town. I'm still looking for place."

"Your name is Laurence Lantz, isn't it?"

"It sure is."

"Employed?"

"Abe's Shoe Repair, on Regent Street. I'm on my lunch hour."

The squad car swung off the square onto East Washington Avenue and the driver turned off the flashing red light. They went past the turn-off to the downtown police station and Lucky saw the long boulevard descending ahead of them, then leveling out for its long run to the horizon. You could see all the way to the cornfields of Sun Prairie from up here and he wondered if that was where he was going to wind up.

"Abe's—that's a sheeny joint, ain't it?" the cop asked. "You wouldn't catch me workin' for no Jew. Bet most of your customers are niggers, too, ain't they?"

"We have some colored customers," Lucky said. "It's a mixed neighborhood."

The cop made a face. "You wouldn't catch me handlin' no niggers' shoes."

"Maybe he likes the smell," the cop at the wheel said.

"Maybe he does," the young cop said. "Maybe he likes the smell of his own shit, when it comes dribbling out his ears."

They were just passing the sooty-brick walls and blue glass windows of the Oslo Machine Shop—Leo's place of employment. Right now Lucky envied his brother that nice safe hospital bed. He wished he were back in the san, where crap like this never happened, but he made an effort to talk sensibly to the policemen:

"Look, I think I know what this is all about."

"He says he knows what this is all about," the young cop said to the driver, as if he couldn't hear what was being said in the back seat. "Should we ask him to tell us?"

"Sure, let's hear what the nigger-loving asshole's got to say for himself," the driver said good-naturedly.

"Speak up, pal," the young cop said, and slipped his night-stick from his belt.

"Well, you're worried about me and Glenda," Lucky said. "But there's nothing going on between us—I just dropped by to say hello. We hadn't seen each other for eight, ten years. I didn't even know she was married."

"He says there's nothing goin' on between him and Glenda," the young cop repeated for the driver, then turned with a snarl: "Who's Glenda, punk?"

"Your friend's wife, I believe."

"You bet she is," the cop said, and rapped his night-stick across Lucky's knee. The pain made him wince, and stars danced behind his closed eyelids.

"You think you're pretty smart, don't you?" the cop asked him, prodding his ribs with the night-stick. "You think you're one smart son of a bitch, am I right?"

"No, I don't think that at all," Lucky said, blinking out the window at the suddenly bright street. They were approaching Schenk's Corners and the shopfronts looked like over-exposed snapshots, the world flooded with harsh white light. When they swung onto Atwood Avenue, he began to wonder if the cops were taking him out to Lake Edge. Lots of cornfields still in Lake Edge. Maybe he could crawl as far as Leo's place when they were done with him.

The squad car drove the length of Atwood Avenue, passing some of his favorite hangouts from days gone by, joints where he was known and liked, where they would have told the cops Lucky Lantz was all right. But the squad car didn't stop at any of those places. It kept right on going, over the hill and out of town on Monona Drive, and by this time Lucky thought he knew where they were taking him, and it wasn't as far as Lake Edge.

Sure enough, just over the bridge the squad car turned onto a gravel road that ran along the creek, past a string of decrepit boat houses. Weeping willows lined the road on the other side, screening a soggy plain that was once the city's dumping grounds. The squad car bounced over several rusty railroad tracks with weeds sprouting between the ties and pulled up before an abandoned factory, out of business since the thirties. The hot mid-day sun lay on the old brick and wood buildings like a coat of shellac. Their windows were broken, their interiors dark and quiet. No one around to hear his screams. Lucky was glad he hadn't eaten any lunch, since it was likely he would soon lose whatever was in his stomach.

The cop returned his license. "Get out of the car," he said.

Lucky climbed out, into the heat and dust. Beneath the strong odor of the stagnant creek, he caught the ghostly aroma of tar and oil, the rotting wastes of the abandoned factory. Probably more than one body buried around here. Maybe the cops would decide they'd bullied him enough and just leave him. But no, the young cop put on his shades and climbed out after him. Lucky saw him slipping on a pair of leather gloves and thought, *Please don't break a tooth.* He couldn't afford any dentist bills just now.

The cop pushed him across the lot to the edge of a ditch where muddy water glinted up through the weeds. Then he turned him around, took him by the lapels and put his face so close Lucky could see himself twinned in the dark circles that hid the cop's eyes. "All right, you rotten old piece of shit, we got enough to do without messin' around with bums like you, so you better listen real good. Are you listening?"

"I'm listening," Lucky said, but the cop gave his lapels a shake anyway.

"You want to walk the streets in this town, and keep that shitty job of yours fixing nigger's shoes, you stay the hell away from the Cambridge Hotel, understand me?"

"I understand," Lucky said. His neck ached and the taste of bile was in his mouth.

"And you stay the hell away from Glenda Royce, too, you got it? Harry don't want nobody messin' with his wife. It makes him damn unhappy, and when he's un-happy, *we're* unhappy, you hear me?"

"I hear you," Lucky said, the bright daylight dancing with blue and white butterflies all around him.

The cop held him steady for a moment, as if to help him maintain his balance. At first Lucky was grateful for a little kindness after such rough treatment; then he saw the kid cock his fist. You could try to slip the punch, but the cop would just hit you again. Better to let him have one clean shot. Lucky braced himself and the blow caught him on the cheekbone beneath his left eye. His face went numb and his knees buckled; he dropped to all fours on the biting gravel and, before he could turn away, the cop's knee nailed him squarely on the mouth. He pitched over and into the ditch, where he rolled to a stop in several inches of muddy water.

"Take it easy, pal," the cop said and went back to the car.

Laurence heard the car door slam, the tires spit gravel. He heard the squad car swing around in the lot and head back up the road. After a while he found the strength to raise his head and spit the muddy water from his mouth. Then he pushed up from the ditch and crawled to the top of the gravel bank. The front of his shirt and most of his trousers were caked with black mud. He tasted blood and ran his tongue over his lips, finding the gash the cop's knee had opened at the corner of his mouth. At least he seemed to have all his teeth. Then he realized his left eye was swollen nearly shut. The sun beat down on his bare head and the old factory buildings stared at him with empty black windows.

He felt weak and light-headed, but found he could walk, one careful step at a time, across the gravel lot and into the shade of the big willows. He leaned against a trunk to rest a moment and let his head clear, then started up the road past the ramshackle boat houses. Old men or little kids used to come down here to fish, but there was nobody on the riverbank today. It was too hot, and the creek stunk.

Lucky reflected that the world was not a very pleasant place. Sometimes the best place to be was in a nice soft bed in a cool, breezy room, looking out on a long stretch of sunny lawn. But a guy got bored just lying there. He got the urge to get out in the world again and try his luck—which so far wasn't running any better than usual. Win a few, lose a few, that's how it went. Make peace with your brother, and he has a heart attack. Get a job you can handle, that you even kind of like, and your boss tells you he needs three fifty to stay in business. Try to collect on an honest debt and the fucking roof falls in on you.

Lucky paused in the shade of the last willow, the glare of the open park just ahead of him. Clearly, a man lost touch with reality, living in the san. He forgot a few basic rules, such as: ask for what you think you've got coming and you'll be told to forget it, it was never yours in the first place. Tell a guy what you're after and he'll find some way to hide it before you get there. But there were other ways of collecting on bad debts. You just had to use a little subtlety; you had to disguise your hand.

I can play this game, Lucky thought. *I've been playing it all my life.*

He watched the traffic buzzing along Monona Drive and tried to decide what his next move should be. It wasn't likely he could thumb a ride, the shape he was in, but it was still a long walk out to Leo's place. Who else did he know on the east side? Those bars he'd passed, they wouldn't know him there anymore. Besides, he hated to show up at one of his old hangouts looking like a bum—that wasn't Lucky's style.

Then he saw a Yellow Cab coming down the hill from town, heading right toward him. He stepped out into the sun and raised his arm. At least he still knew how to hail a cab.

9.

Seems Like Old Times

AT FIRST it seemed the taxi was going to pass him by, even though its back seat was empty. Then the driver got a good look at Laurence and pulled over. He leaned out his window and called across the roadway. "You all right, pal?"

Laurence felt dizzy in the bright sunlight; he wasn't sure he could make it across the four lanes of whirring traffic. "I could use a little help," he said, "but I've got money—I can pay your fare."

"Stay there," the cabby said, and came to get him. "Jesus, who worked you over?" he asked when he saw his face up close.

"Madison's finest," Lucky said. "They were having a slow day."

"Sons a' bitches! We got some damn mean cops in this town."

"So I noticed."

The cabby helped him across the street and into the back of the cab. "So where do you want to go? I was answering a call out in Monona Village, but I could drop you someplace along the way."

Laurence gave the driver Leo's address, figuring it was still his best bet, and settled back as the cab pulled into traffic. Nothing like a cab ride to make a man feel better about himself. Bums and losers couldn't afford taxis, which was why Lucky took them as often as he could. Some of the best times of his life had taken place in the backseat of cab. A little cramped, but better than a hotel room, if the gal was skittish. He'd even composed a tune once called "The Yellow Cab Blues":

> *Oh baby, tell me, why do I get so blue*
> *When I'm riding in a Yellow Cab with you?*

He noticed the driver eying him in the rear-view mirror. "Do I know you, friend?"

"That's what I was wondering," the driver said. "Ain't you Lucky Lantz? Used to play the 'lectric gee-tar at the Wagon Wheel over on Gilman Street?"

"My country-western phase," Lucky said. "Were you a regular?"

"No, but my old lady used to wait tables there. You took a few bucks off me at craps, after hours. Name's Bert Wiley."

"Sure enough. How you doin', Bert? Still rattlin' them dry bones?"

"Nah, there's no action in this town any more. The new police chief, he took the boys off the take, and that goddamn wrecked everything. You can't find a good craps game this side of Chicago these days."

"Must be why the cops are so mean," Lucky said. "It's a rotten job, if you can't skim a few bucks on the side."

"You know it," Bert said. "A little action is good for

everybody, that's my opinion. A guy comes into town on business and the first thing he wants to know is, where's the action? Cards, dice, pussy—whatever he's after, he expects me to take him there, right? Cab drivers are supposed to know these things. But these days, nine times out of ten, I can't do a thing for him. Consequently, I get lousy tips. The whole thing stinks. It gives the city a bad name."

"What about the Cambridge Hotel? Don't they still have games up in the high-priced rooms?"

"Oh sure, but you're talking big money there. East-coast money, west-coast money—I pick up a lot of fares outside the Cambridge, I know the type. High-rollers—they'll get a game if they want one, but who's got the dough for that kind of action?"

"Not me," Lucky said. "They must have pretty high table stakes, huh?"

"You know it," Bert said. "Five, six clams if you want a chair. And no I.O.U.s, neither. You pay up when you leave or you're cat-food."

They were nearly to their turn-off. Lucky leaned forward and rested his arm on the back of the front seat. "Tell you what, Bert, I'm no gambling man anymore, but I know a couple guys who might like to get into one of those games at the Cambridge. If you hear of something good in the works, would you let me know?"

"Sure thing, Lucky, but where do I find you?"

"There's a little shoe repair shop on Regent Street: Abe's—you know the place? I'm working there."

"I can find it," Bert said. "I usually meet the trains at the Milwaukee Road station, when I got nothing better to do."

The cab swung off Monona Drive onto the shady

streets of Lake Edge. It was nearly one thirty when they pulled up before the brown-shingled bungalow and Laurence was relieved to see Leo's car in the open garage—he'd been a little worried that Maggie and Jack might be off somewhere. He paid the fare and added a dollar tip.

"Hey, thanks, Lucky. I'll let you know if I hear anything."

"You do that," Lucky said. He didn't know what use he'd make of the information, but he figured he'd find some angle. He was not normally a vengeful person, but sometimes you had to fight back, at least a little bit, just to save your self-respect. It had been a long time since Lucky Lantz had cared very much about self-respect, but being sober did that to a person. It made him feel there might be something worth sticking up for, after all. Which was, Lucky supposed, just one more way a guy could get himself in trouble.

~§~

An hour later he was sitting in Leo's shady back yard, a glass of lemonade at his side and an ice bag pressed to his swollen eye. Maggie and Jack had gone out to the hospital, but not before Maggie attended to his wounds, gave him some of Leo's clothes to wear, and put his own muddy duds in her washing machine. Laurence appreciated the mothering, even though he'd had to accept a scolding in the bargain.

"The police wouldn't have done this to you if you hadn't been breaking some law," Maggie insisted as she applied Mercurochrome to his cuts and abrasions. "They don't beat up on innocent people."

"Not in your world," Laurence said. "In mine, it happens all the time."

"Well, you live in the wrong world," she said, and he was inclined to agree with her on that. But it was his world, after all, and maybe it was time he started making use of the opportunities and allies it could give him. Eddie King was a crude, moronic son of a bitch, but he knew how to handle cops—that was how he'd managed to stay in business all these years, preying on honest musicians. A friend like Eddie could even up the odds. So could Frank Holiday, if he was still interested in giving Lucky a job. After all, it didn't have to be a career. A few nights' work at the Blue Swan would cover Abe's debt, and if he should hear of a hot game at the Cambridge Hotel—well, Frank would find some way to show his appreciation for a tip like that.

He left his lawn chair and went into the house—which, somewhat surprisingly, Maggie had left open for him. The dog growled but didn't leave his bed in the kitchen, so Lucky made himself a baloney sandwich and poured more lemonade, then went to the telephone in the dining room. There was no listing for the Blue Swan, nor for Eddie King, but at this hour of the afternoon Eddie was usually to be found at the Leisuretime Billiard Emporium. Laurence dialed the number and asked for Eddie.

"Who wants him?" a gruff voice asked. "Tell him it's Lucky—Lucky Lantz." When Eddie came on the line, he said, "You fellas still looking for a piano player?"

"You bet we are—the damn club opens tomorrow night and Frankie's still not satisfied with anyone we've heard. He thinks it's the piano's fault the dumb broad can't stay on key."

"It probably is," Lucky said. "I can keep her on key."

"You tellin' me you've changed your mind about retirement?"

"Let's just say I might be able to manage a few nights—enough to get your club rolling, anyway. When can I audition with Savannah?"

"This afternoon, if you want. I'll call Frank and set it up. Where are you?"

"At my brother's place—where you dropped me off the other day."

"Be there in half an hour," Eddie said.

Laurence knew it would be more like an hour, which gave him time to get his shirt and pants out of Maggie's washing machine, run them through the wringer and hang them out on the line to dry. He thought Maggie would appreciate that. Then he called the Hiawatha and asked for Ginger, figuring she'd want to know what time he'd be home for dinner. If you were going get along with women, he saw, you had to take care of the little things.

~§~

"So what do you think?" Eddie asked as they pulled into the parking lot outside the Blue Swan. "Pretty classy joint, huh?"

"Yeah, very classy," Laurence said. As it happened, he knew the place. It was one of those old roadhouses that had more lives than a cat and a different name for every one of them. Back in the 20's, when Lucky was just getting started in the business, it was called the Riverside Inn, and it featured a basement speakeasy and several little cabins down by the river for private parties.

After Prohibition, the Riverside was reborn as the Stardust Ballroom and Lucky signed on as an week-night bartender, just so he could hear some of the big-name bands that booked the Stardust for one-night stands. Glenn Miller, the Dorseys, Artie Shaw—some of the best swing bands in the country played the old Stardust in its prime. Teddy Harrigan and his Royal Troubadours weren't in that league, by any means, but they had a lead singer who was in way over her head, and so scared she needed several stiff drinks before she could approach the bandstand. Her stage name was Ruby Devine; Lucky never learned what her real name was—not even after she started calling herself Ruby Lantz.

A crew of workmen were on the roof, installing a large plywood sign cut in the shape of a swan and out-lined in blue neon. There were bright blue awnings over the front windows and a blue marquee over the front entrance. Otherwise, the place hadn't changed much from the old days: it was a long, low structure of white-washed log siding, stretching back toward the river in a series of tacked-on additions. There were several willows along the river and a few picnic tables half-buried in the long grass.

Laurence climbed out of the car and approached the front door, feeling a bit like an animal sniffing out a trap. Because that's what the past was—a little box that lured you in with a promise of sweet memories, then slammed shut, trapping you inside with a lot of things you would rather leave forgotten. The Blue Swan was a crypt and Lucky knew all the ghosts.

Beside the door stood a hand-painted signboard:

LIVE MUSIC EVERY NIGHT
Opening this Thursday:
Miss Savannah Jones

Late Show Friday and Saturday:
Red Ford and the Hot Rods.

"Red Ford and the Hot Rods?" he asked Eddie. "What the hell are they—auto mechanics?"

"It's a rock and roll group," Eddie said. "Like I told you, that's the new sound. You gotta get your ass in gear, Lantz—you're about ten years out of date."

Eddie yanked open the door and the new sound came blaring out at Lucky, along with a blast of machine -chilled air. At first he thought maybe the workmen were still refurbishing the interior, because what he heard sounded more like power saws and jackhammers than music. Then he recognized the scream of over-amplified guitars, the high-pitched whine of a frantic adolescent voice: *"Oh since muh babee left me, Ah found a new place tuh dwell . . ."*

Lucky pulled back and turned to Eddie. "This is the 'new sound?' What happened to playing in the same key?"

"If it's loud enough, nobody cares," Eddie said with a grin. "You got to rev up the decibels for this kind of music. That's why Frank installed a new sound system— loud enough to blast you right out of the fucking joint. That's how the kids like it."

"Kids?" Lucky asked before Eddie could open the door again. "I thought this was a night club for grown-ups. You can't serve liquor to kids."

"Out here you can," Eddie said with a wink and gave

the door another shove.

Lucky stepped reluctantly into the refrigerated air, tainted with stale cigarette smoke and pulsating with noise. Like a Chicago subway station, he thought—never one of his favorite places. Beyond the entrance foyer with its cloakroom and hostess' stand, there was a horseshoe shaped bar, and beyond that a large dining room and dance floor, mostly dark, though its bandstand was illuminated by several spotlights. Lucky saw that all the racket was being raised by four young men in blue jeans and tee-shirts. They looked like scrawny farm boys, barely out of their teens, with greased-up hair and acned complexions, and they were performing with great seriousness, as if they thought they really knew what they were doing. One was torturing an electric guitar, one mistreating a base, one stomping around the stage behind a tenor sax, while the fourth pounded the hell out of a set of drums.

"I'll wait outside," Lucky said to Eddie, but then, his eyes adjusting to the gloom, he made out Frank Holiday and Savannah sitting at the far end of the horseshoe bar. Holiday motioned them over, and somehow, when Frank Holiday made that little gesture with his index finger, you felt inclined to approach. Lucky took his time strolling down the bar, stopping to inspect a few of the photos on the walls—musicians and entertainers who had never seen the inside of the Blue Swan. Maybe Frank was showing off his Las Vegas connections.

Holiday put out his small, manicured hand, then motioned Lucky to a stool. Savannah sat on his other side. She was wearing a tight pink skirt and one of those peasant blouses with the elasticized neckline a gal could push off her shoulders if she wanted to show more cleavage. Savannah had pushed hers well down her slim brown arms and Lucky tried not to gawk at the two mounds of creamy caramel she was putting on display. She sipped her tall drink through a straw and ignored the newcomers.

There was no hope of conversation until the barrage from the bandstand had run its course. When bombardment let up, Holiday spoke to the bartender who was stocking the bar for opening night. "Hey, Sid, tell those clowns to knock off their rehearsal. I've got a new piano player here I want to try out with Savannah."

"Sorry," Lucky said, his ears still ringing, "if that's the kind of music you want to book in here, I'm not your boy, Frank. My style's a little different."

"I know your style," Holiday said. "The Hot Rods are for the weekend late shows when we expect a younger crowd. You and Savannah can do the supper hour and a few weeknights. That's an older group, more sedate. Jazz standards and blues, just the stuff you like, Lucky."

"Yeah, but I couldn't play every night," Lucky said. "Not at my age. Eddie said maybe two or three nights a week."

Savannah gave him a long cool look over Holiday's shoulder. "I'm sure you're good for more than twice a week, Lucky. The kind of songs I sing, you won't have to work much at all. I like 'em nice and easy, sweet and low. Just take your time and—" she blinked innocently— "let it happen, you know?"

Eddie guffawed. "You better watch this dame, Frank. Like I told you, old Lucky here's a real ass-bandit."

Holiday's smile was as thin and brittle as the swizzle stick he twirled in his agile fingers. "I'm sure Lantz knows better than to fool around with any woman that belongs to me. Where'd you get that shiner, pal?"

"Talking sweet to the wrong woman," Lucky said. "You can bet I won't make that mistake again."

"I'll decide who I belong to," Savannah said. "Are we going to do a song, or do we sit here gabbing all afternoon?"

"Do a song," Holiday said amiably. And then he took hold of Savannah's arm, his fingers digging into her soft flesh. "You keep telling me you'd sound a lot better with a decent piano behind you, so let's hear it. I can still cancel your engagement, if I don't like what I hear."

"You can go to hell, too," Savannah said, and pulled her arm free. She stalked to the bandstand in her high heels and tight skirt, her tight little butt making motions that caught in Lucky's throat. He turned to Holiday.

"I thought I was the one getting the audition, not her."

"She's counting on you, pal. See if you can save her bitchy little ass."

Lucky followed Savannah to the bandstand, where a grand piano had been rolled out to replace the electronic apparatus of the rock and roll group. In the gloom he could see white-clothed tables and red plush booths, fake palms in pots, a dead strobe above a small dance floor. The large room still seemed to echo the Hot Rods' thunder and Lucky imagined the ghosts of Dorsey and Shaw plugging their ears and praying for a change of pace. He sat down at the keyboard and took a cigarette from the pack Savannah put on the piano ledge. "So what'll it be, lady?"

Savannah considered. "How about 'Stormy Weather', key of G."

Laurence put his hands on his lap. "No, not that

one. Anything but that."

"You don't like that tune?"

"I have problems with it." Especially here, Laurence thought, where he first heard Ruby singing that song in her tremulous, wavering soprano. When Teddy Harrigan discovered she was too drunk to sing her last set, he fired her on the spot. That was when Lucky, who'd been mixing her seven and seven's all night, took pity on her and asked Howie Richards, the manager, if they could use one of the little cabins out back. It wasn't for sex—the poor kid just needed a place to sleep it off, and by the time she woke up the Troubadours were long gone. The next weekend Lucky broke her in with his own group, the Swinging Six (soon to become the Swinging Seven), and the rest, as they say, was history—but not a very happy history, from his point of view.

"All right, then," Savannah said, "'The Man I Love', key of B flat."

"Gotcha," Lucky said, and launched an eight-bar intro.

Savannah had one of those soft, breathy voices that needed a mike to make itself heard in a crowded dining room, but she was pretty much on key and she knew how to phrase a song. Lucky didn't confuse her with anything fancy; he just built a strong, steady structure of chords and rhythm beneath the melody, followed her lead, let her take the tune her own way. By the second chorus, Savannah was looking over at him every so often, giving him a smile that said she liked what he was doing and maybe, if he played his cards right, those words might take on a special meaning, just for him. The beginning of a beautiful relationship, Lucky thought, if I was crazy in the head. Not being crazy, he tended to his business and returned Savannah's smile with a polite nod. She came on strong for the last chorus and finished with a nice, sustained wail of longing and frustrated desire.

Frank Holiday and Eddie King clapped enthusiastically. "Not bad," Savannah said, brushing a lock of hair back from her dark eyes. "You know how to play that thing."

"I've been at it for a few years," Lucky said. "What's your next number?"

"What about 'As Time Goes By', key of F?"

"Nice tune," Lucky said, and did an intro.

Savannah's voice grew stronger as they went along, and Lucky found it easy enough to match his style to hers. He could play this kind of music in his sleep, though producing two or three hours of it every evening might get a little boring. The trouble with ballads, they were always about somebody's broken heart, and they gave you too much time to think, to dream at the keyboard. And dreaming, Lucky reflected, was always what had gotten him in trouble.

Looking up from the keyboard and seeing Savannah's full figure in silhouette against the spotlights, he could almost imagine he was playing this tune for someone else: for the only woman who ever got the better of him, who could always hurt him more than he could hurt her. *A kiss is still a kiss, a sigh is still a sigh—* and a fool, goddamn it, is still a fool—*as time goes by.*

Savannah sat on the piano bench with him for the last chorus. Though Lucky slid over to give her room, she still managed to rest her thigh snugly against his. Good thing Frank Holiday couldn't see them playing kneesies from across the room. He and Eddie applauded the end of the number and Lucky said softly, "Take it easy, kid—the guy you have to impress is sitting over there."

"I don't care about him," Savannah said, loud enough for Holiday to hear. "He's just a guy with a job, as far as I'm concerned."

"Yeah, and I'm a guy with one foot in the grave," Lucky said. "You'd get more rise out of a corpse than you'd get out of me, sugar. What's your next number?"

She considered. "Maybe 'That Old Black Magic', how does that grab you? Good for raising the dead?"

"Only if it's done right," Lucky said. "A little more up-beat, this time?"

"Sure, make it swing," Savannah said, and snapped her fingers to set the tempo.

Lucky knew she'd have trouble keeping up with that beat, but he gave her a brisk, brief intro and told her with a nod when to jump in. The first chorus went all right, but halfway through the second Savannah lost the beat, then the melody, and Lucky had to finish the chorus without her. He reined in the tempo for the last chorus, giving her a chance to redeem herself, and she scrambled back on board, then gave him a sheepish smile. Altogether, she wasn't as bad as Eddie had led him to believe.

"That's enough," Holiday said, coming over to the bandstand. "You can save the fast stuff for after you've played together for a while. It's the slow, torchy stuff the audience will want, anyway. Come on back to my office, Lantz—we'll talk terms."

The manager's office had been remodeled as well, and considerably expanded from the old days. In addition to a big mahogany desk, Holiday had several leather sofas, a bar, and a hexagonal poker table with a green felt surface. The windows looked out on a row of ancient willows along the river.

"Sit down, Lantz," Holiday said. "Get you a drink?"

"I'm still on the wagon, Frank," Laurence said.

Holiday fixed himself one and sat down at his desk. "So how much do I have to pay to coax you out of retirement? Fifty a night sound about right?"

"Fifty a night sounds pretty good, if it's for three hours' work. But I can't do more than three nights a week, seven to ten thirty, with a couple of fifteen-minute breaks. And just till I get back on my feet, you understand. If I hang around joints like this too long, I'll be digging my own grave."

"Have it your way," Holiday said. "I like a man who knows his limit. Once we get Savannah launched, you can quit any time you like." His eyes sharpened, zeroed in on Lucky's shiner. "You haven't got your eyes on my woman, do you?"

"Frank, she'd take one look at me with my clothes off and bust a gut laughing. She was just trying to get your goat back there—I think she's nuts about you."

"She's a dumb cunt," Holiday said. "I could get another dozen like her, if I wanted 'em, but I don't like bein' played for a sucker, you know what I mean?"

"You bet I do," Lucky said. "Nobody likes that. I'm sure you could find another singer—and another piano player, too, if I can't hack it."

"Right. So is it a deal?"

"I could use an advance," Lucky said.

"An advance?" Holiday cocked an eyebrow and Lucky saw that, despite his big talk, he was not a man to part easily with his money. "I don't usually pay my musicians until after they've performed, Lantz. You know you'll get paid."

"Yeah, but the thing is, I've got to get a certain sum together by the weekend. That's the only reason I'm here, to tell you the truth."

Holiday smiled. "Heard of a big game, have you? Eddie tells me you've got connections at the Cambridge Hotel."

"Used to," Lucky said. "I was reminded today that my connections with that over-priced flea trap have been severed. I just want to get set up in my new trade: repairing shoes."

"Oh yeah, Eddie told me you'd become a cobbler. So how much do you need?"

"Three fifty." Holiday looked dubious, so Laurence explained Abe's problems with his mortgage and taxes. "We've got till Saturday to raise the dough or Abe's Shoe Repair gets sold to some realtor and I'm out of a job."

Holiday sipped his drink and drummed his fingers on the desk. "Three fifty—that's seven nights' work. How do I know you won't take my money and skip town? Eddie says you used to be quite a con man."

"The first thing a con man learns," Laurence said, "is who to con and who not to con. I wouldn't con you, Frank. You'd kill me without blinking an eye."

Holiday smiled. "You've got me wrong, pal. I don't kill people. But I got friends who do."

"That's what I meant," Laurence said.

Holiday got to his feet. "All right, tell you what. You open with Savannah tomorrow night. If the crowd likes her, you can do Friday and Saturday—seven to ten-thirty, just like you want. I'll have three-fifty for you Friday night and you'll owe me five more nights. If she bombs, you'll still get your fifty a night and the chance to earn more when I find another singer."

"Savannah will be okay," Laurence said. "I can get her through an evening."

"That's what I'm trying to make sure of," Holiday said. He ran his fingers over his green felt tabletop. "Care for a few hands of poker before you go?"

Laurence shook his head. "I'd have to be a damn-site richer than I am right now, Frank, before I'd sit down at a table with you."

They went back to the bar, where Eddie was brutalizing the pinball machine. Savannah was watching a cartoon show on the bar's TV. All the little mice were getting sucked up in vacuum cleaners by big bad cats. Nice saxophone soundtrack—Lucky thought he'd seen that cartoon twenty years ago.

"Take the man home, Eddie," Frank said. "We've cut our deal."

Savannah didn't turn around, though Laurence thought he saw her back stiffen.

"Sure you don't want to hang around for a while, shoot a little pool?" Eddie asked. "Frank's got some nice new tables in the back lounge."

Laurence checked his watch. It was after five, and he'd told Ginger he'd be home for supper by six. "Another time, Eddie." He could see there would be plenty of opportunities to shoot pool with Eddie King in the near future.

"Say goodbye, Savannah," Holiday told her, as Laurence and Eddie made for the door.

"Goodbye, Savannah," she repeated in a dead voice, and kept her eyes on the TV. Frank Holiday was obviously pleased.

"So," Eddie said, as he spit gravel pulling out of the parking lot, "you're back in the music business. About time, if you ask me. I hope you know what a goddamn big favor I've done you, pal."

"You're a real friend, Eddie," Laurence said, as the hot air from the open window began to blow against his face. Sometimes he wondered why, with friends like Eddie King, a man just didn't spend his entire life on Easy Street.

10.

That Old Black Magic

THE NEXT DAY Laurence brooded at his workbench, sewing welts and straps, applying half-soles and rubber heels. A storm had passed during the night and the morning was cool and bright, with a feeling of autumn in the air. It was tough being cooped up in the dark, airless shop, and every so often Laurence left his bench to stand in the open doorway, gazing at the row of shabby houses across the street.

"What's the matter, Lucky?" Abe called from the back. "Looking for more customers? We got enough work to keep us busy."

"Just taking a breather," Laurence said, and lit a cigarette from the pack he'd purchased yesterday evening. "You know, it would be a lot easier working in here if we put a fan in that back window, blew a little fresh air through the place."

Abe laughed. "Sure, Lucky, sure—once we know we're going to be here after Saturday, we can invest in one. That will be soon enough, I think." He went back to his work, whistling a tuneless melody through his teeth as he bent over his stitching machine. Laurence spit a tobacco crumb from his tongue and remained at the door.

He hadn't told Abe yet that he'd cut a deal with Frank Holiday, that the three fifty they needed was practically in the bag. He didn't want to get the old man's hopes up, because he was having some second thoughts about working at the Blue Swan. If it hadn't been for those cops roughing him up yesterday, and for the stiff-arm they'd given him at the Cambridge, he never would have taken that gig, because it had trouble written allover it.

So how else was he going to raise the dough? Any other time, he might've swallowed his pride and asked his brother for a loan, but that was out of the question now. He'd seen a piece in the morning paper, which he'd skimmed over breakfast at the Hiawatha: STRIKE LOOMS AT OSLO. The union had given the company until midnight Monday to sweeten its latest offer, or else they'd walk and Leo would lose his benefits. Some Oslo big-shot was quoted as saying the union's demands were unreasonable and would bankrupt the company. *Times were hard all over*, Laurence thought; if you had a chance to make fifty a night playing the piano, you damn-well ought to take it.

If only I still had that pearl-handled banjo, he thought, returning to an idea he'd toyed with yesterday, then set aside. That banjo was a dandy—worth eighty to a hundred bucks at a good pawn shop, more if he could find a buyer for it himself with the fifty Joey March had promised him and the one forty-seven in his coin purse, he'd be nearly there. He could quit the Blue Swan after one weekend, get out clean before he got to liking it too much, before the temptations became too much for him.

Of course to claim that banjo he'd have to go see his ex-wife, and he'd been telling himself for two days now that would be a big mistake, maybe the biggest one of all. Yet seeing Ruby again didn't *have* to be such a god damn big deal. She'd been growing older these past fifteen years, just like everybody else—chances were she wouldn't mean a thing to him.

Laurence flicked his cigarette butt toward the gutter and went back to his workbench. Sometimes a guy's worst mistakes weren't the ones that took him by surprise, but the ones he could see coming a mile off, like a freight train that gave you plenty of time to get the hell off the tracks. Old Ruby was like one of those freight trains—he'd seen her coming for a long time now, but he was pretty sure he could jump clear in time.

At noon, when Abe broke out his aromatic hunk of salami, Laurence finished the job he was working on and turned to his employer. "Well, I guess I'll break for lunch, too, Old-Timer. I may be gone for awhile again this afternoon—I've got to make a few calls."

"Sure, Lucky, sure—only don't get beat up this time, okay? I don't want you should get hurt on my account."

"Don't worry," Laurence said. "I learned my lesson yesterday." He didn't want to call Ruby from the Hiawatha so he stopped at the little grocery next door, where he'd noticed a sign in the window: "Home-Made Sandwiches." At the end of a cluttered aisle, he found a small deli counter and a heavy-set black woman, who waited patiently while he read the chalkboard menu above her frizzled gray curls.

"So what's good today, darlin?" he asked when he'd finished.

She gave him a gap-toothed grin. "I makes it myself,

so I can't rightly say. The ham is fresh."

"Great, I'll have a ham sandwich. With a slice of Swiss cheese, on rye bread, with maybe just a little lettuce and mustard—that sound all right to you?"

"You the fella eatin' it," she said. "If tha's what you want, tha's what you get."

She set to work and Laurence spotted a pay phone over in the corner. A battered phone book was dangling from a cord. He paged through it and, sure enough, there they were, Chester and Ruby Claymore. An address out in Nakoma Hills, too—one of Madison's better neighborhoods. With an address like that, Ruby's temper may have improved. He fished out a dime and dropped it in the slot, then dialed the number.

A woman's voice came on the line. "Claymore residence."

He recognized Ruby's down-home twang beneath her snooty tone. He said, "Ruby, hi, this is Laurence."

There was a momentary pause, just long enough for an intake of air or a lost memory to click into place. "Why Lucky, what a surprise! What brings you back to town?"

She sounds friendly enough, he thought. As if they were just old friends. As if they hadn't been man and wife for nearly five years—the worst five years he'd ever known, it seemed now, but in some ways maybe the best. You never knew with Ruby—was it heaven or hell, or some strange mixture of both?

"Just passing through," he said, letting her think he might still be on the road with a good band. "I got your married name from Glenda at the Cambridge and thought I'd give you a call. I was hoping maybe we could meet somewhere for a cup of coffee."

"Coffee?" Ruby asked. "Does that mean you're on the wagon?"

"That's what it means," Laurence said. "Going on two years now."

"Well . . ." he could hear her thinking—you could always hear the wheels turning in that crafty little brain of hers—"why don't you come out here? I can give you a cup of coffee, and a piece of cake, too."

"Sounds great. How do I get there?"

He was hoping she would offer to come pick him up, but instead she gave him directions from the nearest bus stop and said she'd see him in half an hour. *As easy as that*, he thought, hanging up the phone. A happy reunion for one thin dime.

The old woman was wrapping his sandwich in waxed paper. "Say, ain't you the fella that went to work at the shoe repair shop next door?"

"That's right, darlin. C'mon by—we got special deals for our fellow tradesmen."

"Oh, I ain't no *tradesman*," she said with a deep, throaty chuckle, "but I sure could use some new soles on these nurse's oxfords. You do that kinda work?"

"Course we do. Why, nurse's oxfords happen to be my specialty. You got a Coke to go with this sandwich, darlin?"

She got a bottle from the cooler, opened it and put it on the counter, eyeing him suspiciously the whole time. "You sure do look familiar to me, son. Don't I know you?"

Laurence had been thinking the same thing. It was that rich contralto laugh that brought it back to him. "Well, if your name is Nellie Hopkins, and you used to sing the blues with Henry Washington's band, you might remember an old broken-down piano player by the name of Lucky Lantz."

The old woman's eyes narrowed to slits, then opened wide in recognition and surprise. "Why, bless my bones, Lucky Lantz—it *is* you!" She reached across the counter with her flabby arms to grasp his shoulders. "Now what you want to go and fool an old woman for? Why, I'da knowed you if you walked up to this counter wearing a wedding gown, 'stead a that shiner! Where you been hiding all these years, son?"

"Oh, here and there. That is me at Abe's shop, Nell—I'm his new apprentice."

"Apprentice? Shoot, old Abe can't afford no 'prentice!"

"This one he can," Lucky said. "You tell all your friends and neighbors to come on by—we'll have some hot deals for 'em."

"I'll sure do that," Nell said. "But what you gone an' give up your music for, Lucky? You one of the best blues pianos in the business."

"Thanks, Nell, but I was getting too old for the life and what it leads to. I gotta reform my ways." He gave her a dollar fifty for the sandwich and Coke. "So tell me, do any of the boys still jam around here?"

She rang up the sale and gave him his change. "Sunday afternoons—a place down by the tracks called Shorty's. That's about the onliest time we get together any more—those of us what ain't dead yet."

"Well, since I'm still among that number, I'll try to drop by some Sunday. Say hi to everybody for me, will you, Nell?"

"Sure thing, Lucky. You come join us now, y'hear?"

Laurence took his sandwich and Coke up the street,

where there was a bench he could sit on while he ate. Work crews were out, cleaning up the debris of last night's storm, and the whine of chain saws and grinders arose from the next block. Not his choice of dinner music, but it was nice sitting in the sun after his long morning indoors. The cool air was sweet in his nostrils and the sky was so blue it seemed to hum inside him. It was as though the dying summer had come back in all its glory for one last fling.

One last fling, Laurence thought, watching a dump truck full of branches and wilted foliage go up the street—now there was an idea for a tune:

> *Honey, you said our love is through,*
> *And I know there's nothing I can do.*
> *But listen, baby, here's the thing—*
> *All I want is one last fling.*

Kind of corny, but he was in a corny mood just now, probably because he was going to see his ex. Ruby loved sentiment—she wallowed in it, like a pig in a trough—though underneath that gushy exterior she hid a heart of solid brass. He would have to be careful not to let her see how he still felt about her, or how much he wanted that banjo, because when had Ruby ever let go of anything she thought was valuable?

She let go of Laurence easily enough—in fact, she pretty much tossed him aside—but that was because she knew what *he* was worth. At the end, when he was sick again and back in the san, she gave it to him straight, and he'd always admired her for that, even though he'd wanted to wring her neck at the time.

I know it's over, I'll set you free,
But honey, darlin', hear my plea.
There's one last thing you can do for me.
Honey, give me one last fling.

Laurence finished his lunch and walked up Regent Street another six blocks to Monroe Street, where he knew he could catch the Nakoma bus. Waiting on the corner across from the stadium, he could hear the UW marching band, the sonorous bleats and blats of the brass, the *thumpa-thumpa* of the big drums. Getting ready for their first game of the season. Lucky had played a lot of gigs on campus, especially when Leo was a student and knew guys who could get them jobs. He remembered those football weekends: the excitement in the air, the cheers and chants, and then the dances and homecoming parties . . . it made him a little sad that he'd never been a part of all that, except on some band-stand, watching the frat boys party with their tipsy sweeties. *They never would've let me in the joint*, he thought—not with his sixth-grade education. Besides, it wasn't his style. Those college kids didn't know what life was all about.

The bus came and carried him out Monroe Street past a stretch of large older homes, smug behind their hedges and picket fences. He recognized the stop from Ruby's directions, pulled the cord, and shambled to the rear exit. Even though he'd been looking forward to this reunion for years, he felt like a man about to leap from an airplane without a parachute as the doors folded open and he eased himself down the two steep steps.

"Turn right at the Mobil station," Ruby had said, "and walk two blocks along Cherokee Drive. Turn right again on Chippewa Drive." *A lot of dead Indians around here*, Lucky thought. Maybe he'd turn out to be another one. The terrain was hilly and he had to go slowly up the steep streets, pausing every so often to catch his breath. Massive oaks spilled shade over generous, ivy-bordered lawns. In the sunny gardens storm-battered lilies drooped from their long stems like elegant ladies looking for lost treasures in the grass.

I always knew that gal had a nose for money, Laurence thought. The day she lost interest in Lucky was the day she realized he wasn't going anywhere. A smarter dame would have seen that a lot sooner; a better one wouldn't have cared. Ruby wasn't especially beautiful, but she had a quality both sweet and gritty, like wild raspberries, or like some scrawny baby bird kicked out of its nest, its feathers all ruffled and a wing busted, a thing you wanted to care for and protect, even while it pecked your hand. It was a quality Lucky found hard to resist—at least when they were getting started.

That would have been 1936, her first year in the band, and Lucky built a lot of numbers around her reedy, slightly off-key voice. Some of the best things he'd ever done, really, not counting those months in Chicago with Gary Ames. Of course, it didn't take him long to learn that Ruby was quite a bit older than she looked and every bit as tough as she sometimes seemed. He had no idea how many lovers she'd had before their marriage, or how many since, yet even now the thought of another man screwing Ruby was enough to make him wince.

I shouldn't be doing this, he thought, pausing at the corner of Chippewa and Cherokee. Yet how could he back away now? And what else had he been waiting for these past fifteen years?

Christ, fifteen years since that day in 1941 when she showed up at the san and told him she was filing for divorce. He had nothing to give her, not a cent to his name, so there was nothing for them to fight over; he didn't even have to show up for the hearing, and so lost his chance to see her one last time. *Probably all dolled up in one of her little-girl dresses*, he thought, *flirting the ass off some old idiot of a judge.* No, he shouldn't be doing this. The pain was still too sharp.

And yet over all the years Laurence had felt sort of good about the pain, had even been proud of it, in a way. Because he knew that for most of his life he had been a bad man with women, had taken what he could get and left a lot of dames brokenhearted, so it seemed only right that, finally, one of the female sex would take her revenge for all the others, would make him fall hopelessly and foolishly in love, then put her brand on his heart for the rest of his life. Sometimes Lucky could still feel her initials carved into the juicy red meat of that peculiar organ—"R.L." for Ruby Lantz. This heart is mine.

He paused outside the gate that led to a red brick house with the number 817 on its glossy black door. It was just one o'clock. He wondered if she had perked the coffee yet, and maybe added a dash of cyanide. As he got closer to the front door its rectangular shape took on the look of a coffin lid. There were a lot of dead Indians buried behind that door.

He rang the bell, heard a chiming response from somewhere within the house. Classy. He wondered if she would even let him in the door once she got a look at him. He smoothed back his hair and pasted that old

Lucky Lantz smile on his face. But when the door opened Laurence figured he'd gotten the wrong house, or maybe Ruby's mother had come to visit. Then he remembered that Ruby didn't have a mother, and that she was *supposed* to look older—he'd been counting on that.

"Lucky—come in! It's so good to see you!"

She didn't, thank God, offer her cheek for a kiss. Laurence would have been afraid to kiss anything so well-preserved, like a specimen under glass. Not that Ruby didn't look terrific. Her mousey brown hair was now blonde and attractively styled; her figure filled out a demure navy-blue dress with a mature shapeliness it had never boasted in the old days, when her scrawny body used to drive him wild. Even her teeth had been fixed—they were a string of pearls, white and even, where once they had been as crooked as an alley fence, stained brown with nicotine and graying at the gums. Maybe it was her new teeth, or maybe just a clever use of cosmetics, but Ruby looked younger at forty-eight than she had at twenty-eight, when they first met. Only the eyes remained the same—those bright, moist, starry-dark eyes he'd fallen in love with—and it was the eyes that persuaded Laurence he'd come to the right house.

She saw the appraisal he was giving her and responded with that same shrewd, mocking smile. "So, do you like the way I look, Lucky?"

"You look lovely," Laurence said, but he was pretty sure he was safer with this woman than he would have been with the old Ruby—a woman bruised, battered, full of folly and mischief, the kind of dame who could caress your dick with one hand and pick your pocket with the other.

"But what happened to you?" she asked, gazing up at his black eye.

"Oh, that," Laurence said. "Just a little accident. Slipped in the shower the other morning. Otherwise, I'm fine—the best I've been in years."

She looked a little skeptical but led him without comment into a formal living room. Marble-faced fireplace, flowered upholstery, lots of sleek dark wood still smelling of furniture polish. Laurence sat uncomfortably on the sofa and Ruby perched prettily in a little armchair just across from him. "So . . . should I bring out the coffee, or would you rather start off with a little snort?"

He was a little surprised at the offer of a drink, because he'd told her he was on the wagon, and most people respected that. So far only Eddie King had tried to pull him off the wagon, but Ruby was a lot like Eddie in some ways—she would never urge a man to give up his bad habits, because it was his weakness that gave her an edge. He said politely that he would stick to coffee.

"So you've really quit drinking," she said, as if she hadn't quite believed it.

"You betcha," Laurence said. "I've had to change my entire life, Ruby—although it looks like I got started a few years later than you did."

"Well, we all have to start sometime," Ruby said, and went to get the coffee.

Laurence looked around the living room. There were ceramic pixies and Chinamen on the end tables, framed paintings on the walls—fruit baskets and country scenes—and on the mantel, between a pair of gold candlesticks, a tinted photo of Ruby and her husband, this Chester Claymore cat—a very distinguished gentleman with wavy gray hair and a square jaw. *Probably a goddamn bank president or something*, Lucky thought. He could hear a clock ticking and music softly playing somewhere in the house. Though tone-deaf, Ruby had always loved music.

She returned with a porcelain coffee service on a tray. Even a little plate of sugar cookies. She put the tray on the coffee table and poured a cup for each of them. *Well, no cyanide*, Laurence thought, observing that they were both drinking from the same pot. She handed him his cup and resumed her seat.

"Well. To what do I owe the pleasure of this visit, Laurence? Just checking in for old times' sake?"

"You could say that," Laurence said. "I just got back in town, you see. I was out of commission for a couple of years."

"The usual problem?"

He nodded. "Only worse. It gets worse every time, which is why I can't let it happen again. I've given up the music business, Ruby. While I was still inside they taught me a trade, so I could earn an honest living. I'm a shoe repairman now."

Somehow, he did not take the same pleasure in telling her this that he had with other people, and he felt sure she would scorn his last-ditch effort at reform. He could see the mockery in her smile, hear it on the tip of her tongue, though her words were kind enough: "That's wonderful, Lany—I'm so glad for you!"

"You are?"

"You know I always wanted you to settle down and take care of yourself. That's why I finally decided we had to split up. I was no good for you, and I knew it. The life we were living, it was killing both of us."

"That's true," Laurence said, impressed by her insight, "but it was a great life while it lasted."

"For you, maybe. Not for me. I simply couldn't take it any longer. I had to break out of it for my own sake, if not for yours."

That sounded more like the old Ruby, always watching out for herself Laurence smiled. "Well, you never would have gotten a house like this if you'd stuck with me. What does your husband do, anyway?"

"Oh, he owns a company. They make something industrial—I never figured out just what, but apparently it's very profitable. You should meet Chester sometime—you'd like him. Of course, he doesn't know that much about my former life. We'd have to be very—" she searched for the word—"discreet."

"He doesn't know you were a singer?"

"Oh, he knows that. I mean, he doesn't know about us. He doesn't know I was ever married."

"Where does he think you spent the first thirty-odd years of your life, in a convent?"

"Of course not, but Chester doesn't know how old I am, exactly. There are certain things, darling, a wife doesn't have to tell her husband. That's what I learned from being married to you—that sometimes it's better if people don't know each other too well. There's so much less than can use against each other, you see."

She looked so pleased with this pronouncement that Laurence wanted to protest. Then he remembered how Ruby used to accuse him of humiliating her in various, mostly imaginary ways. Whenever he tried to talk seriously to her, to work out the problems in their marriage, she wound up making him feel like a brute. It was the last time he'd ever tried talking sense to a woman.

"I decided I wanted to leave all that behind me,"

Ruby went on. "I had a terrible childhood, as you know, and my twenties were a disaster. I've been seeing a psychotherapist for the last several years and I've finally come to understand how I always let men use me and abuse me, ever since I was a kid. Women do it to get love, you know, but it never works—it just attracts guys like you."

He started to say something, but she warned him off with a particularly bright and confident smile. "When I realized how exploited I'd always been, I decided to remake my life. It can be done, you know. People really can change, Larry. All they have to do is make up their mind, and then stick to it."

"It sounds so easy," Laurence said. "Don't you ever get nostalgic for the old days, Ruby? Don't you ever feel like a phony, living in a place like this?"

She flared up at once. "Are you calling me a phony? You, of all people?"

Laurence saw he would have to be careful if he wanted to get what he had come for. "No, no, of course not. It's just that, you and me, we weren't like most people. We got out of the barnyard where all the cattle were kept and had ourselves a little romp in the meadow. Once you've done that, don't you find it hard to go back in your pen?"

"So now I'm a cow," Ruby said, and looked off across the room, as if trying to take all this with good humor. He remembered that look, having seen it often enough in the old days.

"Bad choice of terms," he said. "What I'm trying to say is that most other people live like cattle, whereas you and I, we were free spirits. At least we tried to be."

"Free," she said, "but enslaved to a bottle. Don't

forget that. The booze, and the drugs, and the wild parties . . . and the *sex—!*"

"Yeah, it was fun while it lasted," Laurence said with a smile. "But I was thinking of the music we made together, too. I had a damn fine band in those days, Ruby, and you were a big part of it."

"You said I couldn't sing on key."

"You couldn't, but you knew how to sell a song. And we knew how to cover for you. People loved you, that was the main thing. You had a lot of charm, a lot of sex appeal. You still do, obviously. I'm not knocking you, babe. I'm glad to see you doing so well, and I don't blame you one bit—"

"Blame me?" she asked, glaring at him. "Blame me, for saving my own life?"

"If that's what you want to call it," Laurence said. "At the time, it felt more like you were destroying mine. Sometimes it still does. There hasn't been a day in the past fifteen years when I haven't thought of you—when I haven't missed you or hoped for a chance to win you back."

The moment he spoke these words, he realized they were true and therefore embarrassing, almost shameful, but his confession certainly had the desired effect on Ruby. She softened at once, gave him one of her sweetest smiles, and came over to sit beside him on the sofa.

"I'm sorry, honey, really I am. And we shouldn't fight, it's been so long since we've seen each other. I missed you, too—a lot, at first, then less and less as the years went by. But I've always remembered you—" and here she put her small, scarlet-nailed, ring-sparkling hand over his— "with affection."

"Did you keep," Laurence asked, "any of our things?"

He had nearly said his things but realized in time she might take offense at that. In order to get his banjo back, he'd have to pretend she had a right to take it in the first place.

"Oh, I may have a few mementos in a trunk in the attic," she said. "But I couldn't keep much, Larry—nothing I didn't want Chester to see."

Lucky's heart sank. "Then, I suppose that banjo's gone?"

"Banjo? What banjo?"

"You know, the one I bought back in '39, with the silver trim and pearl handle—the one I was always so fond of."

"Oh, *that* banjo," she said, and left the sofa.

"I was hoping you might still have it," Laurence said. "You see, I need to raise a bit of money this week. The guy I work for, he's gonna lose his shop if he can't pay his mortgage and taxes, and that banjo ought to bring in a few bucks."

He watched as she went to a cabinet and extracted a package of cigarettes. She lit one, took several puffs, and then turned to him. "I'm sorry, Larry, really I am. But I sold that banjo a long time ago."

"Oh," Laurence said, and took out a cigarette of his own.

"I had to," she said, "in order to pay for the operation."

"The operation? You mean, on your teeth?"

She smirked. "You think a crummy banjo could pay for a new set of teeth? No, dear, Chester paid for that, bless his heart, and for just about everything else you can see from where you sit. The operation you paid for was the one you were obligated to pay for, though I never wanted to tell you about it, and I knew you had nothing else, anyway, so I just took whatever you left behind. I'm sorry, but I was desperate."

Laurence tapped his cigarette on the crystal of his watch. "The operation I was 'obligated' to pay for?"

She walked over to the window and spoke with her back to him, looking out at her shrub-sheltered, oak-shaded lawn. "Six weeks after you went in the san, I found out I was pregnant. It was your kid, no doubt about that—I hadn't been with another man since that time we . . . well, you remember what we did. Anyway, it was yours, and you were in the bug-bin for God knows how long, so what was I going to do? I couldn't raise a kid on my own—I was working forty hours a week to pay off our debts."

"Jesus," Lucky said softly. "Jesus Christ."

She whirled around. "You don't have to sound so *stricken* by the idea. I knew you never wanted kids, and in your condition, what the hell did you care?"

"How do you know I didn't want kids?" Laurence asked her. "Did we ever talk about it? Did you give me a chance—?"

"A chance to do what? To come home from the san and get a steady job? To give up your drinking and your whoring around? To live like a normal man, like those *cattle* you despise so much?"

"I never whored around when we were married," Laurence said, putting a match to his cigarette, "except with you."

"What does *that* mean?" Her voice rose to a pitch he remembered all too well from their ancient quarrels. For a gal who couldn't sing on key, Ruby had a way of hitting a note that could make your hair stand on end.

"Nothing," he said, "it means nothing." But it suddenly struck him that his whole life might have been different if he'd become a father. Like his brother Leo, who was so damn proud of that fine, strapping son of his—as any man would be, if he had a son like that—if he had people to live for, people who loved him, who counted on him. If Laurence had been offered *that* chance—the chance to become a father—it might have changed his entire life.

And now it came home to him that Ruby had stolen not only his beautiful, pearl-handled banjo, and not only his unborn child, but also the chance to reform his life when it still could have meant something. For a moment he was too bitter to speak and he sat there on the sofa, dragging fiercely on his cigarette, wanting to pull the smoke into the last few air sacks of his only good lung until it, too, gave up the ghost.

Ruby had turned back to the window. He could see her sculptured face in profile, the pert nose and prominent cheekbones, the pouty lower lip and slightly receding chin. He was surprised at the force of his anger, at the old feeling of rage and betrayal. *It was always like this,* he thought. Just when he would start to love her again, to trust her, she would find some new way to destroy him. She might have been the only person in the world he had ever wanted to kill.

He imagined getting up from his chair, walking across the room and grabbing a handful of that curly yellow hair. He imagined striking hard at that painted, that prefabricated face, imagined breaking that sheet of glass in which she had encased herself. But the moment he pictured himself doing that he also saw her startled, frightened eyes, and he realized that what had always made those eyes so beautiful, so appealing, was the fear they held. Fear of him, of all the men she had betrayed and reduced to his murderous state.

And then he realized that it wasn't really Ruby who had betrayed him. Because if he had been a better man, a man more like his brother, he would never have dumped good old Lou to take up with a tramp like Ruby. And he wouldn't have left his wife alone and penniless to deal with an unwanted pregnancy. *It's the same old story,* he thought sadly. The chickens always came to roost. You got what you deserved in this life, and he had never deserved the honor, the dignity, of fatherhood.

Ruby went to the cabinet which had produced her pack of cigarettes and took out a bottle of scotch. "I think I'll have that little snort after all," she said, pouring some into a glass. "Join me?"

He had never wanted a drink more in his entire life, but he shook his head. She took it down in a swallow, from which he could conclude that she still did a fair share of drinking, then poured another.

"I'm sorry, Lucky," she said in a husky voice. "It must be a shock. You see, I got over it a long time ago. I paid the price for all our mistakes, but maybe the bill is just catching up with you."

Laurence tried to shrug it off. "Oh well—I never was much good at paying my bills. What difference does it make now?"

She looked at him steadily over her glass. "It might have made a difference to us once, if we'd been better people. That was *my* last chance to have a kid, too."

He waited for her to go on, certain she would.

She looked away. "There were—complications. They wound up taking out the whole business. Chester and I wanted to adopt a kid, but I was afraid the agency would check into my background and then—well, it ain't always easy covering your tracks."

He didn't know whether to believe her or not. Maybe she just wanted him to think that she shared his loss, that its pain weighed as heavily on her as it did on him. But even for that he was grateful. You had to give people credit for small favors. He got to his feet. "I think I better be going, Ruby."

"So soon? You just got here."

"Any longer, and we might start clobbering each other with those gold candlesticks. Or—" he considered his words carefully before he spoke them— "I might try making love to you."

She gave him her old shrewd smile. "Keep looking at me with those hang-dog eyes of yours, and I might let you."

For a moment it was there between them once again —that old black magic. That almost supernatural force. For two people who had spent a good part of their lives together making one another miserable, they certainly felt a strong mutual attraction, and even now, with him a shrunken, misshapen, used-up husk of a man, and her a gorgeously retooled and restyled fabrication of a woman, they felt the pull. For Laurence it was like looking down into a deep pool of very cold, very clear water from some spring high in the mountains, and at the bottom of that pool, looking up at him through the frigid medium, he saw her face. If he dove in after her, could he fight his way to the bottom, bring her up in his arms? For a moment he was tempted, but then she looked away from his questioning gaze.

"Just kidding, of course," she said, putting her drink

on the table. "We're too old for that stuff."

"Yes, we're too old," Laurence said. "And too wise. Thanks for the coffee, Ruby. Thanks for talking to me."

"My pleasure," she said, and followed him to the door.

As he opened the door he heard something snap behind him and turned to see her hand go into her purse. For a moment he thought she might bring out a gun and shoot him, but her hand emerged with a wad of bills. "If this would help you out—"

He shook his head. "I can't take money from you, Ruby. Besides, I'll be all right. You know old Lucky—he can always raise a few bucks when he needs to."

She put the purse down and came to him at the door, her face raised for a kiss.

"Take care of yourself, Lucky. It was good seeing you again."

"It was hell seeing you," he said, "pure hell. But I wouldn't have missed it for the world."

On his way back to the bus stop, Laurence finished writing his song:

> *Honey, we know it's all been said,*
> *And everything we cared about is dead*
> *The harm we did can't be undone,*
> *And the life we got, it ain't much fun.*
> *But before I go, I ask one thing—*
> *Honey, give me one last fling.*

11.

Blue Moon

GINGER had made pot roast for supper. Laurence moved the pieces of meat, potato and carrot around on his plate, trying to appear busy with his knife and fork. The gravy began to congeal on his mashed potatoes.

"What's the matter, you don't like pot roast?" she asked him.

"It's great," Laurence said, and put a large piece of meat into his mouth. He chewed for awhile, then delicately removed the gristle and put it on the edge of his plate. "Just a little chewy in places, that's all."

"That damn butcher, he promised me a good piece of meat. You got problems with your teeth?"

"My teeth? No, they're pretty good, considering I never saw a dentist after sixteen or so, except in the san." He remembered Ruby's teeth, that string of white pearls. *You think a crummy banjo could pay for this set of teeth?*

"I've got good teeth," Ginger said, helping herself to more of the vegetables. "Always took care of them. Figured it was one thing I could do for myself."

"Smart," Laurence said, and swallowed some mashed food. It went down hard, like a lump of clay. *Claymore,* he thought. *Chester Claymore.* A little red wine would wash this grub down, make it all taste a lot better. Maybe someday, if he felt sure of himself, he could risk a glass of wine with his dinner.

"So what time is your gig?" Ginger asked.

"Seven o'clock," Laurence said. "Eddie's picking me up at six thirty."

They ate in silence for a while, the low sun slanting in through the kitchen window. Laurence observed the dust motes dancing in the rays, smelled the onion skins rotting in the sink. Three days in Ginger's apartment and already it was starting to get on his nerves, especially the way she left her clothes all over the place. Nylons hanging in the bathroom, a bra and undies on the bedroom chair, a forgotten sweater on the living room couch. He'd always lived in small rooms, easy to keep clean. What more did a man need?

"So how did things go at the shop today?" she asked.

"Just fine," Laurence said. "We got a bunch of new orders. Abe's as happy as a kid with a bunch of presents under his Christmas tree."

"That's nice," Ginger said. "If you can help that old guy, it will be one of the best things you ever did."

"Oh, I don't know. I've done some pretty good things in my time. I wish I had some records of that group I had back in the thirties—the Swingin' Seven. Better than the Gary Ames stuff, I think."

"I meant, the best thing you ever did for somebody else," she said, and then, when he gave her a puzzled look: "You know what I mean. A musician, a good one like you, he usually plays just for himself, doesn't he?"

He put down his knife and fork. "Tell you the truth, I don't know what the hell he plays for. He's just got this music inside him and it has to come out, somehow. Like fish gotta swim and birds gotta fly—that's all there is to it. I never believed in keeping things bottled up inside me."

He reached for his cigarettes and Ginger got up to pour the coffee. "I guess there was a lot of musical talent in your family," she said, and he could tell she was trying to set him up for something. Even so, he didn't mind talking about it.

"Well, my mother had a good voice, used to sing solo for weddings and funerals at the little Swiss church in our hometown. She could play the piano and organ, too—gave me my first lessons. When silent movies first came in, we used to play for the Saturday night flicks in New Glarus. Ma played the piano, Leo played the drums, and I played the banjo. Winter of 1913, that must've been—almost forty-three years ago."

"And your brother, was he as good as you?"

"Leo?—one of the best. He could get music out of a clarinet you wouldn't believe. A damn shame he gave it up, but then, that's often what happens when a guy falls in love. Everything else takes a back seat."

Ginger had been picking up the dishes, but now she sat down and looked at him. "Did you ever feel that way about anybody—like they were most important thing in the whole world?"

"Yeah, once," Laurence said, "but I got over it." He took a sip of his coffee and waited for what he knew what was coming next.

"I wish you hadn't taken this job at the Blue Swan, Lucky. Couldn't you raise the money Abe needs some other way?"

"I tried all the other ways—that's how I got this shiner. This town is full of deadbeats. Deadbeats and crooks. Frank Holiday is giving me an advance Friday night, so Abe will have his three fifty by Saturday."

Ginger peered intently into her coffee cup. Then she said, "I could lend you the money. I hate to see you borrowing money from someone like Frank Holiday."

Laurence had been expecting that. Very carefully, he said, "It's an advance, not a loan—seven nights and I'll be square. I appreciate the offer, sugar, but I couldn't take money from you."

"Why not? What's wrong with my money?"

"Nothing, I just don't think it would be a good idea, that's all. I borrow money from you and it will mess up our whole romance. I'll be like an investment you made or something—"

"People can invest other things besides money," Ginger said, going to the sink. "Maybe I already have."

"Well, then you'd better un-invest it," Laurence said, as she ran water in the dishpan. "I'm not a good risk, Ginger. Not for you or anybody. Jesus, you think I want you on my conscience, too?"

She turned around, a look in her eyes Laurence had seen before. It was never a good sign, that look. "You sound like you're planning to run off."

"Not if you don't push me," he said. "Just let me handle this, okay? I can raise that three fifty my own way."

"Sure, but what is it going to cost you? Being around booze and drinkers every night, hanging out with guys like Eddie King and Frank Holiday—how long do you think your health is going to last this time?"

"About as long as I want to. The trouble with women is, they always think they know what's best for a man. They don't know beans about that, sugar—they never have and they never will."

"For Christ's sake, my name is *Ginger*."

"I know your fucking name." He ground out his cigarette and went into the bedroom, where he took off his shirt and sniffed the armpits. It was still all right. Good thing, because all his other shirts were wrinkled from the suitcase and this wasn't a good time to ask Ginger to iron them. He went into the bathroom and used some of her deodorant. Then he shaved the silver stubble he'd grown since morning, combed his hair and patted a little aftershave on his cheeks. It wasn't likely his black eye would show on the bandstand, but he dabbed a little talc around it to lighten the skin.

When he returned to the kitchen Ginger was still doing the dishes. Last night he had helped her, but it was already twenty-five after. "Gotta be on my way," he said. "I won't be late—probably eleven or so."

"I'll be sound asleep by then," she said. "Try not to wake me up."

He could tell she was still sore. He went to the sink and put a hand gently on her rump. She tightened her buns but otherwise didn't protest. "Look, I'm sorry," he said, stroking gently. "Sorry I didn't have much appetite, and sorry I made you feel bad. I still think we've got a good thing going here, babe, if we just play our cards right."

"I'm not a gambler, Lucky. I like a sure thing."

"Tell you the truth, I'm not a gambler either. If I can't win, I don't play. I think I can win with you, baby."

"Sure, you've won so much over all these years," she

said, and he could see a tear working its way down her
cheek.

He leaned over, kissed away the tear, and went to
the door. He was half-way down the stairs when he
heard her voice behind him: "Good luck tonight. And
take care, you hear?"

He turned at the door. "Sure, sugar. I always take
care."

~§~

Eddie's Cadillac was muttering at the curb. "Get
your ass in gear, Lantz. Frank hates it when the show
goes on late."

Lucky settled down beside Eddie and the big car
took off with a squeal of rubber. "I thought you were his
partner, not his chore boy," he said.

"Shit," Eddie said, "I ain't nobody's chore boy. It
just so happens that Frank's got most of the money in
this operation, so he gets to call the shots. But he needs
me because I know the music business, and I know this
town."

"So he takes your advice, does he?"

"He hired you, didn't he?"

"I think he may have made his own decision on that
one," Lucky said. No point letting the big jerk take too
much credit—next thing, he'd want a ten percent commission.

They drove down Park Street into the glare of the
setting sun. At the Beltline, Eddie roared through the
underpass and up the ramp, then handed Lucky a bag of
cannabis and a roll of cigarette papers. "Roll me a joint,
would you, pal?"

"Sure you want my spit on your reefer?" Lucky asked him. "I might be carrying a few germs, you know."

"Shit, that's right—fuck it," Eddie said. "I can have one when we get there. You could toke up yourself, though—a guy who don't drink booze has gotta have some fun, for Chrissakes."

That's right, Lucky thought, *he does*. Old Doc Steinmetz had never said anything about marijuana. The hipsters in the music trade always said pot wasn't habit-forming, and Lucky himself had always been able to take it or leave it. On the other hand, he knew well enough that one vice often led to another. Get high on grass and he might want to try something else, something more to his taste.

He started rolling the joint, just to see if he remembered how, and to have something to do with his hands. It came out pretty well—a little thin in the middle, but smokable. He reached over and pushed in Eddie's dashboard lighter.

"So, you're not a plaster Jesus, after all," Eddie said with a chuckle.

"I never claimed to be no plaster Jesus," Lucky said. "I'm just a guy trying to get through life with a whole lot of past dragging along behind me. You remember Ruby, Eddie?"

"Your old Missus? Yeah, I remember her. A wildcat, wasn't she?"

The lighter popped out and Lucky lit his joint. "Wild enough. I saw her today—kind of knocked the slats out from under me, you know?"

"Good," Eddie said. "Your piano ought to be nice and bluesy tonight. Nothin' like a mean-assed dame to bring out the best in a guy."

"That's what we think, isn't it?" Lucky took a tentative drag on his joint. "Is that why we always go for the ones that are bad for us? Why can't a man ever love the good ones, for Chrissake?"

"Because they're fucking boring, that's why," Eddie said.

Lucky had never thought Eddie was much of a philosopher, but he recognized the wisdom of his reply. Goodness was boring, that was the whole damn trouble. The Garden of Eden must have been one big drag till Satan showed up, and the joint had been jumping ever since. He took several quick drags on the reefer, sucked in the smoke and held it there. Almost at once he felt that tingle in his spinal chord that wasn't alcohol or nicotine but something all its own. He coughed out the smoke and tossed the reefer out the window.

"Hey man," Eddie said, "that's good grass! That cost a pretty penny."

"One hit will do me for now," Lucky said. "I ain't used to the stuff"

"Well, roll yourself another. You'll probably want it during the break. It's going to be a long night, even if you get to knock off early."

Yes, Lucky thought, *no doubt it would.* Jamming with Leo or sitting in for a set at the Buccaneer was one thing but carrying an inexperienced singer for three hours was going to be tough. It was hard to believe he was letting himself in for this again. When was he ever going to learn? Still, he felt better for having taken a hit off the joint. It had been so long since he'd looked at the world through rose-colored glasses, he'd forgotten how it could pick up your mood.

Eddie had turned off the Beltline onto U.S. 51. The

sun was settling into a pinky-orange haze over the marshes south of town and the smell of the open fields came in the window on a cool breeze. A dim and ghostly moon was rising to the east. Lucky knew that if he stared at that moon long enough he would begin to believe he was on it. That was what grass did for you. Personally, he never felt he played any better when he was high, but sometimes being on the moon had its advantages, especially on a long night. He rolled the second joint and put it in his pocket.

They were still a mile or so from the Blue Swan when Lucky noticed the blade of light cutting through the violet sky—Eddie had gotten one of those spotlights they used to advertise premiers and grand openings. It seemed to have done its job, since the parking lot outside the club was already nearly full. The big neon sign on the roof was shedding blue light on the glossy car-tops, and to Lucky it looked as if you could peel off that blue sheen and eat it. "Looks like your grand opening's going to be a success," he said to Eddie as they left the car.

"Yeah, Frank'll be pleased," Eddie said. "You play good tonight, Tiger, and old Eddie might just give you a little bonus."

A new signboard had been set up at the door. *Appearing Tonight: the Fabulous Savannah Jones.* There was a black-and-white glossy of Savannah in her low-cut gown, and below that Lucky saw to his surprise an old publicity photo of himself, taken back in the days when he looked more like Valentino than Bela Lugosi.

Special Added Attraction:
Lucky Lantz, Madison's Own "Sheik of Swing."

"Hey, you remembered my old title," Lucky said.

Eddie slapped him on the back, a little too hard. "A'course I did! So do a lot of people. Why you want to bust your dumb ass in a shoe repair shop, when you could be a fucking celebrity, is beyond me."

The bar was jumping and most of the tables in the dining room were occupied. Waitresses in black uniforms moved briskly, clearing away plates, delivering coffee or drinks. A spotlight encased the grand piano on its little stage before red velvet curtains. Frank Holiday, looking like a river-boat gambler in a white dinner jacket with a red carnation in his buttonhole, came forward to meet them.

"Just in time, Lantz. We've got a full house, so let's get cracking."

"Terrific," Lucky said. "Where's the star?"

"Oh, she's still powdering her nose. Why don't you go ahead and do a few numbers, warm up the audience?"

"I didn't know I was going to have to solo," Lucky said. "I haven't got that much material, Frank. It's been awhile."

"That's all right, just start the ball rolling. Savannah will be out in a few minutes."

He put a fatherly hand on Lucky's shoulder and guided him toward the bandstand. Lucky saw the faces at the surrounding tables look up from their dinners. Some of the faces were vaguely familiar, though he recognized no one by name. That didn't really matter, because he understood the kind of audience it was: middle-aged, middle-class, moderately well-heeled—a nice group. Lucky knew the kind of music they liked, knew what they'd come to hear.

He went up to the grand piano and found a small microphone mounted just above the keyboard. Apparently he was expected to provide a little patter between numbers. Well, he could do that. He'd been a bandleader, off and on, for thirty years. He sat down on the bench and the noise level in the restaurant immediately dropped. Lucky could hear dishes rattling in the kitchen, a few female voices still chattering away, but otherwise the floor was his. He leaned over the microphone and spoke softly, letting the sound system amplify his crooner's baritone:

"Good evening, ladies and gentlemen, and welcome to the Blue Swan. We're real pleased to have you with us for our grand opening and we hope you enjoy the show. My name's Lucky Lantz—I guess a few of you old-timers might remember me. I used to play a lot of clubs 'round these parts, but it's been a while and I need a chance to warm up my pinkies, so I hope you won't mind if I try out a few tunes until our singer arrives."

There was an encouraging patter of applause. Lucky positioned his hands above the keyboard and then, without having thought about his opening number, launched into "Blue Moon", always good for a solo, with some nice chords to savor. He played three choruses and the blue notes shimmered in the smoky air. In his mind he saw a blue swan gliding down a river of smoke and he let the swan just swim along, its long elegant neck held erect, its plump body parting the smoke. A big moon was rising on the horizon. Owls were hooting in the trees. Somewhere on the shore couples were making love. It was going to be, he could see, an enchanted evening.

The audience applauded and Lucky leaned over the microphone. "Thank you, ladies and gentlemen, thank you. Not too bad for an old-timer. A guy has to start slow at my age, as I'm sure some of you understand. I thought maybe I'd tease your memory a little bit tonight, see if I can bring back any sweet recollections. Here's a tune my brother and I used to play back in the twenties. I guess a few of you might be old enough to remember this . . . it's called 'Deep Purple'."

A few people clapped to show they approved his choice, and Lucky had the song rolling before the applause subsided. He played two choruses and, getting a little bored, modulated into "Me and My Shadow." Ah yes, the golden oldies. A stroll down memory lane. I could play this stuff all night, folks. It flows out of me like blood from a vein. Suddenly Lucky saw blood on the keyboard and knew that reefer was still messing up his brain. Easy pal, we've got work to do here.

He finished off with two choruses of "All By Myself," and as the audience clapped he spotted Savannah making her way toward the bandstand. He could tell by the way she swayed on her high heels that she'd had a few too many. Shit, just like Ruby—couldn't go on if she wasn't half-smashed. Well, she wasn't the first lush he'd ever accompanied, that was for damn sure. He'd get her through the evening.

Savannah's strapless yellow evening gown showed off her full breasts and smooth tan shoulders, her long, slender arms. The sheath clung to her hips and molded itself to her tummy and backside in ways the men in the audience would surely enjoy. Even if she couldn't hold the beat all night, a lot of guys wouldn't care. Lucky took a deep breath and spoke into the mike:

"And now, ladies and gentlemen, the treat you've all been waiting for—a wonderful little lady I know you're going to like. This is her debut in a Madison-area club, and I hope you'll make her feel real welcome. Let's hear a nice round of applause for *Miss Savannah Jones!"*

The burst of applause gave Savannah the courage to mount the bandstand and approach the mike. She smiled nervously at Lucky and said, "'The Man I Love'—like we did it yesterday?"

"Gotcha," Lucky said, and gave her an intro.

She started poorly, slightly offkey and much too soft and breathless, but gradually, as Lucky coaxed her along, giving her plenty of freedom with the tempo, she began to strengthen. He found that if he put in a few runs it helped her timing, gave her a chance to think about the lyrics and how to bring out their meaning, phrase by phrase. By the last chorus she was putting her heart into it and the audience, Lucky could see, was responding. There was a nice round of sustained applause and Savannah beamed and bowed, showing off her cleavage and extending the applause by another full minute.

Lucky lit a cigarette and wished he had something to sip, because his throat was dry. He signaled one of the waitresses, who came up to the bandstand and gave him her ear. "Sweetie, could you bring me a 7 UP or something?"

"Sure—nothing in it?"

"Well . . . no. Just something wet and sweet, okay?"

The applause had died down and Lucky returned to the microphone. "Well now, folks, wasn't that something special? I promised you'd like this little lady. What'll it be next, sweetheart?"

Savannah asked for "Sentimental Journey" and snapped her fingers to give Lucky the beat. Lucky had a

nice little choo-choo train base he used with that number, and every once in a while he blew the whistle way
up high in the treble. It was corny, but what the hell, this
was good-time music and Savannah was a good-time
gal, now that she was rolling, and the audience liked the
way she swung her hips to Lucky's beat. In fact, Lucky
didn't dislike it much himself Savannah looked better to
him tonight than she had at their audition: a little wild, a
little reckless—just like old Ruby, a gutter-snipe in an
evening gown.

The waitress brought his drink and Lucky waited till
the end of the number to quench his thirst. With his first
sip he knew he'd been had—the goddamn bartender had
added a double shot of whiskey to his 7 UP, probably at
Eddie King's request. A shiver of pleasurable shame
went down Lucky's spine. Ah, now *that* was what he'd
been missing these past three years! That and a lot more
like it.

"'These Foolish Things'," Savannah said, "key of B
flat."

Lucky played, Savannah sang: *A cigarette with lipstick traces . . . an airline ticket to romantic places . . .*
And all through the number that glass of whiskey-spiked
7 Up sat there waiting for him, teasing him, tormenting
him, telling him that life wasn't much good without a
little booze to brighten it up, and what the hell, this was
his world, his milieu—this was the kind of work he was
born for, and what the hell did he want with a fucking
cobbler's bench and a bunch of goddamn smelly shoes?

During the applause Lucky called the young waitress over and gave her the drink. "Take this back, and
tell the bartender I asked for a *soft* drink, okay?"

Savannah asked for "Someone to Watch Over Me,"

and Lucky said, "Just what I need," and rolled his eyes, ala Groucho Marx, which got a few laughs from the audience. Savannah played along and kept her dark eyes on him as she sang, gave him those smiles a man couldn't miss, and they had a little act going now, something the audience was quick to catch onto. It was all good fun, showmanship, but Lucky promised himself that tomorrow evening he'd make damn sure Ginger was in the audience.

At eight fifteen they took a break. Savannah sat down beside him and said, "It's going pretty well, don't you think?" Her eyes were radiant with that glow of giddy pleasure only performers ever know. *And then only young performers,* Lucky thought—*the ones on the way up.*

"It's going great," he said. "You've got them eating out of your hand, kid."

"Your piano helps a lot. I was pretty nervous at first."

"Yeah, and a bit sloshed, too. Go easy on the sauce and you'll be all right. I've got something in my pocket that's just as good."

"You got some grass? Enough to share?"

"I've been straight for so long, it doesn't take much to give me a buzz. Let's get some fresh air."

They left by the rear exit and walked down to the river. There, with the moon above the willows and crickets chirping along the grassy bank, Lucky lit the joint and they passed it back and forth. It had been a long time since he'd smoked grass with a woman and he liked the sense of intimacy it created. Always a good way to get a little love-stuff going in the old days, if you could find a gal who wasn't afraid to try it.

"So," Savannah said, "you're not so standoffish as you were the other day. Not afraid of Frank anymore?"

"I'm scared to death of Frank," Lucky said, "but you and I need to work on our rapport, if we're going to be a team."

"I thought you only agreed to do seven nights."

"That's all I'm signed up for now, but we'll see how it goes. If my health can stand it, and you and I hit it off, I could be talked into a few more dates."

"Oh, I think we'll hit it off just fine," Savannah said. She inhaled deeply, then let the fragrant smoke slip out between her pursed lips. "You're pretty cute, for an old guy."

"Thanks," Lucky said. Obviously she hadn't noticed yet the odd slope of his shoulders or the hollow place on his left side. They didn't do that operation anymore—too risky, and it left too many hunchbacks. It was a radical procedure even back in the forties, used only on desperate cases. What had Lucky Lantz ever been but a desperate case?

"I like older men," Savannah was saying. "They've got a certain class, you know? And they act like gentlemen, most of the time."

"Most of the time," Lucky said. "It's when they stop acting like gentlemen that things get interesting."

"Do they . . . stop?"

He saw her face in the moonlight, a pale oval framed by her lush dark hair. He leaned forward and brushed her lips with his. "Easy, Tiger," she said. "Frank Holiday owns these lips."

"Oh yeah? I thought you said you'd decide who you belong to."

"That's right, I will," she said, moving a little away

from him, "and I'm still making up my mind about you. Time to go back in?"

At the back door, Lucky turned and looked at the row of cabins along the river. Apparently Frank hadn't thought to rent them out, as they did in the old days, because they were all dark. But Lucky marked the one he and Ruby had used, those many years ago.

~§~

By ten thirty he was exhausted, flying by instinct, his fingers so numb he could barely feel the keyboard, his eyes so dry and eyelids so heavy he could barely keep them open. Three hours on the piano bench had given him one hell of a backache, and the afterglow of the joint had been replaced by a nasty headache, nearly as bad as some of his old hangovers. He made his way to the bar and asked the bartender for a glass of water and a couple of aspirins.

"Sorry for the booze-trick, Lucky," the bartender said. "I know you're on the wagon, but Eddie made me do it."

"That figures," Lucky said. "The only wagon Eddie King ever heard of is the paddy wagon. Where is the big lug? I want my ride home."

"He's in the back, I think—playin' poker with Frank and some of his pals."

"Would you send someone back there? I gotta go to work tomorrow morning, for Chrissake."

Savannah slid onto the barstool next to his. "I'll give you a ride home, Tiger. I've got the keys to Frank's car in my purse, and I could use a little fresh air."

"Fine," Lucky said, and downed his aspirins with a

long swallow of water. "This place is starting to give me the creeps."

She lit a cigarette. "So why'd you take this gig? You don't like the joint and it keeps you up past your bedtime."

"It's for my apprenticeship—so the old man I work for can stay in business long enough to sign my papers. Would you believe it? I can make fifty a night playing piano, and here I am taking a job where I'll be lucky to make fifty a week."

"I don't see much sense in that," Savannah said.

"Sometimes I don't either, but that's what they want me to do—that's what's supposed to be good for me."

"Who says?"

"Oh, my brother. And the doctors. And the woman I live with. Everybody. They all know what's best for Lucky Lantz. Sometimes it gets to be a pain in the ass."

"Come on," Savannah said with a smile, "let's get out of here before Frank finds out I'm borrowing his precious car."

~§~

Frank's car was a black Mercury convertible, a year or two newer than Eddie's Caddy and in much better shape. Savannah drove fast, the wind in her hair, and Laurence huddled inside his light-weight sports coat. He was full of that dead, empty feeling you always got after a night on the bandstand, that sense of having used up something precious inside of you by sharing it with people who couldn't appreciate what you'd given them, who never really understood why you played or what it all meant. Laurence remembered the feeling and remembered now why he had never liked to go home to bed after a gig. You didn't want to take that feeling to bed with you, for fear it might still be there in the morning, so you had a little something to eat, then a few more drinks, maybe a card game or another jam session —anything to round out the evening, to fill up the emptiness.

"So, I thought we sounded pretty good tonight," Savannah said.

"We sounded terrific," Laurence said.

"I think Frank was pleased."

"Wonderful."

"You don't like him much, do you?"

"I hate the bastard. Guys like him are what's wrong with the music business. To them, it's just another racket, another way to sell liquor, to set up those little sidelines in the back room. They don't respect musicians —they'd buy us and sell us like cattle, if they could. And once they get sick of us, they hang us out to dry. Behind every club like the Blue Swan there's a graveyard full of dead musicians."

"You sound like you've had the course," Savannah said.

"I have. I've had it several times. And yet, like a fool, I keep going back to it. Because how else can you play your music, if you don't work for guys like Holiday?"

And it occurred to him that if he hadn't taken this gig he might never have remembered how much it once meant to play his kind of music, and how much it could mean still, if he let it. Of all the problems poor dumb Ginger had been worried about, she hadn't known enough about musicians to add that one to her list.

"I hate the little shit myself," Savannah said abruptly. "He beats up on me, you know."

"Oh yeah? The bruises don't show."

"That's because he knows where to leave them. Why do you think I wear such skimpy outfits? So there'll be fewer places for him to hurt."

"I thought maybe you liked guys looking at you," Laurence said. "Beautiful women usually do."

She turned to him. "Do you think I'm beautiful—really?"

"Sure, a good singer, too, but keep your eyes on the road. You wouldn't look like much in a ditch."

She swerved back into her lane and they drove in silence for awhile, beneath a big blue moon and a field of solemn stars. Entering the outskirts of the city, Savannah said, "You've played the clubs in Chicago, haven't you, Lucky?"

"Several years ago," Laurence said. Sometimes it seemed as if he had simply imagined that part of his life, or dreamed it during one of his long stays in the san.

"You think I'm good enough for the big city?" she asked. "Could I make it in Chicago?"

He thought it over. "With a good accompanist, or a good group backing you up, you could. You'd need to work with them quite a lot—polish your material, broaden your repertoire. It's take a lot to hold a big-city audience."

"My repertoire is pretty broad already. We just scratched the surface tonight, pal."

"Well, then I'll look forward to going a little deeper the next time. Maybe I'll see how far I can push you."

"I'd like that," she said. "I'd like that a lot." And it was clear she was talking about more than music. A cheap little tramp, but she knew how to sell a song, and how to rile a guy's blood. His blood hadn't been this riled in a long time.

She exited the Beltline and he directed her to Ginger's flat. He was glad to see, as they pulled up at the curb, that Ginger's windows were dark. "So," she said as she killed the engine and turned to him, "I guess we'll take up where we left off tomorrow evening, huh? Building our 'rapport'?"

"I guess so," Laurence said. "Unless you want to get together some afternoon for a little rehearsal. I don't mean at the club."

She gave him a long look. "You've got a woman waiting for you in there, pal."

"And you've got a man waiting for back at the Blue Swan. Any reason why, some afternoon, we can't let them both wait?"

She smiled. "I guess not—but where would we find a place with a piano?"

"I'll bring my guitar," he said. "Tell me, do those lips still have Frank Holiday's name on them?"

She leaned forward, practically spilling her big tits in his lap. "You tell me, Tiger—try 'em and see."

He felt her kiss like a mousetrap closing on his lips. Their teeth grated together; her tongue probed like a quick flicker of electricity—the blue-white spark of a short circuit. Breathless, Lucky couldn't hold the kiss as long as he would have liked, but it was long enough to raise the old goblin from its lair—and to tell him something he didn't want to know.

"Well," she said, sitting back and smiling like a woman who had just proved her point, "what do you think?"

"I think Frank's days are numbered," Lucky said,

"but you'll have to find a younger stud than me, baby. I couldn't take you to Chicago—not at my age. You'd burn me to a crisp in a matter of days."

She glared at him. "Too bad for you, old-timer. You had your chance."

"Yes, I reckon I did," Laurence said sadly, and climbed out of the car. He watched as she pulled away from the curb, made a U turn and headed back up the street.

Weary, aching, an empty man with an empty heart, Lucky climbed the stairs to Ginger's flat, let himself in, groped his way through the dark rooms to the bathroom, where he closed the door and turned on the light. The face he saw in the bathroom mirror looked to be about a hundred, and he saw that Savannah's teeth had opened the cut at the corner of his mouth. There was a thread of blood trickling down his chin, as if he'd been feasting on someone's throat.

God help me, Laurence thought, and wished for once there really was a God, any god, he could turn to for support. But he had lived his life for so long now without a God, he didn't know where to begin looking for one. It was all darkness, muddle, confusion. You did what you could to make sense of your life, and then they found some way to screw up your head once again.

He undressed to his underwear, then turned off the light and entered the dark bedroom, where the glow of moonlight from the window showed him Ginger's sleeping shape beneath the covers. He slid in beside her and tried to feel the healing presence of her warmth, but it was a long time before he stopped shivering and an even longer time before he could stop thinking about the blue-white fire of Savannah's kiss.

12.

Inside Straight

SO HERE'S HOW IT GOES. Laurence gets his three-fifty advance from Frank Holiday and turns it over to honest Abe Slovinsky, who pays his mortgage and taxes and signs Lucky's papers. Lucky plays five more nights at the Blue Swan, paying off Holiday, and then calls it quits. Eddie and Savannah try to persuade him to stay on— especially Savannah—but Laurence knows what's good for him. And what's bad for him. He's out of the music business for good.

Meanwhile, the state has started supplementing his apprentice pay and he's able to move out of Ginger's apartment and into a little place of his own—nothing fancy, but comfortable, quiet. He still sees Ginger, of course; they go out to dinner and a movie every Saturday night, and Lucky gets a squeeze pretty much whenever he wants one. Abe's business continues to improve and Laurence is able to save up a bit of money. And one day, when Leo and Maggie least expect it, he presents them with an envelope containing eight hundred dollars —full payment for the furniture he lost to the finance company those many years ago.

Okay, that's it, he's quits with the world. Nothing to do now but sit back, take it easy, and live as long as you can. That's how it goes.

Only Laurence knows his luck isn't running that way. Not this time around—maybe some other time. But this time, he knows, something is going to go wrong—he can feel it in his blood. You can't take money from guys like Frank Holiday and expect to pay it back without some kind of interest. And you can't flirt around with a fiery dame like Savannah Jones and not get burned. It's like trying to fill an inside straight. You know the odds are against you, but sometimes you have to give it a try. Because that's the only way you can stay in the game, and he's going to stay in this particular game as long as he can, play his hand the way it's dealt, and see what he can make of it. Who knows? Maybe for once in his life he'll actually come out a winner.

~§~

On Friday Laurence got to work a little late but spent almost the entire day in the shop, helping Abe finish up the orders that had come in during the week. By three thirty they had emptied the shelves of shoes waiting for repair and moved them all to the "waiting for pick-up" shelves. A few new orders had come in during the day, but Abe said they could do those Saturday morning. He was open till noon on Saturdays, and that was usually his slowest day.

"Why don't you take off early," he said to Laurence. "Get some rest before you go to your second job this evening. It don't seem right you should work so hard, so soon after you got out of the sanatorium. I heard you coughing a lot today—more than before, I think."

"It's just these damn cigarettes," Laurence said. "I should give 'em up, but what the hell, a guy's gotta have *some* vices."

Abe's mild eyes peered at him through speckled glasses. "The only vice I got at my age, Lucky, is staying alive. You should try it."

Laurence chuckled. "You're a wise man, Pops. Hope some of that will rub off on me, if I'm here long enough. Maybe I will knock off early today. I'd like to drop by the hospital, see how my brother's doing."

He hadn't seen Leo since Wednesday, and he was hatching a plan he wanted to try out on Maggie and Jack, if everything was going all right, so he hiked out to St. Mary's and, sure enough, Maggie and Jack were in Leo's room.

"So when are you getting out of here?" Laurence asked, when Leo reported no recurrence of his chest pains.

"The doc still won't say. He wants me to get used to this new medicine, and I guess there's a few more tests they have to run. All this time in the hospital is going to cost us an arm and a leg."

"Well, better an arm and a leg than a heart," Laurence said. "I hear you can't get by without one of those." He turned to Maggie, who was trying to smile at his joke. "Say, I've got an idea. Why don't I take you and Jack out to dinner this evening? I'm playing piano at a new club, place out of town a ways called the Blue Swan. We can have a nice dinner and you can stick around to catch the show. You folks have had a rough week—it might cheer you up."

This was the first Leo and Maggie had heard of his job at the Blue Swan, so he had to explain, after a fashion, how that had come about. "It's just for seven nights, you understand, just to get the club rolling. I guess they think I'm some kind of draw, and we actually had a pretty good turn-out last night."

Leo put on his serious face. "Are you sure that's a good idea, Larry? You're taking a considerable risk, going back into that kind of work."

"I know I am, Leo. I didn't want to do it, but Abe needs three hundred fifty by tomorrow or he'll have to sell the shop, and there just wasn't any other way to raise the money. I sure wasn't going to ask *you* folks for it—not with the tight place you're in!"

Leo and Maggie exchanged a look that seemed to mix relief with a touch of guilt. Then Leo said, "Couldn't you serve your apprenticeship in some other shop?"

"Sure, if I could find a place that would take an old lunger like me. That might not be easy, and I'm anxious to get started. Besides, I like Abe, and I like the location. It's a good deal for me, Leo. All I have to do is work seven nights at the Blue Swan and I'm home free. So what do you say, Maggie—couldn't you use a night out?"

Laurence knew Maggie; she could *always* use a night out. She looked at Leo, who told her silently that it was up to her. "But can you afford it?" she asked Laurence. "If you're working there because you need the money for your other job, you shouldn't be spending it on us."

"Hey, the Friday fish-fry is a buck ninety-nine," Laurence said. "Toss in a couple of drinks—for you, Maggie, not for me or Jack—and it'll set me back ten bucks at the most. That's not much more than cab fare, especially if you stick around for the whole show and drive me home afterwards. We'll be out of there by ten forty-five."

"Come on, Ma," Jack said. "I'd sure like to hear Lucky play. Are you doing a solo, Lucky, or is it some sort of combo?"

"Well, actually, I'm backing up a singer," Laurence said. "She's a bit of an amateur, but I think she's got possibilities." *And she'll pop your eyeballs out, junior.*

"What about your friend?" Maggie asked. "The one you're staying with—won't she be jealous?"

"Oh, we'll take her, too. She's been wanting to meet you, and she's a really nice gal—you two will hit it off just fine." *Probably too well,* Laurence thought. If one woman knew what was best for a man, two women usually knew ten times as much.

"Well, I think you ought to go," Leo said. "I've given you both a rough week, and you should have a little fun. Besides, you can keep an eye on my brother here—make sure he behaves himself."

Laurence gave Maggie a wink. "That's what I'm counting on, Leo. That's the point of the whole deal— keep the old reprobate out of trouble!"

They left the hospital at five and drove to Ginger's flat. Maggie and Jack waited in the car while Laurence went up to tell her they were going out to dinner. Fortunately, Ginger hadn't started to cook supper, but she said, "You could've given me a little warning, for Pete's sake! My hair's a mess, and I need a bath . . . I should iron my good dress—"

"You'll look fine," Laurence said. "Maggie's not dolled up, either. Come on, if we leave now we'll have plenty of time for a nice dinner before I go on. You've been wanting to meet my family, haven't you?"

"Give me ten minutes," Ginger said.

Laurence called Eddie King to let him know he wouldn't need a ride, and then he went down to wait in the car with Maggie and Jack. They were arguing, as usual. "What is it now, you two?" he asked.

"Nothing," Maggie said, but her eyes were bright with tears.

"Have you been giving your mother a hard time again?" Laurence asked Jack, hoping to make peace before Ginger came down.

"Heck, no," Jack said. "I just told her I could help you pay for our dinner. I've got money from my lawn mowing jobs, so why should you have to pay it all?"

"Well, that's real kind of you, Jack," Laurence said, "but I sort of wanted this to be my treat. It's been a big week for me, you see—getting back in circulation, getting my first steady job in, Lord, I don't know how long. Seems like I ought to celebrate. Tell you what, though. Since I don't have a car, I need some way to get out to the Blue Swan for these dates. If you're free tomorrow night, and your Ma will agree, you could give me a ride out there and back—that would save me another big cab fare."

"Sure—can I stay and see the show?"

"Not without your mother—I don't think that would be allowed. Of course, if she wants to come, too—"

"We'll see," Maggie said. "One night out's probably enough for me, but I guess Jack could give you a ride—if his father says it's all right. We don't like him driving on the highway, but I suppose he does it anyway."

"Like I do a lot of things," Jack said, and lit a cigarette.

"You see?" Maggie said. "His father's in the hospital with a heart attack, and he starts acting like a thug. And he used to be such a good boy!"

Jack blew smoke out his nose with satisfaction.

A few minutes later they saw Ginger coming down the driveway, looking pretty nice for a gal who only had ten minutes to get dressed. Laurence got out of the car to meet her, then provided introductions. Ginger got in back with Maggie, who always preferred the back seat, believing it was safer, and Laurence sat in front with Jack. Before they were well out of town, the two women were launched on a friendly conversation, and Laurence thought his plan might work out pretty well.

~§~

The Blue Swan's fish-fry was routine—breaded perch, French fries, coleslaw, and rye bread. Washed down with a few beers, it would have tasted great, but Laurence stuck to 7 UP. Maggie and Ginger each had several drinks and chattered away like old cronies. Maggie loved eating out, Laurence recalled, and she was always jolly after a few drinks. Jack obviously didn't approve; the cheerier his mother became, the more he sulked, as if he thought one of them ought to be in mourning. Laurence tried to get him talking about music and then told a few stories from the old days, when he and Leo spent summers on the road with their own band, and that seemed to cheer him up.

"You guys must've had a great time," Jack said. "I wish I could do something like that."

"Oh, you'll get your chance," Laurence said. And then, seeing Maggie's anxious glance, he added, "Just don't be in too big a hurry—your folks need you around home right now."

Eddie King stopped by their table and insisted on buying a round of drinks. Laurence had to introduce the big jerk and Eddie let on he was a big-time promoter who could put Lucky's career back on the tracks, if only he would co-operate. "I could make this guy a lot of money," he said, glaring around the table, as if he'd punch the first person to disagree.

"*That's* your boss?" Ginger asked, when Eddie finally left.

"One of them," Laurence said. "The other one's got the money and the brains—he's probably more dangerous than his stooge."

"Dangerous?" Jack asked. "You mean, they're like gangsters?"

"The music business is full of unsavory characters," Maggie said to her son.

"That's why your father and I don't want you to go into it—you'd have to deal with people like that all the time—wouldn't he, Larry?"

"I'm afraid so," Laurence said. "It goes with the territory."

"Hey, I thought he was a nice guy," Jack said, just to irritate his mother.

At seven o'clock Savannah had yet to make an appearance, so Laurence figured it was up to him to get the show rolling. He left some money with Ginger and went up to the bandstand. They had another good turn-out; the dining room was full and Lucky thought he saw a few familiar faces from the night before. The noise level dropped as he took his seat at the piano and adjusted the microphone. "Good evening, ladies and gentleman, and welcome to the Blue Swan . . ."

He did his usual patter and then a few solo numbers. The applause was generous and Lucky felt he was among friends. He played "Whispering" for Maggie and "I've Got A Crush on You" for Ginger, then a little "12th Street Rag" for Jack. At seven fifteen Savannah came out in her glistening gold sheath and Lucky gave her an introduction, then gladly receded to the background. From now on, it was her show.

Savannah opened with the same numbers she'd used the night before and Lucky gave her what she expected, without any new wrinkles. She sang with more confidence this evening, and she pitched her songs more at the audience than at the accompanist, which was fine with Lucky. The applause was generous and a couple of times he spotted Frank Holiday watching from across the room. Holiday seemed to be pleased, if you could tell anything from his gambler's impassive face.

At their first break, Savannah sat down on the bench with him. "I see you brought your fan club tonight. Do I get to meet them?"

"Of course," Lucky said. "I was just going to take you over to their table."

Maggie was friendly enough, but Savannah got a hard stare from Ginger. As for Jack, he was so flustered by the immediate presence of so much exposed female flesh he could barely look at her. Prolonging the general discomfort was all part of Lucky's plan: the more these folks saw of each other, he somehow felt, the safer he was from all of them. So they all had a drink—Laurence sticking to 7 UP —and made awkward small-talk until it was time for Lucky and Savannah to return to the bandstand.

"So that's the old bag you prefer to me?" Savannah asked before they turned on their mikes.

"Hey, take it easy," Lucky said. "Ginger's a good gal, and I ain't exactly Rudolph Valentino, you know."

"Who the fuck is Rudolph Valentino?"

He could tell she was pissed, but fortunately she put her anger into her vocals, giving them an undercurrent, an edge, they hadn't had before. Lucky caught the mood and used it as part of his accompaniment, taking a few more riffs than he had before, challenging her with some trickier rhythms. They had a kind of jazzy feud going now and it punched up the music, gave it a little bounce. Some people even got up to dance. Lucky figured his strategy had worked like a charm. Scratch a romance and find some good blues.

Savannah went off by herself on the second break and was gone longer than she should've been. When she came back Lucky could tell she'd been smoking grass again and was high as a kite. Her timing was off, her voice broke on a few high notes, and more than once she wandered off key. Fortunately the dinner crowd was thinning out by now—the old-timers wanted to go home before the rock and roll band took over at ten and the Blue Swan became an entirely different sort of club. Lucky didn't blame them.

Between numbers, Savannah sent the waitress for another drink. "Haven't you had enough?" Lucky asked her, his hand over the mike.

"Is that any business of yours?" she snapped back at him.

"Just trying to keep you out of trouble," Lucky said.

"I'll take care of myself, thanks."

He got her through the last set by taking more choruses for himself, with longer and intros and breaks, until finally she wasn't singing much at all. When they finally limped to a close on their last number Savannah gave him a withering look and left the bandstand. *Well, that solves that problem*, Laurence thought, though he wasn't entirely happy with the resolution.

While Ginger and Maggie were using the ladies' room, Laurence went looking for Frank Holiday and found him in the bar, surrounded by his cronies. After awhile he managed to pry loose an eyeball and Holiday stuck out his hand. "Nice job, Lantz. She was shaky at times, but you kept her going pretty well. The crowd liked her, so she's still got a job and so do you."

"So do I get my advance?"

Holiday snapped his fingers at the bartender, who produced an envelope. Holiday passed it to Laurence. "You owe me five more nights, you understand."

"Understood," Laurence said, and took a quick peek inside the envelope.

"It's all there," Holiday said with a smile. "So who's the good-looking brunette you brought along tonight?"

"Oh, that's my sister-in-law. You wouldn't like her, Frank—she's a devout Catholic, very straightlaced, and she doesn't approve of gamblers."

Holiday sneered. "Did I say I was interested? She's a little old for me—I can get all the young stuff I want."

Laurence was glad to hear it; nonetheless, he decided he'd better not bring Maggie out to the Blue Swan again.

The Hot Rods were just getting set up as they made their exit from the club. Jack wanted to stay and hear a few numbers, but Laurence told him he wouldn't like it. "I've heard better car wrecks," he said.

They drove back to Madison beneath another big round moon and, as they neared the city, Maggie said, "Thanks, Larry, for the night out. It was good hearing you play again—I enjoyed it, but I couldn't help wishing that was Leo up there with you."

"Me, too," Laurence said, and without mentioning that it was for her sake that Leo gave up the business. "So can I count on a ride tomorrow night?"

"Of course, but after that I'm not so sure. We'll see what Leo thinks. Jack starts school next week—he won't be going out on school-nights."

She spoke with such confidence that Laurence expected Jack to protest, but the kid brooded silently at the wheel. *Probably seeing visions of sugar-plums in shimmering gowns,* Laurence thought. The evening had certainly given him plenty to think about.

It also put Ginger in a romantic mood, as Laurence discovered when they were back in their flat and getting ready for bed. He was tired and not exactly in the mood himself, but Ginger knew what to do to get him going and they wound up having a pretty good time. Afterwards, as she lay curled in his arms, she said, "You're such a good guy, Lucky, you deserve a break."

"I got one," he said, "when I met you." And he was nearly able to believe it, all the way up to the threshold of sleep, when he looked through the open door and saw Savannah waiting like a tigress in his dreams.

~§~

The next morning Laurence came up Regent Street a few minutes after nine. A shiny blue Chrysler was parked outside Abe's shop and he figured he knew who that belonged to. He quickened his pace and pushed into the shop, where he found a large, heavy-set man in a loud plaid jacket taking up most of the space before the counter. He had a round shiny dome and a thick dark moustache, and his dark eyes jabbed at Laurence like a pair of inquisitive crows.

Abe was bent over the counter examining some printed forms. He looked up at the sound of the bell and gave his apprentice an anxious smile. "Lucky, this is Mr. Wulfsham, the man I told you about. He brought me his offer—the papers are all drawn up." The old man spread his hands, as if there was little he could do to resist such efficiency.

Laurence eased around Wulfsham's bulk and put the envelope Frank Holiday had given him on the counter. "Better not sign anything until you've had a look at this, old-timer. Go on, open it—it's an early Christmas present."

"Hey, we're doing business here," Wulfsham said. "Can't it wait?"

Abe opened the envelope and took out the bills. He wet his thumb and peeled back the corner of each one, then looked at Laurence in disbelief "You did it, Lucky! You raised the money we need!"

Wulfsham glared at Lucky. "Who *is* this guy?"

Abe seemed to gather himself up, to stand a little taller against Wulfsham's imposing bulk. "This is my new partner, Mr. Wulfsham. This is an angel from God, the answer to an old man's prayers."

"Oh, I wouldn't go that far," Laurence said, "but I've cooked your goose, pal. You can be on your way—we've got work to do this morning."

The developer couldn't believe what he was hearing;

first he laughed, then he got sore. "Now see here, Slovinsky, you'd better think this over carefully. You won't get a better offer, and next week my price goes down. If necessary, I'll have this property condemned."

"Condemned?" Abe asked, suddenly frightened again. "You can do this?"

"He's bull-shitting you," Laurence said. "He can't do a thing if you pay your taxes. Besides, we're going to organize the neighborhood, Wulfsham. We'll keep guys like you from tearing everything down and putting up all those ugly concrete boxes."

Wulfsham gave him a contemptuous look. "I don't think *you'll* do much of anything, mister, but you just cost your partner a nice settlement. Next time you see me, I'll be looking over the front end of a bulldozer."

He stalked out of the shop and Abe watched with worried eyes as the blue Chrysler pulled away. "Maybe we shouldn't have made him angry, Lucky. A man like that has powerful friends, maybe."

"Aah, he's a bully and a blowhard," Laurence said. "I know the type—think they can use their money to push people around. I wouldn't mind getting a guy like at the poker table—he'd be easy pickings, Pops. He wouldn't know what hit him."

Abe stared at him. "You do this often, Lucky— gamble at cards with rich men?"

"Not anymore," Laurence said. "Though sometimes I get the itch, especially when somebody gets my goat. Say, you'd better take this money uptown and pay your bills. I'll tend the fort here."

Abe motioned to the shelf of shoes waiting for repair. "Better we get these done first, Lucky. They were promised for this morning. I got till noon—both the bank and the tax office stay open till twelve."

"Well, don't put it off too long." Laurence figured it would take the old man some time to drag his bum foot all the way to city hall, and to whatever bank held his mortgage.

They worked side by side for the next two hours and, though they finished the shoes scheduled for pick-up, more work came in, including a rush job for two college boys who wanted their black dress shoes back by noon. Some big frat party that night, Laurence guessed. He got both kids to agree to a special rush-order charge of five dollars over the regular price.

"That's how you make money in this business," he said to Abe after the kids left. "Find out what the customer wants and how much he's willing to pay. There's not another shop in Madison that would get these shoes back to them by noon."

Abe shook his head. "You got different ideas, Lucky. To me, fair is fair, but to you, fair is whatever you can get away with."

"That's the way the world works, old-timer. I didn't make it the way it is—I just try to get by in it."

They went back to their tasks and at eleven thirty Abe realized it was already too late to get uptown before the banks and city hall closed. "Well, I guess I got until Tuesday morning," he said. "They haven't come to kick us out yet."

"And they won't, either, until that fat-ass Wulfsham gets after them about it. But you'd better not leave that three fifty in the till over the weekend. What do you usually do with your receipts?"

"To tell you the truth, what little cash I got, I usually just take it home with me on Saturday afternoon and put what I don't need in the bank on Monday morning. Most weeks the bank don't get any of it—that's why I'm in trouble. But this week we've done a lot better. We ought to count what's in the register and split it up between us, like we agreed."

"Except for the three fifty," Laurence said. "You keep that."

"No, no," Abe said, "you take it. Until I pay my mortgage and taxes, it's still your money. What if I lost it?"

"I trust you, Pops. You won't lose it."

"But this neighborhood isn't so safe anymore. What if the word got around that we're starting to make a little money here? Somebody gets an idea, follows me home I'd feel better if you took the money, Lucky."

"Well, let's count the till and see what's in there," Laurence said. "Then we'll decide."

So at five past twelve they locked the front door, pulled down the shades, and took the cash drawer out of the register. Laurence counted the bills while Abe did the loose change. When they were done they added the two together. It came to ninety-seven dollars and thirteen cents. Abe said he'd started the week with ten dollars in the till, mostly in change, so that was a total of $87.13 in new receipts.

"Unbelievable, Lucky! That's nearly twice my best week in this shop since I been open, going on nine years now. I said you'd bring me luck."

"Well, one good week isn't going to put us on easy street," Laurence said, "but it's a start. So what did we agree on? Anything over twenty a week is mine, right?— up to forty, and then we split the rest down the middle. So let's see: we'll leave thirteen cents in the till for good luck, along with the ten you started out with, and that comes to—" he did a little long division on a scrap of paper— "forty-three dollars and fifty cents apiece."

Abe agreed and counted out the money, to which he added the three hundred and fifty from Frank Holiday. "There! Now we're even. I'll sign your papers right now, if you got them with you, Lucky. You been like an angel from God to me."

"Better wait till we've paid those bills," Laurence said, putting the three fifty back in its envelope and the rest in his wallet. "I'll meet you uptown Tuesday morning and we'll take care of it together, okay? Nine a.m. in front of city hall."

"But we open at nine," Abe said.

"So put a sign in the door. Tuesday we'll open at ten. It's the beginning of a new life for both of us, Pops. Now you have a good weekend."

"You, too, Lucky—and God bless you for all the help you've been to me."

Laurence wasn't sure God listened to Jews any more closely than he listened to Christians, but he figured he could use all the help he could get.

~§~

Saturday was Ginger's day off and she'd fixed them a picnic lunch. Laurence got his guitar and they walked over to Brittingham Park, where they found a place to spread their blanket overlooking Monona Bay. The lake was smelling better after several days of cooler weather, but the sun was still warm enough to bring out the picnickers and sunbathers.

Labor Day weekend, Laurence thought—the end of summer. Always a slow weekend in the music business, with folks off on family outings, but the big dances of fall were just around the corner.

"I really enjoyed last night," Ginger said. "Thanks for taking me. I liked your sister-in-law, too. She seems like a good, down-to-earth sort of gal."

"Yeah, Maggie's all right," Laurence said, gnawing a hunk of Ginger's fried chicken. It was a bit tough, but the potato salad was all right—it came from a deli.

"What's she got against you?" Ginger said, looking off across the bay so she wouldn't have to meet his eye.

"Oh, we used to be great chums," Laurence said. "Then . . ." he paused; there was just too much ground to cover, so he tried to sum it all up: "I ain't always been the most responsible guy in the world, Ginger, but I'm trying to make up for it now."

"I can see that," she said, and put her eyes on him, looking so long that he began to feel uncomfortable. "You're like a man with a suitcase full of regrets, and every one of 'em is heavy as a rock. You've got that easy-going manner that fools people into thinking you don't have a care in the world, but I never saw a man lug around as much grief as you. When are you going to unload some of it and give yourself a break?"

"When I payoff a few debts," Laurence said. He finished his lunch, wiped his fingers, and picked up the guitar. Ginger's words had given him an idea for a tune—you could call it *A Suitcase Full of Blues*. He'd tried out a few chords and the words fell easily into place:

> *I keep on a-travelin' from town to town,*
> *But this suitcase full of blues*
> *Keeps draggin' me down . . .*

Ginger saw he was absorbed in his music, so she picked up the remains of their lunch and put it in her basket. Then she stretched out on the blanket and closed her eyes. Laurence grew bored with his composition and played a few more tunes. He watched a family of ducks gliding along the shore and thought how you ought to be able to make a life out of such nice, quiet afternoons as these. For some guys, it might be enough, but he knew that, for guys like him, it would only be half a life.

Still, wasn't half a life better than none?

13.

Shake, Rattle, and Roll

LAURENCE was done with supper and ready to leave by six thirty. Ginger gave him a kiss at the back door. "Watch out for that torch singer," she said. "Looks to me like she could give a guy first-degree burns."

"Don't worry," Laurence said, "I'm wearing my fire-proof suit."

"Yeah, well maybe I'll apply a little first-aid when you get home," she said. "Don't be late."

He went down the back stairs and along the driveway. Jack was waiting at the curb in his father's Plymouth.

"So how's your pa?" Laurence asked, settling down beside him.

"Doing fine—the doc said he can come home early next week." Jack paused, then added, "I'll sure be glad of it, because Ma and I are driving each other nuts."

"You're too much alike," Laurence said, knowing that was the standard explanation for parent-child problems. People used to say the same thing about him and his father, but not because they couldn't get along.

Jack swung onto Park Street and accelerated, though the speed limit was still 25 miles per hour. "The trouble is, she just doesn't want to see me grow up. She can't get it through her head that I'm sixteen years old."

"Wow, that's old!" Laurence said. "When you going on pension, old-timer?"

Jack grinned. "Aw, come on—I'll bet you were already playing in dance bands at my age, or maybe in some speakeasy."

"Not quite. Prohibition didn't come in till I was nearly twenty." Laurence was tempted to reminisce about those early days, when he first went off on his own and found he could support himself playing rag-time piano in saloons and hooky-tonks, but then he remembered Leo's plea—*Don't encourage the boy!*—and decided on a different tack.

"Anyway, you don't want to measure yourself by me, Jack. Here I am, trying to start my life all over again at the ripe old age of fifty-five. You could spare yourself a lot of misery by not making the same mistakes I did. Dropping out of school, for instance—"

"Oh, I plan on going to college and all," Jack said. "I imagine I'll settle into some other career eventually. But I'd sure like the experience of playing in a jazz band for awhile—you know, just bumming around the country, like you and Dad used to."

"It's a tough life," Laurence said, "even when you're young. Your old man was smart to get out when he did. Guys like me, guys who couldn't give it up and settle down, we paid a high price. We lost the chance to lead a normal life."

"So who wants a normal life?" Jack asked, and Laurence saw he wasn't getting very far. But it wasn't

easy, telling somebody your whole life had been a mistake. Because what if, maybe, it hadn't been? What if it
was the only life you wanted, the only one where you
could be yourself and do the things you were born to do?
A guy had to use his gift, whatever it was, or it could
turn rotten inside and kill him, and at least Lucky Lantz
was still alive.

It was five to seven, the sunset fading behind the
trees and the parking lot already full, when Jack
dropped him off outside the Blue Swan. The first thing
Laurence noticed was that Savannah's photo had been
removed from the signboard by the entrance and strips
of masking tape covered her name. His own name and
photo were still there.

He found Eddie King at the crowded horseshoe bar,
puffing his cigar and playing the big shot, as usual. "Hey,
what gives with the poster?" Laurence asked.

"You're doing a single tonight, Lantz. The dumb
broad finally went too far—Frankie fired her ass."
Eddie's satisfaction was evident from his smirk, but
Lucky thought he saw something else, too—something
you didn't often see in Eddie King's stupid dark eyes: a
flicker of fear.

"Fired her? What'd she do?"

"Well, she was drunk as a skunk by five this afternoon, for one thing. Frankie hates it when she gets
stinko, but I reckon he found out she's been playing
around, too . . . old Frank don't take that kind of shit
from no woman. She's lucky she got her whore's ass out
of here in one piece."

"But Frank knows I can't do a solo for three whole
hours!"

"You won't have to. The rock and roll kids agreed to

come in early tonight. All you gotta do is hold the audience till eight, eight thirty, and then they'll take over."

"Great," Laurence said, thinking that, unfortunately, Jack wouldn't be back for him until ten thirty. Maybe he could find some earplugs. "I still want this to count as one of the nights I owe you guys," he said, knowing there was little hope it would.

"You'll have to talk to Frank about that," Eddie said. "But after the show. People are waiting for some entertainment, so get your ass up there."

That was one of the things Lucky loved about being a musician—the way you got pushed around by ignorant, no-talent bums like Eddie King. He went up to the bandstand and took his place at the piano, then spoke into the microphone.

"Good evening, ladies and gentleman, and welcome to the Blue Swan. I'm afraid I've got some disappointing news for you. Our featured singer, the fabulous Savannah Jones, was taken ill this afternoon and won't be able to perform this evening. Nothing serious—just some kind of flu, most likely—but I'm afraid you'll have to make do with old Lucky Lantz as a solo for an hour or so, until our house band, Red Ford and his boys, make their appearance—"

There were a few groans from the audience. Lucky could see this wasn't the crowd for a rock and roll band, but he got his first number rolling before they could start leaving the tables. For some reason, he played an old favorite: "Don't Get Around Much Any More." For Savannah. Poor kid, he hoped Holiday hadn't been too rough with her. He'd seen that nasty glint in the gambler's blue eyes and knew he was a sick son of a bitch. And he didn't even want to think about what it might take to shock Eddie King.

He segued into "Hard-Hearted Hannah, the Vamp of Savannah." The kid would be a natural for a torchy song like this—even had her name in the title. He'd have to teach it to her, if he ever saw her again. Funny how much he missed the little monkey, as green as she was, and as much trouble to cover for. Lucky had never liked doing solos; he preferred to see someone else in the spotlight, so he could work in the shadows, finding ways to compliment and support the lead performer. That was his talent, his gift. But hell, who was he trying to kid? The damn woman had gotten under skin.

He played "I've Got You Under My Skin" and then a few other Cole Porter favorites, and the audience of old-timers seemed reasonably satisfied with their dinner music. At eight o'clock he took a break and went to the bar for a 7 UP. The bartender was the same guy he'd talked to the other night, an older fellow who remembered Lucky from the old days. He leaned over the bar and spoke softly, close to Lucky's ear.

"If you're looking for a certain lady, you might try cabin number one out back."

"Cabin number one? Is that where Frank put Savannah after he beat her up?"

"*Shhhh!*" The bartender's eyes slid across the crowded barroom. Then he produced a paper bag from beneath the bar and slid it toward Lucky. "Here's the key, and something else she might need. Tell her it's from Sid."

Lucky peered inside the bag and saw a pint of vodka and a motel key. "Thanks, Sid." He left the club by the back door and took the path down to the river, then along its bank to the first cabin. The moon was just rising behind the trees and the crickets were chirping. Now and then a bull frog croaked back in the reeds. He could hear traffic on the highway, the whir of the kitchen's exhaust fan as it scented the night with grease.

It was dark along the river, but there was enough moonlight to see by, and to see that the cabins were in bad shape. Their steps sagged; paint was peeling and window screens were bulged out and torn along their frames. He climbed the steps to number one and tapped on the door, listened for a moment and then tapped again. This time he thought he heard a faint groan from inside. He put the key in the door, turned it, and stepped into the dark interior. A bad smell of boozy vomit mingled with the must and mold of the disused cabin.

"Savannah? Hey, it's me, Lucky."

Another groan, louder this time. He didn't want to turn on the overhead light, but after a moment he made out a lamp near the door. He reached under the shade and found a switch. The dim light showed him the rumpled bed, the figure lying on her side with her back toward him, the dark mass of her hair.

"Hey, kid, you doing all right? I brought you something to ease the pain."

She groaned and rolled over, showing him her battered face.

"Shit," Lucky said. "Goddamn it to hell."

He sat down on the bed beside her and put his hand on her hip. The bruised and swollen face was barely recognizable. Both Savannah's eyes were swollen nearly shut; blood was crusted around her nose and mouth. "Gimme," she croaked, "somshing to drink."

He uncapped the vodka and poured some into the

plastic glass on the bed stand, then put it to her lips. "Compliments of Sid," he said. "Easy, it might sting."

She took it down in a swallow and lay back. "More," she said. "More drink."

"In a minute," he said, and went into the bathroom. There were no towels or wash cloths, but he soaked his handkerchief in cold water, wrung it out and brought it back to the bed. Sitting down beside her again, he dabbed at her nose and mouth, put the cool hanky to her forehead. She gave him half a smile. "Thanksh, pal."

"Did Frank do this to you?"

She gave a slight nod.

"For God's sake, why?" Then, seeing it was too difficult for her to speak, he said, "Never mind, I can guess why. Did he think you were fooling around with me?"

Her head moved a bit, side to side. "You ain't . . . only fish . . . inna shee."

Lucky patted her arm. Somehow he felt as if this whole thing was his fault. She might not have gone off on a spree if he hadn't thrown Ginger in her face the other evening—that was probably what set her off. No woman liked being put in her place—especially not a gal who thought she was pretty hot stuff.

"I'm sorry as hell about this," he said finally. "I gotta go now, but I'll be back."

"Leave the bottle," she said.

When he got back to the Blue Swan he found that the rock and roll band was already on stage, setting up. The Hot Rods had exchanged their blue jeans and tee shirts for matching red blazers, which gave them a slightly more professional look than they'd had at rehearsal, but Lucky didn't expect them to sound any better.

He went back to Frank Holiday's office and knocked on the door. Eddie King opened it. Over his shoulder Lucky could see Holiday sitting at the poker table with three other guys. A game was in progress, the table strewn with chips and cards. The air was filled with smoke and charged with the electricity only high stakes poker can bring to a room. Something inside Lucky made a sharp, convulsive movement.

"Yeah, what is it, Lantz?" Eddie asked.

"The Hot Rods are here," Lucky said. "I want to talk to Frank so I can get out of here."

"Deal me out," Holiday said, and rose from the table. He strolled over to the door, looking at his watch. "It's only eight fifteen, Lantz. You still owe me two and a quarter hours."

"You don't need me, Frank. You've got the shit-house quartet."

Holiday barely smiled. "I know you don't dig their kind of music, but I expect my employees to honor their contracts. Our deal was verbal, but it still holds. You work till ten thirty, or you give me back two hundred and fifty smackers."

"Hey, wait a minute," Lucky said. He should've known Holiday would be looking to get out of their deal, now that he no longer had a singer. He hadn't brought the money with him, and besides, it wasn't his money anymore. It was Abe Slovinsky's money; the old man had gambled his shop on Lucky's honor.

Somehow, Laurence was not greatly surprised by this turn of events—he'd known all along he would wind up getting screwed. "So what do you want me to do?" he asked Frank, hoping for a compromise. "You don't really want me to play piano with that bunch of grease-monkeys?"

"Sure, why not? You're an old pro—maybe you can teach 'em something," Holiday said. "Teach 'em to play in the same key, for a change."

"You ever try teaching music to a gang of apes?"

That nasty light came into Holiday's blue eyes; he enjoyed making people do things they didn't want to do. "You took my money, Liberace, so you'll give it a shot—unless you want to try paying off your debt at the poker table."

Lucky looked at the green felt table, the red, white, and blue chips scattered across it, the bright white cards lined up before each player. Nothing would have pleased him more than the chance to buy into that game, but he couldn't go down that street, not this time, not again.

"Okay, I'll stick it out until ten thirty," he said, "but what about next week?"

"Next week I'll have a new singer for you," Holiday said, "if I can find one. Hey, maybe you'd like to set up an audition for your sister-in-law—I'll bet she can swing that plump little ass of hers."

"You go to hell," Laurence said and walked away from him.

He half-expected Holiday to come after him, or to send Eddie out to punch his face in, but the bastard just laughed and slammed the door. Lucky entered the dining room, crossed among the tables to the bandstand, and sought out the acne-faced redhead he took to be the leader of the group. The kid was testing the amplifier for his guitar, which produced a shriek like the death rattle of a butchered hog.

"Hi there, you Red Ford?"

"Yeah, how ya doin', man?"

"Not so hot. I'm supposed to play with you guys to-night."

"Oh yeah? Who says?"

"The boss man. He wants me to earn my pay, so I got to hang in here till ten thirty. I don't like it any more than you do, but that's the deal."

The kid grinned. "Shit, man, I don't give a rat's ass— we'll drown you out, anyway. We ain't got no sheets for a piano."

"I can fake it," Lucky said. "Just tell me the key, when you know it."

"Sure thing," the kid said. "We generally start with 'Rock Around the Clock', key of F. Then we do 'Shake, Rattle, and Roll', same key, and then some Elvis numbers—'Jailhouse Rock', 'Blue Suede Shoes', 'Heartbreak Hotel'. After that we just jam, do whatever comes into our heads."

"That's quite a repertoire," Lucky said. "How about a little Fats Domino or Louie Prima for a change of pace?"

"Who the hell are they?" Red Ford asked, and then poked Lucky's arm to show he was only joking. "Tell you what, Pop—we'll let you do a few solos once we get rolling."

"Wonderful," Lucky said.

The piano had been rolled to the side of the stage, behind the drums, and Lucky got the drummer to help him push it out where he could see what the rest of the band was doing. Not that he wanted to see their shenanigans, but he didn't want those cymbals crashing in his ear, and he thought he might be able to pick up a few visual cues when the music itself made no sense to him.

When they were ready to go, Red Ford snapped his fingers to set the pace and they tore into "Rock Around the Clock." *One o'clock, two o'clock*—there wasn't much to do with music like this but pound out the chords, four to a bar, and Lucky did it, even though he knew no one in the dining room, including himself, could hear what he was playing over the shriek of the amplified guitars, the fog-horn bellow of the tenor sax, the ceaseless pounding of the drums and cymbals. It made no sense, playing piano in a group like this, but he did it, because he owed Frank Holiday five nights' work and he knew what could happen to him if he reneged on the deal. Guys like Holiday loved it when you reneged, because they were always looking for a chance to hurt somebody. And Laurence had been hurt enough over the years—his broken old body couldn't take any more hurt—but his spirit, it seemed, was still a glutton for punishment.

Lucky settled in for a long evening. Amazing how boring music could be if you played the same song over and over again, which was essentially what the Hot Rods did. Over the years he had played in some pretty bad groups—corn-ball German polka bands and hick country -western bands, rag-tag assemblies of worn-out veterans and green kids—but he had never played with a group of musicians more tone-deaf or limited in their skills than the Hot Rods. He looked in vain for some spark of talent, originality, or feeling in their music, but it just wasn't there. It was all toot, toot, pound, pound, shriek, shriek, *gonna rock, gonna rock, all around the clock tonight!*

What made it all the worse, from Lucky's point of view, was that many of the older folks who had come to hear Lucky and Savannah were still eating their dinners when the Hot Rods commenced their first set. They were therefore obliged to witness the spectacle of Lucky Lantz up there on the bandstand, shaming himself with this bunch of hooligans, betraying every instinct and every principle he'd ever had as a jazz musician. Lucky thought he saw more than one look of reproach from the tables nearby: *Can't you do anything about these kids? We thought you were* our kind *of musician!*

I was, folks, I was. And then I sold my soul for a lousy three hundred and fifty bucks, so the old man I work for can stay in business and the state of Wisconsin will send me sixty bucks a month, and with that and what I make at his shop I can probably live like a poor man for the rest of my life—which will no doubt be shortened by all my past vices and indiscretions. While in the back room of this very joint, the local high-rollers and hoodlums are pushing chips worth two or three thousand across the table. They're taking money from suckers, folks, and you see the biggest sucker of them all up here on the bandstand, because he's putting up with this shit in the hope of living a sober, quiet life—a life he doesn't even want all that much—for a few more paltry years.

When the band took a break at nine fifteen Lucky went to the bar and asked Sid for a couple of aspirins and another 7 UP.

"Sure you don't want something stronger?" Sid asked him.

"Only if I could put it where it would do the most good," Lucky said.

When they resumed at nine thirty most of the older folks had cleared out of the club and the younger set were beginning to arrive. Girls in full skirts and tight sweaters, boys in blue jeans and sideburns. Few of them looked old enough to drink hard liquor, but nobody seemed to care about that. The kids took over the bar and the pool tables; they crowded onto the dance floor and began to throw their bodies about in some strange parody of dancing. Lucky tried to amuse himself by watching the full skirts swirl up around skinny white thighs and pert little butts in pink panties. That would be the only pleasure he'd get tonight—a blurred glimpse of jail-bait ass. Just the thing for a dirty old man.

At ten thirty he took his numb fingers and battered eardrums back to the bar and told Sid he was done for the tonight. "Tell Frank I stuck it out—the full three hours—but he'd better get himself another singer or he can write off that advance he gave me. I'm not playing another night with the Four Stooges."

"Frank left an hour ago," Sid said. "He doesn't like the band any more than you do. So did you check on our friend?"

"Yeah, she's in pretty bad shape. Are you the fella who got her in trouble?"

Sid looked properly offended. "Who, me? Hell, I'm a married man with six kids. I just felt sorry for her, that's all."

"So who was it? Whoever got her drunk ought to come and get her—Frank ain't going to leave her out in that cabin for long."

Sid put his elbows on the bar and leaned close to Lucky's ear. "It was a black dude, a south-side hustler by the name of Cool Johnny Combs."

"A colored man? Are you sure?"

"I seen him come by for her in his big car. Johnny's a gambler, but Frank won't let him in his games, 'cause he's black. But Savannah's part Negro, you know—one of them Creole half-castes."

"Does Frank know that?"

"He does now. That's another reason he beat the shit out of her. Eddie filled him in on all the dirty details —how she used to be one of Johnny's hookers when she first came to Madison."

"That son of a bitch," Lucky said. If he had been twenty years younger and forty pounds heavier, without a permanently damaged lung and a medical history that had taught him to avoid violence, he might have told Eddie King just what he thought of him. Good thing the big lug was no longer on the premises.

He left the Blue Swan and found Jack leaning against his father's car. The rock band had started their next set and Jack was listening to the noise, which was slightly more tolerable outside the building. "Hey, they're not bad," he said.

Laurence glared at him. "I've been meaning to tell you, kid, you've got lousy taste."

Jack looked a little hurt, but didn't argue with him. Laurence got in the car and Jack took the wheel. They left the parking lot and set out for Madison, but Laurence was still thinking. He watched the moon dodge through an onslaught of scrappy clouds, like a boxer trying to duck a flurry of fists, then saw the lights of the city reflecting off the cloud cover up ahead. The sky over Madison was brownish pink, like an old bruise.

"Stop the car," he said to Jack. "We've gotta go back to the Blue Swan."

"What's the matter? You forget something?"

"Yeah, what's left of my self-respect," Laurence said.

Jack turned the car around on the highway and they

headed back. When they arrived, Laurence directed him around in back, then down the old service road that ran behind the cabins. "Turn your lights off and take it slow," he said. "You'll be able to see the road by moonlight."

Jack did as he was told and Laurence told him when to stop. "Wait here for a minute," he said, and went to the first cabin. He could hear the muffled booms and squeals of the Hot Rods, happily pounding out "Rock Around the Clock" for the twentieth time that evening. There were other sounds now, too—a squeal of brakes out on the highway, the bleat of several horns in the parking lot. A kid's voice yelled some taunt or threat. Laurence supposed they had fights outside the Blue Swan every time the Hot Rods played. Good thing the club was surrounded by miles of open farmland.

He entered the cabin and found Savannah had passed out. The pint bottle of vodka was half full. He gathered up her clothes and purse, then wrapped her naked body in the sheet and blanket she was already tangled up in. He took her things out to the car and asked Jack to come in with him. "Buck up, kid—this ain't very pretty."

Whatever Jack thought of their mission, he was too awed to voice an opinion. Together, they managed to lift Savannah's limp body off the bed and then over Jack's shoulder; with Laurence leading the way, he carried her out to the car, where Laurence helped him get her in the backseat.

"Holy shit," Jack said, when he got a look at her face beneath the dome light, "it's that singer! Who did this to her, Lucky?"

"The guy who owns this joint. I told you it was a rough life, kid. You get to work for assholes like Frank

Holiday all the time."

"So where we gonna take her?"

"I'll think of someplace," Laurence said. "Come on, let's get out of here."

They made their way around the Blue Swan and past the knot of kids milling around the front entrance. Somebody yelled at them but Laurence told Jack to keep going. Once they were on the highway Jack floored the accelerator and Laurence didn't tell him to slow down. The more miles they put between them and the Blue Swan, the better he liked it.

Neither of them spoke on the drive back to Madison. Laurence knew his nephew had plenty of questions, but he was in no mood for talking. All he wanted was the peace and quiet of the closed vehicle whirring along the highway, following its headlights down a tunnel of darkness. Entering the city on Park Street they passed a shabby motel that still had its "Vacancy" sign on. Another sign said, Singles: $4.50.

"Pull in here," Laurence said.

He went into the office and booked a room, paid for it with the bills in his wallet, then came back with the key. They drove down the row of mostly empty parking spaces until they found the right door. Together, they got Savannah out of the backseat and Jack carried her into the room. They put her down on the bed, where she groaned, mumbled something, and promptly went back to sleep. Laurence put her clothes and purse on the room's only chair. He put the paper bag with the half-empty bottle on the nightstand, then found a pad of paper on the desk and wrote her a quick note: "I'll check in on you tomorrow—Lucky."

He propped it up against the paper bag and they left

the room.

A few blocks further down Park Street Laurence saw the pink neon of an all-night restaurant. "Pull in here," he said, "I need something to eat." He wasn't exactly hungry, but he didn't know how else to fill that old empty feeling—worse tonight than it had been in years. Besides, he wanted to make sure Ginger was asleep when he got home. He was in no mood for that "first aid" she'd promised him.

They sat in a booth of padded, cherry red vinyl, and Laurence had a milk shake while Jack wolfed down a burger and fries. Afterwards Laurence smoked a cigarette and shared a memory with Jack—a memory so old he sometimes wondered if it had actually happened or was maybe just another one of his sanatorium dreams.

"I got in this poker game once, down in Dubuque, which can be a pretty tough town. Least it was in the thirties. The game went all night and on through the next day and into the second night. Guys were paying two, three hundred dollars for a seat at the table; and at one point I was up six thousand dollars. Never had a run of luck like that in my life. At the end it was like a runaway train—I couldn't control it, couldn't stop it, couldn't get the hell off. You see, there were guys at that table that would've knifed me in the alley if I'd tried to walk away with that much money. The only way I could get out of there alive to was to lose some of it back to 'em, but it took a long time for my luck to run out. Finally, when I got so sleepy I couldn't see the cards, I lost every damn cent."

"Jeez," Jack said, "I wouldn't want to get in a game like that."

"I learned a good lesson," Lucky said. "You always

have to give yourself a way out before you start. That's the only way you'll get to keep your winnings. Remember that, kid, when you go out in the world. Always give yourself a way out."

"I'll remember it," Jack said, but Laurence could see he wouldn't. Kids never thought they'd make the same mistakes their elders made.

When they pulled up outside Ginger's place, it was nearly midnight and the lights were out. "I guess I don't have to tell you to keep all this under your hat," Laurence said.

"I won't tell anybody," Jack said. "But what are you going to do with Savannah? Will you need another ride?"

"Don't know yet. I'll let you know if I do. You take good care of your Ma now, you hear? And drive home safely."

He climbed out of the car and went up the driveway to the rear entrance. There was no moon to light the alley.

14.
September in the Rain

HE was back in the san and the guy in the bed next to his was coughing his lungs out. *Shut up and die, why don't you, and let me get some sleep*, he thought—and then realized the guy coughing was himself. He woke with a start and reached for the box of tissues he kept by the bed. Somewhere church bells were ringing—Sunday morning, and Ginger had already gone off to work. He coughed up a gob, spit into the tissue and examined it carefully. No blood. Just the usual phlegm from his damaged lung. He crumpled the tissue and pitched it across the room, then sank back on his pillow with a sigh. Not dead yet, but pushin' it, pal, pushin' it.

The bells continued to ring and Laurence was reminded of the flat on Sommer's Avenue where he'd lived with his mother after the divorce. They were near a church there, too—St. Bernard's—and its bells would rouse him first thing in the morning—usually with one hell of a hangover. The bitter aftertaste of regret: all those drinks you wished you'd never taken, all those things you wished you'd never done.

Yeah, like hauling off Frank Holiday's woman and stashing her in a fleabag motel on the edge of town. What the hell got into him? Even if Holiday didn't care about the dame, he wouldn't let anyone pull a stunt like that. Guys like Holiday always got pissed when you took something they thought belonged to them. That was the only way you could hurt the bastards—by stealing their money, screwing their women, beating them at their own game, whatever it was. The better they thought they were, the more it hurt when you showed them you were better.

Of course it didn't always work that way. Sometimes their luck beat yours and you had to expect that. But Lucky had won often enough in his younger days to remember how good it felt. He knew Frank Holiday could be had. All it required was a bank-roll big enough to stand up to Holiday's bluff, to out-last his hot streak and catch one of his own. He remembered the electric spark that shot through his body when he saw that green-felt table strewn with cards, and he knew he still had his nerve, his old instinct for the kill.

But that was my old life, Laurence mused, listening to the bells. *I don't play those games anymore. I don't take those risks, those crazy long-shot chances. Yet how much shit did a man have to take before he finally said "enough"?* He had never worked a gig that had shamed and disgusted him as much as last night's. If Frank Holiday expected him to play off his advance with more of the same, he could have his money back—even if it put Abe Slovinsky out of business.

It's not like I owe the old guy anything, Lucky thought. He'd given him a week's work—well, most of a week, anyway—and punched up his business. Abe had paid him a fair wage and now they were quits. Of course, he couldn't get around the fact that Abe had passed up a chance to sell his shop, that he was counting on that three fifty to pay his bills. Goddamn it, he hated it when people started depending on him, because then what choice did a guy have? Either you gave them what they wanted, or you let them down. Your life was no longer your own—you were screwed.

He heard a growl of thunder, followed by the splatter of raindrops against the windowpane, and rolled out of bed. Raising the window shade, he looked out on a dark and dismal day. Only the second of September and already several trees in the neighboring yards were starting to show some yellow leaves. Laurence wondered if he would live long enough to see another spring, another summer. Death didn't really scare him as much as it once had. In fact, sometimes it even appeared to have its advantages: *A man gets weary, and sick of tryin', tired of living and afeared of dying . . .*

In the san he had decided that life was better—even a life without booze. But there were some things he wasn't prepared to give up, and one was his self-respect as a musician. Another, apparently, was his freedom. Ginger was a good enough gal but she just didn't understand the kind of guy he was—or if she did, she was still going to try to change him into something else. *One week back on the outside*, Lucky thought, *and already they've got you by the balls.* Why did this always happen to him?

Of course there was a way out, if he was man enough to take it. Last night Holiday had offered him a chance to win back his debt at the poker table. It was tempting, but to have a chance against Holiday he would need a considerable stake. Right now he had the three fifty Frank had given him, plus the one forty-seven in his coin purse and the forty he'd earned at Abe's—that was well over five hundred bucks, but he'd need at least twice that much before he went up against Holiday's fat bankroll.

Still mulling it over, Laurence made himself a light breakfast, then dug in his suitcase until he found the cheap plastic raincoat he'd bought up at Tomahawk. He put it on and left the apartment, trudging through the rain with his head down and hands in his pockets. He walked past Abe's shop, his hand-painted signs still in the darkened window, and reached the Milwaukee Road station just after ten. The express train from Minneapolis, the Hiawatha, was due in at ten fifteen, and the taxicabs were lined up behind the station house, waiting for fares. Laurence walked down the line, checking the face of each driver. It was a long shot, but in the third cab he found Bert Wiley reading the Sunday paper. He bent down and tapped on the window.

"Hey, Bert—how you doin'?"

"Hey, Lucky. Get in, pal—it's raining out there."

Laurence went around to the passenger's seat. "So, anything happening up at the Cambridge?"

"As a matter of fact, a trio of live ones pulled in yesterday. I went by your shop, but you'd already closed. Didn't know where to reach you on a Sunday, so I sort of gave up on the idea, but they looked plenty ripe to me."

"Oh yeah? Tell me about 'em."

"Well, I picked 'em up at the airport around noon, took 'em to the Cambridge. Said they were from Kansas City, but one of 'em had an accent that sounded more like Texas. Big wheels with McGruder Industries. You know what they make?"

"No, I can't say I do."

"Machine tools, for one thing. These guys are here to cut some big deal and I figure I know what it is. See, after they checked in I took 'em out to the general offices of the Oslo machine shop and they told me to come back around six. You know what's going on at the Oslo, don't you?"

"Yeah, they're about to go out on strike. My brother works there."

"So maybe you know the company's got till midnight Monday to come up with a better offer. I heard one of these guys say they had to stick around until Tuesday."

"Tuesday? You think they're waiting to see if there's a strike?"

"Like vultures waitin' on a carcass," Bert said. "The Oslo's been operating in the red for years, and the major stock-holders have been looking for a chance to unload that turkey. No doubt they'll get sweet deals for themselves—those guys always do—and the guys who work there will get screwed."

"Screwed? Why screwed?"

"Because if McGruder buys that plant, they'll probably shut it down and transfer all its business to Kansas City. That's the way things are done these days—you eliminate the competition and increase your profits in the long run."

Laurence was impressed with Bert's savvy. You could learn a lot, driving a cab. "Do you suppose the union knows about this?"

"Probably not, or they would've settled by now. See, most of that stock is owned by some old Madison families. They wouldn't have the nerve to put half the east side out of work. The strike's their excuse—they can say the union drove 'em to it."

"Hell, I ought to tell my brother about this. Maybe he can warn somebody."

"Just don't tell him where you got the information. A cabbie's supposed to keep mum about anything he overhears in his cab—sort of like a priest in the confessional, you know?"

The Hiawatha's horn sounded from up the tracks. "I gotta cut this short," Bert said. "What I wanted to tell you was, these guys were pissing and moaning about being stuck in Madison over the weekend—kept saying what a dead, nothing town it was. They wanted to know if I could find them any action."

"What kind of action—cards?"

"Poker," Bert said. "One of 'em, guy named Ducaine, came on like a real tinhorn, bragged about the big games he'd been in down in Memphis and Mobile, places like that. He figured he wouldn't find anything up to his standards in a crummy little burg like Madison."

"So what'd you tell them?" Laurence heard the approaching rumble of the Hiawatha's twin diesels, though the engine itself was still screened by the station.

"I said I'd see what I could dig up," Bert said. "Told 'em I knew a guy who knew a guy, that sort of thing. They were interested. Said they'd be at a private party Saturday night, but they'd be free Sunday evening. Said I should come by the hotel around five if I had anything for them."

The rumble had increased to a roar, and now Laurence saw the sleek yellow body of the Hiawatha glide past the station and come to a stop further down the platform. Steam gushed from its undercarriage as the roar of its twin engines subsided. After a few minutes' stop, Laurence knew, the Hiawatha would continue on its way south to Chicago. A three hours' ride to the big city, the bright lights of Rush Street and the Loop. He felt a wild impulse to grab a ticket and climb aboard before the train left the station.

"Okay," he said. "It might take me awhile to set up a game, but I'll work on it. You know a place out near Stoughton called the Blue Swan?"

"Used to be the Stardust? Yeah, I've heard of it, but I think these guys would rather play at the hotel. They got a big suite on the top floor—nice set-up for cards."

"I remember those suites," Lucky said, watching as one of the coach doors opened and the conductor climbed down with his little stool. "That would suit me just fine, if my friends and I can get past the house dick. That's one of the things I'll have to work on. Where can I reach you?"

"Best thing would be if we could meet back here around five," Bert said. "I'm behind in my fares this week, so I gotta keep cruising the streets, even though there ain't much doing on a Sunday."

A single family had emerged from the coach. One of the red caps picked up their bags and started toward the taxi stand. Bert's cab was the third in line, so he wouldn't be getting this fare. A few more people got off, but they were heading toward the parking lot, not the taxis. Several people boarded the train and then the conductor slammed shut the doors and signaled ahead to the engineer. The rumble of the big diesels rose and the train began to glide out of the station.

"Looks like I'm out of luck," Bert said. "The trains

just don't bring in the business like they used to. It's
them goddamn freeways."

"Well, I've got a fare for you," Lucky said. "I need a
ride out to the Rest-Awhile Motel on Park Street."

"Hell, why didn't you say so? Your money's as good
as theirs."

"Yeah, but it's not very far—I figured you'd prefer a
further trip, if you could get one."

Bert started his engine. "You know, Lucky, you're a
pretty decent guy."

Yeah, a prince, Laurence thought, but he didn't like
very much what he was thinking of doing.

~§~

There was a diner across from the motel. Laurence
made sure it was open, then went back to the motel. He
had to knock several times before Savannah came to the
door. She had simply pulled the sheet off the bed and
wrapped it around her naked body, and she stood in the
doorway, in the dim light of the rainy day, as blowsy and
seductive as any woman he'd ever seen. Her bruised and
swollen face only added pity to the confused mixture of
feelings she stirred in him.

She blinked, then managed a smile that matched
her sarcastic tone. "Hey, it's my knight in shining armor!
Come to claim your reward?"

"Knights in shining armor don't expect rewards,"
Laurence said. "I just thought you might like some
breakfast. There's a little place across the street that
looks like it could do some decent ham and eggs."

"I'd probably barf all over 'em," she said. "But coffee
would be okay. You bring my clothes last night?"

"They're on the chair," Lucky said. "I'll wait for you across the street."

He went into the diner and took a booth near the front, where he could watch for her. The waitress brought a menu and he asked for coffee. "We'll order breakfast when my friend gets here," he said. "What's good this morning?"

The waitress refused to crack a smile. "It's all the same every morning," she said. "Depends on what you want."

"Yes, I guess it does," Laurence said and watched her walk away. It was just as well she wasn't as friendly as Ginger—he was feeling guilty enough already. He picked up a discarded paper from the next booth and browsed through it until he saw Savannah coming across the street. She'd draped a bath towel over her head and shoulders to keep off the rain and she walked stiffly, as if her body hurt allover. The paper bag he'd given her last night was cradled under an arm—the last of her vodka, Laurence supposed. She came into the restaurant and slid into the booth next to Lucky.

"I'd a been here sooner, but I couldn't find my damn panties. You must've left 'em behind."

"Didn't know you wore any," he said, though he thought he remembered scooping up a lacy black thing last night. "How are you feeling?"

"How do you *think* I'm feeling? I'll feel a lot better if I can get some tomato juice to spike with this vodka."

Laurence signaled the waitress, who came and took their order. She looked hard at Savannah's bruises, but didn't comment. She also didn't ask about the contents of Savannah's paper bag but brought the coffee and tomato juice promptly.

"So let's talk about your boyfriend," Laurence said, when Savannah had fortified herself with some hair of the dog.

"Who, Frank?"

"No, Cool Johnny Combs. He's the fellow who got you in trouble with Frank, isn't he? How'd you get mixed up with him?"

"That's a long story," she said. "Where'd you hear about Johnny?"

"From the same source that provided the vodka you're drinking. Sid said you used to be one of Johnny's girls, and that he came by yesterday to pick you up. Thinking of going back into your old trade?"

She glared at him—as much as she could glare, with her battered eyes. "It ain't quite like that. I suppose Sid told you I've got some colored blood in me, too."

"Honey, all blood is colored," Lucky said. "I've got no problem with that. But if your friend Johnny got you started on hard drugs, you're gonna need more than coffee and bloody Marys to get straightened out."

"Naw, it was just some high-grade grass and several Beefeater martinis. I never messed with the hard stuff—and I never was one of Johnny's hookers, either. See, we grew up together in the same shitty neighborhood down in East St. Louis. Johnny was a friend of my brother's and he came back to visit a year or so ago. Put on a big show around the neighborhood, flashing his bankroll and gold jewelry. Told us he was a 'sportin' man' up north, where it was real easy to pass for white. Said he had connections in the music business and could help me get work—this was after he heard me sing at a local club—so I came on up and that's when I found out about Johnny's real line of work. Sure, he gambles and pushes a few drugs, but mostly he furnishes girls to some of the local hotels—you know, when they have a guest who wants that sort of thing—"

"Like the Cambridge?" Lucky asked.

"Yeah, I guess the Cambridge. Anyway, that's where I met Frank."

"You met Frank Holiday at the Cambridge? No kidding! So he knew you and Johnny were connected."

"Not really. Eddie King set it up. Johnny and Eddie do a lot of business—that's why Johnny thought he could get me some bookings. The only reason I agreed to date Frank Holiday was that they told me he was opening a night club and wanted a singer—I figured a girl's gotta get started somehow. Besides, he seemed like a nice guy, at first. It was a month or two before I found out what a creep he was—"

She broke off as the waitress approached with their breakfasts. Laurence had persuaded Savannah to try a little toast, which she nibbled at while he dug into his ham, eggs, and hash browns, thinking over what she'd told him. When he was done he signaled the waitress for more coffee, then lit a cigarette and peered at Savannah through the smoke.

"Honey, you wouldn't be the first singer to get her start in somebody's bed. I don't fault you for that. But you've been selling yourself too cheap, and if you go on letting guys like Frank Holiday use you for ass-wipe, you're going to have a very short career. Your friend Johnny sounds like he isn't much better. You need a decent manager—somebody who really knows the business, and who cares about what happens to you. Somebody who can keep away the sharks—"

"That's what I thought I had," she said, "when you

came onto me so strong the other night. Then all of a sudden you backed off, said you were 'too old for me' or some dumb shit like that. I figured Eddie must've been whispering tales in your ear. It pissed me off—"

"So the next day you went off with Johnny and got smashed. That wasn't very smart, you know. Johnny was just trying to get back at Frank, because Frank won't let him play at his table."

"Hey, some guys *like* me, you know? *Some* guys think I'm pretty hot stuff."

"I'm sure they do," Lucky said, "and I'm one of them. Why do you think I came back for you last night?"

She pondered that for a minute. "Because you felt sorry for me?"

"I felt a lot sorrier for myself, playing with that ragtag bunch of hayseeds Eddie King put together. But I knew I was partly to blame for what happened to you, and I couldn't leave you there for Frank Holiday to kick around. And I'll tell you something else—I missed you on the bandstand last night."

"You did?" He had put his hand on her knee and she said, "Hey, careful, pal—I haven't got any panties on, remember?" But the smile she gave him didn't seem to require that he remove his hand.

"I've been thinking it over," Lucky said. "We were beginning to make it click the other night—musically, I mean. Between the time you got sore at me and the time you got too drunk to carry a tune, we weren't half bad. Made me think maybe we ought to give it more of a shot."

"Where? Here in Madison?"

"I don't think Holiday would stand for that. We're probably washed up as a duo in this town. But I might be willing to take you down to Chicago, see what we could line up. Most of the guys I knew in the clubs along Rush Street have probably moved on . . . I couldn't make any promises, but we could give it a try, if you're interested."

"Of course I'm interested," she said, and took his hand, moving it a little higher on her leg. "I'd do anything for a shot at the big time, Lucky."

"Of course we'd need a stake," he said.

"A stake?"

"Something to live on while I look for work. Plus I've got some obligations here in Madison I want to take care of before I could go. I reckon it would take a couple of thousand, anyway, to make it work."

She sagged against the booth and released his hand. "Then I guess it isn't going to happen. I haven't got any money. Frank never gave me more than a few bucks at a time—afraid I'd run off on him, I guess. Hell, he's even got all my clothes out at his place."

"How about your friend, Johnny? Would he help us out?"

"Not to the tune of two thousand dollars. He may feel a little bad about what happened to me, but not *that* bad. Johnny's a businessman."

"And I've got a business proposition for him," Lucky said. "He doesn't like Frank Holiday and neither do I. Holiday won't play cards with a colored man, but he'll play cards with me. If Johnny could stake me—say, five hundred dollars—I could win what we need at the poker table and get some revenge in the bargain. Think he'd be interested?"

She smiled. "Yeah, I think he would—long as he knows you've got a good chance of winning."

"Honey, they don't call me 'Lucky' for nothing. Johnny can ask around town about me if he wants to—a lot of people remember I used to be pretty good. Now where can I find him? I've got a line on a big game—something Frank Holiday's sure to go for—but it has to be this evening."

"What is this, Sunday? Johnny doesn't do much on Sundays. Sometimes he goes to Shorty's for ribs, then sticks around for the jam session."

"I heard about those Sunday jams at Shorty's. What time to do they start?"

"Two or three—whenever folks show up. It's pretty informal—anybody who feels like joining in can have a chair. Mostly they play old-time jazz, New Orleans style."

"That's my favorite," Lucky said. "Can you ask Johnny to meet me there? Be good if you could come, too—that banged-up face of yours is likely to help our cause."

"I guess I can make it, if I can find my underpants. I could use an umbrella or a raincoat, too—it's getting damn chilly out there."

Laurence took out his wallet and gave her a ten-dollar bill. "I don't think there's any stores open today, but here, take a cab. Get yourself a little rest now and meet me there at three o'clock."

"You want me to keep the motel room for another night?"

"Sure, we're going to need it for one more night, at least."

"'We?'"

He paused, then met her eyes. "If this thing is going too fast for you, kid, you can always back away from it. I'm not saying we have to become sweethearts, but I can't spend another night with Ginger—not if I'm leaving her in the morning, that just don't seem right. Besides, I may wind up spending the night at the poker table."

She slipped an arm through his. "Listen pal, we can start using that motel bed right now, if you want to. Just go easy on me—I'm still pretty tender in a lot of places."

"I'll bet you are. Thanks, but I think I'll wait till we're sure this deal is going to pan out the way we want it to. I don't need any more bad debts. Besides, it might give me a little extra incentive—something else to play for, you know what I mean?"

She squeezed his arm. "Then you got it, pal—you got it. Hey, what happened to your ribs?"

Her arm had brushed the hollow place in his side. "Ah, that's another long story," Lucky said. "Maybe we'll save it for the train ride to Chicago."

~§~

Visiting hours at St. Mary's didn't start until two, but Laurence wasn't stopped as he past the nurses' station on the third floor. He was hoping for a little time alone with Leo before Maggie and Jack arrived—there was a whole lot he wanted to talk about. If anyone could talk sense to him, it was his kid brother. Leo had always had the good sense in the family, and Laurence would have been the first to admit that he should've listened to him more often over the years.

"Why can't you be more like your brother?" That was what his old mother used to ask, though Laurence knew she'd stuck up for him as best she could. Wasn't her fault that time Leo kicked him out. As long as she

had a place of her own, he'd been welcome to stay with her—the last time he'd had anything like a home, or even wanted one.

He walked into Leo's room, came around the screen and saw his brother stretched out on his bed with his eyes shut, as pale and still as a dead man. *My God, he's gone!* Laurence felt a sharp pang of loss—his last link to the old days, to the sweet world of childhood and all the things he used to be, broken! But with that thought there came also a sense of release, of wicked freedom, because now the last person in the world whose opinion really mattered to Laurence could no longer make him feel bad about the things he'd done—or might yet do.

And then Leo's eyes snapped open and the sky-blue gaze he fixed on Laurence was like a spotlight from the world beyond. For a moment Leo seemed to have the omniscient gaze of some eternal spirit—and then he smiled and the spell was broken.

"Larry—c'mon in! I was just taking a little nap."

"Sorry to disturb you," Laurence said. "I was just passing by the hospital, so I thought I'd drop in—"

"I'm glad you did. Jack and Maggie won't be out for an hour or so—we can have a nice, quiet talk. Want to crank up my bed?" As Laurence was doing so, he added, "I got some good news yesterday. I can go home on Tuesday."

"Say, that's great." Laurence pulled up a chair. "Clean bill of health?"

"Well, not exactly. Doc wants me to give up cigarettes and fatty foods, and I've got all these prescriptions I'm supposed to take . . . and no heavy work for six months. I can go back to my job in six weeks, if I have a job by then."

"That's one of the things I wanted to talk about," Laurence said. "I heard something today I thought might interest you. Fella I know met these three out-of-towners up at the Cambridge Hotel yesterday. Turns out they're with McGruder Industries, and they're hangin' around Madison this weekend to see what happens at the Oslo. What does that sound like to you?"

"Like McGruder's planning to buy us out—but there have been rumors to that effect for some time. Everybody knows the Oslo's in trouble. It stands to reason that this strike will hurt business, drive down the value of its stock and attract a competitor like McGruder. Sharks always smell blood in the water."

"The union knows that, and they're still going out on strike?"

"Well, there's a lot of bad feeling against the company just now. Some of the men probably think a new owner would do a better job of running the company than the present bunch of old cronies."

"But what if McGruder intends to close the place down and move all its business to Kansas City?"

"Then we'll all be out of work," Leo said. "Except for the big shots and maybe some of the managers—they'll get nice, cushy jobs with the home office. If the men *knew* that McGruder was waiting in the wings, all set to buy us out and maybe shut down the plant, that *might* make a difference."

"Can't you call somebody?" Laurence asked. "The tip I got came straight from the horse's mouth, Leo. I think it's solid."

"Could be it is, but I don't have many friends in the union these days—not since I got booted upstairs. Most of the guys think of me as management now, since I do

the payroll. I wish I'd never accepted that damn promotion, Larry. My life hasn't been the same since."

"Well, I'll leave it up to you," Laurence said. "Seems
a shame to let it happen, though—unless you *want* to
look for a new job."

"I may not have a choice," Leo said. "The doc says
it's probably the job—the long hours and the stress—that
brought on my attack. He wants me to ask the company
for reassignment—if there *is* any company to ask, after
next week." He was silent for a moment, and Laurence
could see him thinking. You could always tell when Leo
was making a decision, because the muscles in his jaw
twitched.

"I guess I owe it to the men," he said finally. "They
probably won't believe me, but I'll call somebody.
Thanks, Larry. It's too bad the *Cap Times* doesn't know
about this. A little bad publicity would put a lot of
pressure on the company—they might back away from
the deal."

Laurence knew *The Capitol Times* was the more
liberal of Madison's two newspapers. Its reporters often
hung out at the Cambridge, looking for a hot tip or
maybe some dirt on the politicians who stayed at the
hotel when the Legislature was in session. Some of those
reporters were sporting types, and Lucky wondered if
any of his old cronies were still on the beat.

"Maybe that can be arranged," he said. "But you
know, Leo, I agree with the doc, for what it's worth. Find
yourself an easier job. You need to ease up a bit if you're
going to make it to retirement."

"That's easier said than done," Leo said. "I've got
Maggie and Jack to think about—and Jack starts college
next year. Besides, a guy my age can't change careers

that easily—but I guess you know all about that."

Laurence nodded. This was the point at which he could bring up his own problems, if he wanted to. He could tell Leo all about it and get his honest opinion—but before he could find a way into that topic, Leo brought up another.

"You know, I've had a lot of time for thinking this past week, Larry. I guess I've relived my whole life twenty times and worked it out twenty different ways. But there's one episode I keep going back to—one week, really, that's all it was. I wonder if you remember it, too?"

"Was I there?" Laurence asked.

"Not exactly, but you were part of it. Remember, back about 1927—the second or third year we took the band up north—we arrived at the Eagle Waters Resort in early June to find the place had gone out of business?"

"Yeah, I remember that," Laurence said. "Feds busted their speak and put the owners in jail. We were booked in for three weeks' and had nothing else scheduled until later in July. We thought we could line up more dates while we were still at the Eagle, but we were shit out of luck—six musicians with no money and no work."

"Yes, and do you recall what we did about it?"

"Well, let's see. We talked about going home, but it was a helluva long drive in those days, and we would've had to come back up north in July . . . I think we decided to split up for awhile."

"That's right. You and Earl Clevinger were supposed to take the touring car and all the cash we had between us and go out in search of more bookings. The other four of us were going to hide out in the woods for a week, live off the land like hobos, and wait for your return. I don't mind telling you, Larry, I was plenty nervous about that. I figured you'd take that money to some damn poker game and lose it all, and that we'd wind up stranded in the north woods—"

"But it didn't happen that way, did it?" Laurence asked, remembering it now. "We got the bookings, two or three of 'em anyway, and came back for you at the end of the week. You were the sorriest looking crew of wood-rats I ever did see!"

Leo laughed. "Yes, I suppose we were. But I loved that week in the woods. We had a couple of pup tents, and we pitched them on the shore of the prettiest little lake I ever saw in my life. We had just a few provisions— coffee, matches, salt, flour—and some fishing tackle. We caught plenty of fish, found some nuts and berries in the woods, and Bill Jensen even shot a grouse with a sling shot. It was a pretty good life, all in all—like something out of *Robinson Crusoe* or *Huckleberry Finn* . . ."

When Laurence looked blank, Leo added, "You know, survival in the wilderness, that type of thing. I guess northern Wisconsin wasn't quite a wilderness in 1927, but it came pretty close. There wasn't much up there in those days but scrub pines and poplars, and of course lakes teeming with fish . . ."

"So you had a good time," Laurence said. "You ought to do more of that kind of thing. Learn how to relax—this is your big chance."

Leo smiled at the thought. "I'd like to take Jack fishing this fall and go camping with him next summer— it's been a while since we've done that sort of thing."

"Don't miss the chance," Laurence said. "Jack's a good boy, but he needs the things you can give him, Leo.

He needs a dad."

"I'm aware of that," Leo said, "and I'm going to take more time for him, and Maggie, too. But you know, I keep going back to that week in the woods—how quiet and peaceful it was, how close I felt to something at the heart of life. It was the best week of my life, Larry—I was almost sorry when you came to get us."

Laurence laughed. "So I could have lost that money playing poker, after all! You see, Leo, bad habits have their uses. You've spent your whole life wishing you could've stayed out there in the woods, whereas me, I've never left them."

Leo obviously didn't like this interpretation; his brow furrowed and the muscles in his jaw twitched. "I wouldn't call your kind of life 'living in the woods,' Larry. A man's got to make certain choices in this life— he's got to own up to his responsibilities."

Laurence sighed. He could see that Leo would never escape the yoke he'd placed around his neck. No number of heart attacks would ever force him to give up his precious conscience. And he also knew this wasn't where he wanted to turn for advice.

"Well, you're right, Leo—of course you're right. A man does have to make choices, but sometimes those choices aren't as easy and obvious as they look. How does he know when he's doing the right thing?"

"He knows," Leo said. "Deep inside, he knows."

Laurence looked at his brother with sadness, and pity, and also an undiminished admiration. You came out of the woods at your peril, he saw. You came out and they caught you, and then they put a yoke around your neck and set you to work plowing their fields, and you were theirs for the rest of your life. He got to his feet.

"Well, Leo, I've got to be going. I hope everything goes well for you once you get home. Remember the doctor's orders—take it easy."

Leo took the hand Laurence offered but looked up at him with puzzlement. "But we'll be seeing you again, won't we, Larry? We'll call you about coming out for dinner one of these evenings after I get home."

"Sure," Laurence said, "sure, but I'll be moving to my own place soon. I'll let you know my new number." And he made his escape from the hospital room before Leo could ask any more questions. He felt as if he'd gotten the advice and clarification he'd come for—not from Leo directly, but from deep inside himself. It was just like Leo said: deep down inside you always knew the right choice.

15.

Struttin' with Some Barbeque

LAURENCE picked up his guitar and left Ginger a brief note. It was only a few blocks from Ginger's apartment to Shorty's, which turned out to be another place he knew well. When he first came to Madison, the ramshackle old building next to the switch yards had been a boarding house for railway-men with a speakeasy in its basement. Later it became Luigi's Spaghetti House, and Chicago gangsters used to stop for dinner on their way up north. During the war it was the Mustang Lounge, a servicemen's club where Lucky and his High Flyers played a record thirty-straight Saturday nights. 1943, one of his best years in the business. In those days you could always get a room upstairs for a few hands of poker or a quiet tête-à-tête with a lady, and Lucky figured you still could, even though the neighborhood had changed its complexion since the war and Shorty's now served southern and Creole specialties.

"*Sundays: All You Can Eat for $1.50,*" said the sign at the door. Below that another, smaller sign: "*Jam Session Today, 2-5.*"

It wasn't yet two, but a sizeable crowd had already gathered in the big, barn-like hall. Lucky saw a few white faces—old-time jazz fans, or college kids from the campus neighborhoods across the tracks—but the majority of Shorty's customers were black. Large family groups all decked out in their Sunday best, as if they'd just come in from their morning church services, Grandpa and Grandma and all the kids. Lucky hung his dripping raincoat on a peg near the door and took a small table near the bandstand. A crew of waiters were still delivering platters of fried chicken and barbecued ribs to the surrounding tables, but he wasn't hungry after his big breakfast. A beer would have been nice, but he ordered a Coca-Cola and a bag of peanuts, hoping that would hold him until supper.

The trick, he saw, would be getting through tonight's game without taking a drink. If he could do that, he could do all the things he wanted to do and never go back on the bottle. But if he couldn't, it wouldn't much matter whether he won or lost at the table, because he'd still come out the biggest loser of all. Of course *one beer* wouldn't make or break him, and maybe the day would come when he could have a beer with his meal and not worry about what it might lead to, but for the time being he'd stick to soda pop.

Two o'clock came and the first musician to approach the bandstand was Papa Lester Holmes, who had to be well over eighty and so crippled with rheumatism he could barely climb the short flight of steps. Once seated at the battered upright piano, Papa uncurled the fingers of a much younger man, thick and strong, with knobby knuckles and powerful tendons rippling the backs of his large hands. He strolled through a few down-home rags at an easy pace, as if he wanted to give folks plenty of time to digest their dinners. Meanwhile his nephew, young Tyrone Holmes (who wasn't so young anymore, Lucky saw), was setting up his drums, and by the time he'd built his little fortress of bass drum, high hat, and assorted skins, Henry Washington had arrived on the bandstand and taken out his instrument. A few toots and Lucky could tell that Henry's comet still had its pure golden tone. Tyrone ripped off an extended drum roll and the trio jumped into their first number, "When the Saints Go Marching In."

As if summoned from their graves, other elderly musicians, both black and white, now came out of the audience, crossed the dance floor, and took their places around the piano. Lucky recognized most of them: Charley Cooper, a solid trombonist when he wasn't on the sauce, and Fatso Hogan, the only guy in town who still played a jazz tuba. And there was Kenny Sloan, whose banjo was even livelier than Lucky's in his prime, and Sid Martin, always a reliable sax man. With each new arrival the music grew in volume and density, the pace quickened, the many voices merged and blended, the old jazz numbers came alive: "Down by the Riverside". . . "Way Down Yonder in New Orleans" . . . "Back Home in Indiana."

By now Lucky was tapping his foot and itching to join in, but no one had noticed him sitting at his little table against the wall and he decided to wait for an invitation. These fellows had been jamming together for years and they didn't need his feeble contribution. Then big Bill Williams, who was just setting up his base fiddle, saw Lucky and motioned him to come on up. Lucky took his guitar from beneath his chair and joined the others around the piano. He got a few nods, a smile and a wink, even a couple of hand-slaps. "Hey, man, grab a chair," Henry said. "We ain't got no leader here. One guy jus' picks a tune and runs with it, and then the rest of us join in. You feel like takin' a chorus, you jus' stand up and take one."

"Sounds good to me," Lucky said, and perched on a stool.

He knew his cheap little guitar couldn't make itself heard in the full ensemble, but that was all right, he was happy just being part of it, sitting in with his kind of musicians, playing his kind of music. These guys had been playing in jazz bands for most of their lives, and they all knew how to add those little touches, those harmonies and counter-melodies, that enriched and filled out the sound. This was the way jazz was supposed to be played, Lucky thought—not as a raucous slugfest of oversexed adolescents, but a free-flowing collaboration of savvy old pros.

By now most of the people in the big room had finished their dinners and were sitting back to enjoy the music. They were a good audience—not jabbering among themselves or trying to out-shout the musicians, but listening to each number with soft smiles and half-closed eyes, sometimes nodding as if they really appreciated what the musicians were doing. And Lucky strummed along through some of his favorite numbers: "Riverboat Shuffle," "High Society," "Struttin' with Some Barbecue"—all the great old Dixieland tunes, though he knew there were those in this group who didn't like that term. "Dixieland" was what white musicians called it, and here they'd rather call it New Orleans jazz, or Chicago jazz, or maybe even Kansas City jazz, but it was all the same music, with the same heart and soul, no matter what name it went by or what color skin the musicians wore.

Papa Holmes took a solo chorus on "Royal Garden Blues," and now that he was fully warmed up and maybe felt a bit challenged by the younger musicians, he put on a display of "stride piano" that had the others standing around to watch his large hands flying over the stained and chipped keyboard. Being a piano-man himself, Lucky was perhaps best suited to appreciate the virtuosity and power the old man displayed. Not a beat was missed, not a note slurred; it was a disciplined outpouring of energy and passion. And just so no one might think it was done by rote—the same tune played the way Papa had played it for fifty years—he took another chorus in an entirely different style, doing all new things, variations and inventions springing from his nimble fingers like water from a fountain.

Now that's what music is, Lucky thought—a fountain of pure fresh water from somewhere deep inside a person's soul. He himself had never tapped a well as deep and pure as Papa Lester's. He'd never had as much power in his fingers, not even in his younger days, nor had he achieved the degree of skill Papa displayed. Maybe he hadn't worked hard enough at it, or maybe he hadn't given up enough (though it seemed to him that he had given up a great deal over the course of his life) but mostly, he thought, it was just a matter of talent. He lacked the passion, the heart, the soulful genius that distinguished the old man's music.

Laurence had never believed that jazz, great jazz, was the exclusive property of anyone group of people, but he could see that, however you explained it, there were fountains and then there were fountains. Some produced a towering pillar of steaming spray, others a mere tepid trickle. As an artist, Lucky Lantz was more of a trickler than a geyser, a guy who got what he could from his limited resources, but even that was nothing to be ashamed of. Because underneath the surface of every man's life there ran an underground river of love and death and lost hopes, and every musician tapped into it as best he could. If you could tap it for as much as a trickle, you'd never die of thirst.

The audience was still applauding Papa Lester's solo when somebody said, "Nellie's here," and then somebody else said, "Hey Nellie, get on up here!" And then the crowd began to clap and Lucky saw the large black woman who had made his sandwich at the grocery store come out of the audience and approach the piano. She was wearing a bright orange dress with ruffles and flounces galore, and she seemed to have recaptured the glow and spirit of her youth. "Well, I see you found us," she said to Lucky.

"I sure enough did, darlin'. I'm having a ball up here."

She turned to Papa Holmes. "How about a little 'Big Butter and Egg Man'—you up to that one, Lester?"

"I'm your man," Papa said, and hopped into it.

Nellie still had her voice. She belted out that number with the same lusty, gutsy force she'd always given it, and Henry and the boys knew her phrasing, knew just when to sidle in and when to stand aside. The crowd loved it; there were cheers and whistles to spike the applause, and one big black woman stood up and bellowed, "You tell 'em, sister!"

"Oh, I'll tell 'em, honey, but they won't believe me,"

Nellie said. Tyrone did a drum roll and Charley's trombone gave a horselaugh. The crowd laughed, and Lucky thought, *Now this is how it ought to be—good-time music for good-time folks.* The world had enough trouble and sorrow. When people had a chance to enjoy themselves, they needed the right kind of music to make it happen—his kind of music. Lucky's blues.

Of course there had to be sad songs, and Nellie could sing those, too. She sang a moody, lonesome "All By Myself," and then a feisty, furious "One of These Days." But she finished her set with another rouser, an old Ethel Waters number, "My Handy Man."

> *He shakes my ashes, greases my griddle,*
> *Churns my butter, smokes my vittles,*
> *My man is such a handy man!*

As Nellie was taking her bows and blowing kisses to her fans, Lucky spotted Savannah in the audience. *Good timing, gal.* If anyone could teach Savannah how to belt out the blues, it was old Nellie Hopkins.

Savannah was sitting with a slender, handsome young man with light brown skin, a pencil-thin moustache, and straightened, shiny black hair. He wore a cream-colored summer suit with a black shirt and pink tie, and there was a gold watch chain on his vest, a pink carnation in his buttonhole. He had the regal air of a man who had women lined up and waiting for his call, and Laurence figured this was the fellow he'd come to meet. He left the bandstand and crossed the room to Savannah's table.

Savannah had disguised her bruises with some powder and make-up, but still had a noticeable shiner and a puffy face. "This how you spend your day off?" she asked him. "Jamming with a bunch of broken-down old musicians?"

"Honey, these old-timers have a lot to teach us." He turned to the young man. "I'll bet you're the fella they call 'Cool Johnny.' I'm Lucky Lantz."

Cool Johnny looked Lucky over with a gambler's eyes—not black, but amber, with slightly clouded whites. He moved his toothpick from one corner of his mouth to the other and stuck out his chin. "I hear you want to talk to me, Lantz. So speak your mind—I'm a busy man."

"I appreciate that," Lucky said. "Maybe Savannah mentioned that I've got a proposition for you—a business proposition. There's a fellow here in town I think you know—a gambler by the name of Frank Holiday—"

"Yeah, I know the motherfuck," Johnny said, and looked as if he would have spit on the floor if he hadn't been too well-bred. "What about him?"

"I hear he won't play poker with a man if he doesn't like the color of his skin. Is that what you heard?"

"Yeah, I heard something about that. Lotta white folks feel that way—so what?"

"So he's also happens to be the guy who messed up this lady's face, you know that, too, don't you?"

Johnny looked at Savannah. "She ain't one of my ladies no more, so I ain't responsible for her . . . but yeah, I see what he done. Mean sumbitch, ain't he? What you aim to do about it, Lantz?"

"I'd like to take his money away from him," Lucky said. "That interest you?"

"Sure, it interest me, if I get some of it."

"That's the general idea," Lucky said. "I can take Holiday at poker, but I need a stake—one large enough to keep me going until I can get a handle on his game. I figure a thousand bucks ought to do it."

Johnny stared at him. "And you want me to give it to you? *Shee-yit!* Do I look like I just got here from the farm?"

"You can ask around about me," Lucky said. "I used to have quite a reputation in this town."

"I already done that. Folks I talked to say you were good enough, in your time, but they also say you been out of circulation for quite a few years. How do I know you ain't lost your touch?"

"You don't know that," Lucky said. "That's where your gamble comes in. You bet on me, I bet on the cards. If I win, you get your thousand back, plus ten percent of my winnings. If I lose, you get to stomp on my face."

Johnny sneered. "You think I wouldn't?"

"I'm sure you would. That's why I don't intend to lose. Anyway, this will be a six-handed game. If I can't beat Frank Holiday, there'll be somebody else I can beat. I won't lose my stake, Johnny—not with Eddie King at the table."

"Eddie King? That dumb-ass lard-ball!" Combs thought it over. "Okay, but five hundred's my limit. You lose five hundred, I won't have to stomp on your face— just break a few fingers. And I want a quarter of your winnings."

"Fair enough," Lucky said, figuring a quarter would be whatever he said it was. He hadn't expected to get a full thousand out of Johnny. Five hundred would do. With the five hundred he already had, it was a sufficient stake. You could play a lot of poker with a thousand dollars.

Johnny peeled five C-notes off his roll and Lucky

put them in his wallet. "Now, there's another thing you might be able to help me with—"

"And why should I do that?" Johnny asked.

"Well, let's just say you're protecting your investment. This game is being held in one of the suites at the Cambridge Hotel—three fat cats rolled in yesterday and they're looking for action. I can get Frank and Eddie up there, but I may have some trouble getting into the place myself. You see, the house dick is an old enemy of mine."

"Tom Cotter? I guess I can take care of him," Johnny said. "My ladies work the Cambridge from time to time. Cotter's got a soft spot for one of 'em. Tell me what time you want to show up and I'll make sure he's otherwise occupied."

"That's just what I was hoping," Lucky said. "If Cotter's out of the way between seven and eight, that ought to give me time to get the game rolling. I don't care if he comes back later in the evening—in fact, I'd just as soon he did."

"So how do you get out of there with your winnings —assuming you got any winnings to get out with?"

"I've got a plan for that. I used to work at the Cambridge, and I'll have a friend waiting for me in a taxi in the alley. You and I can settle up tomorrow at the Milwaukee Road depot, before Savannah and I leave on the 10:15 for Chicago."

She squeezed his arm. "Sounds great, lover, but how do I get my clothes from Frank's house? I can't go to Chicago wearing this one crummy outfit—and no under-pants!"

"Johnny can take you out there this evening while Frank and Eddie are at the Cambridge. Then he can bring you back to the motel and I'll meet you there after the game."

Johnny's eyes narrowed. "You got me runnin' all over town for you, don't you, Lantz? I used to takin' orders from no honky—"

"Hey, you owe me on this one," Savannah told him. "If you hadn't got me so damn stoned yesterday, Frank never woulda beat up on me so bad. And who fixed me up with the creep in the first place?"

"Okay, okay," Johnny said. "But I'd better see you at the Milwaukee Road station tomorrow morning, Lantz, or I'll know where to find you. You won't want to hang around this town owin' me money."

"I don't intend to," Lucky said, and it suddenly struck him as sad and predictable: one week in his old hometown and already he'd had enough. When would he ever find a place where he could settle down and grow old gracefully, like a normal human being? He shook off the dreary feeling and turned to Savannah. "So how do I get a hold of Holiday on a Sunday afternoon?"

"He'll be at his home number," she said. "It's unlisted, but I can write it down for you." She found a pen in her purse and wrote the number on a napkin.

Lucky took it and stood up to go. "If there's a problem, I'll call you at the motel and you can let Johnny know the deals' off. Otherwise I'll see you sometime after midnight—don't wait up."

"I'll keep your bed warm, lover," she said, and blew him a kiss. "Win big."

Win big or lose big, Lucky thought, *sometimes it was hard to tell the difference. All you could do was place your bet and wait for the cards.*

The jam session was still going strong and he didn't want to call from the restaurant, so he got into his raincoat, picked up his guitar, and set out through a cold drizzle for the Milwaukee Road depot. Along Regent Street he found a phone booth and huddled inside, shutting the door against the chill wind. He dropped a dime in the slot and dialed the number on the napkin. It took several rings before Frank Holiday's gruff voice came on the line.

"Hi Frank, this is Lucky Lantz."

"Lantz, you broken down Padarewski, I want some words with you. Where's that piece of trash you took home with you last night?"

"I didn't take her home with me, Frank. I just put her where you can't beat up on her. You see, she doesn't want to be your singer anymore. She's taking her career in another direction."

"She can take it straight to hell, for all I care," Holiday said. "I got no use for the lyin' little bitch, but I'm not in the habit of letting my employees walk off with my property—it sets a bad example for the rest of the staff."

"You've got a funny notion of property, Frank. Slavery went out about a hundred years ago, I hear. And by the way, I'm no longer one of your employees, either. I quit last night."

"Then you owe me two hundred dollars, chum."

"I know I do, and I've got a plan for paying you back. You in the mood for a little poker tonight?"

Holiday's voice changed. "I'm always in the mood for poker. Who wants to play?"

"Three fat cats from out of town—big shots with MacGruder Industries. They're stuck in Madison over the weekend and eager for some action. Sound interesting?"

"Of course it does. Bring 'em out to the Blue Swan. We're closed tonight, so it'll be nice and quiet in the back room. Drinks on the house."

"Sorry, that's not what they want. They've got a suite at the Cambridge and they want to hold the game up there. I suppose they're a little cautious, being out-of-towners, but they're loaded, Frank, and ripe for the picking. I'm giving you a hot tip here."

"Yeah, and how do you come by this information?"

"I've got a lot of friends in this town, you know that. Also connections at the Cambridge—I used to work there in the old days."

"Yeah, Eddie said you used to be a bellhop. You gonna be in this game, too?"

"I thought I might sit in for a few hands, just to see how it goes—till you guys drive me out, of course. I can't go real high on the bets, you understand."

"You'll be playing with my money, so you'd *better* have a good night. Otherwise, you and Eddie will have a few words when the game's over."

"Oh, you bringing Eddie along?" Lucky asked innocently.

"I expect he'll want in," Frank said. "But first we gotta meet these guys, set some house rules. I don't play with no candy-ass, penny-ante types. And no cry-babies, either. I play a man's game."

"I know you do, Frank, and that's what these fellows are looking for—good honest poker. Why don't we all meet in the Cambridge bar about seven tonight so we can get acquainted and lay down the rules? If you don't like their looks, or you can't agree on the game, you don't have to stick around."

"Sounds all right," Holiday said. "But this better not

be a set-up, Lantz. Eddie says you're a sneaky son of a bitch. If you try to pull a fast one on me, it'll be the last goddamn stunt you ever pull on anybody, you hear me?"

"I hear you, Frank. Loud and clear. You tell Eddie I appreciate the good word—I'll try to make sure he gets a little something out of the evening, too."

He hung up and was at the taxi stand just after five. Bert was waiting in his cab.

"All set," Lucky said, and explained his arrangement with Frank Holiday. "If these McGruder fellas have made other plans in the meantime, let me know at this number—" he gave him Ginger's telephone number— "and we'll call the whole thing off."

"What else are three out-of-towners gonna do on a Sunday night?" Bert asked. "They'll be rarin' to go, but say, do you really think you can hang in there with these guys? You ain't been in a high-stakes game like this for a long time, have you?"

"Too long," Lucky said. "I figure I'll need a couple of hours to get rolling. If I'm not raking in the chips by midnight, I'll know I'm in big trouble. In fact, I may be in trouble anyway—Eddie King's a sore loser and Frank Holiday's not the sort to let anyone walk off with his money. A little diversion might come in handy. Can you raise the cops on that two-way radio of yours?"

"Oh sure, no problem—I know their frequency. But what the hell—you want a raid on your own poker game?"

"It's not my game," Lucky said. "Let the big shots take the heat, and the hotel, too. I owe those bastards one. Anyway, it might not be necessary. You'd better start checking the alley behind the hotel about eleven. Come back every fifteen minutes or so—can you do that?"

"Hell, on a Sunday I could sit there all night."

"If I'm not down to meet you by twelve thirty, put in the call. Tell 'em there's a high-stakes game in progress in one of the top-floor suites. Mention that there's drugs and weapons on the premises, that ought to get them moving. Then sit tight—I'll be down as soon as I can."

"And what if you can't get out of the hotel in time?"

"I used to work there, Bert. I'll get out, and I'll make sure I have something for you, too. That goes without saying."

He started to get out of the cab, then had to stop for a prolonged spell of coughing. It occurred to him that he'd been coughing a lot today—it must have been the cold, wet weather. That was always tough on the old lung.

Bert said, "Hey buddy, you're soaking wet! Can I take you someplace?"

"Yeah, I guess it's time to go home and face the music," Lucky said, and he gave him Ginger's address.

16.

Dealer's Choice

GINGER was in the living room, reading the Sunday paper with her shoes off and feet up, but Laurence could tell she was wound up tight and ready to pounce. "So where have you been all afternoon?" she asked, her voice a shade too bright, her eyes aglitter behind the paper.

Her portable TV was on—some variety show. Laurence sat down across from her and couldn't help noticing how misshapen her bare feet were—bunions and corns, the consequence of all those years behind the counter. He appreciated her kindness and didn't want to hurt her, but there was no point in dragging it out. The sooner he got out of here, the better.

"I left you a note," he said. On the little TV, a man in a shiny suit was juggling plates and cups and knives.

"Some note," she said. "'Home around five'—you call that an explanation?"

He looked at his watch. "So, it's five thirty. I don't have to explain anything. I think maybe you've gotten the wrong idea about us, Ginger."

She flared up. "Oh, I think I've got the idea, all right!

You eat my food, you sleep in my bed, and you do as you damn please. Is that it?"

"I need my freedom," he said, not bothering to point out that he'd taken her out to dinner Friday night and brought home a few groceries earlier in the week. "If you can't put up with the way I am, then I guess it's time for me to move on."

She stared at him for a moment, and he saw that what he'd taken for the glitter of anger was actually the first bubbling up of tears. "You bastard," she said, and the tears began to trickle down her cheeks. "Go on, get out of here then—see if I care!"

She hid her face in her hands—large, work-roughened hands—and he resisted the impulse to go to her, to put his arm around her and tell her he was sorry. Women always pulled this weepy stuff on a guy. You had to harden yourself against it. On the TV screen, the juggler had switched to flaming torches.

"Look," he said, "you've been good to me, but I've been a bachelor most of my life. The woman I married, she wasn't much of a wife, and I wasn't much of a husband, so I never really got the hang of married life. Maybe I'd be a happier man if I had, but it's too late now. You can't teach an old dog new tricks."

She took a Kleenex from the box beside her and dabbed at her eyes, and he saw several crumpled tissues on the floor. He sensed there was something else, something she hadn't accused him of yet, even before she took a pair of black lace panties out from under the sofa cushion.

"I guess this old dog still knows all his old tricks," she said and flung them at him. "I found those in your jacket pocket this morning."

Laurence caught the panties inches from his face, along with a hint of Savannah's distinctive scent. He tossed them aside. "I suppose you want to know where they came from?" He could've asked her why the hell she'd been going through his pockets, but he decided to let that one pass. Maybe she deserved an explanation.

"I don't really give a damn," she said. "I know a whore's panties when I see them, and I can guess whose butt they came off."

"Frank Holiday beat her up," Laurence said, "and left her in a cabin behind the Blue Swan. I had to get her out of there, so I stuck her in a motel for the night. She was too drunk to get dressed, so I brought along her clothes and left them there—I guess I forgot that particular item."

"It'll make a nice souvenir," she said. "You must have had some night, an old buck like you with a young piece of tail like that!"

"Actually, it was murder," Laurence said. "Frank made me play with his house band—those friggin' Hot Rods. You want to hear four guys murder a tune, you should hear them. I was in no mood for sex after that, believe me."

Ginger softened a bit, as if she almost did believe him. "You knew what you were getting into. I told you not to take that job, didn't I?"

"Yes, babe, you told me."

"I suppose you've started drinking again, too."

"No," Laurence said, "I haven't. But your fussing over me won't keep me from it. You don't seem to hear what I've been telling you. I can't change the way I am."

"You're goddamn right you can't," Ginger said. "Guys like you never change. I should've known that the first morning you walked into the diner with that ass-kissing look on your face. You ain't just a musician, Lucky. You're a loser. You can't help losing, because you love it so goddamn much."

"And you know all about winning?" he asked her, more stung by her words than he wanted to admit.

"Well, I sure as hell know more than you," she said, and picked up her newspaper, as if their conversation was at an end.

The juggler on TV had been replaced by dogs riding bicycles. He watched for a moment, thinking the feat only slightly more difficult than the things he was required to do. You tried to be nice to people, to show them a good time, and they wound up thinking they owned you. Worse, they even thought they understood you.

At least Ginger wasn't crying anymore, so this seemed like an opportune moment for a get-away. "I'll go pack my bag," he said, and rose from his chair.

He had unpacked only a few things, so there wasn't much he had to replace in the suitcase. Still, he hadn't quite finished folding his shirts when she came into the bedroom and stood behind him with her arms crossed. "So where will you go?" she asked.

"I'll find a place," he said.

"With her?"

"Maybe. First I've got a score to settle with Frank and Eddie."

"A score? What do you mean by that? You're going to play cards with them, aren't you?" And then, when he didn't answer: "Jesus, Lucky—you *are* a loser!"

He spun around. "Look, babe, you call me that one more time and I'll—"

He was caught by a sudden spasm of coughing and had to sit down on the bed. She looked down at him sadly. He turned away from her, his face in his handkerchief, and waited for the spasm to subside.

"You'd better stay here tonight," she said. "It's cold and rainy out there—not a good night for you to be trudging the streets with your bum lungs."

"I'll be all right," he said. He was glad to see there was no blood in his handkerchief and put it away. "What you don't understand about me, Ginger, is that I do win at cards. It's the one weapon I have against guys who are bigger than me, tougher and richer, too. I may be a loser in most ways, but I can beat Frank Holiday at poker and I'm going to do it."

"Why? What will that accomplish?"

"It'll get me off the hook, for one thing. I owe the bastard two hundred dollars—four nights' work—and I'll be damned if I'm going back to the Blue Swan, not after last night. The little fucker humiliated me, Ginger. He made me share the bandstand with those no-talent greasers, made me play along with them, as if I really thought that crap they spewed out their hind ends was music—"

"Hey, some people like that kind of music," Ginger said. "Just because it doesn't appeal to you—"

"If it doesn't appeal to me, it's garbage. Listen, I've spent thirty-five years as a musician. It's the one thing I know, the one thing I've got to be proud of in this stupid, fucked-up mess of a life, and if I can't tell a good band from a rotten one, or real music from phony schlock, I ought to quit."

"I thought you *had* quit!" she said and walked out of the room.

He finished packing his suitcase, then took the coin purse from the lining of his guitar and transferred the bills to his wallet, where they made a considerable wad. He hadn't had a wallet this thick in years. Over a thousand bucks cradled between two thin pieces of leather, and all his to win or lose.

So what if he just took off with this bankroll? The easy way out, always the first thing he thought of—just take the money and run. But there was no satisfaction in that. He was determined, for once, to do things right, to payoff his debts and honor his obligations. Then he'd be a free man.

That's all a man needs, Laurence thought, buckling the straps that secured his suitcase. *Freedom. I got plenty a' nothin', and nothin' is plenty for me!*

Even without his box of shoe-repair tools, the suitcase was too heavy to lug all the way to the train station, so he called for a cab and then waited at the bottom of the stairs. He half expected Ginger to come down and try to talk him out of leaving, and maybe he almost wished that she would, but she didn't, and eventually the headlights of the taxi came up the alley. Laurence dragged his suitcase outside and the driver helped him get it in the trunk. He thought he saw Ginger watching out the window as the cab backed out of the alley.

~§~

At the Milwaukee Road station he got a baggage trolley and wedged first his suitcase and then his guitar into one of their large lockers. Then he purchased two tickets to Chicago and reserved two seats on tomorrow's 10:15 express. They cost $10.50 a piece, but if there was one thing he knew about playing poker with guys like Eddie King, it was the wisdom of setting up a quick exit in advance. Of course you never knew what chance was going to throw in your way, but that was all part of the fun, the excitement, of a big game. He hadn't realized how much he'd missed that sort of thing, but now he knew. His blood was humming—it had been humming all day.

He had a sandwich at the station and then walked through the rain up West Washington Avenue toward the Capitol Square. Illuminated by floodlights, the big gray dome of the state capitol glowed dimly in the dusk, a gigantic iceberg riding on a mist-covered sea. Headlights and neon signs swam on the wet pavement like rainbow-colored eels, and Lucky felt the cold drizzle penetrate his cheap raincoat, sending shivers down his spine. More than once he paused to cough into his handkerchief.

He walked past the Cambridge Hotel on the other side of the street and saw there was no doorman on duty tonight. Just as well—he wouldn't want old Ernie to get in trouble because of him, and he had a hunch everybody on duty at the Cambridge tonight would be in a peck of trouble by morning.

The cocktail lounge had a separate entrance on Fairchild Street. It was still a few minutes before seven and Bert's cab was parked just up the block, though Eddie's Cadillac and Frank's black Mercury were nowhere in sight. Good—Lucky wanted a chance to get acquainted with his three lambs before the lions arrived on the scene. He entered the lounge and saw Bert sitting with three men at a table near the back. The place was quiet, as usual on a Sunday evening—just a bartender, waitress, and a couple of guests with nowhere else to go. Lucky strolled up to their table and Bert said, "Here he is—the guy I was telling you about. This is my friend, Lucky Lantz."

Bert was drinking a beer. The three out-of-towners were drinking cocktails—a martini, a Manhattan, and what looked like scotch and soda. Lucky pulled up a chair. "Howdy, fellas. Bert tells me you've got an evening to kill."

"That's right," the scotch-drinker said. He was a tall, lean man in his forties with straight dark hair and a handsome, sharply chiseled face—a poker player's face that would show no more than he wanted it to. "We were thinking of a little card game, and Bert says you're the man who can help us out. My name's Ducaine, Cal Ducaine. These are my associates, Charley Thorpe and Ray Spaulding."

Lucky shook hands with each of the three, registering their characters through their smiles and their grips. Ducaine was clearly the ringleader, a strong, confident man used to asserting his authority and obliging other men to surrender on his terms. Not an easy mark, by any means, but if you lulled him with some easy victories, you might take him by surprise. He wouldn't expect much resistance from the likes of Lucky.

Charley Thorpe was short and chubby, with curly reddish-brown hair. He seemed the most relaxed and friendly of the trio, with a quick grin and affable manner—probably not a regular gambler and not likely to stick it out when the going got tough. Guys like Thorpe were easy to bluff, but you had to be careful not to scare them off too early. A few good hands and he'd start playing reckless poker at least until he'd lost a lot of money.

Ray Spaulding was something else again. A dry little man with a few scraps of graying hair on his otherwise shiny dome, an accountant's thick glasses and a scruffy little moustache, he seemed particularly tense, as if he suspected already that he'd fallen among thieves. *A nervous Nellie,* Lucky thought. He hated playing cards with guys like that, but he'd have to take the bitter with the better. On the whole, he found them a manageable group.

"So what sort of game did you have in mind?" he asked. "You fellas in the mood to risk some money?"

"We didn't come here to play bridge," Ducaine said with a thin smile. "Bert here tells us you're a serious poker player, Mr. Lantz."

"We're legitimate businessmen," Spaulding put in. "We want an honest, straight-forward game with respectable people. Maybe that's not your kind of poker, Mr. Lantz."

"Call me Lucky. I like that kind of poker myself, when I play, which isn't often, anymore. But I've got a couple of acquaintances—local businessmen—who might be interested. I asked them to drop by so we could all get acquainted. They should be here any minute."

The waitress had approached and Lucky requested a 7 UP.

Ducaine looked at him sharply. "You're not a drinking man, Lucky?"

"Oh, I've nothing against it, for other people," Lucky said. "I just find that alcohol clouds my judgment. A few drinks and I'll bet on anything!"

Charley Thorpe chuckled. "That's me, too, which is why I'd like to keep the stakes reasonable. Maybe a dollar a chip?"

"We'll set reasonable limits," Ducaine said, "and appropriate house rules. How did you get your nickname, Lantz?"

"Oh, I made a few lucky bets in my youth," Lucky said. "You know how that sort of tag sticks to a guy. I've been a musician most of my life—" Just then he spotted Holiday and King passing the bar's big window. "Ah, here come my friends now."

"Good thing," Thorpe said. "I don't want this game to run too late—we've got a busy day tomorrow. Eighteen holes of golf, if it stops raining."

Tough life, Lucky thought. Golf, poker, and sitting around waiting for some company to fall into your hands. Cleaning these guys out would be a pleasure.

"Well, I guess I'll be going," Bert said, as Frank and Eddie entered the bar. "Hope you fellas have a good game." He gave Lucky a quick wink as he headed for the door. There was a narrow passage between the tables. Frank Holiday stepped aside to let Bert pass, but Eddie King rammed him with his massive shoulder.

"Watch where you're goin'," he snarled as Bert scurried around him.

Lucky rose to make the introductions. "Frank Holiday, gentlemen. Frank owns a nightclub outside of town, the Blue Swan, which just happens to be closed on Sunday evenings. And this is his associate, Eddie King. Eddie's a promoter, among other things." He didn't add Eddie's other lines: thug, hooligan, general all-around big-mouth.

Ducaine introduced himself and his friends. Lucky could see that he and Holiday had already recognized one another as serious gamblers. He'd been counting on that. Nothing intrigued an expert like the presence of another in the game. While those two were taking one another's measure, Lucky could pick off the others one by one.

Frank and Eddie ordered drinks and the six men engaged in a bit of small talk. "So how are you enjoying our fair city?" Holiday asked the out-of-towners.

"Hmm, not much going on, is there?" Ducaine asked.

"I like the lakes," Charlie Thorpe said. "I wouldn't mind a house on one of those lakes, if I were to move here."

"Thinking of opening a branch office?" Lucky asked him.

"Whatever gave you that idea?" Spaulding asked, his eyes narrowed.

"Oh, just guessing. I hear you guys are with McGruder Industries. Same line as our own Oslo plant—of course, they may be about to go out on strike, so I'm told."

"That's nothing to us," Ducaine said. "We're just here to look at some blueprints. So let's talk poker. I hear you guys might be interested in a little game this evening."

"I'm always interested," Holiday said. "My club is available, if you'd like to come on out—"

"We'd rather stay here," Spaulding said. "We've got a nice big suite upstairs. It's quiet and private, and the room service is good."

"That's fine with me," Lucky said. "What kind of stakes did you have in mind?"

"Well, where I come from," Ducaine said, "we usually play table stakes of five hundred—that gets you in the game, and where you go from there is up to you. Minimum bet is five dollars, maximum fifty. Three raise limit, dealer sets the ante. That sound all right to you?"

"It's tame, but acceptable," Holiday said. "I assume side bets are permitted?"

"Of course—and we can raise the stakes later, by common agreement, if you're getting bored."

"Gee, a fifty-dollar bet is a bit rich for my blood," Charley Thorpe said with his nervous chuckle. "Couldn't we make it a twenty-dollar max?"

"Dealer's choice," Ducaine said, ignoring him. "Deal goes around the table. If you sit out more than two hands, you're out of the game. We'll have drinks and snacks sent up to the room, so nobody has to go anywhere, except the john. I went to the bank yesterday and got several packs of five's and ten's, so we won't need chips."

"Wild cards?" Eddie asked. "I don't like them fucking wild-card games."

"Dealer's choice," Ducaine repeated. "If you can explain the rules, you can call the game. Anybody who wants to sit out the hand loses their ante. Table talk strictly prohibited. The cards speak."

"All right, that all sounds good to me," Holiday said. "You boys want to set a quitting time, or do we go all night?"

"Not hardly," Thorpe laughed. "We have to get up early tomorrow. Tee-time at nine a.m."

"We'll go until midnight," Ducaine said, "and then we'll discuss a quitting time. If anyone gets sleepy, they're free to drop, except right after a winning hand."

"Fair enough," Lucky said. "I may not last very long myself—late nights aren't good for me anymore. By the way, it might be better if we don't all go up to your suite at once, Cal. The Cambridge has a nervous house-dick."

"I've already taken care of him," Ducaine said, "but you're probably right—no point in raising suspicions. You fellas finish your drinks and then come on up—we're in rooms 917, A-B-C."

Lucky knew the suite. It had been the site of some fabulous, high-stakes games in his younger days, when there was a poker marathon on the ninth floor of the Cambridge nearly every night. He'd had some of the best nights of his career in good old 917—it was his lucky room!

Things were looking good. The rules of the game as Cal Ducaine laid them out were all to his liking—exactly what he would have called if he'd been running the show. And using cash instead of chips was good, too—he'd been wondering how he could cash in his chips early without raising suspicion. He was a little surprised Frank and Eddie hadn't quibbled about the betting limits or the dealer's choice rule, but now that they were alone in the bar, Frank turned a grim face on Lucky and put a grip on his arm.

"And now, my friend, we need to have a few words. You were talkin' pretty big on the phone this afternoon. Where'd you come up with the five C's to get in this game?"

"That's my business, Frank. Maybe I got a rich daddy."

Eddie guffawed. "That's a laugh—your old man died fifteen years ago. He was a drunken bum, just like you."

Lucky was going to respond, but Holiday said, "Shut up, Eddie. Lantz and I got things to talk about. Where's that black gal you took away with you last night? You got her stashed somewhere?"

"She's nursing her wounds, Frank. You were pretty rough on her."

"I'll do worse'n that, if she starts shootin' her mouth off about me and my backroom operation. You tell her that. She'd better get her chocolate ass out of town, if she knows what's good for her."

"Better check the till back at the club, Frank," Eddie put in. "Maybe the bitch took some money with her when she left. Maybe that's where Lantz got his stake."

"You're full of shit, Eddie," Lucky said. "Savannah was too beat up to go near that till, and I wouldn't take money from her if she had. I got the three-fifty you advanced me, Frank, and another one fifty I saved up in the san, plus a little cushion from a friend. That's it, believe me—my whole stake."

Holiday's blue eyes turned to ice picks. "That's not much of a stake, my friend. If you want to stay in this game, you'd better keep a low profile. These guys are loaded, I can tell that just by looking at them, and old Frank intends to win big tonight. Don't get in my way. If I take enough off these patsies, I might forget about that two hundred you owe me. I might even overlook your other miscues—like walkin' off with my woman."

"That's real generous of you, Frank," Lucky said, "but I hope to win enough tonight to cover my debts— from the other guys, of course."

"It *better* be from the other guys," Frank said, and downed his drink.

"It better not be from me, either," Eddie said, as they rose to leave. "I ain't your fuckin' patsy, Lantz."

"I hope you brought your switchblade," Lucky said. "You might want to carve your initials on some of that fine Cambridge woodwork."

"Get smart with me and you'll find out," Eddie said.

As they were leaving the lounge, Lucky spotted Phil MacDonald, a beat reporter for the *Cap Times*, eating his club sandwich at the bar. Lucky waved and smiled and Phil's eyebrows went up, a sure sign he remembered Lucky and the games he used to run. *He'll check back later tonight*, Lucky thought happily. Old Phil could always smell a story.

Tom Cotter was nowhere in sight as they crossed the lobby, which was about as lively as a funeral parlor between wakes. That's how it was on a Labor Day weekend—even the bell hops got the night off, and the young desk clerk seemed not to notice the three men waiting for the elevator. The Cambridge had installed self-service elevators since Lucky's day and the first to open its doors was a small box lined with mirrors. Lucky was surprised to see how thin and frail he looked, wedged in between his two companions. His eyes looked hollow and sickly and his skin had the pallor of a corpse. The doors slid shut, the elevator rose swiftly, and Lucky felt a thickness in his lung he didn't like, a tickle in his throat.

The doors opened on the ninth floor. They left the elevator and followed a thick oriental carpet to the black walnut door with the gold letters, 917A. Ducaine answered on the first knock and ushered them into the familiar room. The Cambridge may have redecorated its suites since Lucky's time, but they hadn't changed the basic furnishings—two sofas, several easy chairs, a hexagonal table with six chairs, and a bar over by the far wall. A large window looked out on the city, but you couldn't see the capitol dome from here—it was on the other side of the hotel. Three doors opened off the sitting room—four bedrooms and a bathroom.

"Drinks are on the company," Ducaine said, indicating the several bottles on the bar. "Help yourselves, gentleman, and then we'll get started."

"Mind if I use the bathroom first?" Lucky asked.

Ducaine pointed to the appropriate door, which Lucky had already spotted. He went in, shut the door, and looked around. Pretty much as he recalled. There was a small broom closet next to the shower stall, and in the back of the closet there was a dumbwaiter. Not many people knew about this feature, since meals were usually delivered by the room service staff. The dumbwaiter was mainly used by the maids when they were cleaning up the suite and had dirty dishes to return to the kitchen. Lucky slid up the door and saw the shelf was in place. A stout rope on a pulley would lower the shelf nine floors to the dishwashing area.

Once, in his bellhop days, he had wedged himself into the little compartment—a tight fit, but he was skinny enough, even then—and lowered himself all the way down, just to see if it could be done. He had never needed this particular escape route at the conclusion of a game, but tonight maybe he would.

He went back to the sitting room and found the others beginning to gather at the table. He poured himself a glass of soda water and then grabbed the second chair on Frank Holiday's left. That way he could watch Frank closely, and on four out of every six hands he would see Frank's bet before placing his own.

Ducaine took a seat directly across the table and produced a leather briefcase. He snapped it open and began to extract wrapped packs of five's and ten's. "All right, gentlemen—I assume you'd all like the required five hundred dollars' worth to start?"

"Gimme a thousand," Holiday said, and tossed a roll of hundreds across the table. Ducaine counted it before giving Holiday several packs of five's and ten's.

"I'll start with five hundred," Lucky said, and produced Cool Johnny's five c-notes, which he placed before Ducaine like a sacrificial offering. *Bring me luck*, he prayed, though he didn't really believe there was a God who paid much attention to the prayers of poker players. Whatever gods ruled this game, they were the crazy, cock-eyed gods of chance and luck, as indifferent to their human puppets as tornadoes and lightning bolts.

The others all bought five hundred dollars' worth of smaller bills. Meanwhile Holiday had placed an ashtray, lighter, and pack of cigarettes beside his chips. Both Ducaine and Thorpe smoked, but when Eddie King lit one of his big, smelly cigars, Ray Spaulding looked disgusted and got up to open the window. Charley Thorpe munched potato chips and pretzels and beamed at everyone, as if he expected a nice, friendly game of Parcheesi.

Ducaine broke open a new deck of cards, shuffled them once and fanned them out face down across the table. Each man drew a card and Lucky got the high card, a queen of clubs. "Your deal," Ducaine said and passed the deck to Ray Spaulding. "The man to the right of the dealer shuffles, the man to the left cuts. Lucky, you shuffle a deck for Charley—that speeds up the game."

They were nice cards—standard Cambridge hotel playing cards, plastic-coated, with an English fox-hunting scene on the back. Their edges had a crisp bite;

their faces were bright and bold. The hearts and diamonds gleamed like drops of blood on new-fallen snow, the spades and clubs like dabs of tar. Lucky felt his confidence rise as he shuffled the second deck for Charley. This was where he belonged, doing what he understood. If you could decide everything in life with a deck of cards, a guy would at least know the odds. He'd understand the rules of the game.

Spaulding shuffled his deck competently, but a few more times than necessary, then gave it to Lucky who passed it to Thorpe for a cut. Then he tossed a five-dollar bill onto the table. "Five card stud, nothing wild— a nice simple game to get us started."

Everyone tossed in a five and Lucky dealt the first cards around the table, sailing each one with a deft flick of his wrist so that it landed precisely in front of the player, face down. Oh, but it felt good to do that again! A sense of his old power, a tingle of recovered pride, passed up his arms and produced a feeling of warmth in his ravaged chest. With it came the sudden urge for a drink—something to stoke that fire and keep it burning. *Never mind that*, Lucky thought, and dealt the second card face up, without looking at his own hole card. Again he flicked each card so that it landed neatly alongside the first. Thorpe got the high card, a king of hearts. Lucky's card was a four of spades. He checked his hole card and found a ten of diamonds. "Your bet, Charley," he said.

"Well, that king looks pretty good," Thorpe said with his nervous chuckle, and bet five dollars. All around the table five-dollar bills were added to the pot. Lucky dealt a third card, face up. Charley got a nine of clubs to go with his king; Ducaine paired his sixes; Frank Holiday got a second heart and Lucky got a ten of spades. Ducaine bet ten dollars on his sixes—an aggressive bet— and Holiday promptly saw him. Lucky decided to test Ducaine's resolve and raised him ten. Thorpe and Spaulding dropped; Eddie, Ducaine and Holiday all stayed, bringing the pot to one hundred and forty dollars.

The fourth round gave Ducaine a queen of clubs, Frank a jack of hearts, and Lucky a five of diamonds. Ducaine bet ten dollars on his sixes, telling Lucky he had either a third six in the hole or another queen—or else he was testing the others with a bluff. Holiday raised him back ten, suggesting his hole card was another heart. Lucky decided to drop.

On the fifth and last round, Ducaine got a queen of spades and Frank a two of hearts. Now Ducaine showed two pair and Frank showed four-fifths of a flush. Lucky checked the card that would have been his and found it was a ten of clubs. Too bad—he might have won with three tens. Ducaine bet twenty-five dollars on his two pair and Holiday considered carefully, then raised him twenty-five. Ducaine met the bet and Holiday displayed his hole card—a five of hearts. He had his flush.

"Nice, but I've got a full boat," Ducaine said, and turned over a six of clubs.

"Well, I had to see it," Holiday said with an affable smile. Neither man had been bluffing and Lucky figured he was fortunate to have gotten out when he did—either hand would've beaten his tens. But now he was down thirty bucks. He shuffled the deck, passed it to Spaulding, and lit a cigarette.

Thorpe took over the deal. "Same game," he said, "only deuces wild. Ante five bucks."

"Fuckin' wild cards," Eddie King said, when a deuce went to Spaulding.

Spaulding glared at him. "Do you have to use such coarse language, Mr. King?"

Eddie looked amazed. "Fuck, it's poker, for Chrissake!"

"No table-talk," Ducaine said sternly, and they both fell silent.

Lucky caught a pair of kings early and stayed with them to the end, hoping for a third, but Spaulding won with two pair. Now he was down seventy-five bucks. At this rate his first five hundred wouldn't last long, but he told himself not to panic, and not to start counting his money after every hand. You had to go with what the evening gave you. Sometimes the cards just weren't there, but you had to keep plugging away until something changed and you hit a hot streak. When the streak came, you had to know how to play it. You had to know the most it could give you, since one hot streak a night might be all you'd get.

To that end, Lucky studied the other players, concentrated on learning their styles and mannerisms, looking for habits or foibles he could use against them. The three out-of-towners played true to type, no surprises there, and Eddie King's style of play hadn't changed from the old days. He got up often to refill his glass—free liquor was something Eddie couldn't pass up—and the more he drank the more over-bearing and belligerent he would become. Lucky just hopped he wouldn't get out of hand too early. When the time came, he was counting on Eddie to blow his stack.

Frank Holiday was the real puzzle. A cool professional, he hid his feelings behind a haze of cigarette smoke, maintaining a relaxed, affable manner through good hands and bad, as if he really didn't care whether he won or lost. He lost several hands early, then won just enough to keep his pile of crumpled bills from shrinking any further. Lucky could tell Frank was setting his three marks up for the kill and watched him closely, but though he knew most of the tricks crooked gamblers used, he could detect no evidence of cheating. Of course Eddie, that stooge, often bet into Frank's best hands, sweetening the pot with a raise or two when his own cards weren't that good. If Ducaine noticed this, he didn't say anything about it.

The evening wore on, and Lucky managed to win a few hands with mediocre cards—nothing like a streak, but enough to keep him going. From where he sat he could see the bar with its little army of liquor bottles: scotch, bourbon, brandy, gin, along with mixers and a little pyramid of clean glasses. Now *that's* what he was missing—the warm, confident, on-top-of-it feeling that came with a few drinks. Not that he had ever played poker drunk—that was a fool's game. No, his serious drinking came later, when he was winding down after a big night. A celebration or a lament—at some point it was all the same.

He looked away from the bar, toward the window, but Spaulding had pulled the drapes and Lucky had to imagine the scene—the rooftops of surrounding buildings cradled in fog, the sky above them filled with a hazy pink glow from the downtown lights. Streets angled off the square like the spokes of a wheel, each marked by its necklace of lights, and in the center, rising into the haze and brooding over the city like a mountain of ice, the pale-gray dome of the state capitol.

17.

Down and Dirty

BY TEN THIRTY Lucky knew he was in trouble. He hadn't won a hand in over an hour and the little stack of bills at his side was just about gone. He had two hundred still in his wallet and told himself not to panic. A guy could recoup his losses quickly in a game like this, yet even worse than the cards he was getting was the way he was playing them. His head just wasn't in the game, and on a couple of hands he'd flat out lost his nerve, letting himself be bluffed out with cards that would have won.

Frank Holiday, on the other hand, was on a roll and the jumbled pile of bills beside his ashtray had grown to a small mountain. Every so often Frank would smooth out some of those bills and tuck them neatly away in the leather wallet he kept in his inside jacket pocket. Then he'd take a sip of scotch—Lucky noticed that he actually drank very little—light up another cigarette, and let his fingertips dance lightly on his silver-plated lighter as he calmly surveyed the table with narrowed eyes.

Holiday's run of luck and aggressive betting had the

other players buffaloed; even Cal Ducaine had begun to shy away from a confrontation. Thorpe and Spaulding had clearly lost heart, and Lucky was afraid they would drop out of the game before he could recoup his losses. He was going to need them, and their money, once his luck changed—but first he had to change the rhythm of the game, break Frank's streak, and get the others back into it. One hand could do it, one good hand, but where the hell was it?

Right now they were playing seven-card stud and Frank was showing a possible flush—three hearts and a diamond. Eddie had nothing on the board but a pair of deuces, yet he bet into Frank's flush, driving up the cost of staying in the game. Lucky didn't know how, but he was convinced Holiday was signaling Eddie in some way—when to raise and when to layoff. Ducaine dropped and Holiday took the third and last raise for twenty bucks. With a pair of queens showing, Spaulding had to call Frank's bet, and that allowed Lucky and Thorpe to drop. Eddie dropped as well and Frank turned over his hole cards to reveal the fifth heart.

"What did you have, Mr. King?" Spaulding asked as Eddie tossed in his cards.

"That's my business," Eddie said. "I dropped, didn't I?"

"You were betting as if you had something," Spaulding said. "Or were you betting your partner's hand?"

"That's bullshit," Eddie said. "Why the hell should I do that?"

"Frank Holiday can bet his own hands," Frank said, calmly gathering in his winnings.

The next deal was Frank's and Lucky stood up. "Deal me out," he said, and walked over to the window.

He drew aside one of the curtains and leaned close to the glass. The rain had let up and he could see lights twinkling across the city, the dark band of Lake Monona, a couple of TV towers flashing their red lights to the south. Bert's cab was out there somewhere, patrolling the streets, but soon now he would start checking the alley behind the hotel. Lucky's avenue of escape. Maybe he should just cut and run, take what little he had left and blow town for good.

Sure, and say goodbye to his pride and self-respect, and to every good thing he hoped to do with that money—not to mention the sweet little piece who was waiting for him at the Rest-Awhile motel. Too bad he hadn't taken a serving of that pie when he had the chance, because gals like Savannah had no time for losers. Nobody had time for losers—not Ruby, not Ginger, not Maggie and Leo. They all had him pegged. They knew the book on Lucky Lantz. He was the only one who continued to believe that he still had a chance to come out a winner. But if he ran away now he'd only prove everybody right and, looking back on his life, he would see nothing but failure. Broken promises, bad debts, one big zip.

He walked over to the bar, put some ice cubes in his glass, then poured in the seltzer. He took a sip, considered, and then added a splash of bourbon. He took another sip and nothing drastic happened. The world didn't spin or stand on its head. The lights didn't dim and his heart didn't stop beating. *I can handle this. Just a drink or two to get me going. I can handle it.*

He had to admit that the taste was sweet, like the smoky flavor of a whore's kiss. It was the dark, deadly taste of his first love—the sweetest, wickedest, most dangerous mistress he'd ever known, the one who'd been leading him to his ruin these past forty years. Neither cards nor dice nor any other game men played for money could compare to the kick this little lady delivered. Lucky took another sip and felt a pleasurable shiver of surrender. *But I still can walk away from it, if I have to,* he thought, and added another splash of bourbon to his glass before carrying it back to the table.

Eddie King grinned at him, then rearranged his cards with a knowing smirk. Frank Holiday's serene expression didn't change, yet Lucky felt he was also smiling behind his veil of cigarette smoke. The others seemed not to notice the different color of the liquid in his glass, or thought nothing of it if they did. *Lots of guys take a drink now and then. It's no big deal.*

They had just started a game of five-card draw and Lucky had to wait for the next hand, when it would be his deal once again. On the first round of bets he noticed a sound he'd been hearing of fand on all evening, but hadn't really zeroed in on before—the light tapping of Frank Holiday's fingernails on his silver cigarette lighter. Perhaps Frank wasn't quite as relaxed as he seemed; maybe those taps were a nervous habit that could give him away. Lucky decided to pay special attention to Frank's taps from now on, and on the next round of bets he noticed something else. Eddie King was listening to them, too—in fact, they seemed to have a direct influence on the way he bet his cards. By the third round Lucky was sure: the taps were a code. They told Eddie when to raise and when to layoff By the end of the hand, Lucky thought he had the code figured out. It was simple enough—easy for a jerk like Eddie to remember—but likely to escape notice by the others, since Frank's fingers were always drumming on something.

Lucky felt a surge of confidence. *Okay, you bastard, I've got you now!*

Spaulding passed him the pre-shuffled deck. "Your deal, Lantz. See if you can't change my luck."

"I'll do that, Ray," Lucky said as he passed the deck to Thorpe for a cut. "You fellas seem to be getting a tad sleepy—let's try something different. Ante ten big ones . . . for baseball."

"Hey, now there's a game with balls," Eddie King said and grinned around the table to see if everyone got his feeble-minded joke.

"I hate that game," Spaulding said. "Too many wild cards screw up the odds—a man doesn't know what he's got."

"Hey, it's a man's game," Eddie said, forgetting his own dislike of wild cards. "Besides, it's dealer's choice, remember? If you don't like it, you can drop."

"America's Pastime," Lucky crooned as he began to deal the first card face-down around the table. "In case any of you are unfamiliar with the rules, baseball is just like seven-card stud, with a few variations. Nine's and three's are wild, four gets you another card, and a three, face up, means you have to equal the pot to stay in the game."

"That's the part I like," Eddie chuckled. "No chicken-shit bastards allowed!"

"Glad you approve, Mr. King," Ducaine said drily, and exchanged glances with his associates.

When he had dealt two cards face down around the table, Lucky sailed a third card, face up, into place before each player. Thorpe got a ten of clubs, Eddie a jack of diamonds, Ducaine a seven of clubs, Frank a nine of spades—a free wild card—and Spalding a five of spades. Lucky got a five of hearts. He checked his hole cards and found a six of hearts and a nine of diamonds. Already he had three cards to a straight, but if he couldn't make them all hearts it wouldn't be much of a hand in this game—not with all those wild cards.

"Jack bets," he said. Eddie hesitated and in the silence Lucky heard the soft tapping of Frank Holiday's fingernails. One, two, three. *Bet something, flea-brain.*

Eddie tossed a ten-dollar bill on the table. Ducaine stayed and Frank raised another ten. Everyone saw the raise and Lucky dealt out the second card. Thorpe got a king of diamonds, Eddie a six of clubs, and Ducaine another seven. Frank got an ace of hearts to go with his wild card, and Spaulding a queen of clubs. Lucky gave himself the seven of hearts and now he was only one card away from his straight flush. With nine hearts and seven wild cards still unaccounted for, he knew he had an excellent chance.

"Aces bet," he said, and met Holiday's icepick eyes.

Frank put twenty dollars on his aces, a strong bet, but Lucky liked his own hand and raised him twenty. A few eyebrows went up around the table. Thorpe groaned but he saw the raise and Eddie, responding to the tap of Frank's fingernail on his cigarette lighter, raised twenty more. *Too much for those jacks, Eddie—Frank's leading you by the nose!*

Ducaine debated, then tossed in three twenties. Frank met the raises, and then, looking hard at Lucky, added another twenty. Lucky had to go into his wallet, but he saw the raise. Fortunately, it was the last for that round. "Getting too rich for me," Thorpe said and tossed in his cards. Eddie and Ducaine met the bets. Okay,

Lucky thought, here's where we separate the men from the boys.

Eddie's next card was a three of spades. Everyone laughed—everyone but Eddie, who looked at Lucky with disbelief shading toward rage. Lucky ignored the look and counted the pot. "Three hundred and eighty dollars," he told the big lug. "I think you said something about balls, Mr. King."

Everyone chuckled, and Eddie glared at the pile of bills in the center of the table, then looked up at Frank, who gazed off across the room as if he couldn't care less, though his fingernail tapped twice on the lighter. Frank wanted Eddie to stay in the game.

"Fuck," Eddie said, and went into his wallet for the money he needed. He put the bills on the table and the deal continued. Frank got an eight of clubs and Lucky the six of spades. That gave him three sixes, but he didn't expect them to stand up, since it was pretty certain Frank had a third ace or a wild card in the hole. It was the straight flush he needed—one more card.

"Ace's bet," he said.

Frank tossed a twenty-dollar bill onto the table.

Lucky promptly saw the bet and raised another twenty. He couldn't show weakness now—he had to believe that straight flush would come, and the others had to believe it, too. Luck was yours if you took it; it passed you by if you didn't.

"Damn you, Lantz," Eddie said, but when Frank tapped just once on his lighter he met the bet. He had to stay now, with so much of his own money in the pot. The others were likely to stay, too, since Eddie's three eighty was a tempting prize. That was the thing about baseball —it hooked you one way or another. Ducaine stayed and

Frank considered another raise, then simply met Lucky's bet. *So maybe he doesn't have a wild card in the hole,* Lucky thought. *Or maybe he just wants me to think he doesn't.* Another round would tell the tale.

On the last up-card, Eddie got another jack—probably not enough to beat Frank's aces—and Frank got an eight of diamonds, giving him two pair on the board. Lucky drew a four of clubs, which gave him a straight, but not the straight flush. It also meant he got another card, which he lay face down alongside his two-hole cards. Without looking at it, he turned to Holiday for the bet.

Frank pondered the meaning of Lucky's indifference to his extra card, then dropped two twenties on the table. *Overkill,* Lucky thought. *He's trying to find out if I'm bluffing the straight flush.* Spaulding dropped. Lucky checked his third down card, saw it was a useless queen of diamonds, then slowly picked up four twenties —the last bills he had on the table—and lay them atop the pile, his eyes steady on Frank's.

Hearing just one tap on Frank's lighter, Eddie tossed in his cards. "Fuck this shit," he said, and went to get himself another drink.

Ducaine dropped. Frank simply saw Lucky's raise. *He might have raised me again,* Lucky thought. *If he's got that wild card in the hole, why didn't he raise?*

He dealt the last card face down. "Your bet," he told Frank, without looking at his last card. It was either there or it wasn't. Either way, he knew how he had to play the hand.

Frank glanced at Lucky's up-cards, then bought a moment's thought by reaching for his cigarettes, shaking one out and sticking it between his lips. He snapped his lighter beneath it, then casually tossed a pair of twenties onto the table. It was a strong bet, but it came a bit too late—Lucky had seen his indecision. With a really strong hand Frank wouldn't have hesitated, because the odds were against Lucky's straight flush and a gambler like Frank always played the odds. Lucky felt a glow of triumph as he went into his wallet and extracted four twenties. "Raise you forty," he said, and put them on the pile.

Spalding grunted and Thorpe giggled nervously. "Jeez, I'm glad out of this game," Charley said and grabbed a handful of corn curls.

Frank had a raise left, if he wanted it, and he'd seen Lucky go into his wallet twice already. He put two twenties on the table and then, with a shadow of a smile, he added two more twenties and a ten—the maximum raise of fifty dollars.

"Jesus, you play mean, Holiday," Ducaine said. "You can't drive a man out of the game like that."

"Can't I?" Frank said. "We agreed on a fifty-dollar max and a three-raise limit. If Lantz can't meet the bet, he can fucking well drop."

Lucky had sixty dollars left in his wallet. There was one raise left but he wanted Holiday to show his cards, win or lose, so he simply called the bet. If he lost this hand, he'd have ten bucks left—Bert's fare and tip. "Let's see 'em," he said.

After a moment's pause, Holiday pushed his hole cards aside, leaving only his aces and eights—a mere two pair. "That's what you have to beat," he said, and looked off across the room as if the game no longer interested him.

Lucky lined up his five and seven of hearts. Then he

turned the six of hearts and put it between them. Then he turned the nine of diamonds and put it beside the seven. There were two down cards left and Lucky knew one of them was the queen. He turned the other, the one he hadn't looked at yet. It was a nine of clubs. He placed it next to the five to complete his straight flush.

"Nice hand, Lantz," Ducaine said.

"Yeah, a beauty," echoed Thorpe.

"Goddamn," Eddie said as Lucky dragged in his pot, "I thought sure he was bluffing you, Frank, but even my jacks coulda beat your two pair!"

"Shut up, Eddie," Holiday said, and inspected his fingernails.

The deal passed to Spalding. Meanwhile, Lucky scooped up his money. No time to count it, but he figured the pot was close to twelve hundred dollars. He was back in business. More important, he'd shown these losers that Frank Holiday *could* be beat. He'd made the great gambler look bad on three separate counts—first, because he'd tried to bluff a weak hand and failed; second, because he'd tried to drive Lucky out of the game and failed at that, too; and third, because he had shown his irritation at the loss. The spell was broken and from now on, Lucky knew, the other players would challenge Frank more freely. He took a sip of his drink and felt that delicious warm feeling spreading through his body.

"Shit, you got lucky, Lantz," Eddie said as he resumed his seat. "It's those fuckin' wild-card games—that's bullshit poker, if you ask me."

"I thought you said it was 'a man's game,'" Spaulding sneered. Lucky took another sip. He figured that three of spades he'd dealt Eddie from the bottom of the deck more than made up for the old entry in his little black book. It was against his principles to tinker with the deal, especially when there was a sharpie like Frank Holiday in the game, but once in a great while, when the game was rigged against you, it was worth the risk. He'd mark Eddie's debt paid the next time he went over his accounts. "September 2, 1956 –$150 plus interest."

The deal continued around the table and Lucky won three of the next four hands. You couldn't push a hot streak too hard or it would blow up in your face, so on the next hand he dropped early and took his empty glass back to the bar. *Easy now—you haven't had this stuff for a while.* He poured a little bourbon over ice—just enough to keep the taste in his mouth—then filled the glass with seltzer. The first sip didn't go down just right and he was still coughing when he came back to the table.

"That's quite a cold you got, pal," Charley Thorpe said as Lucky resumed his place. "You been hacking away all evening."

"Sorry, it's just this damp weather," Lucky said. "Always bothers my allergies."

"Don't you believe it," Eddie King said. "Fucker's got TB—better watch out he don't cough his germs on you."

"Are you serious?" Thorpe asked, and pushed back his chair.

Suddenly everyone's eyes were on Lucky. His face felt hot—maybe he was running a fever. "Eddie's full of crap," he said. "I was in the san, but that was a long time ago. I'm a cured man now."

"Hey, what's with all the table talk?" Ducaine asked. "Let's finish this hand."

Thorpe won a modest pot and the deal returned to Lucky, who called for Mississippi, or Pass the Trash. Each player passed three cards to the player on his left, then two, then one, keeping his best five—or his worst, since high and low hands split the pot. The cards were stacked and rolled, one at a time, so there were plenty of bets as the players tried to calculate who was going high and who was going low. Lucky had only a mediocre low to work with, but after three rolls it was clear Thorpe was the only other low. Lucky chased him out with a couple of late raises. The others fought over their high hands and Lucky wound up splitting a large pot with Ducaine—over seven hundred dollars a piece.

"Hey, let's play that game again," Thorpe said, taking up the deal. "Only this time pass 'em to the right."

"Bullshit poker," Eddie commented, but everyone ignored him.

The mood at the table had changed considerably in the past half hour. Ducaine and his mends had hope again, Frank and Eddie were on the outs, and Lucky now looked like the man to beat. Which was just the way he wanted it, because the more these suckers believed in his luck, the more of it he would have. Luck was a myth—it didn't exist. But stealing it from somebody else made it seem to exist for a little while and, once you got the whole table believing in your luck, it was as though you had them believing in ghosts. They were spooked, and men who were spooked didn't play the cards in their hand, didn't see what was on the table, didn't calculate the odds or believe them when they did. One way or another, they let you take it all away from them.

All his life Lucky had known about stealing luck, just as he had known about stealing music from the air and pleasure from the arms of a woman. None of it really belonged to you, the music least of all, being the breath of angels and joyful laughter of the gods, who were thieves themselves, since they took it all back in the end—the money, the music, the love, the moon and stars. Yet while the game was still in progress it was possible to have a pretty good time, and Lucky was having a good time now, raking in the pots and stuffing the bills in his jacket pockets when the pile at his elbow became too large. The more chances he took the more he looked like a winner to the others, who gave him that leeway that opened the door to more of that luck that didn't really exist but which filled the warm, smoky room like the presence of a ghost.

Even Frank Holiday, who should have known better, having pulled the same trick plenty of times himself, was beginning to believe in Lucky's luck. He didn't like losing to a broken-down has-been of a piano player, and the more he lost the madder he got. And the madder he got, the worse he played. Even Eddie King had turned against him and was ignoring his taps on the lighter, so after a while Frank stopped tapping. He lit a cigarette and gazed levelly at Lucky through the smoke. "Having quite a run of luck, aren't you, Lantz?"

"I've had better," Lucky said.

"Just don't push it too far," Holiday said. "Guys can run out of luck awful damn quick, sometimes."

"So I've heard," Lucky said, and began shuffling his deck. You couldn't beat a guy like Holiday if you didn't make him mad at you. Of course making Frank Holiday mad had its risks. Good thing he was leaving town in the morning.

He calculated he was up over four thousand dollars

by midnight. By the time he took care of his debts—and something extra for Johnny and Bert—he'd have a clear three grand to use in Chicago. Not a bad evening, he thought, going back to the bar for another drink, not a bad evening at all. He made this drink a little stronger, because they were nearing the end and the toughest part still lay ahead.

What he needed now was a way to shut things down. Bert would be calling the cops in less than twenty minutes. A local patrol car would get the call, but they'd request back-up from the nearest station house, which was ten minutes away, on the other side of the square. Lucky figured they would all be assembling outside the hotel by twelve forty-five. It would take them another five minutes to get the room key from the desk clerk and come up on the elevator. That meant they'd be pounding on the door by twelve fifty, and Lucky hoped to be long-gone by then.

"What do you say, boys," he asked as he resumed his seat. "You up to another three, four hours of poker?"

"No way," Charley Thorpe moaned. "I thought we were going to set a quitting time at midnight, and here it is already a quarter past."

"Shit, we're just getting started," Eddie King said. "Don't you want to win back some of the money this fucker Lantz has been taking off us?"

Spaulding appealed to their leader. "What do you say, Cal? We *did* say we'd set a quitting time at midnight. I think I've lost enough for one night."

"Well, maybe once more around the table," Ducaine said. "Would that be acceptable to everyone?"

"Suits me," Lucky said, though in fact he was afraid it would take longer than half an hour to give everyone a last deal.

"Shit, what a bunch of pansies," Eddie King said. "When I get in a good game, I like to go all night."

"Well, Mr. King," Spaulding said, "some of us have to earn an honest living. I don't suppose *you've* ever had that problem."

"What is that supposed to mean?" Eddie demanded. His fat face was flushed with liquor and he looked about ready to show off his switchblade. Nothing capped an evening for Eddie like a good fight.

"Take it easy, Eddie," Frank said. "Mr. Spaulding didn't mean anything. Are you going to deal the cards or aren't you?"

"Mississippi," Eddie said, a stub of cigar clamped belligerently between his teeth. "Ante twenty-five bucks."

"I've lost too much on that game already," Thorpe said. "Deal me out." He got up to replenish his drink and bowl of snacks.

"Asshole," Eddie said under his breath.

Charley ignored him but Spaulding said, "You know, Mr. King, I'm getting awfully sick of that foul mouth of yours. Why don't you try keeping it shut for awhile?"

Eddie put down his cards. "Yeah? You gonna make me . . . *asshole?*"

"All right, calm down," Ducaine said. "If you can't play a civilized game of poker, Mr. King, we'll call it an evening right now. You guys can just clear out of here."

"Relax, Eddie," Frank said, in a tone of voice that his partner couldn't ignore. "We'll take it one hand at a time. Anybody who wants to drop out can, provided they haven't just won a hand. Wasn't that your rule, Ducaine?"

"That was the rule," Ducaine said.

Eddie dealt the cards and they made their passes. Lucky went high with jacks and fives. He could see Holiday had a good low and they kept raising one another's bets to fatten a pot they would eventually split between them. It was twelve twenty-five by Lucky's watch when they turned the last card and, sure enough, Lucky won high and Frank low. Though not one of the largest pots of the evening, it was close to a thousand.

"Tell you what," Lucky said as Holiday reached out for his share of the money, "let's leave it all in there and play one last hand, winner take all."

"What, just the two of us?"

"Nah, let's let the other guys play, too. It's been a long night and we're all getting a little tired—this could be our last hand. What do you say, boys? Want to add a hundred dollars to the pot for a chance to win it all?"

"What game?" Ducaine asked suspiciously.

"Five-card no-lookie," Lucky said. "No wild cards, no funny stuff, we just turn 'em and bet 'em, one at a time. What do you say, Frank? Want to be a sport? Give everybody a chance to end up a winner."

Holiday didn't want to look like a piker. Besides, he could calculate the size of the pot for the eventual winner. Between two and three thousand—enough to make up for a long losing streak. "Okay," he said, "but I get to shuffle the deck."

"Hey, you don't think I shuffled 'em?" Charley Thorpe asked.

"It's my money in the pot and I want to shuffle the goddamn deck," Holiday said.

"Okay, okay," Ducaine said. "You shuffle, Spaulding cuts, and I deal—fair enough?"

"Fair enough," Frank said, and took the deck from

Ducaine.

Lucky suspected a trick but could spot no treachery in Frank's expert shuffle. That didn't mean there hadn't been any. The easiest way to cheat would be to palm one of the cards, then use it later in place of one of those you'd been dealt. But how would you know *which* card to extract?

"Hey, it's my money in the pot, too," he said as Frank completed his shuffle.

"How about I get a cut?"

"I guess that's fair," Ducaine said. "Pass him the cards, Holiday."

Lucky cut the deck, then passed it to Spaulding, who also cut it, and finally Ducaine dealt the cards out face down around the table. "Remember, nobody looks at their hand," he said. "We'll turn them one at a time and bet on each card."

It was twelve-thirty when they started. On the first turn Charley Thorpe was high with a queen of clubs and bet ten dollars. Eddie promptly raised him ten and Frank Holiday raised him another ten. Lucky, who had a three of spades, took the last raise for ten dollars.

"What the hell are you betting on, Lantz?" Eddie asked him.

"You want my money, you'll have to bet," Lucky said.

After three cards had been turned, nobody had so much as a pair, but the size of the pot, and the fact that it was the last hand, kept everyone in the game. Lucky checked his watch: twelve thirty-five it was going to be close.

On the fourth turn, Ducaine paired his sixes, but everyone else had at least one higher card they could hope to pair on the last turn. Holiday had a king and Lucky an ace; they both bet into Ducaine's sixes and only Spaulding dropped. Then it was time to turn the last card. Lucky saw what might have been the flicker of a flashing red light between the drawn drapes.

"Trade you cards," he said to Frank Holiday, before he could turn his over.

"What?" Holiday asked sharply.

"I'll trade cards with you," Lucky said. "Neither of us knows what we've got, so what difference does it make?"

"You're crazy," Holiday said, "this is my card."

"Do you know it's a king?"

"Of course not."

"Then trade with me."

"Go fuck yourself," Holiday said.

"Then count the cards," Lucky said to Ducaine. "I'd like to make sure we're playing with a full deck here."

"Are you calling me a cheat, you rotten old weasel?" Holiday asked. "Count 'em!" Spaulding said sharply. "He insisted on shuffling the deck, didn't he?"

Ducaine had dealt thirty cards around the table. That meant there ought to be twenty-two in what was left of the deck. He snapped them rapidly down, one at a time, and they all counted along with him. There were only twenty-one cards.

"Where's the twenty-second card, Frank?" Lucky asked. "Up your sleeve?"

Holiday's left hand whipped out and rapped Lucky hard across the mouth. Lucky felt Frank's ring rake across his upper lip and the lower part of his face went numb. "Nobody calls me a cheat," Holiday said. "Eddie, kick this bum outa here."

"This isn't your suite, Mr. Holiday," Ducaine said. "I'll decide who stays or goes, and I think you and your friends had all better go."

"Not without our money," Holiday said, and nodded to Eddie, who stood up, the switchblade having miraculously appeared in his hand. The others froze at the sight of the nasty weapon with its tapered, five-inch blade.

"Come on, you cocksuckers," Eddie said gleefully. "Make a move on me, just make a move! Turn your card, Frank."

Holiday turned his last card, which was indeed a king. "I'll take my money and go home," he said, and reached out to pull in the pile of bills.

"Say, what's this?" Lucky asked and picked up a card from the floor. He tossed it onto the table, a worthless four of hearts. "Now where did that come from, I wonder?"

Ducaine brought a small revolver out of his briefcase. "I had a hunch you two were a couple of thugs. Everybody sit tight. Nobody touches that money until we get this thing straightened out. Charley, call downstairs and get the house dick up here, on the double."

Charley got up to use the phone but Eddie King grabbed him, put one arm around his throat and the knife to his belly. "Drop the gun, Ducaine, or I'll slit your pal's gut wide open."

Before Ducaine could react, Lucky stood up, pushing down hard on the edge of the table as he rose. The table tipped toward him and all the objects on its surface, including the pile of money, began to slide off. Frank Holiday made a move to grab the bills, but his weight added to Lucky's only hastened the table's fall. It went over with a crash and scattered cards and money across the floor. Holiday went down on his hands and knees to grab what he could, and first Spaulding and then Ducaine fell on him. They rolled over on the floor, kicking and squirming, and Ducaine's gun went off: bringing down a shower of plaster from the ceiling.

While the others were scuffling, Lucky calmly picked up two handfuls of bills—about his share of the original pot, he judged—stuffed them in his pockets and started toward the bathroom. Eddie King saw him go, but he was still struggling with Thorpe and couldn't do much about it. "Go on, hide in the john, you broken down bugfarm," he yelled after him. "I'll deal with you later."

Passing the bar, Lucky grabbed the bottle of bourbon and took it with him into the bathroom. He locked the door, leaned against it, and took a long swig from the bottle. Booze dribbled down his chin and wet his shirt. It burned in his stomach and made him cough. He threw the bottle into the bathtub, where it shattered, splashing the dark red liquid over the white porcelain. No problem, there would always be more—he knew that now.

Good thing he'd found that card on the floor. Of course, it had come from his own sleeve, not Frank Holiday's. You couldn't count on a crook like Holiday to cheat when he was supposed to, so Lucky had done it for him.

More sounds of violence from the next room—curses, breaking furniture. A heavy object struck the bathroom door. Lucky was about to slip out through the adjoining bedroom when he heard a commotion in the hall, the tramp of several feet. A fist or nightstick began pounding on the door to the suite. "Open up! It's the police!"

Okay, too late to use that exit. He left the door ajar and went to the closet that hid the dumbwaiter. He slid aside the panel. The opening was small, but he was able to wedge himself in, his legs drawn up so his knees were nearly to his ears. As he reached out to shut the closet door, he heard the door breaking down in the next room, more commotion, shouted commands. Then the magic words: "You're all under arrest!"

He slid shut the panel and, in utter darkness, began to work the ropes that would lower him to the kitchen. Having managed this feat once in his younger days, he knew it was possible. But he had forgotten how dark and suffocating it was inside the little box, how cramped he would be, and how much weaker he was now than when he first tried this stunt fifteen years ago. The waiter was balanced so that he didn't have to haul his entire weight, but the ropes had enough resistance to make his muscles ache after a few pulls and he had to pause every so often to give them a rest. His back began to ache; his legs cramped. Sweat broke out across his brow and lathered his back and shoulders. His breath came in gasps. He was afraid he would start coughing and lose control of the ropes. He fought back panic, rested, then worked the ropes, lowering himself another five, ten feet. Then he rested again.

Suspended somewhere between the middle floors of the big hotel, Lucky could hear the murmur of voices from the rooms adjacent to the shaft. Sometimes he heard snoring, laughter, cries of pleasure or anguish, flushing toilets, running showers and faucets, snatches of TVs and radios—the whole world humming in his ears, as if he were sealed up in his coffin and buried deep in the earth, which had begun to talk to him in its varied tongues, its strange, mysterious, but musical language.

    The blues, Lucky thought. Even the old earth had the blues, and this was its melancholy song—a song that only dead men ever got to hear.

18.

Bye Bye Blackbird

JACK woke to hear voices in the kitchen—his mother's voice and a man's familiar baritone. His first thought was that his father must have gotten out of the hospital a day early, but that didn't make sense, because how would he get home without a ride? And if it wasn't Dad, who else could it be, gabbing away out there at—Jack reached for his watch—jeez, 7:30 in the morning?

It ticked him off, because this was Labor Day, the last day of summer vacation, and he had planned on sleeping until noon, at least. He rolled over and tried to go back to sleep, but fat chance with all that jabbering in the kitchen. Besides, he could smell coffee now, and bacon frying, so he knew his mother was fixing breakfast for whoever it was. And that just didn't seem right, because, after all, if your old man was in the hospital recovering from a heart attack, your old lady shouldn't be fixing breakfast for some other guy at seven thirty in the morning, should she?

Jack sat up in bed and tried to hear what the voices were saying, but he couldn't quite make out the words.

He lay back on his pillow and gazed up at the ceiling with its familiar pattern of cracks—that road map to nowhere he followed every morning, that was beginning to look like a picture of his own life. He knew he was probably being too hard on his mother—there had to be some perfectly reasonable explanation for this guy's presence in their kitchen at seven thirty in the morning—but it only added to the many grievances he had against her. They had been feuding all summer, and this past week, without his father there to keep the peace, had been worst of all. Jack couldn't quite understand it. He *wanted* to be a good son, to stand by his mother during this family crisis, but he seemed incapable of controlling his own irritability, or the sudden bursts of anger that led him to say and do things he was later ashamed of.

Things will be better, he thought, *when I'm back in school*. It had been a rough summer, hanging around the house those first two months, waiting to turn sixteen so he could finally get his driver's license and a full-time job. Now he had the license and the job, and he was actually looking forward to the start of a new school year. New classes, new teachers, and, most important of all, new girls. This year, he had promised himself, he would screw up his courage and start asking girls out, and maybe he would eventually get himself a *real* girlfriend. And then, he somehow knew, all these problems with his mother would take care of themselves.

By this time Jack was pretty sure he knew who that voice in the kitchen belonged to, and all those breakfast smells were starting to make him hungry, so he rolled out of bed, put on his bathrobe, and shuffled out to the kitchen. Sure enough, Uncle Lucky was sitting at his father's place, just about to tie into a big stack of pancakes. Ma was standing at the stove in her housecoat, and Jack noticed that she'd combed her hair and put on a little make-up. She smiled and said, "Oh, good morning, honey—look who just dropped in for breakfast." Lucky flashed his old, debonair smile and said, "Good morning, young man. Sit yourself down and have some of these pancakes—they're mighty good!"

Jack noticed the tone and inflection—almost exactly the same as his father's—and he felt a little resentful, as if Lucky actually thought he could take the old man's place. He was also surprised by Ma's display of cheerful hospitality. Why, she hardly ever got up to make breakfast for her husband anymore! And after all the bad things she'd said about Lucky over the years—it just didn't make sense. It was Jack's considered opinion that his folks just weren't being fair to his uncle. They weren't giving the poor guy a chance. Of course, that business at the Blue Swan the other night had made him wonder . . .

"So, I hear you were out pretty late last night," Lucky said, putting a comical note of reprimand in his voice. "Your ma thought you might sleep till noon, and I was afraid I might miss you. I wanted to be sure I said goodbye."

"Goodbye?" Jack sat down at the table in his usual place. "You're leaving town again, Lucky?"

Ma set a glass of orange juice in front of him. "Larry's decided the shoe repair business isn't right for him, Jack. He's been offered a job in Chicago, playing piano in a nightclub, and he's decided to take it. And I must say," she added, going back to the stove to flip more pancakes, "after hearing you at the Blue Swan, I can understand why you're reluctant to give up your career in music."

"Well, it's a lousy life," Lucky said, dipping a strip of bacon in the pool of syrup on his plate and popping it in his mouth, "but it's what I know, Maggie. It's what I'm cut out for—maybe *all* I'm cut out for, though I'd like to learn watch repair sometime, if I get a chance. That was what I wanted to go into last spring, but the gal at the san talked me out of it."

Jack knew at once the job offer in Chicago was a fabrication, and that Lucky's abrupt departure probably had more to do with the singer they'd rescued on Saturday night than anything else. He had given that episode a good deal of thought—especially the part where Lucky had him carry Savannah's inert body to and from the car. Good God, she'd been naked under that sheet, stark *naked*, and he could still feel her soft woman's body under his hands. She was also dead drunk, and pretty beat her up, and all this suggested that Lucky was mixed up, once again, in some bad business with some pretty bad people.

Which seemed to confirm what Dad always said about him. Lucky was a hell of a nice guy, when he was sober, and a marvelous piano player, but he had the wrong kind of mends. And those mends always led him into trouble. And once he was in was trouble, you just couldn't trust him anymore—he'd do anything to anybody, if his back was against the wall. Or if he needed a drink. And that was the other thing Jack had begun to notice about Lucky this morning: there was a faint aroma of liquor about him, not on his breath so much as on his clothes, as if he'd spilled some on himself and hadn't had time to change.

The odor brought back an incident that had lived in

Jack's memory for the past eleven years—that summer after the war, when Lucky lived in their attic along with Grandma Belle, who'd lost her flat to the housing shortage and had nowhere else to go. He and Uncle Lucky were great chums in those days, and one hot afternoon when Jack was coming home from the store with a popsicle melting all over his hand, Lucky happened to come sputtering down Buckeye Road in his Model T coupe. He stopped to offer Jack a ride, and he smelled then the way he smelled now—as if he'd been drenched in a vat of booze. He couldn't seem to focus his eyes or keep the car on the road. It went down into the ditch and out again, weaving all the way down Hegg Avenue until it missed the Lantzes' driveway and wound up in his mother's flower bed. Jack banged his nose on the dashboard and it began to bleed, and his mother came shrieking out of the house . . .

A day or so later Jack's father marched upstairs to the attic and told Grandma Belle that Lucky had to go. Dad thought Lucky was out somewhere at the time, but he was actually dozing on his cot behind a screen and he heard most of what Dad had to say. Jack and his mother were in the kitchen when Lucky tore out of the house, jumped in his car and drove away—and that was the last the family saw of him for two or three years.

"Something wrong, pal?"

Jack turned from his uncle's questioning gaze and his eyes fell on an envelope on the kitchen counter. It was just an ordinary business-size envelope, but it was stuffed so full the flap wouldn't close properly and some of its contents had spilled onto the linoleum. Jack recognized the gray-green color of money, though he couldn't read the denominations. He looked up at his mother, who was just putting a plate of pancakes and bacon down in front of him.

"Your uncle brought us a wonderful gift, Jack—our money worries are over, at least for the next couple of months."

"It's not a gift," Lucky said quickly. "I'm just repaying an old loan—God knows it should have been paid off a long time ago, Maggie. You and Leo have every right to that eight hundred, and I want you to use it any way you see fit."

"Well, it will keep us going, I can tell you that," Ma said. "It's a true God-send, Larry. I don't know *what* we would have done—"

"You just make sure Leo lets you keep it," Lucky said. "That's why I brought it out here instead of stopping by the hospital—I knew you'd be more sensible about it than he would. Besides, this way I get one of your wonderful breakfasts."

Now Jack thought he understood. He had heard the story of Lucky's infamous loan—how he had used Grandma's furniture as collateral, and then defaulted, so the furniture was lost to the finance company, and how his folks first found out about it when they had to put Grandma in the nursing home. He knew his mother in particular had held that offense against Lucky for years, and he also knew how worried she was about money. Why, the way she carried on, you would have thought she cared more about the goddamn insurance than she did about her husband!

There were still, of course, a few unexplained mysteries—such as, where had his uncle gotten hold of eight hundred dollars, after working for just one week in a crumby shoe repair shop? And wasn't he going to need that money, and a whole lot more, if he was running off to Chicago with a wild woman like Savannah Jones? Jack had a hunch Lucky had gone back to another of his old pastimes—you couldn't really call it a profession— but he hadn't gotten his nickname playing the piano. Jack's folks seldom ever talked about that part of Lucky's life, because they disapproved of it so much.

Lucky must have guessed what Jack was thinking, because he said, "Eat your pancakes, boy. I was hoping you'd give me a ride to the train station this morning— and the Hiawatha leaves for Chicago at 10:15." And then, when Jack wouldn't stop staring at him: "All right, so I got a little lucky at the poker table last night, but don't tell your pa. He doesn't believe you can make any money gambling, just like he doesn't believe in Santa Claus."

"Well, you're certainly *our* Santa Claus, Larry," Ma said, beaming at her brother-in-law from the stove, and an at once Jack understood what his father had meant when he said, just the other day, that any time his brother was involved, there were certain questions that were bound to come up—questions Lucky had never been able to answer satisfactorily. You couldn't depend on the man—you were a fool if you did—but once in awhile, under just the right circumstances, he could give you a nice surprise.

By the time Jack finished his breakfast, Ma had gotten out the cribbage board and she and Lucky were already engaged in a last game. That gave him time for a quick shower and, coming out of the bathroom, he happened to glance down the hall toward his parents' bedroom. The door was open, as it usually was when nobody was in there sleeping, and the bed was still unmade. There was nothing so odd about that—his

mother often didn't make the bed until she'd had breakfast—but there was something about those tangled bed-
clothes and flattened pillows that gave Jack a sudden,
bad thought. How long had Lucky been in the house,
anyway, before their voices in the kitchen woke him up?
He told himself he had a dirty mind and went into his
room to get dressed.

They left for the train station at nine fifteen. Maggie
decided not to ride along, saying she had to make potato
salad for the big family picnic later that day, so Jack and
Lucky had some time alone together on the drive into
town. Jack was full of questions, yet found it hard to
open his mouth. He was intensely conscious of the
bright, breezy day, the crisp, clean air of autumn. The
lake glittered like blue marble, its surface flecked with
white caps. Billowy, snow-white clouds moved rapidly
across the sky and the trees in the park were ruffled by
the wind. The entire world seemed to be on the move, or
straining at its moorings, and Jack reflected that his
uncle's vagabond life was more in tune with nature than
the settled existence his parents had arranged in their
snug little home. He yearned to be off and away, a free
man like his Uncle Lucky, yet he could see the sadness
and loneliness of that life, too. Lucky had no one, really,
and his flings and friendships were as short-lived as his
easy-come, easy-go riches.

Halfway into town Lucky was taken by a fit of
coughing and Jack saw him spit surreptitiously into his
handkerchief. It came to him that his uncle might not be
free to roam for long. In fact, he was an odd symbol of
freedom, having spent half his adult life cooped up in
sanatoriums. There was a price for his kind of freedom,
a very high price, but it wasn't one Jack thought he

would ever have to pay. He was sixteen, and on a day like this he felt that he would live forever.

They were going up Atwood Avenue when Lucky asked Jack to stop at a drug store so he could pick up the morning paper. Jack waited in the car and after a few minutes Lucky came out with the newspaper under his arm, a paper bag in his other hand that looked as if it might contain a bottle. It could have been a bottle of cough medicine, but somehow Jack doubted that.

Lucky paged through the newspaper as they continued across town. "Ah, here it is!" he said, and folded the paper so he could read one of the articles. He chuckled a bit as he read it and then tossed the paper in the backseat. "Well, you can tell your dad the Oslo might not be going out on strike after all—they're about to get some really bad publicity."

"Yeah? What's that all about?"

"You can read it for yourself, after you drop me off. Just remember, Jack—you can't believe everything you read in the papers!" Lucky began to hum an old tune, "Lady Be Good," as he watched the old two-story houses on Williamson Street go by. Then he said, "Son, you'll have to tell your pa goodbye for me—we won't have time to stop at the hospital. Tell him I'm sorry to be leaving so soon, but I'll be back one of these days. Remind him of that week he spent in the woods, and how I came back for him then. He didn't think I would, but I did. Old Lucky always comes back. You tell him that."

"I'll tell him," Jack said, and he thought he knew the incident Lucky was referring to, because it had always been one of his father's favorite stories.

As they neared the railroad station, Jack saw the taxi cabs lined up waiting for the Hiawatha's arrival.

There were a few people on the platform, but the station was quieter than usual, because of the holiday. Lucky told Jack where to park, just down from the taxi-stand. When they got out of the car, a woman got out of the last cab in line. Jack saw it was the nightclub singer, Savannah Jones. She was all dressed up for traveling in a flowery summery dress, with white gloves and white high heels, and she looked gorgeous, as usual, though even from a distance he could tell her face was still quite bruised and swollen. She shaded her eyes against the bright sun.

"Wait here a second," Lucky said to Jack, and went to meet her. They talked for a few minutes while the cab driver got her suitcases out of the trunk and put them on the dolly of a waiting porter. Lucky gave her a train ticket and what looked like the key to a locker. Then he sent Savannah into the station with the bags, paid the cabdriver and shook his hand, as if they were old friends. The driver got back in his cab and Lucky returned to Jack, who was waiting beside the car.

"No need to come in with us, Jack," he said. "We can say our goodbyes here." He took another envelope out of his coat pocket, not quite as thick as the one he'd left on their kitchen counter. "I need you to do another favor for me. This is for Abe Slovinsky, the old guy I was working for. I don't know where he lives, and he won't be in the shop today, but I promised to meet him tomorrow morning at nine sharp outside City Hall. He's going to need what's in here to pay his mortgage and taxes—can you make sure he gets it?"

Jack knew he was supposed to report to his new homeroom at eight thirty Tuesday morning, but he said he would take care of it and accepted the envelope.

While he was putting it in the back pocket of his jeans, Lucky slipped a folded bill into his shirt pocket. "A little something for your trouble. Get yourself some new records—but none of that rock and roll crap, okay?"

Jack nodded and left the bill where it was—he didn't want Lucky to think the money mattered all that much to him. "I'm sorry we didn't get to have another jam session," he said. "I learned a lot from that first one."

Lucky smiled and put a hand on his shoulder. His touch was light and gentle, like his voice and his music, but his usually merry eyes were as solemn as Jack had ever seen them. "Tell you the truth, son, I don't think you'll ever set the world on fire as a jazz musician, but hell, music is really more for the pleasure it gives us than for anything else. Your dad's got the right idea on that score—play for fun and not for money and you'll like it a lot better, and live longer in the bargain. But I'll want to have another jam session with you two next time I visit, so keep practicing."

"I will," Jack said, and he scarcely noticed that one of his boyhood dreams had just been dealt an all but lethal blow. Perhaps he'd known all along that he didn't have the talent his father and uncle were blessed with, and he was beginning to realize it was a gift he was probably better off without.

"You be a good fella now," Lucky was saying, "and take good care of your folks. Do what you can to help your dad around the yard, and don't fight with your ma so darn much. They both think the world of you. Why, they've built their whole life around you."

"I know that," Jack said, with more regret than gratitude. "I'll do my best." They heard the bellow of the Hiawatha's horn approaching the station. Lucky stuck out his hand. "Thanks for everything, pal. Put her there!"

They shook hands and then Lucky went into the station. Moments later the long yellow train glided past the station house and came to a halt a little way down the track. The big twin diesels sat there rumbling, steam hissing out from their undersides, and the passengers began climbing down from the coaches. In a few minutes Jack spotted Lucky and Savannah on the platform. A young black fellow in a flashy white suit was with them. He and Lucky had a quick conference while the red cap put their bags on board. Then Lucky and Savannah climbed on the train and the flashy dude gave them a wave. The conductor came along the platform slamming doors, calling "All aboard! All aboard!" Then he signaled ahead to the engineer and blew his whistle. The Hiawatha's horn bellowed in response and the rumble of its great diesel engines rose to a roar.

The train began to move—slowly at first, then faster. The long yellow cars rolled out of the station and across West Washington Avenue, then one by one disappeared around a bend in the track. The red crossing lights stopped flashing and the gates went up; traffic began to move along the avenue again, and then it was as if the train had never been there, had never disrupted the quiet of this bright, suddenly empty morning.

Jack waited in the car as the people on the platform dispersed. The young Negro was counting a role of bills as he came out of the station. He tucked the role in his vest pocket and waved to the last cab in line at the taxi stand. The cab driver gave him a thumbs-up sign in return. Then the dude got in a pink convertible and drove away. The taxi left as well, and Jack reached into the backseat for the newspaper Lucky had discarded.

It was folded open to the local news page, where a headline caught his eye: FIVE MEN ARRESTED AT CAMBRIDGE HOTEL. He knew his uncle had once skipped bells at the Cambridge, so he skimmed the accompanying story and learned that an anonymous tip had led to an early-morning raid on one of the hotel's luxury suites. Five men had been taken into custody and charged with gambling, disorderly conduct, possession of marijuana, and carrying concealed weapons. Three of them were guests at the hotel; their address was given as Kansas City, Missouri. The other two were Madison residents and Jack recognized their names. One of them he'd met at the Blue Swan; the other he'd seen from a distance and heard his uncle mention with contempt. He didn't know what the raid had to do with the strike at the Oslo, but he thought he knew where Lucky had gotten his bankroll. According to the newspaper, police were seeking a sixth man who left the hotel shortly before the raid, and whose identity remained unknown.

When he got home, Jack clipped the article and put it in his box of boyhood souvenirs, where he kept some other mementoes of his uncle's career. Then he remembered the bill in his shirt pocket and took it out. "Holy shit," he said aloud, and went out to the kitchen, where his mother was putting the finishing touches on her potato salad.

"Look what Lucky gave me," he said, and showed her the fifty-dollar-bill.

"That man!" she said. "What would a boy like you do with fifty dollars?"

"I'll think of something," Jack said, and put it out of reach before she could claim it for family expenses.

He went into the dining room and sat down at the

old upright piano. He could still see his uncle's long, slender fingers dancing lightly over the keys, and he longed for the natural grace and elegance that lived in those talented hands. He played a chord and heard the notes, pure and strong in their harmonic simplicity. He played another chord, and then another, letting each chord suggest the next, playing not what his mind told him to play but what his fingers found on the keyboard, what his ears wanted to hear. He let the chords modulate from a major key to a minor, through a progression of sevenths to a diminished fifth and back again to the tonic. The sequence suggested a melodic line and his right hand picked the notes out of the treble, letting them fall easily down the scale as the chords suggested. He repeated the phrase, keeping it clean and simple, the way his uncle would have played it, and pretty soon he had a tune. An easy, bluesy tune that anyone could play. He added a little rhythm with his left hand, picking up the pace just a little. He played the tune over, embellished it here and there, then played it again.

"That's a nice number," his mother called from the kitchen. "What's that called?"

"Oh, it's just something I made up," Jack said. He thought he knew what name he'd give it, if he ever got it just the way he wanted it, but for the time being it didn't need a name.

THOMAS BONTLY'S

CELESTIAL CHESS

The ghost story you have been yearning for . . .

40th Anniversary Edition

Introduced by Thomas Kent Miller

www.bruinbookstore.com